Louisa Heaton lives on Hayling Island, Hampshire, with her husband, four children and a small zoo. She has worked in various roles in the health industry—most recently four years as a community first responder, answering 999 calls. When not writing Louisa enjoys other creative pursuits, including reading, quilting and patchwork—usually instead of the things she *ought* to be doing!

Once making her home in sunny Brazil, **Luana DaRosa** has since lived on three different continents—though her favourite romantic locations remain the tropical places of Latin America. When she's not typing away at her latest romance novel or reading about love, Luana is either crocheting, buying yarn she doesn't need, or chasing her bunnies around the house. She lives with her partner in a cosy town in the south of England. Find her on X, @LuDaRosaBooks.

Also by Louisa Heaton

Resisting the Single Dad Surgeon
The Surgeon's Relationship Ruse

Cotswold Docs miniseries

Best Friend to Husband?
Finding a Family Next Door

Also by Luana DaRosa

Pregnancy Surprise with the Greek Surgeon
Falling for Her Miami Rival

Buenos Aires Docs miniseries

Surgeon's Brooding Brazilian Rival

Valentine Flings miniseries

Hot Nights with the Arctic Doc

Discover more at millsandboon.co.uk.

ONE NIGHT TO TWIN MIRACLE

LOUISA HEATON

FAKING IT WITH THE DOCTOR PRINCE

LUANA DaROSA

MILLS & BOON

First published in Great Britain 2025
by Mills & Boon, an imprint of HarperCollins*Publishers* Ltd,
1 London Bridge Street, London, SE1 9GF

www.harpercollins.co.uk

HarperCollins*Publishers* Macken House, 39/40 Mayor Street Upper,
Dublin 1, D01 C9W8, Ireland

ISBN: 978-0-263-32518-8

09/25

FSC www.fsc.org
MIX
Paper | Supporting responsible forestry
FSC™ C007454

This book contains FSC™ certified paper
and other controlled sources to ensure responsible forest management.

For more information visit www.harpercollins.co.uk/green.

Printed and Bound in the UK using 100% Renewable Electricity
at CPI Group (UK) Ltd, Croydon, CR0 4YY

ONE NIGHT TO TWIN MIRACLE

LOUISA HEATON

MILLS & BOON

To my twins, Becca and Jared x

CHAPTER ONE

DR AURORA DOTSON wasn't used to having a thriving social life. Most of her hours were spent at London's St Henry's Hospital, in scrubs, hair tied up in a messy bun with a pen poked through it, grabbing a Belgian chocolate from the box on Reception whenever she had a moment and sharing a dirty joke and a laugh with the midwives.

So tonight she was out of her comfort zone, attending a charity auction to raise money for the NICU at the Augustine Hotel, and scrubs simply would not do. The Augustine was one of the oldest and finest hotels in London, five star, à la carte dining, marble floors and *suites*—all of which had names—rather than rooms. It demanded a dress, heels and make-up, of which she'd had none—unless an ancient mascara counted, which she was sure it did not.

Luckily, her sister, Maylee, had stepped in to rescue her, offering Aurora one of her dresses to wear and the use of her make-up bag for the big night.

'Honestly, Rory, what would you do without me?'

She'd chosen a simple, little black dress with an asymmetrical neckline that fell just above the knee. She'd teamed it with some dainty black heels that threatened to break her ankles from their vertiginous heights, and had sat patiently whilst Maylee had painted her face, because Rory had no idea in what order everything should be used.

When her sister was done, she had looked in the mirror and marvelled at her own reflection. 'How did you do that?'

The heels were taking some getting used to. One dangerous wobble near the hotel lifts had her considering taking them off, going barefoort and walking into the venue swinging them from her fingers, but she wasn't sure her bosses would be that impressed, so she'd simply reminded herself to walk really slowly. And it was a decision she was glad of because, when the doors opened and she stepped inside the room, she gasped at the marvel before her and needed some time to take it all in.

The Augustine had a beautiful function room, with hints of the old theatre it used to be. There was a stage for the VIPs, a pit for the orchestra that was playing…who on earth was paying for that? There was also a large space decorated with red curtains, candles, a massive candelabra dripping with crystals that hung from the ceiling, and gilt-framed pictures on the walls of all the past artistes who had performed here over the years.

A waiter appeared at her side holding a silver tray laden with champagne flutes. She took one and slowly began to make her way into the throng of people. As an obstetric surgeon at St Henry's, the NICU was an area dear to her heart, and it needed funding for the state-of-the-art incubators and other equipment that it wanted to buy. Her bosses had made it clear that she was to attend, schmooze the guests and make it clear how important their donations could be. She thought it best to find one of the board first, just to make sure that they could see that she had *at least* attended. She wasn't sure how persuasive she'd be in making people part with their money. All she had to do was find them.

Luckily one of them, Charles Holloway, had quite the distinctive braying laugh. Once she heard it, she set off in that direction, excusing her way through the crowds and making her way over to a large group of black suits, where Charles held court.

'And she was just stood there! Without a stitch!' Charles burst into a loud, donkey-like laugh, knowing that all the sycophants surrounding him would laugh too. She assumed he'd been telling one of his bawdy jokes, as he was prone to do when surrounded by gentlemen, but she made her way into his inner circle and raised her hand in greeting.

'Mr Holloway. Good evening.'

'Dotson! Hardly recognised you in your glad rags. Good to see you here.'

She felt his hungry gaze assess her and waited for it to be over. Later on she'd take a shower, but for now she would endure it. Charles, weirdly, was a friend of a friend who had known her father's family for years. He was a bit of a pig, but she'd been told he had put in a good word for her when she'd applied for her post at St Henry's. It had been made clear to her that she had him to thank, even though she felt very strongly that her application had been strong enough on its own, without his greasy input.

Charles introduced her to the gentlemen of his circle and she nodded and smiled at them all, shook a few hands, fulfilled her duty and was about to mention that she'd seen someone she needed to speak to when Charles took her to one side.

'There's someone I need you to schmooze.'

'Really?' She didn't want to schmooze anyone.

'Yes, see that fella over there?' He pointed at a stooped old man with a cane in a dark-grey suit, talking to a woman of similar age in a crimson dress. 'Billionaire. William Stride. Deals in diamonds, would you believe, but his grandson needed an incubator when he was born, which is why he is here tonight. Feels the need to give something back. I think you should go and talk to him.'

'Oh, I'm not sure if I—'

'Course you can! He's always been a sucker for a pretty face, otherwise I'd be talking to him.' Charles chortled at his own self-deprecating yet sexist joke as he nudged her forward.

Rory hated being used this way. But weren't they all here to charm people into opening their wallets and purses and pouring money the hospital's way? That was part of the job, whether she liked it or not. And what would it hurt to say hello and introduce herself—maybe tell the gentleman a few stories? He might be nice, sweet. And anyone at this point would be better than Charles. 'Fine.'

She made her way through the crowd, grabbing a second champagne flute after emptying the first, and surreptitiously made her way towards the old couple. As the crowd began to clear and she got closer, she could see that they were not standing talking to one another alone. There was someone else there—a guy her age. A guy with a charming, bright smile who seemed genuinely interested in something the older man was saying, laughing with them.

She couldn't help but notice how good he looked in his

tux, the colour of it pairing beautifully with his dark hair and bright-blue eyes. Eyes that seemed to glance briefly in her direction and catch her gaze. In that millisecond of connection she felt a fizz of something explode within her and her heart began to pound, before he turned back to the older man and laughed again. She knew what that connection meant. She understood her attraction to this man…and why wouldn't she be attracted? He was gorgeous, whoever he was.

The unexpectedness of this other man already had her slowing and faltering. If William Stride had been alone, she simply would have gone up to him and said, *Mr Stride? Hello. I'm Dr Dotson. I'm an obstetric surgeon with this hospital; very pleased to meet you.* Then she'd have launched into her party patter, being polite, being political, selling the hospital and all the wonderful things they achieved there, in the hope of greasing the wheels a little bit.

But this other guy there, he'd see right through it. To be fair, so might William, but manners would simply prevent him from mentioning her obviousness out loud, because his need to be polite to a young lady would subdue anything else.

So, how to approach? Rory looked back and saw that Charles had already forgotten about her and moved on back to his cronies. Would he know, if she chose to avoid Mr Stride? *Probably not.* So she turned and headed in the other direction, hoping to find something to eat at the buffet table.

Smiling at last, she found a veritable array of delicious delights awaiting her: salmon bites; mini arancini; vegetable sushi; petits fours. And, strangely, tiny sausages on sticks with chunks of apple. Rory picked one up and tasted it, her mouth exploding with flavour.

'Changed your mind?' a voice said close to her ear.

Rory turned to see who it was, blushing madly when she realised it was the young man who had been talking to William Stride. The man who had caused her to divert because, well, he was quite the distraction.

Rory liked a good-looking man. A good-looking man was usually quite happy to join her for an hour or two of fun and then go his separate way. And, whilst she was happy for that to be her modus operandi, it had not been scheduled for tonight. Tonight wasn't for the hospital—not really. Tonight was for all those future babies who would be born and rely on the hospital's equipment and trained staff to look after them so that they got past their difficult start in life and grew up to live their best lives.

She smiled at him. 'About what?'

'Talking to my grandfather.'

'That was your grandfather?' Too late she realised she'd admitted that his grandfather had indeed been her target. But it also meant that she'd learned that this young man might just be the grandson who had needed a NICU incubator when he had been born, as Charles had informed her.

'Yes.' The man opposite her smiled and there was something about his smile that did strange things to her insides. This guy was utterly charming. Dangerously so, without even trying. His looks ought to come with a sign: *warning—irresistible.* His blue eyes sparkled, yes, but beyond that they seemed able to see deep into her soul, making her want to look away before he saw too much. His mouth was wide, generous and genuine. His eyes crinkled at the corners and his jawline was square and already prickling with the stubble that would be his five o'clock shadow. At the thought, her mind happily provided her with an image of his face resting on her lovely white bed pillows, those eyes gleaming at her with devilish wickedness at the memories of what they'd got up to the night before…

'I was going to say hello, sure, but then I saw you talking to him and I didn't want to interrupt. I had no idea you were related.' She hoped he'd believe her.

Whether he did or not, he made no indication. 'So, why are you here this evening?'

Rory smiled and sipped her champagne, running her gaze up and down his body. The man knew how to wear a tux. 'To raise money for a good cause. You?'

'Same.'

She could tell he was admiring her dress. Or maybe what lay *beneath* the dress. The thrill of their instant connection was electrifying. 'I see. And what is it that you do for a living?' The grandfather was in diamonds. Maybe he was too. She could imagine him sweating beneath the hot sun, bare-chested, his hands and clothes covered in dirt as he prised a rare diamond from the rock and held it up to the light.

'I'm an obstetric surgeon. Caleb Stride.' He held out his hand.

An obstetric surgeon? Now her mind saw him in scrubs, and that did wonders for her libido, too. Fighting it down, she smiled at him and shook his hand, thrilling at the electric shocks that ricocheted up her arm at the contact. 'Rory Dotson. I'm an obstetric surgeon too, here at St Henry's. Where are you based?' she asked, hoping he'd confirm he was safely at a hospital far, far from her own, as she *never* indulged in workplace flings.

'I've been working in San Diego the last couple of years, but I'm looking for new opportunities to present themselves.'

San Diego? Excellent. *So no chance of me running into you ever again after tonight and that makes you* perfect.

She licked her lips, drawing his eye and seeing the hunger in his expression, exactly as she'd expected. The need that she also felt. Rory didn't socialise often and when she did it was usually with a particular cause in mind: to connect with someone. It didn't have to end in sex, though if it did then that was a bonus. It was more about chasing the connection. About being someone's focus. About the flirting, the banter, the back and forth. That feeling of being special.

And if she decided to take it further? She chose her partners with care, making sure that they were someone who understood her one-night-only rule. There was no exchange of phone numbers. No exchange of email addresses or social media. It would be one night. That was it. Rory had no time, or inclination, to get into a complicated, difficult or disappointing relationship with anyone.

'And are you here alone tonight, Caleb?' She liked his name. It suited him. It was a strong name.

'I'm here with my grandfather.' He smiled, preferring to be a mystery man, clearly.

'That's not what I meant, and you know it. Are you in a relationship? Married?' He wore no ring, but that meant nothing these days.

'No.'

He looked directly into her eyes. His answer told her

everything she needed to know. Charles's instruction to schmooze the fabulously rich diamond guy was forgotten, as was the idea that she'd mingle and feel as if she was still on the clock at work, even though she was at an evening function. Her nerves before coming here were forgotten, and the worry that she'd turn an ankle and end up on crutches. The intent in his eyes and, no doubt her own, was all that mattered. She knew that she did not want to stand here for much longer holding this empty champagne flute. She could think of something much more interesting to hold…

His expression told her, in no uncertain terms, that he felt the exact same way.

'Good. Well. I think I'm going to go to the ladies' room. Maybe I'll see you out there?'

She never used to be this forward with men; she'd always been passive. But, since her humiliation at the hands of her ex-fiancé, Leo, she'd made a vow that she would never let a guy make the decisions ever again. Which meant that she'd had to take control. Always. The first couple of times she had felt awkward, unsure if she could even be that kind of strong and assertive woman. But she figured if she could advocate for women at work, for her job, then she could advocate for herself too. And that meant leading the way herself, making it clear to any man she got involved with exactly what she wanted and expected from him. No more, no less.

Rory gave Caleb one last lingering and flirtatious look before she turned and walked away, knowing that he would watch her go, so adding a little sway to her hips. Not too much! She still wasn't sure with these heels. But enough to draw the eye and make him hunger for her.

She headed over to the ladies' room, her eyes scanning the hallway. There was another function room next to the one that they'd been in, and it looked empty. Good to know. In the bathroom, she checked her make-up, touched up her lipstick and added one more spray of perfume to her wrists as she gazed into the ornate mirrors above the sinks and adjusted her appearance. She made her hair just right and smoothed out the tight skirt, making sure it hugged her curves perfectly.

I'm ready.

She hoped beyond hope that, when she left the bathroom, Caleb would be waiting for her outside. She'd thought this evening would be boring, meant for networking, and she'd get home exhausted and ready to crawl into bed. But now this night looked a little more promising and she was here for it. It would be incredibly disappointing if he wasn't waiting for her as she hoped, after she'd made it clear to him what she wanted. Her need to feel a physical connection with him was almost overpowering. He was handsome, effortlessly sexy, and she had not been with a man for just over six months. It was time and he was perfect, because she'd never see him again after this evening. He worked in San Diego!

Inhaling a deep breath, she opened the door to the bathroom and smiled instantly at the sight of Caleb leaning casually against the doorjamb right outside. 'Hello.'

'Hello.' Okay—rule setting time. 'You should know that I don't make a habit of this and that anything that happens tonight between us is a one-off. One night only. No commitments. Do you agree?'

He didn't take any time to think about it. 'I agree.' Clearly he was a creature much like herself.

She had laid down her invite and he had accepted. There was nothing more to be said. She reached for his hand, felt her fingers tingle at the touch and drew him towards the empty function room, closing and locking the door behind them. It was darker in here, the sound muffled by the heavy red curtains.

She turned to face him. Her eyes searched his in the shadows of the room. The tension between them was taut, like a bow-string. She hadn't even touched him yet and already her body was thrumming with need, her every nerve-ending alight with sweet anticipation.

Rory reached for the bow-tie at his neck and pulled it loose.

He reached for her but, no, she took hold of his forearms and pushed them down. She would control this and she would only let him touch her when she was ready. She'd make him wait. Make him hold back, so that when she did release him he would be an animal—just the way she liked them to be at the end, their wildness controlled by her so that, even if they felt strong, they would in fact be powerless.

She slowly undid the buttons on his shirt, opening it up to reveal his strong, masculine chest, and pulling the shirt from his waistband. She slid his tux jacket off him, letting it drop to the floor. Then she opened his shirt, slowly revealing his powerful chest and his neat, flat stomach. He was a joy to behold. A feast for her eyes. A carved statue of manliness who looked as good as he smelt.

Again, he reached up to touch her and she stilled his hands. 'Not yet,' she whispered, smiling. Reassuring him that his time would come.

She stepped back, letting him see. Her fingers reached

for the hem of her dress, pulling it upward to reveal her underwear. She'd put on a matching black lace number. Maylee might have cocktail dresses and heels ready to go, but Rory had always bought herself nice underwear, having read somewhere once that if a person felt good underneath their clothes, that confidence could carry them forward.

She knew she looked good. She'd never been a woman to flaunt her body, or womanly curves, but she knew she had them. Men appreciated her ample breasts, the curve at her waist and the bloom of her hips. She wasn't skinny, but average. The dark, lacy knickers drew his gaze exactly to where she wanted it. Her shapely thighs made her legs look longer than they were.

'Let me touch you?' he asked softly.

'Not yet,' she said, feeling the full, delightful force of her control over him and stepping back towards him, reaching for his belt and sliding it free to drop to the floor like a leathery snake. His erection stood proud in his trousers. She reached for it and watched with satisfaction as his eyes closed in bliss as her hand stroked him through the material. It felt large, hefty. Enough that she could imagine it inside her, and the thought thrilled her.

But the knowledge that they weren't in the privacy of a hotel room, with the luxury of time, forced her to move quicker than she usually would. This was a moment in time that she did not want to have disturbed. Now that she'd set her sights on him and decided upon him, she wanted to consume him, as much as she wanted him to consume her. Anyone could try the door at any moment. Anyone could fetch a key to unlock it. The illicit thrill added to her arousal.

'Do you want me?' she whispered, her lips against his skin before she let her tongue lick around his neck.

'I do,' he breathed.

'Do you have protection?'

'In my wallet.'

'Is it in your jacket?'

He nodded.

She let him retrieve it and took it from him, finally undoing the zip over his large erection and allowing his trousers to fall to the floor. He wore boxer shorts and he was just as impressive below the waist as he was above it. She wanted him inside her. As soon as possible.

Rory gazed into his eyes as she reached inside his boxers to stroke him some more, feeling the warmth and weight of him in her hand before she lowered them and revealed him. His need for her was clear and she dropped to her knees to tease him with her tongue and lick him for a moment, hearing him groan and moan before she slid the condom onto the length of him. Then she pulled him down to lie back upon the carpet and told him to take her, finally releasing him from his constraints.

He was over her in an instant, a predatory alpha-wolf standing guard over the meal that was his, before he lowered the weight of himself onto her. He kissed her, softly at first and then passionately, his lips, his tongue, tasting her mouth and her neck, hungrily feeling for her taut nipples through her dress. He trailed his mouth down over her stomach, lower and lower.

Rory arched her back at the contact, closing her eyes, losing herself in the bliss of surrender. As much as she loved to be in charge of these moments, there was something deliriously wonderful about submitting to them too. Of allowing the guy to do with her what he willed. But it was only because she felt safe with him that she allowed it, telling herself that she was still in control of this…somehow.

And then he was inside her, filling her, stretching her, making her gasp as he rode her, and rode her hard. Her shoulders and backside rubbed against the carpet, and she knew she would have carpet burns, but she didn't care. Every mark, every sore spot, would simply cause her to smile secretly to herself at the memories she would feed on for the next few months, until she felt the need for a connection once again.

As their movements became more frantic, as she felt her arousal building to its climax, she pushed herself up against him so that his body rubbed her just so, until her excitement exploded into a multitude of stars. Urged on by her orgasm, he came moments later, gasping and groaning, until he slowed then stilled, kissing her, breathing heavily and finally, sadly, withdrawing.

As always in these moments, Rory felt a thrill—power that she could make him do this, feel this. He was good. Exactly what she'd needed. Making him hold back in those early stages meant that, when she'd released him, when she'd let him touch her, it had been all about her. His need to hungrily explore, to touch, to taste, to caress, had made *her* thc focus. Had made her feel as if she was precious. As if she was the one who'd got more: more attention, more soft touches. It had allowed her to revel in the feeling of being special. That was what this had all been about for her.

He'd been amazing, actually, and she found herself wondering what their encounter might have been like if they had had the security and privacy of a hotel room. Would it have lasted longer? Most definitely. But it hadn't. Adjusting her underwear, she stood and began to get dressed, smoothing her hair and her skirt. She slipped back into her heels as she watched him stand and remove the condom, not sure where to put it.

She had a tissue in her clutch and she wrapped it up in that and slid it into her bag. She would go to the bathroom and dispose of it in a moment. 'I think we should leave this room separately.'

'Agreed,' he said, breathless still, buttoning his trousers once again.

'I don't think we should show that we know each other in the function room.'

'As you wish.'

Rory smiled. Good; he was playing along, letting her control every aspect of this, which was how she liked things. This encounter had been unexpected and delightful, but now they both had to return to being the professionals they were. She would go back into the charity event and do her duty, knowing all the while their little shared secret was theirs alone. And after tonight? She would never have to see him again.

He would go back to San Diego. Leaving her with only a smile upon her face and a sticky sensation between her legs.

CHAPTER TWO

CALEB HAD BEEN born in St Henry's Hospital, so it felt strange to stand there and look at it and realise that his entire, crazy life had begun in this very place. And here he was, returning to work in the very department where his life had been saved.

His mother had come to this hospital in early labour at twenty-nine weeks' gestation. She'd been unwell, suffering from a urine infection that had spread to her kidneys, triggering contractions. The doctors had done what they could to try and prevent the early labour, but nothing had worked: Caleb had been born, struggling to breathe, and was placed into the NICU, plugged into machines to keep his tiny body alive and breathing. He'd had complications. He had developed an infection and had a small brain bleed, which often happened with preemies.

The doctors had gravely informed his mother that he might not pull through, as so much was assaulting his tiny body, but somehow he had. He'd defied expectations, and hearing that story as a small child had made him feel that he would spend his entire life defying expectations wherever he went.

At school, he'd excelled in every subject. He'd got the lead in the school plays every single time. He'd always been the captain of his school sports teams. He'd always been surrounded by girls who flirted with him and wanted to go out with him. And he'd been noticed and admired by everyone, except for the one person whose admiration he'd sought the most: his father.

But he refused to think of that man today. His father wasn't even in his life any more, except as a contact on his phone, and their message history was incredibly short and sporadic, with months between them. His father had made himself a new family, after he'd failed with his first one, and by all accounts he was failing the second one in the exact same way. Caleb wanted nothing to do with him.

Entering Reception, his gaze scanned the multitude of signs, looking for the maternity and delivery ward: floor B. Eschewing the lifts, he jogged up the stairs to the second floor, following the signs that led him to the ward. There was a woman by the doors, holding onto the wall as she breathed through a contraction, her birth partner behind her rubbing her back and coaching her through.

He passed on by and pressed the button to speak to Reception.

'Maternity, can I help?'

'Caleb Stride, obstetric surgeon.'

The door buzzed open and he walked through, eyes scanning the place, instantly noting the layout, how busy they were and how many staff seemed to be working. He was going to be covering for a surgeon who'd had her own baby, and he was kind of excited about the placement, wondering if the obstetrician he'd met at that charity event six weeks ago would be here.

It would be fun to see her face when he appeared.

He'd walked away from that night feeling that she was a woman who liked to control things, and him turning up would be the last thing she'd expect. And he thought it would be fun to surprise her and put her on the back foot. He could be in charge for a change!

She'd told him that she had a one-night rule, which had been just fine by him, because he didn't get into serious relationships either. He'd borne witness to the pain and suffering his mother had gone through when his father had never been around and, though he strived not to be anything like his father, he was not going to risk further pain to someone else with his own demanding job.

He didn't do commitment, so that was something he and Rory had in common. It would be fun to flirt with her and play with the line she'd drawn in the sand. He wanted to show her that her line was just that—in sand. It was something that could be moved, smudged.

'Mr Stride?' The midwife on Reception had red, curly hair and beamed at him.

'Hi, yes. I'm here covering for Ms Bakshi?'

'Oh, of course!' Was she blushing? He knew the effect he sometimes had on women and it always amused him. 'Right, okay. Well, I'm Maddie. The rest of the team are on the ward, otherwise I'd introduce you, but handover is in fifteen minutes. Here, take this.' She passed him a sticky note upon which she'd scrawled a four-digit number. 'It's for the office, which is just down there, end of the corridor on the right. Doctors do their handover in there.' She smiled again, her hand going to her hair subconsciously.

'Perfect, thanks. Oh, by the way, is Rory on duty today?'

'Ms Dotson? Yes. You know her?'

His mind flashed with images from that dark function room: the black triangle of lace against the smooth expanse of her skin; the way her back arched as she thrust upwards to meet him and grind against him; the softness of her; the shadow cast in the dip beneath her belly button. How she'd tasted. How it had felt to bury himself in her. 'A little.' He smiled.

He headed down to the staff room, punched in the number on the door and pushed it open. He found a locker to deposit his jacket and backpack in. Then he turned and surveyed the room proper. It was pretty standard: a desk with a work station, plain walls, a changing room off to the right. There was a couch against the wall with cushions that had seen better days, and a square of tables, lined with chairs for maybe ten to fifteen people, with the remains of crumbs in the middle.

He stood and waited for the door to open.

Normally, she'd take the stairs to Maternity. But not today. She was either exhausted from working double shifts the last couple of days, or she was coming down with something, but Rory wasn't feeling her best. She was tired, mostly, with a weird headache just above her eyebrows. As she sometimes suffered with her sinuses, she hoped she wasn't about to get sinusitis. And, when she'd awoken this morning, her usual cup of coffee hadn't hit the spot at all. Maybe the milk was going off or something, but it just hadn't tasted right.

So she hit the button for the lift and tried to get her mind ready to face another busy day. She was on day shift today: eight until five-thirty. And, though she was exhausted already, she hoped for a busy day so that the time would go quickly. Rashid had informed her last week that they had secured a cover surgeon for Eesha Bakshi, so that was good, and apparently they started today. She would appreciate their skilled hands to help carry the load, as she'd been doing a lot of overtime lately.

The lift pinged open and she stepped inside. Just as the doors were closing, a woman slipped into the lift, overwhelming the small space with her overpowering perfume. Rory wrinkled her nose and turned away to breathe. The scent was sickly and nauseating. *Did she bathe in it? Jeez.* She tried to hold her breath, but it was almost impossible, so when the lift doors reopened on floor B Rory was quick to escape and breathe again. *Why did some people do that?*

As she headed down to Maternity, she spotted Lucy labouring by the door, her partner, Derek, rubbing her back. 'How's it going, Luce?'

Lucy Denby had come in late last night with contractions, just as Rory had gone off shift. She'd only been four centimetres dilated when Rory had left.

'Her contractions stopped for a few hours,' Derek said. 'But they've just started up again. She's at six centimetres.'

'Not long to go, eh? Keep active as much as you can and you'll have a baby in your arms in no time.'

'Let's hope,' Lucy managed.

Rory swiped her card to let her onto Maternity and headed down the corridor towards Reception. Maddie, one of the midwives, was sipping from a cup. 'Do my eyes deceive me?' Rory asked in mock-shock. 'Is there *actual steam* coming from that cup?'

'Yep. Alert the media: midwife consumes a drink that's still hot.'

Rory laughed.

'New guy's here. I gave him the number to the handover room.'

'Oh. Brilliant.'

'You might want to tweak your look.'

Rory paused, confused. 'Huh?'

'He's bloody gorgeous! Looks like someone asked AI to come up with an image of a hot doctor. What with you being single, I thought you might want to do something about…that.' Maddie waved her pen in the general direction of Rory's hair. 'And that.' Next she waved her pen at Rory's face.

'What do you mean?'

'You're looking rough, girl, and I'm being polite.'

'Are you, though?' She smiled and stopped at the desk to get out a compact from her bag to check her appearance. Not that she was expecting to flirt with the new guy; she didn't do work flings, but hey, a girl had to have standards. She did look a little grey and her hair was messy from the wind outside. If this was what too many double shifts did to her, then maybe she ought to slow down.

But Rory adored her job. It gave her life. It was her reason for being and she didn't mind volunteering for extra shifts. St Henry's was her home, just as much as her tiny flat was. But here she got to see happy families, the miracle of birth and cute, chubby babies; and this was a happy place, mostly. 'Ugh. How do I fix this?'

'I think Plastics is on the next floor.' Maddie chuckled.

'You get sassy when you've had a hot drink!'

'Not sassy. Just want you to make a good impression on your friend.'

'My friend?'

'He says he knows you.'

'Knows me?'

'Yeah, um, Stride—Caleb Stride?'

Rory didn't recognise the name at first, her brain searching for the connection. When she did realise who it was Maddie was talking about, she felt her stomach drop and a blush flood her cheeks. She thought of him… *unbuttoning his shirt...caressing the bulge of his briefs. His gasps, his moans... Him thrusting himself into her... The carpet burn... Pleasure and pain…* 'He's meant to be in San Diego…'

'Oh, was that the accent? It was cute. How do you know him?'

She hoped the flush in her cheeks did not give away the answer.

It was many years since Rory had hidden in a toilet to avoid somebody, and she'd never thought that she would do so as an adult, but here she was. The last time, she'd been fifteen years old and hiding because a boy at the school dance had been horrified when she'd made a move to kiss him. Suspecting that all her classmates had witnessed it, she had raced to the nearest loo in sheer embarrassment to work out the easiest way she could collect her coat and escape without anyone noticing.

Now she stood staring at her pale reflection in the mirror, trying to work out exactly how she could fix the mess it reflected before she had to face Caleb once again. Standards mattered! He'd last seen her wearing her sister's finest, in make-up perfection, with her hair styled and her shapely figure on display at its best. Today, she wore a tee-shirt and jeans with an over-sized cardigan on top, because when she got to work she normally just changed into scrubs. It was easier—there were usually a lot of fluids splashing about on Maternity. She'd twisted her dark hair up into a clip, her face was devoid of make-up and she had none with her, except for a year-old lip balm in the bottom of her bag.

Not that she was planning on flirting with the guy, or continuing anything that they had begun, no matter how fabulous their previous encounter. So, realistically, she ought to walk into that staff room looking a state and say, *Screw it. Take me as you find me, mister!* But she felt compelled to make herself look good for a guy that she'd slept with.

Rory began to feel sick at having to meet him again. She'd always been so careful to select sexual partners whom she would have no chance of meeting again, and she'd truly thought she was safe, because he'd said he worked in San Diego!

Damn.

She splashed water on her face, but that didn't help much. She pinched her cheeks to try to bring some colour into them, but she did look quite washed out, and hoped that it was just the bad lighting in the bathroom. She let her hair down from its clip and played with it this way then that, trying to make it look good, only to twist it back up into the clip again. She checked her watch. She couldn't be much longer. Handover would begin soon.

'I'm just going to have to face it out, aren't I?' she said out loud to the empty bathroom. 'Balls.' She did an about turn, and strode out of the bathroom and down the corridor towards the doctors' lounge, the butterflies in her nauseated stomach dancing gaily with delight at the unexpected situation. She paused briefly outside the door, then tapped in the keycode and swung it open.

And there he sat. On the couch, smiling up at her. 'Ms Dotson!'

She gave him a curt smile and nod, trying to show that his appearance didn't bother her in the least. 'Mr Stride.'

But he did bother her. He bothered her greatly. Because he looked just as delicious as he had at their first meeting, if not better, and now he was here and she didn't know how to deal with him. She headed straight to her locker, her armpits sweating, bundled away her bag and grabbed a fresh set of scrubs from storage, before squirrelling herself away into the changing room.

I'm just going to have to get through this.

The handover went as smoothly as they ever did, no matter where it was. The previous shift explained which patients they'd dealt with, if there'd been any developments or complications, who was on the list for surgery during day shift, who was assigned which cases to see on the ward and what jobs needed completing. Caleb sat taking notes throughout it all, sneaking peeks at Rory, who had managed to sit at the table further up from him so that she didn't have to look at him as Dr Marshall gave the handover from night shift.

She looked good—pale, but still beautiful, despite the fact that here she wore no make-up or figure-hugging clothes. She had a natural beauty that he adored to see. If he had to choose between natural beauty or a heavily made-up face, he'd choose natural every time. She'd been stunning the night of the charity event at the Augustine

Hotel, even so. And the way she'd twisted her hair up into that clip… He could imagine letting it loose, watching it fall around her naked shoulders and running his hands through it. Smelling it. Nuzzling the nape of her neck and breathing her in.

Not that she'd let him. She'd made it clear that night that she had a one-night rule, and that was fine by him, but flirting would be fun anyway! Surely she'd enjoy that? And, if not, then she would tell him and of course he would stop.

'And I'd like to take this moment to welcome our new obstetric surgeon, Mr Caleb Stride, to the St Henry's family!'

Everyone turned to look at him, smile, nod or say hi. Even Rory turned, he noted, though she didn't smile or nod. She looked guilty. She looked a little sick. Had his presence here disturbed her that much?

'Mr Stride joins us to cover for Ms Bakshi and will be with us until Eesha decides when, or even if, she wants to return after having baby Zahir. Caleb, do you want to quickly just tell everyone a little bit about yourself?'

He nodded, confident. 'Hi guys, nice to meet you all. I'm looking forward to getting to know you all a lot better.' He looked at Rory as he said this, but she was looking down at the table and didn't notice. 'I've spent the last few years working over in the American healthcare system, but I'm back in Britain now and looking for a place to settle down near family, so here I am.'

Dr Marshall smiled. 'Good. Okay. I thought that Caleb could shadow you for today, Rory, is that okay?'

Caleb smiled at Dr Marshall's suggestion, his gaze drifting to Rory to see how she'd react. He saw her head lift quickly from her lap and her eyes widen briefly before she recovered and nodded. 'Yeah, sure.'

'Show him where everything is, get him accustomed as to how we do things. It might be worth him shadowing for this first week, actually, until he feels ready to settle in and do this UK style.' Dr Marshall chuckled.

'No problem,' Caleb said, finally making eye contact with Rory.

She looked…uncertain. Not the confident, take-charge woman that he'd met previously. Clearly his being here had put her on the back foot and she wasn't happy about meeting up with her one-night stand. He found it terribly amusing.

'Be gentle with me, Ms Dotson,' he said.

Her cheeks flushed with colour as everyone in the room laughed good-naturedly.

CHAPTER THREE

'WHY THE *HELL* aren't you in San Diego?' she asked, turning on him the moment they were alone. He was ruining everything, turning up like this, and she didn't like it one bit. Mostly because it broke her rule, but also because she was mad at herself. Mad for feeling her body react to his presence.

'Because I'm here,' he answered, smiling, a little bit amused by her consternation.

'You know this isn't ideal.' Rory risked a quick glance at Caleb as they headed to the ward to speak to their first patient. 'I don't fraternise with people I work with. It makes life complicated and I don't do complicated.'

'Are we fraternising right now?'

'No.'

'So we're okay, then. What happened was the past, Ms Dotson; you can relax. I'm not going to try and chase you up the aisle, you know.'

'Glad to hear it. This is where I work and I won't have my reputation tarnished by any more gossip.'

Any more? Hmm. 'Understood. So, just flirt with you on the quiet, then?' He chuckled and she stopped to stare at him.

'No flirting! At all!'

He gave her a mock-salute and, flustered, she stomped past him, heading to Room One, sucking in a calming breath and relaxing her shoulders before she gently knocked on the door and pushed it open. 'Mrs Sanderson?'

'Yes?'

Mrs Sanderson had come in overnight on Dr Marshall's shift. Her water had broken at home and she'd been contracting steadily, but a nurse had noticed a rapid upturn in her temperature and suspected a possible infection.

'Hi. My name is Ms Dotson and this is Mr Stride. We're here to check you out and make sure you and baby are okay, seeing as you're not feeling very well. The nurse told you that you're running a fever?'

'Yes. I've been getting some chills too.'

'Okay.' Rory checked the file and noticed that Mrs Sanderson's waters had broken roughly eighteen hours ago. 'Any pain?'

'Yes, down here, but I thought maybe that was because of the contractions, though.'

'It could be.' She smiled, to try and show that she wasn't too concerned yet, though there was a risk of a serious infection here. Some women could develop infections after the amniotic fluids had broken. 'Do you mind if I examine you?'

'Not at all.'

Rory performed a physical examination of the patient. She checked her blood pressure, which was still within the normal ranges, but she had evidence of tachycardia—a fast heart rate.

Caleb, she noticed, was checking the trace. Mrs Sanderson was strapped to the cardiotocography machine. The machine, also known as the CTG, not only monitored the baby's heart rate but also the length, strength and regularity of the mother's contractions. It was a vital piece of equipment in the labour room and could indicate early levels of distress to the baby that a midwife or doctor could otherwise not know about. It didn't hurt anyone, and the monitoring was conducted externally via the mother wearing two elasticated belts around her abdomen. Sometimes, if the baby's heart rate couldn't actively be monitored through the CTG, then internal monitoring would be used, wherein a clip would be attached to the baby's scalp.

'Baby's heart rate has increased. Has he or she been as active as they normally are?' he asked the patient.

'Not as much, no. Is that bad? I thought they all reduced movements during labour.'

'It's just something we need to be aware of, but they're not having decels, which is good.' Consistent decelerations could show that the baby wasn't happy.

Rory was worried about chorioamnionitis, an infection of the placenta and remaining amniotic fluid. 'Do you think you could do a urine sample for me? We can perform a rapid test of that, and I'd like to perform a more intimate exam with your permission to get a vaginal swab and check to see the colouration of your fluids.'

'Whatever you need to do.'

'Okay. I need to check your temp again. It was just over thirty-eight degrees an hour ago.'

Rory used the thermometer and discovered that Mrs Sanderson was still feverish. They unhooked the patient from the CTG machine and waited for her to use the bathroom. She waddled back into the room and passed them the sample. The rapid urine test indicated that there was a high white-cell count and, when Rory got the vaginal swab and performed the physical examination of Mrs Sanderson, she could smell the infection. It made her very concerned indeed.

'Okay. I'm just going to check to see if the bloods you had taken overnight have come back and then we'll formulate a plan, okay?'

'Is my baby going to be okay?'

'We're going to try and make sure of it.' Rory glanced at Caleb to indicate that they should leave, and they headed back out into the corridor.

'You suspect chorioamnionitis?'

'Yes. The maternal fever, the tachycardia, the presence of purulence when I did the vaginal swab… Let's see what the bloods say, but I think we need to get antibiotics on board and this baby delivered asap, rather than wait, if we want to keep them both healthy.' Purulence was evidence of pus.

'Agreed. Want me to order those?'

'Please. Let's get her on ampicillin and gentamicin.'

'Will do.'

She watched him go, glad to feel her breathing return to normal as he walked away to use a terminal at the nurse's station. She opened up her tablet and tapped in her patient's details to bring up the blood results. Mrs Sanderson's CRP, her c-reactive protein, was raised considerably, indicating inflammation. She was also showing signs of leukocytosis, meaning her white blood cells that fought infection were also considerably raised. It was definitely looking like chorioamnionitis.

Returning to the room, they informed the patient of their findings and started her on the antibiotics. 'We're also going to start you on oxytocin to try and increase your contractions. The quicker baby is here, the better. If you consent to that, then we'll need to keep you on the CTG machine to monitor baby and make sure they're tolerating it, which also means you won't be able to move around as much.'

Mrs Sanderson nodded.

'Okay. We'll get your midwife, Sasha, to get that started in the next half hour, hopefully, and we'll keep you monitored and get you cracking on.' Rory smiled reassuringly.

'Thank you.'

'We've got you, okay?' she said, laying her hand on Mrs Sanderson's in a reassuring manner.

Her patient smiled, but her eyes were welling up as she fought to hold back tears.

Outside the room, Rory looked at Caleb. 'Why are you looking at me like that?'

He smiled. 'Like what?'

'Like you're thinking back to our last encounter.'

'I wasn't, but I am now.'

She shook her head in disbelief. 'I'm not sure this is going to work for me. I'm going to ask for you to be reassigned to another doctor to shadow for this week. I can't work with you looking at me like that.'

He held up his hands in mock-surrender. 'I'll stop.'

'You will?' She wasn't sure if she believed him, and a small part of her liked the fact that she'd had such an impact on him that he still thought about their encounter. *She'd* thought about it upon seeing him, so it was only fair…but having him think about it *in front of her* was weird. Because she wasn't used to seeing her very few sexual partners afterwards. And most certainly not at work!

Caleb got her flustered. She felt hot and sweaty and still a little bit sick. Her stomach was churning constantly, putting a weird taste in her mouth. 'I need to get a drink.'

Caleb stared into the NICU as he sipped his coffee on his morning break. Currently four incubators were occupied in the very room where he himself had been taken after his own birth. He wondered whereabouts, exactly. Over in the west corner that had hot-air balloons painted onto the walls? Or the east, where there were trees, bluebirds and a bright-yellow sun? He very much doubted it had been painted like that when he'd been a poorly baby. But, as he stood there and observed the parents sitting by the bedsides of their babies, he wondered how many hours his own mother had sat there and for how long she'd been by herself.

'Oh, God! You're here, too? I can't catch a break!'

He turned to see Rory coming through the security doors to the viewing window that allowed relatives to see into the NICU.

'Oh, I'm sorry. I thought the hospital was public property, but if I'm trespassing…?'

He smiled. There was something sweet about the way he disturbed her—as if their night had had much more of an impact on her than she was letting on, perhaps? Maybe she wanted more from him, but didn't want to admit that to herself, so she acted as though she didn't like him.

It reminded him of when he'd been at junior school and he'd been made by the teacher to sit next to Clare Maxwell. Clare had been really annoyed that he'd been placed beside her, physically drew a line down the centre of the desk and got upset whenever he accidentally strayed over it with an elbow or his pen. It had gone on for weeks, until one day she'd kissed him out of nowhere and they'd been boyfriend and girlfriend for a little while. It had been cute—sweet, innocent.

'It's just, this is my space. Where I come to chill. You're ruining it.'

'My apologies. I just wanted to see the space where I spent so much time as a baby myself.'

She paused from looking annoyed to look intrigued. 'Oh.'

'I was born at twenty-nine weeks. I stayed in here—he gestured at the space beyond with his coffee cup '—for nearly two months. My mother never missed a day.'

Rory came to stand by him. Not too close, he noted.

'And your father?'

Wow. She'd zeroed in on the one aspect that had always bothered him. She was astute. Maybe it had been in his tone when he'd only mentioned his mother. 'He came the first day, apparently, but he was a very busy man.'

Rory frowned. 'It can be hard for a parent to see their child looking so helpless.'

Caleb shook his head. That wasn't how it had been at all! 'I'd rather not talk about him, if you don't mind. Let's talk about us. That appears to be an easier subject,' he said, knowing that to her it was not. She tutted and turned away, glancing through the viewing window.

'So, you come here often?' he joked.

'As a matter of fact, I do. This room, this place, puts the rest of the world into perspective. If something bad happens, I come here and look into this room—at the babies, at the faces of the hopeful parents—and I'm reminded that, whatever I'm going through, it's never as scary as what's happening in here.'

'It makes you less frightened.' He understood implicitly because he did the same thing too.

'Yes.'

'So what brought you here today? Was meeting me again so terrible?' He said it like a joke, but he really hoped her answer wasn't yes. He'd enjoyed meeting up with her again, seeing her reaction, and he was glad to be here. He'd like to think that, somehow, a small part of her was glad to see him.

She smiled at him. 'You're not that important, Caleb. Sorry to disappoint you.'

'I'm hurt.' He grabbed a pen from his pocket and used it to act as if she'd just stabbed him in the heart.

'I had a headache. That's all. I didn't sleep well, and I just needed to come here and look at these families and be reminded of what the struggle is all about.'

'I get that.'

She looked up at him then, assessing him. 'Is what you said earlier the only reason you're here—at the hospital, in general?'

'I have many reasons for returning to London. Family is one of them.'

'Your grandfather… I met him at the charity ball… is he alright?'

Caleb nodded. 'He's fine. In Cape Town at the moment.'

'Good. He seemed a nice guy.'

'He's the best.'

So much better than his own father. But that wasn't a difficult achievement.

CHAPTER FOUR

THIRTY MINUTES BEFORE the end of their shift, they were called in to Mrs Sanderson's room, as she'd begun to push. They'd monitored her closely all afternoon and the monitoring had ramped up after the baby had opened its bowels and passed meconium whilst still inside the womb, indicating that maybe it wasn't as happy as it ought to be.

Rory and Caleb were called in for the delivery, along with the paediatric team and Special Care Baby Unit team, just in case there were any issues with its breathing when baby was born.

They gloved, gowned and got ready, Caleb positioning himself between Mrs Sanderson's stirrupped legs, whilst Rory checked on the CTG tracing.

'Another push, that's it. Deep breath, hold and push—one, two, three…' Caleb counted.

Mrs Sanderson was crowning. The dark smears of meconium could be seen on the baby's scalp. The real worry was whether the baby had inhaled any of it. Sometimes they didn't, but if they had, there'd be signs to look for: yellowish staining of the skin and nails, rapid breathing with abnormal breath sounds, an enlarged chest and signs that the rib muscles were working extra-hard to inhale and exhale.

'Nearly there, that's it…and push! Head's nearly out!'

She watched as Caleb checked for any cord around the baby's neck, but there didn't appear to be, and with one final push, and a gush of stained fluids, Mrs Sanderson's baby boy slithered free and screwed up his face in an attempt to cry.

Caleb was cleaning off the baby's face and using the suction tool to clear any aspirated effects from the nostrils and mouth. Once baby began to cry loudly, Caleb placed him into Mrs Sanderson's grateful arms, before clamping the cord.

The midwives began towelling him off, rubbing hard, helping establish breathing and removing wetness so that he didn't get cold.

Rory leaned over to check on the baby and wasn't totally happy with his colour. 'Cord?' she asked.

'Done,' Caleb responded.

'Mrs Sanderson? I just need to take him to check on his breathing. I'll bring him right back to you.' And she scooped up the baby and carried him urgently over to the cot, where the team immediately surrounded him and got to work, placing a small oxygen mask over his face as Rory listened to his chest. 'SATs?'

His result was borderline okay, but they all wanted to make sure he was fine. He might need a chest x-ray to be sure.

'Is he alright?' Mrs Sanderson called out.

Rory turned and smiled. 'I believe so. He might have inhaled a small amount of stool—not enough to cause any serious issues, but we're just monitoring him to make sure his lungs are clear enough. But he's got good colour and he's not grunting so it's looking good. We're just going to keep him on extra oxygen for a while in the Special Care Baby Unit. Remember we discussed that as a possibility?'

Mrs Sanderson nodded, but didn't seem to relax, and Rory knew that she wouldn't until her baby boy was safely back in her arms.

'Let's give Mum a quick cuddle before he goes up,' she ordered.

Caleb scooped up the baby, now wrapped in many blankets, and carefully handed him to his mother. Mrs Sanderson burst into happy tears and kissed her son on the cheeks. 'Declan. His name's Declan.'

'A good, strong name,' Caleb said.

After a few minutes, they took Declan and handed him over to the SCBU team, who whisked him away and told Mrs Sanderson that she could go and visit him when he was properly settled in.

Rory and Caleb left the room and headed to the staff room to write their final notes and then leave for the day.

As she sat at the desk, typing on her tablet, Rory couldn't help but look at Caleb whilst he didn't know he was under observation. He was clearly a good doctor: kind, calm. She wished she could sit there and create a long list of his professional attributes but, annoyingly, all she could really think of as she sat and surreptitiously gazed at him was how handsome he was, how attractive.

She liked the way his dark-brown hair had been cut short on the back and sides but left longer on the top so that it had this kind of ruffled, 'I just got out of bed' look. She could imagine that gorgeous head of hair resting against her pure-white pillows, his beautiful eyes looking at her with mischief in mind. The feel of him in her hand… A wave of arousal washed over her and she felt herself grow hot.

'You know, if you keep staring, I'm going to start thinking that maybe you do want my number. And round two,' he said, smirking.

Rory blinked. 'What?'

'You're staring.'

'I'm not!' she replied, indignant, feeling her cheeks flush with more heat. *How dare he imply that?*

'Yes, you were. And I'm flattered, but Rory, my eyes are up here.' And he laughed and pointed to them, as if she'd not just been thinking about them.

'You're so full of yourself.' She got up and went over to her locker to get her things so she could go and change back into her day clothes, go home and get away from this guy, whose ego was so huge, she was amazed he could make it through doorways.

Seriously, it had been a long day! Having this idiot following her around, making her feel all kind of things, had simply been an extra load she'd not needed. Running into and having to work with her one-night stand? It was embarrassing—and on a day when she was already tired and irritable. She was hungry too, but also not.

She had this strange craving to eat a really fresh, ripe, juicy mango. Just thinking of that made her all flustered, imagining the taste of it and the way the juice would run down her face and neck as she bit into it. She salivated just thinking about it, but also weirdly felt *sick* thinking about it. Her stomach had felt strange all day, and when she'd had lunch earlier her chicken salad had tasted off. She'd thrown half of it away, not wanting to get food poisoning.

'Well, when someone looks at you as much as you have been doing, you begin to wonder if you have something on your face—but I checked and, as there's nothing between my teeth either, I can only presume you keep looking at me because you either can't get enough, or you're intrigued as to why I make you feel a certain way.'

She scoffed. 'Mr Stride! I didn't know you were a psychologist too. Congratulations. Your parents must be proud.'

'My mother is, certainly.'

She stopped, her hand on the doorknob to the changing room. That was the second time he'd implied that he didn't have a great relationship with his father. *Intriguing.* She could certainly understand the principle of a man letting someone down. She'd had enough experience of that to last her a lifetime and she was never going to let it happen again.

She stomped into the changing room and closed the door behind her, feeling incredibly irritated, and wanting to huff and puff and throw things. Instead, she yanked off her scrubs and threw them into the laundry, then pulled on her own clothes from this morning and spent a moment gathering herself, slowing her breathing, before she opened the door to head back out again, hoping that he would already be gone.

But he wasn't. He was sitting there on the couch, chewing on the end of a pen as he stared at his patient's notes. His lips were slightly parted, the tip of his tongue teasing the end of the pen as he thought. She pushed down as much of her arousal as she could, annoyed by it. It was rudely unwanted!

'Goodbye, Mr Stride. I'll no doubt see you tomorrow.'

'Ms Dotson.'

Was it bad to wish that *he* got food poisoning, so he didn't come into work for a few days?

Because he really was the most irritating man she'd ever met!

Over the next few days, Caleb enjoyed his time spent with Rory. It was fun to flirt with her and, even though she didn't seem so amused by it, she seemed to be enjoying it a little, otherwise he'd stop. He wasn't such an ass that he would force himself on anyone—they were just having fun, snatched in the few moments they had when they weren't dealing with patients.

Rory tried to act outraged sometimes; other times, she'd just laugh cynically and say, 'You wish.' And, yes, maybe he did. He would not be opposed to having a bit more fun with the delectable doctor. Their first night had been.

'We should have another night together,' he said one day, as they were standing on the concourse overlooking the large reception area down below.

Rory laughed out loud. 'You're joking?'

'For closure.' He smirked at her. 'I've heard it's a very important thing.'

'Closure, right.'

'And, forgive me for saying it, but you seem a little… uptight. A passionate night of sex might help you unwind, plus I've heard it can do wonders for the complexion.'

She touched her face. 'Are you saying I've got spots?'

'No.' Though, now he'd said it, he noticed that she did have a little breakout. It could be hormonal—some women got that. She'd done her best to cover it with concealer, but as each day wore on it became more obvious.

'You're saying I'm uptight?'

'Oh, most definitely.' He smiled, back on firmer ground. 'You've been wound as tight as a bobbin. I have a few...*techniques* to help with that.'

He gave her a quick glance, smiling, taking in the pallor of her face after a long day, the way a few tendrils of hair had broken free from her pony tail and the dark circles showing under her eyes. But, even with those imperfections, she was still a beautiful, desirable woman to him. One he'd be pleased to have seen upon his arm. One he'd be thrilled to take to his bed.

Their previous night of passion had not been enough. They'd needed to be quick in case they were discovered. It had been abrupt, frenzied and wild and, though he could do that again, his dreams of her lately had involved a more languorous aspect. *Hours*, rather than minutes, in which she would lie naked upon his bed and he would explore every aspect of her. Maybe he'd blindfold her? Trail her skin with a feather...or his *tongue*? Watch her curl and undulate, and listen to her gasps and moans until he tasted the very heart of her? Drive himself deep into her body with his own?

'I'm sure you do,' she answered, smiling back at him. 'But you're going to have to save them for some other lucky girl.'

'Is there someone else you're saving yourself for?' He doubted it. She'd made it pretty obvious that she wasn't in the market for a relationship.

'Not at the moment.'

'Then why not have some fun? Break that one-night rule of yours. Aren't some rules meant to be broken?'

'Some, maybe.' She looked him up and down, as if

considering him, and he could see in her hungry eyes that she liked what she saw. 'But not that one.'

'You're killing me, Rory.'

'Oh! I get it. You have DSB.'

He frowned. 'DSB?'

She leaned in close and whispered, '"Deadly sperm build-up". I've heard most men think it's fatal.' Then she laughed and walked away from him, and all he could do was laugh and watch her go, gaze focused on her hips and the smooth curve of her bottom in her scrubs. Rory filled her scrubs nicely. But he also had a memory of what those curves were like *unrobed* and he wanted to see them again.

He was about to say something else, to have the last word, but both their mobiles went at the same time and they pulled them from their pockets. They were being called to attend an emergency caesarean section.

She looked at him and curled her finger.

CHAPTER FIVE

OKAY. SERIOUS MODE, NOW. Rory didn't look at Caleb as they began to scrub for the surgery. The patient was already in Theatre, gowned and anaesthetised with a spinal. Her husband would be brought in once she and Caleb were ready to go.

It was Natalie Goldberg. They'd been monitoring her during her labour, as she was pregnant with twins. One of them had been showing some decelerations on the CTG tracing for a few hours, and in the last hour it had become significantly worse, according to the midwife who had spoken to them when they arrived at theatre. Mr Atwood-Green, the consultant, had ordered the emergency caesarean, even though Natalie hadn't technically been his patient, but he'd been called in to check the trace because Rory and Caleb had been on their break at the concourse. Now they would take over and hopefully get these babies out before there was a serious threat to their health.

Rory was on high alert now, even though moments ago up on the concourse she'd been feeling tired and exhausted. It was all she felt lately. Probably some vitamin deficiency or something, because she knew she hadn't been eating right lately. She was determined that this weekend she would reset her eating. Maybe she'd batchcook something, so that she could take some proper meals into work with her. She'd also eat some healthy snacks such nuts or fruit, instead of the sweets she'd been mainlining from the vending machine.

As she headed into Theatre, one of the team helped her on with her gown, tying it behind her, then helping Caleb with his as she got on her gloves and stood over the sterile field of her patient's abdomen.

She took the surgical tweezers and pinched at various parts of the patient's anatomy. 'Feel anything, Natalie?'

'No.'

'Okay, we're going to get started, if you're ready.'

Natalie noddednervously.

Caleb came to stand opposite. 'Scalpel?' She glanced at him once as he took the blade, applied it to the skin and cut the initial incision, then she focused totally on the surgery. He was quick and skilled. He cut through layer after layer with perfection until he exposed the womb, opened it up and began reaching for the first baby. A gush of amniotic fluid burst forth and he had the first twin out in moments.

'Congratulations on Baby A,' he said.

Rory heard Natalie cry as her baby began to wail and she smiled briefly before turning back to watch Caleb retrieve the second baby. The second twin came out a little floppier than the first. It was wet and slick, but the team took him over to the warmer, and pretty soon they heard a second set of lungs join the first, and they all relaxed at the happy sound.

Rory had been feeling so tired, so exhausted, but the sound of the crying babies made that go away briefly. One day, she hoped, she would have the opportunity to have a child of her own. She'd already thought about how she'd do it—alone, through IVF or something—without a guy to let her or her baby down.

Rory glanced up at Caleb, then returned her focus to the incision to assist with the latter part of the surgery: removal of the placentas and stitching the patient back up.

But something else happened. A wave of nausea washed over her as she looked into the open abdomen, and bile rose up in her throat. Rory choked, making a strange, strangled sound as she panic-swallowed it back down and stepped away from the table.

'You okay?' Caleb asked, pausing in his stitching.

'Erm…yeah.' She swallowed again. *What the hell had that been about?* She never got nauseous in Theatre! But in that moment looking at the layers of flesh, muscle and blood had been too much. *Eurgh.* Rory couldn't stand at the table and look. The smell of it all—the amniotic fluid, the blood, the cut flesh, the sheer viscosity and rawness of it—was turning her stomach. She knew she needed to step away or risk vomiting in the body cavity of a patient, which she figured would not be welcomed by the patient, her family or the hospital authorities—though lawyers might be pretty happy about it.

'I, er…need to step away.'

'Okay, go. Get a glass of water; you look a little ashy. Eat some chocolate—get your blood sugars back up.'

She nodded, grateful that he didn't tease her in this moment, in front of everyone. It was bad enough that they were all witnessing this and would no doubt talk about it afterwards. The surgeon who got queasy—that would be a great joke, right? She pulled off her gloves, gown and mask, grateful to breathe easily again, and stepped out of Theatre.

What the hell had just happened to her? Why did she feel so ill all of a sudden? *What did I eat for lunch?* She'd meant to go and get a jacket potato and some salad, just to be healthy, but she'd stuck around for a birth, got called into another case and, somewhere in there, she'd just grabbed a couple of chocolates from the tin on Reception to keep her sugars up. *Damn it, that's why!*

Thankfully, though, it was now home time. Her shift was over and she could go. She would get home, cook something, maybe take a bubble bath and go to bed early. Maybe this nausea would stop once she started taking better care of herself.

After she'd got changed and headed into the staff room, Caleb was waiting for her, looking concerned. 'You okay?'

'Just burning the candle at both ends. I'll be alright once I have something proper to eat at home.'

'What do you have in your fridge?'

She stopped to think and remembered that she'd been working hard all week. She'd not done any shopping. Her expression must have told him everything he needed to know: her shelves would be bare, her fridge, empty.

'Thought so. Listen, let me take you out for a bite to eat.'

She looked at him dubiously.

'As a thank you, for letting me shadow you this week. I know I've been a bit of a thorn in your side.'

'A *bit*?'

He smiled. 'Yeah. A bit. Part of you was charmed, I could tell.'

'Well, Prince Charming, I don't really think I've got the energy to go out to eat. I just want to go home, rest and relax.'

'Then let me cook for you.'

'What?' Was he kidding? Her rules did not allow for her one-night stands not only to start working with her but also come back to hers and start cooking for her.

'Give me your address. You go home, I'll go shop for some real food and then I'll come to your place and cook for you. You won't have to lift a finger.'

It did sound tempting. And, God damn it, she *was* tempted! And exhausted. When had she last had someone take care of her like that—cook for her, shop for her? Even Leo hadn't treated her that way. And would it be so wrong? She'd let a friend do it, if they ever offered, so why not him? All she had to do was not give in to his flirting. 'And what will you be expecting in return for this shopping and cooking experience?'

'Not a thing.' He held up his hands in mock-surrender. 'It's purely a thank you for this week.'

'You're not going to try to seduce me?'

'Not one bit.'

Oh. Is that disappointment I feel? Why the hell am I disappointed? I should feel relieved! 'You can flirt a little bit, if you want. I know you like to.' She gave a grudging smile, as if she were doing *him* a favour.

'Okay. Challenge accepted.'

Rory looked shattered when she answered the door to him, but pale and beautiful in an outfit that made him smile. Clearly she'd put some thought into what outfit would likely be the least sexy to him, but somehow he still thought she looked amazing in it. She wore grey jogging bottoms and an over-sized sweatshirt and her hair was twisted up on top of her head in a messy knot. She wore no make-up.

This was Rory. He could imagine her curled up on the couch looking like this, eating from a tub of ice-cream, licking the spoon as she watched some movie. She was trying to hide her body beneath the over-sized clothes, but it wasn't working, because he already knew what was underneath and it just aroused him even more. To distract himself, he held up the groceries. 'Show me the kitchen.'

He had bought the ingredients for his superfood meal and set about making it: baked sweet potatoes smothered with a spicy chickpea and roast-vegetable stew, drizzled with a light garlic dressing and toasted croutons. They didn't need much. It would be very filling and, as the food cooked, he watched her from his post in the kitchen as she lay on the couch and closed her eyes.

She was beautiful, there was no doubt about it, and there was also an element of vulnerability about her that just pulled at him and made him want to protect her for some reason. There was a blanket over the back of her couch and at one point he draped it over her and watched her sleep for a while before he returned to serve up the food and called out from the kitchen, 'Hope you're hungry!'

He knew that way he could pretend that she hadn't been sleeping, and so could she. She made her way to the small dining table, her face pale and swollen with sleep, and he placed the food in front of her. *'Voilà!'*

'Wow, this looks amazing!'

'Every mouthful will prove to be a scintillating delight.' He smiled, sitting opposite and waiting for her to taste it and give her opinion.

When she did, her reaction was everything he'd wanted it to be: delight, surprise. Deliciousness. Pure wow. 'This is incredible!' she said between hungry mouthfuls. She cleaned the plate in its entirety and he had a sneaky suspicion that, if he'd not been here, then she would have licked it too.

'I, er, have a confession to make,' he said.

She looked at him in suspicion. 'Oh?'

'I may have bought a pre-made, yet decadent, dessert.'

Rory swallowed. 'What kind?'

He got up, went to the fridge and returned with a triple-chocolate mousse in its little pot—milk and white and dark chocolate topped with a chocolate glaze and chocolate sprinkles—and presented it to her with a spoon. 'Got room?'

She smiled wickedly, like a naughty child. 'I have a second stomach reserved purely for desserts like this.'

He watched her devour it—every bite, every spoonful. Every lick of her lips and satisfied moan that he heard her make, turned him on. And all she was doing was eating!

'What?' She looked at him curiously.

'Nothing.'

'No, there's something. Do I have chocolate on my face?'

'No, no, your face is fine. It's more than fine, licking that spoon like that.'

She stopped and blushed, two pink spots filling her pale cheeks. 'Oh. Sorry.'

'No, it's nice. I like it. Do it again,' he said in an amused, low, porn voice.

She put down the spoon and pushed away her plate, irritated. 'Look, you don't want me.'

'No?'

'No.'

'Why?'

'I'm…' She looked away, as if she wasn't sure she wanted to have this conversation. 'I can do fun, Caleb. I can be entertaining for small amounts—it's all I'm good for—but you don't want to know me long-term. I'm not all that interesting.'

'Who says I want to do long-term?'

She smiled sadly.

'Come on. We've already breached your one-night rule. I work with you. I spend time with you on breaks. We laugh. We flirt. We tease. I've cooked for you. Fed you. Tantalised your tastebuds. I would like to think that I tantalised another little bud I can think of.' He grinned. 'We could both scratch that itch we've both been feeling since I walked back into your life. Get it out of our system.'

'You just want to scratch an itch?'

He nodded.

'No strings?'

'Not a single thread.'

He could see she was thinking about it, considering it. He really wanted her to agree to it. It could be fun. It *would* be fun. She was clearly tempted. And what she'd said earlier about him not wanting to know her long-term was nonsense. Why wouldn't he? She was great. *Please say yes. Agree.*

'Okay. But I want a bath first.'

He raised an eyebrow, surprised that she'd agreed. 'I'll run it for you.'

* * *

She took her time in the bath, not wanting to rush it, not wanting to seem too eager to join him in the bedroom, even though she was. It was insanity, having a second night with him, knowing that they worked together, that they were colleagues and she would be see him every day after this at the hospital.

But…there was something about him that drew her to him and, now that she'd eaten, rested and washed, she felt amazing. Her tiredness gone, her arousal took first place in her consciousness. She didn't put on any clothes after the bath except for her fluffy bath robe and a dainty anointment of scent from her small collection of perfumes. Then she padded into her bedroom and found him lying on her bed, bare-chested and waiting for her. He looked like a delicious teddy bear with his dark, hairy chest and dark eyes, waiting for her in half-shadow, the cover slightly thrown back.

She thought about what lay beneath the covers—the parts of him she couldn't see. She felt a flush of desire and need, so strong it almost overwhelmed her, to abandon this slow, sultry walk into the bedroom and just pull back the covers, mount him and ride him into the sunset! But she made herself wait, knowing she was wet for him, and turned, slowly undressing by letting the bath robe drop to the floor, and raising her eyes to look at him.

His eyes widened, just as she'd hoped they would, and she watched him run his gaze over her naked body, not for the first time. But this time it felt better. More alluring. More tempting. She felt like some kind of sexy vixen. She was in control of this. *I am.* She had to believe that. It was important to her that all of this was under her control. She crawled into bed alongside him and let him reach out and touch her. Just because she was submitting to his touch did not mean that she was submitting, or submissive. She was the one allowing it. She was the one giving permission to him.

As Caleb pulled her beneath him and began to explore her body, she allowed herself to succumb to the masterful sensations he was creating. It had been a long time since she'd made love to a man in a bed. After Leo, all her previous encounters had been quickies. An abandoned hotel function room… The one before that had been in the back seat of a car—not as sexy as it appeared in films or on television. The one before that had taken place in a bathroom of a friend's house on New Year's Eve.

Before that, it had been Leo—her ex-fiancé and her first, and only, true love. A man she'd thought she'd be with for ever! A man to whom she had given her whole heart, believing that he would treasure it. A man who had hauntingly humiliated her in front of everyone she knew—every friend, every family member. A man whom she had subsequently discovered had been cheating on her. Since that day, she had refused to let any man have power over her, ever again.

But Caleb? He was not like those others. He was a real man. A solid, well-muscled, well-built and well-hung man who was now causing her to gasp and catch her breath as he explored her body with his tongue and his expert hands. The man could handle a scalpel, that was for sure, but he also knew intimately what to do with the rest of him, and it felt so good!

She wanted to lie there for ever and just let him do whatever he wanted, but she was not a passive player when it came to sex, so when she felt like she couldn't take any more she rolled him over and began to show him what *she* could do.

Together they tumbled, rolled, gasped and came and, after a rest, they did it all over again, and a third time, before falling asleep together, exhausted, sated and feeling that it was a draw. She didn't mean to fall asleep in his arms, but he was so warm, his body felt so right, she was so tired and so it just happened. Her head lay on his chest, her fingers mid-twirl in his chest hair. She was soothed to exhausted sleep by his heartbeat.

She had very sweet dreams that night.

The real nightmare began when she woke up.

CHAPTER SIX

WHEN SHE WOKE, she was still wrapped in his arms, warm, cosy and content. If she'd been a cat, she would have purred. She'd never slept over with anyone except Leo, so to find herself now in another man's arms was a pleasant surprise. She had slept so well. Her body felt sated, her body felt… *Okay, why does my stomach feel off?*

Behind her, Caleb still slept peacefully. She shifted slightly, propping herself up onto one elbow and turned and looked at him. If she'd felt her normal self, she would have ravished him again, as he looked so delicious just lying there, but she was beginning to feel quite sick. Had she eaten too much last night? Maybe the dessert had been too sweet.

I need to drink some water or something.

Carefully, she unwrapped herself from his embrace, grabbed her robe from off the floor and made her way to the landing. Her intention was to reach the kitchen, grab a glass of water and maybe put on the kettle on and make a coffee or something. Maybe eat some dry toast and hope that that settled her. But she never made it that far. As she crept away from her room, bile rose up suddenly into her throat and she rushed to the bathroom and was sick. She tried to be as quiet as he could, not wanting to wake Caleb, not wanting to let him know that she was ill.

When it was over, she wiped her mouth, washed it out with water and gazed up at her reflection in the mirror. She was pale again, exhausted again—now sick. If she didn't know any better, she'd say she was pregnant, but that was impossible, right? When could that have…?

She turned to look towards the direction of the bedroom, where Caleb slept. Her last sexual encounter had been with him, but they'd used protection, and besides she had polycystic ovarian syndrome; she'd been told the likelihood of her getting pregnant on her own was going to be difficult.

Not impossible, though—just difficult. She'd not checked the condom, nor had he. She'd simply taken it from him in that dark room, wrapped it in tissue and disposed of it. What if it had split? What if, right now, she was standing here incubating an embryo?

Heat washed over her and she began to sweat profusely. It all made sense! The exhaustion, the weird cravings, the nausea, the way food tasted off, the odd taste in her mouth… Had her body been sending her signals all this time and she'd dismissed them because she'd been busy or thought it an impossibility?

I need to know for sure.

One thing she did know was that she couldn't tell *him*. Not yet. Not until she was certain, and then she'd decide what to do. Until she knew, she would have to act normal. They had slept together again. It had been an amazing night, but now they had to work together, and this was not a relationship. Neither of them had committed to anything, except agreeing on no-strings-at-all sex. As far as she was aware, 'no strings' usually meant no request from one party to the other that they suddenly become a daddy and play happy families.

Why is this happening to me?

Caleb woke in Rory's bed feeling refreshed and happy. He'd had a great night with a fabulous woman, and he was looking forward to getting something to eat to refill his engine before they started a long day at work together.

But first things first—where was she? He would love to have woken with her in his arms and enjoy a little snuggle before they both got up, showered and dressed. Maybe they could share a shower. The idea of Rory and him standing under some steamy water whilst he soaped up her body appealed to him greatly. But she was already gone. Maybe she was just an early riser. He was, generally. If he'd been at home, he might even have gone for a run. Just a mile or two, to really wake him up and get himself mentally ready for the day.

The bed smelt of her, of sex. He pulled her pillow to his face and inhaled, breathing in the scent of her hair and perfume, before he let it go, swung his naked body from the bed and dressed in the clothes he'd been wearing yesterday. He had a spare set in his car, so he could get changed into a new shirt and tie before he returned to work. No-one would know that they had spent the night together, which was probably how they would both like it.

Hearing sounds filtering from the kitchen, and inhaling the scent of brewing coffee, he made his way there, standing in the doorway, still buttoning up his shirt as he watched Rory clear up their plates from the night before, which had been forgotten. 'Good morning.'

She jumped at the sound of his voice and glanced at him.

'Forget I was here?' he asked with a smile. He'd like to think that he wasn't forgettable. Last night was most certainly not a night he would forget in a hurry. It was a night in which amazing memories had been made and he would cherish them for a long time.

'Of course not. I just didn't hear you get up. Coffee?'

'Please.'

She grabbed a mug and poured him some, passing it over.

'Are you not having one?'

'No, I, er…fancy some juice.' She pulled open the fridge, poured herself a glass of fresh orange juice and took a small sip, pausing afterwards, as if she was checking something, before putting it down and carrying on with the tidying up.

'Let me help you.'

'It's fine.'

'Hey, I made this mess, let me help you clear it up.'

She sighed and stood back, letting him gather things, scrape plates and rinse them before they went into the dishwasher. 'Breakfast?' she asked.

'Whatever you're having is fine.'

'Oh, I was just going to have some toast…. You probably want something a bit more filling.' She checked in the fridge again, but it was appallingly empty except for a questionable pack of pancetta that sat at the back that he'd noticed was out of date when he'd put his food shopping in there yesterday evening. 'I have bacon, if you want me to fry that?' But she didn't sound like she wanted to at all.

Perhaps he had already outstayed his welcome by staying over. Perhaps she'd thought that, after the no-strings sex, he would escape her bed and go home. Perhaps she was embarrassed by this morning conversation. 'Want me to go?' he offered, trying to be a gentleman.

She turned and looked at him, hope filling her eyes. 'That might be best. You'll want to change clothes, I'm guessing, before work.'

Right. She was embarrassed. 'Aren't you worried the neighbours might talk, seeing a handsome man leave your place so early in the morning?'

'I barely know them.'

He'd hoped for a little protest, but clearly she wanted him gone. It stung a little, but it was probably better that way. He didn't want to look as though he was hoping for more here. This encounter was no strings. 'Okay, then. I'll go.'

She smiled. 'Okay.'

'But we're good? It's not going to be awkward at work?' he pressed. He didn't like awkwardness. He liked niceness. He liked flirtatiousness. He liked working with her.

'We're good.'

'Alright.' He took one final slurp of his coffee, put down his mug and then went over to her to kiss her one last time. He couldn't resist. She seemed taken aback, but accepted the kiss and tried her best to not look uncomfortable afterwards. Did he have morning breath? Surely he should have just tasted of coffee? That wasn't bad, was it? She must drink it, as she had it in the house, along with the coffee machine. Or maybe it was just the extended stay. He was meant to have gone and perhaps she just wasn't a morning person. 'I'll see you at work.'

'Yes. See you.'

He grabbed his jacket and left, heading out to his car in the crisp morning air and congratulating himself on giving her a good time. Rory had been everything he had felt she would be. They'd had quick sex, slow sex, passionate sex. They'd had it all and she'd been just as hungry for him as he'd been for her. But they'd scratched that itch between them now and they could just get on with work. It wouldn't stop him from flirting with her, though, because it had been *so fine.*

Maybe they could continue with their no-strings relationship. It would certainly suit him and he most decidedly hoped it would suit her too.

Rory slipped into the ultrasound room unnoticed and locked the door from the inside, switching on the equipment. Her heart was pounding, her blood pulsing in her ears.

She'd bought a pregnancy testing-kit from a chemist on the way in and had slipped into the first bathroom stall she'd found. Her hands had shaken as she'd opened the small package and read the instructions, telling herself that she was being ridiculous even testing; there had to be another reason for her symptoms. One last voice had pleaded for reason in a world that was filled with insanity. She'd peed on the stick, placed the test on the the cistern and waited, trying to ignore her churning stomach, trying to ignore the chatter she heard from other visitors to the bathroom. Eventually, she had picked up the test to look at it, but her hands had been trembling so much, the test had slipped from her fingers and fallen into the toilet bowl.

'No!' she'd cried out, staring at it lying there, submerged on the bottom, the test result unseen.

She'd dithered for a moment, then plunged her hand into the cold water, grimacing as she reached for the test and pulled it out to see two pink lines. But was that because of her, or because of the previous visitor to the toilet? There'd been no time to run back out to the chemist, and she wasn't sure she wanted to spend another ten pounds on something she might drop, so that had only left her with one option: the ultrasound room.

She couldn't do a blood test. If she ran a test under her own name testing for HCG, people would know. Even if she ran it under Jane Doe the staff would ask questions as to who was this mystery patient. So this was the only other way. No-one would think anything of an obstetric doctor going into the ultrasound room. This way, scanning herself, she would know for sure without anyone having to run a test and make her wait for an answer.

It was the not knowing that was awful. Her mind was going everywhere. What she would do if it was positive? How to tell *him*? How to tell everyone that she'd allowed herself to get knocked up when she was an obstetrician and ought to know better? When they were *both* obstetric surgeons!

She turned the monitor so that she'd be able to see it from the bed and placed the ultrasound wand down whilst she lowered her scrubs and squirted some cold gel onto her lower abdomen. Was it her imagination, or did it look rounder, already?

No. Impossible. If there is a baby in there, I'd only be a few weeks—classed as two months, maybe? Her cycle was all over the place from her PCOS, so she could only estimate, but she'd slept with Caleb nearly two months ago now…

Rory grabbed the wand and sucked in a steadying breath before she applied it to her abdomen and moved it around until the screen showed her the black space that was her womb…and there, at the bottom, a bean-shaped embryo, a tiny flicker in its chest.

Oh my God!

She almost dropped the transponder device and, as she did so, her hand jerked and something else flashed up on the screen. She blinked, not sure if she'd seen right. This time she moved it more slowly, wishing she'd done this standing up so that she could use the buttons on the machine for more detail, but…yes. There it was.

A second bean.

A second flicker.

Two babies. Two.

Twins.

This can't be! How was this happening? How was she pregnant with not one baby, but two? They weren't even in a proper relationship! She'd always assumed, because of the PCOS, that she would have to accept a surrogate. Or adopt. Or go through long rounds of IVF. That having a baby, having a family, would be expensive, hard and difficult to achieve. That she would have to go through lots of paperwork and heartache before it happened. Leo had never wanted to stick around to wait, though. He'd found someone else. Someone more fun, more spontaneous. He said she'd got too serious.

Caleb wasn't in the market to have a *relationship*. He enjoyed no-strings fun, like her. That was it. That was the extent of their relationship, if you could call it that.

They were friends and colleagues with benefits at this point, nothing more. She couldn't rely on him to be there for her, so she was already willing to go it alone.

She moved the scanner again and tried to find the one detail she wanted to see, but it wasn't there. There was no line between the twins indicating that they were in separate sacs. And she could only see one placenta—which meant identical twins. And it also meant that carrying these babies could come with a whole load of extra problems she didn't need.

'Hey, there you are! I've been looking for you all morning,' Caleb said when he finally saw Rory emerge from the lift onto the Maternity floor.

'Oh, yeah, I've been busy.' She tried to walk past him, holding a file in front of her stomach.

'Rory, wait.'

She stopped and turned to face him, eyes wary. 'What is it?'

He stepped up close. Close enough that they could have a private conversation, but not so close that people might think they were intimate. 'We're okay, right? After last night?'

They had to be. He really wanted to keep a good thing going with her, because the two of them together were sexual dynamite. And, to put the cherry on the cake too, he really liked her as a person. Respected her and the fact that she knew what she wanted from life and wasn't afraid to ask for it.

'Sure.' She looked away, around them, making sure no-one could hear.

Did he believe her? Right now, no, he didn't. 'Look,

let's meet for lunch. I've got a case right now, but I should be free about one-thirty.'

'I'm kinda busy to be honest with you, Caleb.'

'Please.' He gave her the look. A look that he had carefully cultivated over many years to be earnest and innocent. A 'please trust me' look. A 'please help me' look. A 'I don't mean any harm' look. He'd created it to use on his sisters. Being the only boy and the youngest of four kids, he'd often felt outnumbered by them, left out by them. And, with no dad around, he'd often felt desperate for company and for someone to talk to. Though he'd not dusted it off for decades, he was able to bring it out now and use it to perfection, because she finally caved and nodded.

'Okay. One-thirty.'

He smiled in triumph as she walked off, having got his way, his gaze focusing on the lovely way those scrubs moulded her body. A body that he had again become intimately acquainted with last night. If anything, she'd looked even more amazing than he remembered from the first time. The first time, he'd gone mostly by touch—when she had allowed it—and used his imagination. But last night he'd seen and felt everything, and she'd been so beautiful, so curvy, he'd almost exploded with his desire to consume everything about her: the swell of her hips, the curve of her bottom, her full, large breasts that had seemed so responsive to his touch. She'd tasted amazing and those little sounds she'd made before she'd orgasmed, the gasps as it had built up, had been just as delightful as the orgasm itself.

When she turned the corner and went out of sight, he headed off to check on his patient. The midwife looking after her thought that maybe she was showing signs of pre-eclampsia, a condition that could be extremely dangerous to the mother and baby, resulting in high blood pressure, severe headache, nausea, vomiting and even in full eclampsia or fitting. This patient was considered high risk. She was forty-two years of age and carrying twins, and had been advised to take aspirin since about twelve weeks, but the midwife reported that the labouring mother was experiencing intense headaches and was showing protein in her urine.

'Hi, Daphne, my name's Mr Stride. Morgan has called me in to talk to you about your results.'

Daphne sat and listened to him as best she could whilst having her contractions, but she was struggling. Her headache was bad, her blood pressure was rising and he didn't like what he saw on the CTG machine. The babies showed signs of not being happy in utero.

'In this situation, with the threat of pre-eclampsia, the only thing to help it is to deliver the babies. Normally, I would be happy to give you some medication to increase your contractions and get this baby delivered vaginally. But, as you're having twins, we don't need the complications of delivering one and then having problems getting baby number two out. With your permission, I'd like to suggest we take you down to Theatre and deliver the babies by caesarean section.'

Daphne finished breathing through her contraction and looked up at him, red-faced and sweating. 'Do what you have to do to get them here safe.'

'Alright. We'll get you to Theatre.'

He instructed Morgan and then left the room to call down to the theatres, telling them to prepare for a twin delivery. Daphne was at thirty-seven weeks, so he didn't expect the twins to need too much help after delivery, but he would still have the SCBU team there just in case.

Rory sat nursing a cup of cooling tea in the hospital cafeteria She'd also bought a chicken-salad wrap, along with a small plate of fries, figuring she needed to eat better now that she was eating for three. Three!

My life is crazy right now.

But every time she tried to take a bite of food her stomach lurched in protest. Pre-scan, she'd been able to try and eat the food, but *post-scan*? Now that she knew for sure that she was pregnant, it was like her body had fully acknowledged the morning sickness and was saying *this food will make you sick.*

She knew it wasn't just the food making her feel she couldn't take a bite. It was the knowledge. The knowledge that she was pregnant with two babies. She was in shock, her stomach in turmoil.

It lurched again when she saw Caleb walking towards her carrying a tray, and she managed a weak smile when he slid into the booth opposite her. He had a cup of coffee and a portion of lasagne with a side of broccoli, and the aroma of his food, the sight of it, made her want to hurl. She swallowed the feeling down.

'So…twins!' he said, beaming.

Rory stared at him. *'Wh...what?'*

'I've added two more to my delivery total. A healthy set of bouncing baby boys! Mind you, it was risky there for a moment,' he said, unrolling his knife and fork from the serviette and diving into the lasagne, unaware of the look of relief that spread across her face.

'That's great,' she managed.

She could not tell him about the pregnancy just yet. It was still early days. As an obstetrician, she knew that anything could happen in the first trimester. She could lose the pregnancy, miscarry the twins, and why tell him if that was going to happen? Probably best to keep this to herself until she got past the first twelve weeks.

'Multiples are always such a worry, aren't they?'

'I guess they can be,' she answered, thinking about two cots, two car seats, two lots of nappies, two screaming babies…

'And then, when the delivery is over and they're safe, you can finally breathe again. I'm not saying singleton pregnancies don't worry you as much, but twins and triplets and quadruplets and quintuplets…' He laughed. 'They scare the hell out of you more. Have you ever delivered quintuplets?'

She shook her head. 'No. Triplets a couple of times, but nothing more than that. You?'

'I saw a set of quadruplets born. I was involved in the case over in San Diego. The mother had had IVF and implanted two fertilised eggs and they both split. She carried them to thirty weeks and delivered two boys and two girls. They always send me a Christmas card.'

She managed a smile.

'Not hungry?' he asked, pointing at her untouched food.

'No, I, er…grabbed a snack earlier and kind of spoilt my appetite,' she lied, hating lying to him, but knowing that she could not give him any inkling as to what was going on with her. This was her burden and hers alone, right now. If she got past twelve weeks, then he could carry it with her, and she would just have to hope beyond hope that he would do the decent thing and stand by her and support her.

I guess I need to know more about what kind of guy he is.

'Caleb, can I ask you something?'

'Sure,' he answered, forking in a mouthful of broccoli.

'Do you…like babies?'

He looked puzzled at her question and laughed. 'What kind of weird question is that? Course I do!'

'You always wanted to be an obstetrician?'

Caleb nodded. 'Yes.'

'Even before you did placements in your training?'

Another nod. 'Yes. There were two very strong reasons as to why I wanted to be an obstetrician.'

'Care to share?'

He smiled. 'Alright. I'll play the game of you wanting to get to know the man you've shared a bed with for *two* nights. Not one. I mean, there had to be something special about me, right?' He winked at her. 'Okay, the first reason. My dad was a cardiologist, and he assumed I would be a cardiologist like him, and so I knew I had to pick something other than cardiology because I didn't want to be anything like him. I look like him, I sound like him, I even have his blood type, but I was not going to be his mini-me.'

'Why not?'

Caleb gave a short laugh. 'If you knew him, you wouldn't have to ask.'

'Daddy issues. Okay.' Father issues was a red flag. It probably meant that Caleb wouldn't make a great father either, until he worked to resolve his issues. She'd like to think that he would be great, but her past experiences with men abandoning her and going after someone better told her that this would probably be the same. 'And the second reason?'

'My mum.'

Of course. 'Because you were premature?'

He nodded. Rory stared at him, hoping he'd say more, reveal more.

'My mum went through a tough time, and she told me about it when I was old enough to know. She was scared. All her other pregnancies with my sisters had been fine, but with me she got to twenty-nine weeks and boom—started contractions. She had an infection, and she was scared and going into early labour, and no-one could tell her if I would be strong enough to survive back then. My dad got called to a patient and left her on her own, and so she turned to the staff to keep her calm and comforted. And they were there for her through it all, even when she nearly died. I wanted to be able to do that for someone else, if I could. Pay it forward.'

'She nearly died?' That sounded terrifying.

'The infection in her body was overwhelming and she'd become septic. Thankfully, they managed to save her. And me. They sat by our beds when my father didn't.'

Rory wasn't sure she could do this alone. What if something like that happened to her? Who would sit by her bed and pray for her? Maylee? Her mother? Caleb? And if everything did go okay… One baby was hard enough, but two—how would she deal with two? She would have to stop working! She would have to give her life over to two very demanding children; her life would never be the same again!

'What about you? Why did you become an obstetrician?' he asked her.

'Oh. I, er, wasn't sure what kind of doctor I wanted to be. But my first placement as a medical student was in labour and delivery and I became enamoured of it: the happy stories; the joy; watching people become a family. I know there are a few sad cases, but they're outnumbered by the good, aren't they?' she asked him, wanting to know his answer, thinking about the identical twins she carried.

She knew the risks, the possible issues with twin-to-twin transfusion syndrome when one twin got more of the blood supply and grew bigger, whereas the other one stayed small. Both twins were at risk; even though one would think the bigger twin would therefore be stronger, it wasn't always that way.

Rory had never thought she would end up with a problem pregnancy, because she'd never thought she'd be able to get pregnant anyway! But she couldn't end this pregnancy. It was a miracle, even if it was unexpected, a shock and not something she'd planned. Whatever fate had in store for her, she had to face it. And this was not like the aftermath of Leo's shock decision; this was hers to make and deal with. And, if everything went well this first trimester, Caleb's too.

'Have you ever thought of becoming a father?' she asked him, the question coming from her lips without her thinking about it.

'Me? Hah! I don't think I'd make a good father, and there is no way I'd want to be anything like mine, so... most likely not. Don't get me wrong, I love kids—I love babies and seeing them make other people happy is great—but as long as I can hand them over to someone else at the end of the day, then that's enough for me. I can live vicariously through them.'

Oh. Right. Yeah, the daddy issues. I kind of knew about those.

But it hurt to hear him say it. To hear him say that he wouldn't make a good father, so he'd rather not try.

Well, Caleb, you might just not have any choice in the matter—like me.

Over the next few weeks, Caleb began to notice how Rory kept finding the opportunity to sit down with him and ask him questions about his life. She was very curious! But she kept asking the questions he'd expect from someone who was aiming to be his girlfriend, and that put him on the back foot. So he instinctively did what he felt was right and tried to paint himself as the most dysfunctional person ever, with a terribly broken family, as much as he could aiming to make himself appear as someone with whom she would not want to form a long-term emotional attachment. Because he was good at putting up the barriers. It not only kept him safe, but her too. There was a nice line between enjoying sex with someone and being in a romantic relationship and he knew not to overstep it.

He continued to flirt, as he always did, but she seemed to be holding him at arm's length physically. He kind of liked the hot and cold nature of it, because it was almost like a game—which Rory would he get? And could he be persuasive enough to get her to let him back into her bed, despite him being supposedly dysfunctional?

He dreamed of her, if he was honest. Those two nights with her were very pleasant memories indeed and, though he was not in the market for a relationship, he had to admit that if he were it would be with someone like her. She was beautiful, talented, clever, skilled and sexy. She was fun in bed, fun at work. She made him smile, laugh and feel warm inside. She made him feel that he *mattered.* That was rare, and confusing, because he had to keep reminding himself that they were not going out, nor did either of them want that.

'Your father's in town,' his mother said to him on the phone, as he stood on the concourse during a break between patients.

'And that would be important to me why?'

'He asked to meet with me, to put me in the picture.'

'What picture is that?'

'He's moving back to London.'

'With Ella? And the kids?' Ella was his father's second wife. His second attempt at being a good husband and a good family man. He'd had two more babies with Ella, Caleb's half-siblings, but they'd never met.

'Alone. He and Ella broke up, and he met up with me to say he thinks he made a mistake and wants me back.'

Caleb's mouth dropped open. 'You're joking!' *More dysfunction to add to his family back story if Rory asked.*

'No.'

'And what did you say?'

'I told him that I would always love him, because he is the father of my children, but that I could never put myself back in a situation where I was not as important to him as his job or his patients.'

'And what did he say?'

'That he'd changed. That he'd been having therapy

and that he wanted to make things right, with you and the girls too.'

'Right. Yeah, he left one family to make another, and when that didn't work out left *them* too. Sounds like a decent guy. Jeez, what did you ever see in him, Mum?'

'I loved him and people do crazy things when they're in love.'

He became aware of movement at his side and realised Rory was standing beside him. She must have just arrived. He gave her a smile and raised a finger to let her know he'd be a moment. 'Further evidence as to why you will never find me falling in love. Which hospital is he working at? Just so I know to never go there.'

'I'm not sure. I didn't ask.'

'Oh, well, when you find out let me know. You'd think a cardiologist would have more sense about the human heart.'

His mum laughed. 'You would. He asked if your number is still the same. It's up to you if you answer him or not. Anyway, I'd better let you go. Take care, honey, and I'll see you soon.'

He wouldn't answer. His dad had had enough chances. 'Okay. Bye bye.' He ended the call. 'Hey.' He turned to smile at Rory.

'Hey. Who were you talking to?'

'My mum. Apparently my dad is back in town, alone and wanting a reconciliation.'

'Oh! And that's…bad?'

'Yes! The guy can't commit to anything, unless it's a patient and they're under anaesthetic; then the man can give his all. But if you're anyone else… Did you know that when I was seven years old I developed appendicitis?'

'No, I don't think you've told me that.'

'I'd been to a friend's birthday party and I developed tummy ache. My mum thought that maybe I'd eaten too many sweets and cakes, but overnight I got really bad and started throwing up and became feverish. Dad was at the hospital doing a night shift, and she called him to tell him she was taking me to A&E. My appendix had burst and I had to go into surgery. Guess how many times he visited me?'

'Er…once?'

'Try never.'

'What?' She looked shocked.

'He told my mum that appendicitis was a common surgery and nothing to worry about and that I'd be fine. And I was, but he didn't even come to see me once, because he got the chance to scrub into a heart transplant instead. My mother never forgave him for that and neither did I. He's always been the same way. A tragically distant dad, which is why you will never find me becoming one!'

'I'm sorry,' she said, her voice low.

'Why? It's not your fault he was a screw-up.'

'He hurt you. Doesn't mean you'd be the same way.'

Caleb shrugged. 'I'll never take that chance. I got used to not being important enough.'

'Maybe that's another reason you became a doctor—to become important. To feel like you mattered.'

He smiled at her. She was always trying to psychoanalyse him lately. It was cute! 'Maybe you should have gone into mental health services. You'd be good at it.'

'No thanks. I love the job I have.'

'Good. Because you're amazing at it.'

'Thank you.'

'Did you, er, need me for something? Because I'm available if you're looking for someone to rock your world in a linen cupboard or anything like that.' He winked.

Rory smiled. 'I do need you, but not for that, sadly.'

'Sadly is right.' He let out a dramatic sigh.

'But I do need you to cover for me for an hour tomorrow. I have an appointment that I can't miss.'

'Tomorrow? What time?'

'Nine o'clock. I know you're not on until the afternoon, but if you cover for me then I'll cover for you later and you could go home early.'

'Sure. Everything alright?'

'Why wouldn't everything be alright?'

He shrugged. 'No reason.'

'So you'll do it?'

'Sure. Now have you really given enough thought to what I said about the linen cupboard?'

Rory smirked and walked away.

He watched her go. The woman got curvier and curvier with every day. Or maybe it was just his eyesight appreciating the view, or his brain letting him see more about her, the more he knew. Whatever it was, he liked it very much indeed.

CHAPTER SEVEN

RORY HAD BEEN TO see her GP. She'd had the pregnancy confirmed, had registered with a midwife and, because she'd told the doctor it was twins from having scanned herself, the doctor had arranged for Rory to be scanned properly so that measurements could be taken and the pregnancy carefully assessed. 'I don't doubt your own skills and abilities, but we need to do this right,' Dr Staedtler had said. And so the text had come through to say that, though it was last minute, there was an available slot tomorrow morning for a scan of the babies.

Rory knew she ought to have contacted her GP earlier, but she'd been in shock for a while, getting used to the idea of carrying twins, and then she'd waited to see if anything would go wrong, which she'd been convinced it would. But when she kept waking up, still pregnant and still nauseous, she'd made an appointment and got it sorted.

No more sticking her head in the sand. Shc had to do this right! She'd started taking pre-natal vitamins such as folic acid as soon as she found out. Now she sat in the ultrasound department of a neighbouring hospital to St Henry's, because she'd not wanted Caleb or anyone else to see her name in the system and know before she was ready to tell them.

The other women in the waiting room seemed to be calmly excited. She wondered how many of them sitting there today were there because they'd had sex with a stranger and ended up with more than they were bargaining for. *Probably only me.* She assumed that the others were all happily married, or in committed relationships. She assumed they had a supportive partner, even though, through her own work, she knew the odds of that probably weren't accurate. She saw lots of women come through her department doing it on their own, and with every single one she'd thought about how brave they were and how strong.

Funny how she didn't feel that way herself. There was nothing brave about her right now: she was terrified of what this would mean, trying to parent two babies on her own. Would she have to give up her job? Maybe she'd have to try to wrangle support from a guy, who though sexy as hell, was not going to be father of the year, because he'd already made it quite plain that being a father was the furthest thing from his mind.

A couple of the mothers had toddlers with them. She watched the little ones play, toddling around the chairs and drooling. One touched her skirt with a particularly sticky hand and she smiled politely despite the mother's apologies. Would that be her soon? But, having two, what if they ran off in opposite directions? Which one would she go after? How would she choose? Rory felt sick for a moment, then her name was called and she went into the room with the sonographer, who introduced herself and told Rory to lie on the couch and loosen and lower her waistband.

Rory was about eleven weeks now and she'd already

noticed things getting tight. She'd already gone up a size in scrubs, because she wanted—needed—them to look baggy to hide her growing bump. After today, she'd have a better idea of how everything was going—if the babies were growing appropriately, what might be her risks for certain conditions and her schedule for future checks. But it also meant that after this appointment she would have to start telling people: her mum; Maylee.

Caleb.

She'd tried to imagine it. She'd practised the conversation with him over and over again in her mind, trying out different reaction scenarios. In one, Caleb was amazing and kind and, though shocked, he would be happy to try and be there for her as much as she needed. That was the conversation she liked practising the most. But the one that haunted her was the one in which he looked at her in abject shock and horror and told her that he'd support her financially, but that was all, reminding her of all the times he'd told her that he could never be a father.

'Any history of multiples in the family?' the technician asked.

'No. Not that I'm aware.'

'Well, these are definitely identical twins, but they look great to me at the moment. Measuring their thigh length and head circumference, they're both the size I'd expect to see in normal singleton pregnancies.'

'That's good.'

The technician nodded. 'It's very good. We'll keep track of their measurements with each scan so we can measure their growth along the percentile scale.'

The percentile scale was a way to measure a baby's growth by comparing their measurements to other babies of the same gestation, age and gender. So, if a baby was on the fiftieth percentile for weight, then they were right in the middle and average. If a baby was on the ninetieth percentile, then that baby was weighing more than ninety percent of other babies of the same gestation, age and gender.

'This is Baby A's heart.'

Rory heard and monitored babies' heartbeats every day in her work. But hearing her own child's heartbeat had a broad smile crossing her face at the exact same time her eyes filled with happy tears. She'd not expected such a reaction from herself, but she'd noted of late just how emotional she'd been getting as her body filled with extra hormones.

They listened to both babies' hearts and she cried for each one. The technician told her that the babies were measuring at twelve weeks and one day's gestation.

'Everything looks great. Would you like pictures?'

Rory nodded numbly and sat up, wiping the gel from her abdomen and doing up her skirt. The babies were well and healthy. So was she. There was no reason to keep this news from anyone any more. She wished…part of her wished…that Caleb could have been here to see this. To share in this. By not telling him earlier, she had stopped him from having the chance and now she felt guilty and sad. Would she always do this alone? Probably. Caleb wasn't a good bet for a father.

But the pictures the technician passed her were enough to lift her heart again, and she thanked her and left. She had to get to work.

And she had to tell Caleb that his greatest fear was coming true.

* * *

Caleb had just performed a caesarean on a woman who had failed to progress. He hated that term—as if it was her fault or something, when she had no control over how strong or frequent her contractions were, or how much she could dilate. The baby's heart had begun to show consistent decelerations and the decision had been made by the parents and the team to intervene for the sake of the mother, who was exhausted, and for the baby.

It had been a good outcome and a wise one. The cord had been wrapped multiple times around the baby's neck and a vaginal delivery might have proved incredibly risky for its health. Instead, they had a happy mother and a happy baby, and that was all that mattered.

So he felt on top of the world when he emerged from Theatre and found Rory waiting for him. 'Hey! How's it going?'

'Mmm…good.' She looked apprehensive, as if she wanted to ask him out or something. Maybe she did. He perked up even more and gave her his best smile. 'Could I ask you to meet me for lunch in the hospital canteen?'

'Sure, no problem. What time?'

'Erm…about one? One-thirty, maybe?'

'Of course! I wouldn't miss it.' She had very quickly become one of his favourite people to hang around with in the few short months he'd been working here.

'Great. I'll see you later, then.'

She gave him a weird look before she walked away, and he felt his pulse thrum within his veins. Did she want to suggest that, after all these weeks of flirting, they take their relationship to the next level? Because he would happily meet up with her for intimate relations any time she wanted!

Being friends with benefits with Rory would be amazing and perfect—just what he was looking for. She was a wild cat in bed, and he'd loved every moment of being with her, which was why he'd constantly tried to score a repeat of that second night. And besides, he'd liked spooning her all night. He could most definitely see them both doing more of that. He was a very sexual being, and he felt she was too.

If only she'd allow them both free rein to continue to enjoy the adult fun they had experienced together so far. They'd proved that they could do that and still work well together, so what would be the issue? Nothing he could see. And if they kept it all about sex then there was no danger of either of them thinking that it was going to become something more—though, he had to admit to himself, if he were to pick someone with whom to be in a relationship, she was the kind of woman he'd choose.

When lunch time arrived, he headed up to the canteen, hungry for many things. He scanned the crowd and saw her seated at a booth near the back. He gave her a quick wave, grabbed a chicken Caesar wrap and a cup of tea and headed over to their table.

She had an empty soup bowl in front of her and a side plate of crumbs, from which he figured she'd had a bread roll or two. 'You need to eat more than that,' he said, knowing how busy and hectic their jobs were. They needed energy to sustain themselves as doctors, on their feet all day *and* performing surgeries. They couldn't allow their blood sugar to drop for a moment. And, if they were going to take part in extra-curricular activities in linen closets, then she'd definitely need to keep up her energy levels.

'I'll grab dessert in a minute. I wanted to talk to you first.'

'Okay. What's up? Oh, how did your thing go this morning?'

She smiled and nodded. 'Good. Actually, it's…kind of what I wanted to talk to you about.'

He was intrigued. 'Okay. Shoot.' He bit into his wrap hungrily.

'I've er…kind of been unsure lately about whether to tell you something, but after this morning I know that I can't hold it back any longer. And, whether you like it or not, you need to know something.'

Know something? His smile faltered. Oh. Had she fallen for him? Was that why she'd been blowing hot and cold? Was she struggling with her own feelings for him? Because if that was what had happened here then, despite their chemistry, he was going to have to let her down gently.

'I had a hospital appointment this morning. At Guy's.'

Okay. This was not what he'd expected to hear. A hospital appointment at Guy's? He swallowed his mouthful of food and frowned. He felt a little worried for her, a little concerned. What did this have to do with him? Unless, of course… *Ah.* The *only* reason she'd go to another hospital would be so that she didn't have a patient record here. It had to be something she was embarrassed about. But he'd not noticed any weird or worrying symptoms of his own, so he didn't think that she'd passed anything onto him, if that was what she was worried about.

'Hey, it's okay. *I'm fine*,' he said, trying to reassure her.

'What?'

'I don't have anything and I regularly screen if I have a new partner—which, admittedly, isn't that often. Are you okay?'

She looked a little confused and annoyed, and she shook her head. 'No, Caleb, I'm not talking about an STD here!' she said, low and urgently.

'Then what are you talking about?'

'I'm trying to tell you that I'm pregnant! With your baby! Well, with a little more than that, actually. With *both* your babies.'

He couldn't be hearing her right. She was *pregnant*. Both babies…? Did she mean she was pregnant with twins? *'What?'*

'I'm twelve weeks' pregnant.' She paused to scan his face then slid a picture across the table. 'Congratulations.'

What she said couldn't be right. This had to be a joke. They'd used contraception. He remembered her asking for it that first night in the room they'd sneaked off to when they'd had sex. He'd removed the condom and… he'd not checked it. He'd passed it to her and she'd placed it in a tissue and said she'd get rid of it. It had been dark; he'd not thought to check it. Had it burst? Because they'd definitely used protection!

'*Two* babies?'

She nodded, looking at him with concern. 'Identical twins. I had a scan this morning.'

He looked down at the ultrasound picture. He'd seen many over his years working as an obstetric surgeon, but to be passed pictures of *his* babies… Baby A. Baby B. He looked at them hard and saw Rory's name at the top, her date of birth and her NHS number. These were most definitely her scans… And now they were his! The food in his stomach churned and he couldn't look at his plate.

'I… I don't know what to say right now.'

A father—he was going to be a father. The one thing that he was afraid of being, in case he would be just like his own. All he'd heard growing up from his mother and his sisters was that he was the spitting image of their father. He was the only one of them who even had his father's blood group! They were all O-positive, like their mother, but he was A-negative, like his dad.

And for most of his life, from a teenager onwards, he had tried to do everything in his power to be the opposite of that man who didn't deserve the title of father. He might as well have just been a sperm donor. He'd never been home. Never been to school events. Never supported him in anything. He'd always been at work and, if he was at home, no-one had been allowed to bother him or disturb him because he *needed his space.*

He'd been let down a lot by that man. It wasn't just the appendicitis surgery he hadn't turned up to; he hadn't shown up when Caleb had broken his arm after falling from a tree. He hadn't come to see him when he'd got the lead role of Dracula in a school play. He hadn't turned up for birthdays, because he'd always been working. Christmases had been ruined by his absence. The only thing he had shown up for was to walk his daughters down the aisle, and that had probably only been because he'd got to give them away and publicly prove that they were none of his concern any more.

Even that hadn't happened easily. He could remember hearing his mother shout at him that he'd better be there on the day or it would be the end of their own marriage.

His sad had done his duty there, but at the receptions afterwards he'd seemed withdrawn and absent, even though he'd been right there!

Caleb could count on his hands the amount of times he'd actually sat down and had a proper conversation with his dad, and even then he was being generous in considering those events proper conversations. His father had often gone off on weird tangents and talked about something else entirely.

He had told himself he would not be like his own father and, to prevent that, his entire life plan had revolved around the idea that he would just never have kids himself. It would be one in the eye for his old man, not continuing on the Stride name, but tough.

And yet now Rory was telling him that she was carrying his twins. There weren't enough words in his vocabulary to describe how he felt. Shocked, for sure. Afraid, no doubt. Guilty? Yes. Because already he was letting them down. Most committed fathers-to-be would be thrilled to hear that they were about to become dads but here he was, staring at the scan pictures and thinking of ways he could deny that all of this was happening!

'You're twelve weeks?'

'Yes.'

It tied in with that first time they'd done it in the hotel conference room. He believed her, too. They had to be his. Rory didn't screw around, he saw that—she wasn't that type of woman. She'd done nothing but work hard in the time that he'd known her and any down time she had was used for sleeping.

'I know it's a shock for you, so you need to take some time to wrap your head around it, like I did.'

'How long have you known?'

'Weeks.'

He looked at her. 'And you didn't say a word?' He didn't mean to raise his voice. It just happened.

'How could I?' She leaned in, blushing, her voice urgent again. 'I couldn't believe it myself, and what would have been the point in telling you if I'd only gone on to miscarry? Lots of first pregnancies fail and I was scared stiff!'

Of course. This wasn't just about what he felt but her too. 'You're scared?'

She nodded. 'But I'm keeping them, just so you know. If you don't want anything to do with these babies, then sure, eventually I'll understand, but my hope is that you will want to be involved.'

'Of course I'll be involved!' he said, raising his voice again then checking himself, remembering where they were. He didn't want to bring attention to them and he didn't like raising his voice to her either. It was just the shock. 'I can't not be,' he said, knowing it implicitly. Despite his fears about being a father, he had an obligation here, and he never shirked those. 'I'm just going to have to do my best.'

He couldn't let Rory down. Not her… Why *not her?* That puzzled him.

'That's all any of us can do. Think I know how to be a mother? We both know they don't send you home with a manual for these things.'

'Things?' he asked, trying to make the mood lighter, trying to distract himself from the fact that she somehow meant so much more to him than anyone else.

'You know what I mean.' She gave him a look then. A

look so full of concern that it made him realise that they both felt exactly the same way: shocked and afraid. 'I think we just do what we can, as and when we can. And, somehow, we'll both just muddle through it.'

'Wow. Giving speeches like that, you'll have your own TED Talk in no time.' It was a flash of his old self. It was reassuring to know that he could still make a joke.

She reached across the table for his hand and took it in hers. He was surprised but he liked it very much. He knew no-one could see them back here, so he squeezed her fingers in reassurance. 'We'll find a way to do this.'

'We will.'

'Parenting. It can't be that hard, can it?' Though he knew all too well how quickly a person could screw it up. He knew the love of his mother, but he had not known the love of his father.

What might it feel like to be told by your dad that he was proud of you? Caleb was determined, somehow, that his own children, his twins, would *not* have to wonder how it felt. That he would be able to show them that he loved them, somehow.

He did not know how he would do that, and he feared his ability to do it, not having had a role model himself. But thousands of men became fathers every day and they managed it.

Maybe he wouldn't fumble the bag on this one. Maybe, just maybe, he had the potential within him to be the greatest father in this world.

Now, that would be one in the eye for his dad, for sure.

CHAPTER EIGHT

AS THEY WALKED back to the ward, Caleb stopped Rory just before they went through the secure double doors. 'You know, you and I—we should, um, get to know one another a little bit better. More than this, what we have right now.'

'I've been trying to do that, already.' Get to know one another a little bit better? For weeks now, Caleb had let her know that, though he wasn't a great catch, he would be happy to jump into bed with her at any moment. Whilst she appreciated the blatant fact that he found her sexually attractive, right now, pregnant with his twins, she wanted to know if he could see her as more than just a sexual being.

'I know and I reacted badly to that. But we should talk, spend time with one another, if we're going to be…' he looked around to make sure no-one was listening '…*co-parenting.* I think we ought to know who we're each dealing with a little bit more.'

He was right. She'd thought about that herself. And it wasn't as if he was asking her to be his girlfriend here. He'd nailed it with the word 'co-parenting'. They would parent these babies together, but that was *all* they would do. Except maybe be friends and colleagues. They would be in each other's life a lot! They just wouldn't be living together.

Would he still want to have sex with her, now that he knew? It would be interesting to see if he still flirted with her, or whether he considered her to be off-limits, now that she'd changed from being his hot sex buddy to the mother of his children.

'Okay. I agree. What do you suggest?'

'I was hoping that you might steer that ship. And that maybe, this time, I might be a bit more forthcoming.'

He smiled. He had a cute smile. She could look at it all day, to be honest. But he had to have more than that and a cute butt to do this with her. 'We should, I don't know, go out for a meal, or something? Somewhere we could talk that's not here.'

He nodded. 'Or…you could come to mine and I could cook. I'd like to cook for you for you again. Have I told you before about my world-famous cannoli?'

He had. He'd often bragged that he was just as skilled in the kitchen as he was in the bedroom. What else was he skilled at? Could he hang a roll of wallpaper? Fix a tap? Build a cot? Change a nappy? *I guess I'll find out one day.*

'Okay, dinner at yours. When?'

'When's good for you?'

'Tomorrow? I don't have as much nausea now, so… I could eat.'

'Perfect. Seven o'clock?'

She smiled. 'Seven o'clock.'

They made a pact to meet up and eat together at least twice a week for the next few weeks, as they got to know one another. To begin with, Rory felt nervous each time. What they were doing was stepping way beyond her usual tactic about knowing a guy. She'd had a one-night rule for a reason—she didn't want to have to get to know someone, because what if they let her down again? What if they humiliated her, the way Leo had? What if Caleb walked away and left her to deal with this on her own? And yet here she was, forced into a situation in which she *had* to get to know Caleb, no excuses.

It was scary stuff! *But,* she reasoned, *it's not like I'm getting into a romantic relationship again. It's not like this is going to end with me donning a white dress and walking up the aisle again, only to find it empty at the other end.*

Caleb seemed committed to the idea of co-parenting, to giving it his all, as much as he could, promising that he *would not* let her down. But so had Leo. He had put a ring on her finger and promised to marry her. Promised to be by her side until the end of their days and yet, when she'd turned up to that church, he'd not been there. He'd chickened out at the last moment. Some time later, when they had met to talk, he'd said marriage wasn't for him—and that actually, when he thought about it, marriage *to her* was not what he wanted. That there had, in fact, been someone else, someone *better* than her. Being abandoned had been bad enough, but being abandoned and finding out she'd already been replaced had been another level. It had been a hard punch to the gut, and in front of all her family, all her friends. Everyone from work knew about it and had watched her try to recover her dignity and act as if it had never happened.

What if Caleb said all the right things, promised her

and the babies all the right things, but then abandoned her when the babies arrived? It could happen. And that would be even worse. So this process of getting to know him was incredibly important. She was trying to see inside his soul.

Yes, he was a great cook, he had a nice flat and amazing bookshelves, filled with a wide range of fiction and non-fiction, but what did that tell her about him? His flat was neat and cared for. Pictures of his mum, his sisters and their children abounded, so he was a family-oriented guy. But it was one thing to be a great son or a great brother. Being a father was a struggle for a lot of guys, and he'd told her right at the beginning that he didn't want to be one, that he had father issues—now these babies in her belly had forced them both into a corner.

And what happened to people forced into corners? They fought their way out.

'This looks great,' she said, lifting a lid from a pan to see what was cooking.

She was round at his again, eighteen weeks' pregnant and feeling much better. The glow promised to most pregnant women was an actual glow now, and not just a fine sheen of sweat from her nauseous stomach. People at work knew she was pregnant. They knew that Caleb was the father. It had started the gossip mill going, but they were riding that storm.

'It's white bean stew.'

'Stew?'

'It's good for you, and it has the added benefit of tasting amazing with the Irish potato bread I've made.'

'You're so domesticated. I like it.'

She'd quickly discovered his love for cooking. It was

something he'd taken up during his time away at medical school, needing to find a relaxing, yet creative, outlet. It turned out that Caleb Stride, sex god extraordinaire and father of her babies-to-be, had actually been the resident cook and baker in his halls of residence, filling the building with aromas of fresh bread or apple pies, or knocking on doors to share muffins and slices of lemon tart.

The fact that he'd found time to do that around the masses of studying they'd had to get through amazed her. She had no doubt that Caleb must have been popular, especially with all the young women. But she didn't like to think about that. How many had come before her?

'You find the time for the things in life you love,' he said. 'Cooking, I mean,' he added awkwardly, as if his statement implied that, by cooking for *her*, he loved *her*.

They'd both stayed away from discussing them being in any kind of relationship, except a parenting one. They spent time together. They laughed, told stories, watched movies and bonded over books, music and food, but the big questions… They hadn't really tackled them yet, but Rory knew that needed to happen. She was almost halfway through this pregnancy.

'Oh!' Rory suddenly stood up straight and rubbed at her growing belly.

'Everything okay?'

'Yeah, I think I felt something.'

'Like a kick?'

She'd been aware of some weird swishy feelings, as if something was softly stroking the inside of her belly, but that was all. This was different—more…forceful. 'Maybe? I don't know.'

'Where was it?'

She reached for his hand and placed it on her bump where she'd felt the kick. They stood like that for a while, waiting, wondering, hoping, and were about to give up when it happened again.

A smile crept across Caleb's face. 'Oh my God.'

Rory laughed in shock. 'There's a real person inside me.'

'There's two.'

She looked at him and nodded, still in disbelief that her body was doing this.

'You've got another scan coming up soon, right?'

'Yes. The anomaly scan.'

'I'd like to attend that one, if that's okay?'

'Of course. Why wouldn't it be okay?'

He shrugged. 'I know I couldn't attend the first. You were going through some stuff on your own and I understand that. But I don't want to miss any more. I want to be there for everything.'

'Then you'll be there.'

He nodded and turned away to stir the stew. She felt he had something else he wanted to say. 'What is it?'

'Nothing.'

'No, say it. If we're going to do this, we have to be able to talk to one another. To ask the difficult questions.'

'I don't want to be like my dad. I want to be there for everything. And the idea that we'll co-parent but live apart is doing my head in. Because there will be things that will happen when I'm not there: the first word, the first steps. I'll either be at work or here and, though I could be round at yours a lot, there will still be things that I'll miss. Moments that both parents should see, experience.'

'I know you don't want to be like your dad, but what are you suggesting? It's not like we can live together.'

'Why not?'

'What?' She couldn't believe that he was asking this. *Live together? Move in and actually live together?* 'But… we're not…going out or anything.'

'I didn't say anything about romance, I said living together. Lots of people live together. House mates. Lodgers. We could find a place and do that. That way, we're both there, but we still have our own independent lives.'

'Find a place?'

'Well, your place isn't big enough for all of us and neither is mine. We could rent a place together—move in. That way these babies get their mum and their dad in the same place and I won't feel like I'm missing out on my kids or have to make appointments to see them. Do you know how sad that would be if I had to do that?'

'I get it,' she said, understanding his concern. But moving in together? That was a big thing to decide. A huge life choice!

She'd already fought a bombardment of questions from her mum and family as to who this guy was, why they weren't together or getting married and how the co-parenting was going to work. How would she explain *this* suggestion? Would they think it a good thing, or just tell her she was making another huge mistake in renting or buying a property with a guy who wasn't committed to her, only to the babies? Her mum had already worried about him wanting to take them and go for custody. She'd even suggested she get him to sign something to say he wouldn't take her grandchildren away from her.

'Think about it,' he urged, bending down to open the oven and check on the potato bread.

She nodded. She would. But it was a huge commitment. The last time she'd tried to make a huge commitment with a guy, it had all gone terribly wrong and her life had been ruined. What if the same thing happened here? What if they ended up hating one another, or unable to speak to one another? Would the babies be affected too? Before, all she'd had to worry about was herself. The only person she'd had to pick up and shake down was herself. But this time there was more at stake. She had to think of her children too. What was best for them? And what was the least risky thing for her?

Could she trust him—truly? She had to trust him with the babies—he was their dad and he wanted to be part of their lives, for which she was grateful—but what if he let them all down? What if he couldn't be a good father, the way he feared? Would she be exposing them to possible emotional pain further down the line, when her children would one day blame *her* for putting her trust in a guy who had told her from the outset that he'd never wanted to be a father?

What if he was playing a role? What if this was just some sort of game to him, with which one day he would grow bored, the way Leo had grown bored with her and picked someone else? She saw it in plenty of fathers at the hospital. The babies in their partners' bellies were exciting, fun, and they had all these dreams and hopes. But then during the birth, watching those babies emerge, seeing a real-life person actually get birthed and realising that they were responsible for it hit home. It scared them.

And some of them backed away completely.

Caleb was nervous sitting in the waiting room, waiting with Rory to go in for the anomaly scan. She was a little over twenty weeks now and this would be the first time he would see them for himself. He'd watched her grow bigger, had felt them move and kick, and that was amazing. It was different when it was his own. He'd watched and coached so many women through labour and delivery no matter how it happened, watched a woman and a man transform right before his eyes into a mother and father, a family.

But, now that it was happening to him, he could understand even more all the worries, the fears. The apprehension at holding them right, at taking them in their arms for the first time, terrified that the world might somehow do them harm the second they exited the hospital. Being an obstetric doctor, he'd always assumed that if he ever became a father, which he'd strongly doubted, he wouldn't be that worried at all. He'd been wrong. And it made him question his own father even more. Had he not felt the same thing? Had he not wanted to protect them all?

Caleb had discovered that he was, if anything, worrying excessively, afraid that any misstep would somehow prove to the world that he wasn't good enough to look after them properly. And this anomaly scan—what if it showed something wrong with the babies, something genetic? What if there was something wrong with him at genetic level and he was a carrier of something and had somehow altered his children's lives even before they'd been born?

Being an obstetric doctor, he knew there was so much that could go wrong with identical twins. Twin-to-twin transfusion syndrome, for one. Then there was TAPS to worry about: twin anaemic polycythaemia sequence, in which one twin could be severely anaemic and the other polycythaemic, meaning it received too high a blood count. There could be amniotic fluid issues: too much or too little. What if their cords got entangled? Identical twins statistically had a higher risk of birth defects.

All these worries and more swirled around in his brain, knowing he was defenceless against them all, that he could do nothing about them. He couldn't protect them from any of it!

'Have you had any thoughts about what I said the other week?' he asked to distract himself from the vortex of worry sucking him down. 'About getting a place?'

She glanced at him. 'Erm… I've thought about it non-stop.'

'And? When are we moving in together? Living in sin? Having sex morning, noon and night?' He smiled.

She gave him a playful nudge. 'Is that what you think is going to happen?'

'It'd be fun, wouldn't it? You can't get any more pregnant, though I'd be happy to try.'

Rory smiled. 'It's a big decision.'

'So is bringing babies into the world and we're doing that together.'

'We had no choice in that.'

'True. What's worrying you about getting a place?'

'Who said I was worried?'

'Well, if you weren't worried, we'd be looking already.'

'I just don't want to make a mistake, Caleb.'

'Thanks.'

'No, you don't get to be like that. You're asking for a huge thing from me. Get a place together? Move in with you to raise these babies together? What happens when it all goes wrong? What happens if you meet someone else, or I do? And when one of us falls head over heels with someone else and wants to live with them—what then? People leave when that happens.'

'It's never been in my life plan to fall in love and get married,' he said.

'It was never in your plan to have children and that's happening,' she replied, raising an eyebrow at him, just as her name was called.

They stood up and went into the small darkened room, where the technician introduced herself and Rory lay on the couch, exposing her abdomen to be scanned. She looked healthy, full…ripe. His babies were in there!

But what she'd just said to him was right. What if he did meet someone he couldn't stop himself falling in love with when he was living with Rory? How would another woman feel about him living with his baby's mother, but saying it was totally innocent? Clearly it hadn't been at one point! Would he move out? Would he put this *other* romantic relationship before his kids? Would he make the choice to make his kids take second place in his affections and promise that he'd still visit as often as he could, but would split his time between homes? His father had left one family and made another, and apparently had come back begging for a second chance after realising his mistake. Was he doomed to make a mistake too?

And what if *she* met someone? Someone who loved the babies and her and wanted to slide a ring on her finger and take care of them for the rest of their lives? Would she ask Caleb to move out? Would she just take the babies and go?

There were so many uncertainties and they reminded him that he needed to harden his heart, to put up some barriers just in case, so that he'd be prepared for any eventuality. Maybe moving in together was a bad idea, in that case. Perhaps they *shouldn't* get a place, and he should accept the fact that he would just have to make appointments to be able to see his kids.

'This might feel a little cold,' the technician said, squirting gel onto Rory's belly.

Then she moved the Doppler, he could see his babies on the screen and it was the single most glorious thing he had ever witnessed. His babies! His twins! One was sucking its thumb! His heart melted in that moment and all his fears disappeared for just a second as he sat and marvelled at what he and Rory had created between them. The measurements were good. Both babies were doing well and, at the moment, there appeared to be no sign of anything being wrong, which was fantastic news!

Had his father marvelled at his wife's growing bump? Had he placed a hand on her belly to feel the kicks? Had he cared? Would he have connected with his children better, if he could have seen them like this? Could have heard their heartbeats and watched them slip and slide in the womb?

'Well, everything looks good at the moment. As these twins are sharing a sac and a placenta, we will probably want you to come in weekly so we can keep an eye on them—check for cord entanglement and check their cerebral arteries. Don't be alarmed by it; it's all done for safety, so we can get ahead of any potential problems that may arrive.'

Rory nodded. This was because their twins were MCMA twins—monochorionic monoamniotic twins. They'd the same placenta, same sac.

'Would you like to know the sex?'

They'd not discussed that. Caleb glanced at Rory. 'I don't mind. You choose.'

'I think I'd like to know.'

The sonographer smiled and moved the wand around Rory's abdomen to show them what they were having.

'Twin girls!' he said, surprised. *Daughters*. Daughters were precious. They'd need protecting from this cruel world. He felt a wave of protectiveness wash over him, a wave of duty, care and love.

Rory hiccupped a laugh and that was when he realised she was crying. He passed her a tissue from a box conveniently on a table beside him. 'We'll have an earlier delivery, won't we?'

The technician nodded. 'Usually MCMA twins are delivered on or around thirty-two to thirty-three weeks. You'll be able to discuss this with your consultant.'

'He'll prescribe me steroids—for the babies' lungs to mature?' Rory asked.

'Yes, but again that's something you'll discuss with your consultant. You're under Mr Atwood-Green?'

'Yes.'

'He might also suggest daily foetal monitoring when you reach twenty-four to twenty-five weeks. Babies move all the time and we'll need to check for entanglement.'

'We could do that at our own hospital. We work at St Henry's and he consults there too. It's why we picked him.'

'Then I don't see why that would be a problem.' The technician smiled and passed them a few pictures from the scan.

'So, I'll be a caesarean,' Rory said as she got up into a sitting position.

Caleb nodded. It was the safest delivery for this rare type of twins.

'Thank you.'

They thanked the technician and left, clutching their pictures and feeling happy that the growth of both twins was fine. The risks of Downs was low and, because Rory had a nice long cervix, there was no risk of her going into premature labour.

'So, I've got a few more weeks of freedom, then daily checks for what—nine weeks? Then deliver?'

'Looks like it.'

Rory sighed. 'I knew this was complicated, but now it's just getting more so. What if something goes wrong?'

'I think it's natural to worry, but everything's fine right now. Let's keep that in our minds and carry on as normal. Let's only worry when there's something to worry about.'

She nodded. 'Identical twin girls. Daughters.' She shook her head and laughed. 'Can you believe it?'

He smiled, but as they got to the car, he looked at her over the roof of it. A sudden determination filled his soul. 'I have to be there for them. To protect them. To love them. To marvel in their every day. I don't want to have to make an appointment with you to see them. I know that makes it complicated, and what might happen if one of us meets someone else but, like I said, let's cross that bridge when, or even if, we come to it. We'll work it out then. Let's get a place. What do you say?'

Rory stared at him, biting her bottom lip as she thought. 'I don't want to make a mistake, Caleb.'

'Neither do I. But I do feel that living apart from my children would be a huge one. I can be there for them, we can share the care… I can help. I want to be hands-on. I *have to be* hands-on. I can't do this any other way.'

Rory nodded and got into the car.

'How many weeks are you?'

Rory's patient, Freya Young, was currently on a bed, strapped to the CTG machine and trying to distract herself from her own fear of giving birth by concentrating on someone else. 'Twenty-one,' she said.

'Halfway!' Freya said. 'Do you know what you're having?'

'Twin girls.'

'Twins? Oh, how exciting! Hard work, though, I'd imagine.'

'All babies are hard work,' Rory agreed with a smile as she checked the trace. The baby's movements had reduced somewhat, but the heart tracing was good, and Freya was contracting four in every ten minutes. They were monitoring the baby because Freya had developed gestational diabetes in the last few weeks of her pregnancy, and the baby was large, but had slowed down with its movements. Midwives usually suggested to expect to feel at least ten movements every couple of hours, but all babies were different, and it was important that each individual mother got used to her own baby's movements and noticed if anything changed.

Freya had noticed a drop in the last week and she'd been admitted for monitoring. Her labour had been induced, as her waters had broken with no sign of starting labour on her own, and there'd been some mild green staining in the water, indicating the baby had passed a stool in utero.

'And a worry. I don't know how I'm going to do this on my own.'

'You're not on your own, you've got me,' Freya's mum said, rubbing her daughter's shoulder.

'For this bit. But you live four hours away, Mum. You can't stay for ever. I'm going to be on my own for the majority of it.'

Rory's mum was close enough. Maylee was an hour away. She knew Caleb would want to be by her side for the caesarean and, now that she'd agreed to them getting a place, they would no doubt have to move in with one another soon and get used to living together. Would it be awkward? They hadn't slept together again since he'd found out about the pregnancy, despite the hormones flooding her system and making her hyper-aware of him and his proximity. Would they be able just to stick to co-parenting in their house? Or would they succumb to their desires, slip into each other's beds and make this even messier than it already was?

Since Caleb had suggested they move in, that they take such a big step, she'd noticed herself watching him. Every time he spoke to another woman at work—a midwife, a nurse—or every time he laughed with them or she saw them flirting with him, she felt a warning pang that this could all go so badly for the babies and her. She didn't want to feel jealous or worried. It wasn't as if he was her boyfriend or anything, and she had no right to be jealous, but she couldn't stop herself from noticing. He was an attractive man. He was bound to attract attention.

Caleb had said they'd discuss it later down the line if either of them met someone, but honestly, Rory couldn't imagine meeting someone else. It wasn't as if she was going to be out on the town, or clubbing. She'd either be at work, working or home, trying her hardest to raise two daughters! But Caleb might meet someone. He wouldn't get the maternity leave that she would, so he would be at work whilst she was at home and the hospital was filled with plenty of attractive young women who might flirt with him. And she knew, from her own experience, that he was a very sexual person.

What if, whilst she was at home changing dirty nappies, juggling bottles and laundry, not able to shower, Caleb was at work getting it on with a nurse in a linen cupboard? The thought disturbed her and the fact that she *was* disturbed disturbed her even more! She had no claim on him. It wasn't as if they were courting, going out or boyfriend and girlfriend.

Did she want him to be? Or were her hormones just playing games with her mind? Perhaps, if her brain wasn't sodden with oestrogen, then she wouldn't care about that at all! Yet at the moment her lizard brain was drunk and simply creating the idea that the father of her children was going to be her partner simply by them moving in together.

He'd already found them places to look at. Ever since she'd given him the nod after the scan, he'd scoured websites and noticeboards and found a lovely house, suitable for raising the twins, with vacant possession close to St Henry's, but far enough out that it was big enough. It overlooked a park filled with trees and beautiful walks by duck ponds for the days when they'd be out pushing the twins in a pram. They could move in on Saturday if they liked it. Caleb had done all the searching, all the phone calls and all the scouring of estate agents' websites. He'd even begun to help her pack and get things into boxes, ready.

Her sex god had turned out to be a perfect cook, an amazing doctor, a packer, a caring, considerate person and hugely attractive father-to-be. It was rather disarming and cute and annoying all at the same time. Part of her was waiting for him to falter, just so she could go, *Aha! I knew you wouldn't be good at everything!*

But maybe that said more about her than it did him. She always expected things to go wrong. Her relationships always had. Caleb was only meant to have been a one-night stand who conveniently lived and worked in San Diego, except now they were having a family and would be moving in together and working at the same hospital.

Thank you, fate.

'I'll be here for the first week. Get you into a routine, before I leave.'

'Thanks, Mum.' Freya suddenly grimaced as another contraction hit and Rory watched the tracing.

This contraction was stronger than the others and it lasted longer too. It was a good sign that things were moving on with the labour. She wondered if she would miss this—not going through labour, but having a caesarean.

'You're doing great.'

'I'm glad you think so,' Freya breathed once the contraction was over. 'I still can't believe I got myself into this mess.'

'Well, there's no going back now,' her mum said, smiling and squeezing her hand.

Rory could hardly believe her life now, either. After Leo, she'd believed her chances of trusting someone enough to fall in love with them and create a family were slim to none. She'd always wanted that happy little family, though: a beautiful house somewhere with a gorgeous, loving husband who worshipped the ground she walked on and couldn't do enough for her. Cute little babies to raise. But Leo had ruined it all and she'd not only grieved the loss of him and their relationship but her entire future. She'd believed the rest of it would be spent alone and yet here she was, moving into a rental property with the father of her babies—just some guy she'd had a wild night with. And now they were dealing with the consequences of co-parenting—but not in a loving relationship. She'd be going to bed alone.

But what if that could be different? She liked Caleb very much. He was sexy, talented and clever. She admired him as a doctor and the way he'd stepped up for her. The attraction between them was there, clearly, and if they were together then wouldn't *that* negate the worry of him bonking a nurse in a linen cupboard, or of him meeting someone down the line and wanting to move out?

Would he even want that? He'd never wanted to be a father, but here he was dealing with it. Maybe she could be brave enough to try and trust him and let him be closer—suggest a romantic relationship.

Rory shook her head. No. That was ridiculous.

This was her hormones speaking, not her.

'What do you think?' Caleb had brought Rory out to see an end-terrace three-bedroomed townhouse. It had been newly built in the last decade, so quite modern in its architecture with lots of clean lines, large windows to let in the light, and it was softly carpeted in an oatmeal colour throughout.

They stood in the room that, if they took it, would become the twins' nursery. The windows overlooked the park outside at a view of trees and wide expanses of grass, intersected with narrow pathways. There was a small pond to the left with ducks and what looked like a solitary goose.

It was within their budget, an easy commute to St Henry's and it fell into the catchment area of three great schools, if they stayed here. He'd tried to think of everything—for the present and for the future.

'It's nice,' Rory said, wandering around, one hand on her bump, the other trailing the windowsill. At five-and-a-half months' pregnant with twins, she looked full-term already.

'Nice enough for us to want to put down a deposit? Nice enough to want to christen every room?'

She bit her lip, not going for the retort to his joke.

'What is it?'

'It's too real, is what it is. All of this…moving in. I know we've talked about it, but actually doing it is scary.'

He walked over to her and laid his hand upon her arm. 'I know it is. It's scary for me too.'

'Then why are we both doing something so scary?'

'Because not doing so would be even worse. For both of us. I wouldn't be the father I need to be and you would be on your own.'

She nodded, her eyes welling with tears.

He pulled her into his arms then and just held her. 'Tell me. Tell me who hurt you.'

Rory pulled back to look up into his eyes. 'Who said someone hurt me?'

'The hospital grapevine. I've heard things, but I'd really like to hear your side.' He'd heard vague snippets that had reached his ears after Rory's pregnancy by him had been made public knowledge. Some people were happy for them. Some were surprised that Rory had ended up pregnant after she'd sworn to never be in another relationship. Of course he'd asked them why, and they'd simply said, *ask her about Leo.* She'd never mentioned a Leo. But, since hearing the guy's name, he'd wondered if that guy had anything to do with Rory developing her one-night-only rule.

'Of course. I should have known that you can't have a private life if you work in a hospital.' She sighed, pushing herself away from him, and wiped at her eyes. 'Can we sit?'

There was nowhere to sit. The place had vacant possession. But they went to the stairs and sat down on those.

'I was engaged to Leo. I loved him and we were getting married. Things seemed great between us. I was happy and I thought he was too. Initially, he seemed to be excited about planning the wedding, but as time went on he stopped doing it and left it all to me. Said that he was happy for me to make all the decisions for my big day, and I thought it was because he just wanted to make me happy and let me have the wedding of my dreams. We didn't see each other much. We were both working hard at the same time.'

'Did he work at the hospital?'

She nodded. 'Leo was a general surgeon. He doesn't work at St Henry's now. What I didn't know was that he had begun to see someone else—a nurse who worked in a GP practice. Apparently they met at some party that I didn't go to, because I was working a shift, but like I say,

I didn't know this at the time. But he'd become more and more distant as the wedding got closer, and I just put it down to wedding jitters, you know? I asked him if everything was okay and he kept saying he was fine, so what was I supposed to have done differently?

'Anyway, on the day of the wedding, I was in my dress. I had driven to the church and, when we pulled up, the best man told me that Leo hadn't arrived yet and to circle the block again. Traffic was heavy, so I didn't worry too much—I just thought he'd been caught up in it. But everyone else had made it—all our colleagues at work, our families, our friends… When I turned up again, the best man was looking cagey and that's when he told me to check my phone.'

She paused. 'I didn't have it on me, but my mum had brought it in her clutch bag, and we checked it and there was an email—an apology, to say he couldn't go through with it. He didn't have the guts to say it to my face.'

Caleb shook his head in disbelief. *An email? What a coward Leo was.*

'My mum had to go into the church and tell everyone the wedding was off. I sat in the wedding car, crying my eyes out, heartbroken, with everyone I knew coming out and looking at me with pity through the windows. When my mum made it back out, we drove home. Thank God I'd booked two weeks off for a honeymoon I'd never take, because I needed those two weeks to lick my wounds and hide from the world.'

'I'm so sorry you had to go through that. You deserved more than an email. You deserved a proper apology. A face-to-face apology and an explanation. Did you get one?'

'Eventually. We met for a coffee and he explained he'd

met someone else. Someone who he loved more than me. Told me that they were trying for a baby. That he could see marrying her one day, and that he hoped I'd understand that you can't help who you fall in love with or when. That our time together was never meant to be.'

Caleb was in shock. If he ever came across this Leo…

'And he was right. You can't help it. I'd fallen in love with someone who was unreliable and not committed to get through the tough times with me. I'd fallen for someone who had humiliated me in front of all my colleagues. He left, but I stayed and fronted it out. Eventually, as these things do, other more juicy gossip came along one day, and my trauma got forgotten. Mostly, anyway. And so, yeah, I made a vow to myself that I would never fall in love again. Never get close to anyone romantically again. That all I'd ever have with someone was one night, because one night couldn't humiliate me in front of everyone I knew.'

'Until you fall pregnant with twins,' he said, smiling.

'Until I fell pregnant with twins.' She smiled back, gesturing with her hands. 'I'm afraid that this will go wrong. That you will abandon me for someone else at some point. I mean, let's face it, you're a handsome guy—sexy, clever, available. I've seen the way the midwives look at you, the nurses, the female doctors. Someone is going to come along to claim your heart at some point.'

'Well, I appreciate the compliments, but I really don't see that happening.'

'No? You never thought you'd be a father and yet here you are, wanting us to rent somewhere because it's in a good catchment area.'

Caleb laughed. 'Life has a way of surprising you when you least expect it.'

'And at the most inopportune moments—which supports my hesitation and argument. I can do this alone, Caleb. It'll be hard, but with the support of my family I'll be able to do it. I just don't want to be abandoned in the middle of it.'

'I will never abandon my children.'

She gave him a pained smile. 'And me?'

'You're their mother.'

'Still doesn't answer my question. What am I *to you*?'

Caleb hesitated. How to answer this most difficult of questions? Rory meant a great deal to him and she always would. And, yes, he had feelings for her; how could he not? He was attracted to her sexually. He always wanted to spend time with her. But could he say anything more than that? It wasn't as if they were madly in love! 'I'm… very fond of you,' he managed.

'Fond?' She said the word like it was something ridiculous.

He flushed, feeling bad, feeling awkward, not wanting to show a commitment that wasn't returned. Maybe he could turn the tables in this uncomfortable situation. 'Well, what am I to you?'

Rory looked at him then, intently, sharply. Her eyes were still glazed with tears. But she was looking at him as if she was gauging something, trying to decide something. And then suddenly she leaned in and pressed her lips to his.

Surprised, he hesitated.

But then he began to kiss her back.

When she'd come to view this house, Rory had not thought that she'd be putting her cards on the table and kissing Caleb to let him know that she wanted more from their relationship.

I mean, I'd not really known for sure myself!

Hadn't the worst already happened? She'd been jilted at her own wedding. It had been awful, but she'd survived it, and she'd survive him too if the worst happened, but why not take the chance on a little taste of happiness first? They already had attraction and they'd skipped a few steps to start a family with one another, so why not fill out the middle bit too?

So she kissed him. Because in that moment it seemed like the only way to respond to his question, and it was something she'd been dying to do for ages—kiss him passionately, without it leading to sex. To kiss him because she needed to. Wanted to. To feel his lips upon hers again and savour it. Because it seemed impossible to have two totally hot nights with someone, have her world sexually rocked and not think about it all the time. Not want more of the same—his hands, his lips, his everything!

When they broke apart, breathing heavily, she gazed into his eyes, uncertain, unsure. What would he say?

'Well…that was unexpected.'

'But good…right?' she asked.

He smiled. 'Yeah. Better than good.'

'Okay.'

'Okay. So…we're doing this?'

'We're doing this,' she agreed, hoping that he knew she meant more than just a sexual relationship. She wanted, needed, more from him.

'Putting down a deposit?'

'Yes, and…'

'Having a relationship?'

She smiled and nodded, her heart thumping madly with happiness in her chest. 'Yes.'

'Boyfriend and girlfriend, not just mum and dad?'

'Yes.' He said it, because she couldn't. She'd kissed him instead. It was exciting, nerve-wracking and absolutely terrifying! But Rory felt, in that moment, that it was the right thing to do. She wanted her kids to know their father and, more than anything, she wanted them to be raised in a loving home. Not just one of mutual respect. It had to be more than that. She wanted it all. She wanted the happy-ever-after. Didn't she deserve it? Didn't he?

'Then I guess we ought to phone the lettings agent.'

Rory nodded.

'And then I need to take you back to your place.'

'Oh?'

'Yeah.' He smiled. 'I need to make love to my girlfriend. Is that alright?' he asked, his voice all husky and breathy.

'I can't think of anything better.'

CHAPTER NINE

'WE NEED TO get you to Theatre immediately, there's a prolapsed cord,' Caleb said to the mother whose delivery he'd been overseeing. He had his gloved hand inside the woman, trying to hold the baby off the cord so that it didn't become compressed and starve the baby of oxygen. It was an emergency.

The mother nodded, crying, her face all red and blotchy.

It had already been a difficult pregnancy for Mandy Tennant. She'd suffered hyperemesis gravidarum at the beginning that had hospitalised her, so she could be rehydrated with IVs. She'd gone into premature labour at twenty-eight weeks and been hospitalised again, but they'd managed to stop her contractions and place a stitch in her cervix. Then she'd developed an itch all over her abdomen in the latter weeks of her pregnancy due to a condition called intrahepatic cholestasis, which was caused by a liver condition in the mother. It had been suggested to Mandy that she be induced, as delivery of the baby sorted the condition and reduced the risk of stillbirth, and now the poor woman had a prolapsed cord!

The team managed to take Mandy straight to Theatre, pushing her on the bed all the way round. It was difficult to not press on the cord, but he really needed to avoid touching it to avoid it going into vasospasm, and as such they had Mandy on her knees, face down, to elevate her rear end, which was covered with a thin blanket to protect her dignity as they raced her through the corridor towards Theatre.

In Theatre, he immediately asked Rory to administer tocolytic drugs to help reduce Mandy's contractions as the caesarean was prepped for. The cord was still pulsating, which was good.

'This needs to be a category two section, please,' he instructed the anaesthetist. This was because there'd been no obvious sign of foetal heart distress, and Mandy had not been fully dilated when the cord prolapsed, so there was time for a regional anaesthetic rather than a full general.

Once prepped, they put Mandy on her back, put up the curtain and Rory was already slicing into Mandy's abdomen and was at the womb within seconds of beginning. The baby came out easily, crying lustily—a baby boy—and finally Mandy's crying turned from tears of sadness and frustration to that of happiness. A successful outcome was all anyone wanted in this situation and, yet again, they had cheated the odds and got one.

Afterwards, as they both scrubbed out, they stood at the sinks and smiled at each other. 'We're a good team,' Caleb said.

'We don't do too badly, if I say so myself,' Rory agreed.

They worked perfectly together as a team. They matched each other's energies and wants in bed. She was great to talk to and hang out with and he was beginning to see a future with her—a happy one, if he didn't screw it up.

Had he unexpectedly got lucky? Was it true what they said that, when not looking for something or someone, that thing or that person would arrive in life? He'd not wanted to be a dad and now he was going to be one. He'd not wanted to settle down with anyone and yet he'd rented a place with someone and they were going to move in, in the next day or so. They'd moved their relationship onto the next level. They'd committed.

Life was strange and full of unexpected twists and turns. All he had to do to keep up his side of the bargain was be there. *Not* let her down. *Not* abandon her. *Not* let his babies down—his *daughters.* And if he remained present, if he remained aware, he really couldn't see how any of it could possibly go wrong. He was a good guy. He might look the spitting image of his father, but he would not become him. His father had actually tried to call him recently, but he'd ignored the call. He'd decided that he would make *him* wait for attention for once.

Rory and his girls would always come first. No matter what life chose to throw at them.

Caleb wouldn't let Rory lift a finger as they moved into their new place together. It was sweet, really, the way he was taking care of her, and she could see that he was going all out to make sure that she and his babies were kept safe.

The first thing he moved in was a recliner chair and he made her sit on it, put a packed-lunch box next to her alongside a latte and her favourite book and told her not to worry about anything.

At first, she felt guilty about sitting there as the moving guys and Caleb carried in boxes and furniture, going back and forth from the van outside and back into the property. But after a while she began to enjoy it, especially when Caleb got a little sweaty and stripped down to a tee-shirt and jeans and she could see his biceps bulging and his hair grow a little damp from his efforts.

'How are you doing?' he asked her once, about three-quarters of the way done.

'I'm doing fine. You?'

'Yeah, we're nearly finished. I need to unpack the kitchen stuff, so do you fancy a takeaway tonight, or do you want to go out?'

'A takeaway sounds perfect. How about pizza?'

'Sold.' He kissed her, smiling afterwards as he gazed into her eyes, making her feel special. Then he returned to his work and she sat there, wondering how on earth she'd got so lucky ever since she'd risked everything and kissed him. She'd not known how he might respond, but somehow she'd got everything her little heart desired. They'd rushed back to her place and they had most definitely made love, rather than had frantic sex. And making love to Caleb was everything she had ever hoped it would be. It was different from straight sex. There was something tender about it, something treasured. They'd laughed. They'd smiled. They'd breathed, gasped and moaned…in a good way!

And since that day, since they'd declared their intention to one another, their relationship had shifted onto a different plane—something more devoted, something more open. Her friends at work were so happy for her, especially after the debacle that had been Leo. They wished her all the best in the world.

Maybe it was time for her to get her happy ending after

all. She'd had her fair share of trauma, upset and being alone. Of feeling second best. Of feeling as if she was never quite enough and controlling every aspect of her life since, so that life didn't slip away from her and do its own thing. And now? She was allowing Caleb to take some of that control, and it felt good to let go of the reins and to relax a little. He was doing everything he could to show her that he wouldn't let her down, and it was helping. She didn't feel as tense as before—her main worries now were for the pregnancy, even if she did still find herself watching how the other female staff interacted with him and worrying over every little smile, look or casually placed hand upon arm. Theirs, not his.

That evening, she gorged as much as she could on a scrumptious ham and mushroom pizza that was oozing with cheese and laden with pineapple, green peppers, sweetcorn and jalapenos. It was delicious, and clearly her eyes were bigger than her stomach, which took some doing. Afterwards, she sat on the chair, licking the grease from her fingers, and gave a satisfied smile, only to find Caleb staring at her. She smiled self-consciously. 'What?'

'Nothing.' He smiled back, still eating his own triple-meat feast with spicy chilli beef.

'You think I should have eaten that with more decorum?'

'No, absolutely not!'

'I mean, it's probably going to give me horrendous acid reflux, but it was worth every bite.'

'I could tell.'

Rory laughed. 'You know, there's other parts of me that are still hungry…'

The pizza stopped halfway to his mouth. 'Really?'

'If you've got the energy after a long day hauling boxes and furniture?'

'I'm sure I could find it somewhere,' he said, putting down the pizza slice.

She held up her hands. 'Hold your horses, cowboy. This food needs to go down, first.'

He raised an eyebrow. 'I could do that too.'

Now it was her turn to look intrigued. 'Really?'

'Mmm-hmm.'

'Well, never let it be said that I don't give you what you want...' And she sighed contentedly as his fingers reached for her waistband.

At twenty-five weeks, Rory started her daily monitoring of the twins. She was called to the ultrasound department every day usually in the afternoon, as it was the best time for her, for the twins to be checked. Her fluid was measured, the cords were checked for entangling and the foetal growth-rate checked. There was a worry that, because they shared the same placenta, one twin might receive more blood or nutrition than the other, but so far her daily scanning had not shown any problems. Everything seemed to be going smoothly—the pregnancy, the babies, working with Caleb and living with him.

She'd thought worriedly that living and working together might be too much. That they'd be in each other's pockets excessively and that it might somehow cause friction in the relationship they were trying to build. Her past relationship with Leo had taught her to be on constant alert, always looking for signs of discontent. She'd felt Leo pulling away, but had excused it, blaming it on wedding pressures, not realising it might be something—or someone—else. So she felt that, even though she had to trust Caleb with her happiness, she should also make sure his dedication to her was one hundred percent at all times, because anything less meant that she could potentially lose him.

So when she entered Maternity that afternoon, looking to see if he was free to go to her screening with her, she was alarmed to see him leaning on the desk surrounded by three young, beautiful midwives, Morgan, Shana and Trina, who were all smiling at him and laughing at some story he was telling them.

The surge of jealousy she felt hit her like a wave, but she tried to tell herself that she was being ridiculous. He was committed to the babies and her. There was no reason he'd want to cheat on her with these gorgeous—slim—women. Was there? They were all gazing up at him happily, eyes gleaming, laughing coquettishly—one of them holding out the chocolate tin for him to pick from, as if sharing her own favourite. *I like this one. It's creamy...*

'Caleb?'

He turned and his face lit up even more. He didn't act guilty, so that was good, but then again he was a confident man, comfortable in his own skin, and no doubt comfortable being around women. 'Rory! Hey. Want a chocolate?'

The midwives all seemed to start at her approach, and returned to whatever they'd been doing, one of them giving her an appraising look over the desk. Did she harbour thoughts about Caleb's relationship with her? Because Rory was not going to let any slip of a thing ruin what she had.

'No thanks. I've got my scan in a minute, are you free to come with me?' She didn't mean her voice to sound tense. She just couldn't help it. The midwives had disturbed her.

'Sure.' He turned back to the others. 'You ladies can have me paged if anything urgent crops up whilst we're downstairs, right?'

They nodded and smiled at him, before gathering files and going about their jobs, dispersing because *she* was there now, when they'd gathered like a flock in Caleb's presence.

'They all seem to like you very much,' she observed as they headed to Ultrasound.

'They're a great bunch. A good team.'

'Uh-huh.'

He paused for a moment. 'Have I done something?'

'Not yet. As far as I know.' She hated sounding jealous and churlish, but she couldn't help it. Her body was flooded with hormones and sometimes it meant she thought and acted irrationally.

His hand steered her towards a linen room and he closed the door behind them and turned to look at her. 'What does that mean?'

She flushed, feeling awful, but also unable to stop herself. Her emotions surged, let loose. It didn't help that she was as big as a house and felt cumbersome, not as attractive as she used to, even though Caleb had made it perfectly clear that he found her just as appealing sexually as he had before she was pregnant. 'They all want you, you know! I can tell. I can see it in their eyes!'

'They're just being friendly.'

She scoffed. 'That's what every guy says.'

'Rory. Nothing is going on.'

She wanted to believe him, and she hated that she was being like this, but all the hormones were making her see things that weren't there. She sighed. 'I'm being stupid.'

'No, you're not.' He tipped her chin with his finger to make her look at him. 'What's wrong?'

She shook her head, but then thought of his words. There was a lot at stake and they had to be able to talk to one another. 'I just saw you there with all those midwives and it made me feel jealous.'

'Why?'

'Because they're all young and slim and beautiful and hanging off your every word and I'm…' She sighed. 'I'm not.'

'So you're saying only slim women are beautiful?'

'No! Of course not!'

'Rory…you're the most gorgeous creature I've ever seen in my life. I knew it the second we met. And now, now that I know you even more, now that you're filled with my babies and nourishing them, protecting them and fighting to give them a future with their father, you're even more beautiful. I find you irresistible—sexy, curvaceous. Those midwives are nice. But that's all they are—co-workers. Colleagues. And, if you can't trust me, then I don't know what we're doing—and we're going to have a problem.'

She wanted to believe him. She really did.

But history had taught her not to believe a man when he promised her everything.

'What have you done to yourself?' Caleb stared at their fellow obstetric surgeon, Mr Alex Michaels, as he came into the staff room that morning with his left arm in a plaster cast.

'Can you believe, a trampoline accident?' Alex said, wincing.

'Trampoline accident?' Caleb laughed in disbelief. He couldn't imagine it.

'Oh, don't mock, my friend. You've got all of this to come, when your little girls want their daddy to join them for some backflips.'

'You did a backflip?'

'I most certainly did. Well, I *tried*. I misjudged it and, even though we've got that protective netting around it, it was weathered, it split and I fell out of the side and landed on my arm. Broke my radius and ulna near my wrist, hence this fashion choice.' He raised his arm once again to indicate that his girls had signed his cast with their names, pink love hearts and a message that said, *we love you, daddy xxx*

'So, no operating?'

'Nope. You and Rory will have to carry the load for a little while, if that's okay. Thankfully, it's my left arm, so I can still consult and perform examinations, but I'm limited for a bit.'

'No worries. We all pull together here.'

'Thanks, mate. How is Rory faring?'

'Yeah, good. No problems with the twins as of yet.'

'That's great. I'm glad to hear it. That's the only issue with working in this job. When it's your turn for your partner to go through it, you know intimately of all the terrible things that can happen or go wrong.'

'I know. But we're trying to live in the moment. Enjoy it and not fret too much about what might happen.'

'Very wise. You probably haven't got much longer to go, have you? When's her c-section booked for?'

'When she's thirty-three weeks. She's twenty-six weeks now.'

'Just under a couple of months, then?'

'Yes.'

'You'll both do fine, mate. I have no doubts.'

'Thanks. I hope so too.'

Caleb called Rory that day and told her that when he got home he wanted to take her out for a meal. Said it was important that they still made time for each other and celebrated each other, rather than focus all of their energies on just being pregnant. 'Let's celebrate having moved in together. It's quite a milestone for the both of us.'

Was he going overboard, trying to show her that she was important after her jealous outburst the other day?

At home, she watched him carefully through the reflection in her vanity mirror as he'd slipped into a nice suit. When he went downstairs, she picked up his work clothes from the bed and sniffed them, searching for traces of perfume or lipstick. There was none, and she felt ridiculous. What was she doing? If she wasn't careful *she* would be the one to ruin this!

She tried to take her mind off it by doing her hair and make-up. It wasn't something she did often, and as she did it she wondered why she didn't try more often with her appearance, if it made her feel better like this.

As she eventually came downstairs, he stood at the bottom and watched her, a growing smile upon his face, and when she got to the bottom she did a twirl. 'What do you think?'

'I think every guy out there tonight who sees you is going to want to be with you.'

'If they like whales.'

'You're gorgeous.'

'You *have* to say that.'

'No. I *get* to say that,' he replied, kissing her on the lips. 'Come on. I've got us booked into a nice little Italian place down by the river.'

He wasn't kidding. Dino's was on the waterfront, with an outside dining area lit by lanterns and candles reflecting light onto the water. It wasn't cold, so they chose to eat outside. Caleb pulled out her seat for her and then sat opposite. 'Hungry?'

'As a horse.'

He smiled. 'Good. That's what I like to hear.'

'Italian's my favourite cuisine, I think.'

'Mine too.' He gave the waitress their drinks orders and, when their mocktails arrived, they toasted moving in. 'To our future happiness.'

'Future happiness,' she parroted, trying not to think about how the waitress's eyes had gleamed at Caleb.

The menu was filled with every delight imaginable and Rory wanted to order everything! But in the end she chose an arancini starter and a Catalan lobster main served with green beans and new potatoes. They chomped on sesame-seeded breadsticks as they waited for their food to arrive.

'I see Alex is out of action for a little while,' she said.

'Yeah. He's warned me about getting on trampolines. Apparently they account for as much as half of all A&E admissions for activity-related injuries in children.'

'But he's an adult.'

'Yeah, but he's admitted to me he could be classed as a big kid, so…' Caleb smiled.

'It's a lot of extra work for us to carry. Is the chief going to hire a locum surgeon for cover, just in case?'

'I asked and apparently we don't have the budget.'

'Oh. What about when I'm on maternity leave? That'll be two surgeons down.'

'I guess it means I'll get overtime, if necessary. And our consultant, Mr Atwood-Green, has said he'll fill in for any emergencies, if we're booked.'

'But what about your paternity leave? That'll be three of us away; they'll have to hire a locum.'

'I'm sure the department is aware. We've told them the date for your c-section and they know that neither of us will be there for at least two weeks and then I'll be back. Now, stop worrying about something you don't have to concern yourself about.'

But she couldn't help it. Her worries had grown as exponentially as her waistline.

Their starters arrived, delicious aromas filling her nostrils and making her set aside her previous thoughts. Caleb was right: it wasn't her concern. The hospital was not going to leave the department without an obstetric surgeon. 'These look amazing.'

The restaurant was piping gentle violin music through hidden speakers and the view of the river was beautiful with the Houses of Parliament in the distance. The London Eye reached high into the sky. The low hubbub of conversation at the tables around them was soothing and they were just finishing their starter when a man a few tables across suddenly got to his knee and brought out a ring box to propose to his date.

Rory gasped, waiting to see if she would say yes. She'd never had a romantic proposal from Leo. He'd not gone out of his way to ask her. They'd been living together for a while and they'd spoken about marriage, and one day, he'd said, 'I guess we ought to get engaged if we're going to do this properly.' They'd gone out together and sourced a ring. Leo hadn't wanted to spend too much on it. He'd said the money would be put to better use in planning the wedding, and she'd agreed, just so happy that they were getting engaged.

But, until she'd seen the man on his knee right now, she hadn't realised just how much she envied the woman sitting opposite him. She was getting it all: a romantic riverside proposal. Her loved one down on one knee, taking her out for a meal and surprising her. A ring that he'd chosen all by himself. The woman gasped and said yes, and everyone clapped as the two stood up and hugged each other before sitting down again. The woman kept looking at the ring on her finger in awe, shock and happiness. Rory hoped that these two would have a better wedding than the one that she'd nearly had.

'That made you happy,' Caleb said.

'Of course it did! A little romance brightens anyone's day.'

'It strikes me that maybe you've not had much romance in your life,' he observed.

'How do you work that out?'

'Well, for instance, the way we met. It was wonderful, don't get me wrong, but there was nothing romantic about it. You had a one-night rule, so you'd done that sort of thing before, which means that no other guy would have had the opportunity to date you. And your cowardly fiancé, Leo? I don't know him, but I reckon he wasn't the romantic type.'

'And you are?' she asked teasingly.

'Of course.' There was a small bud vase on their table, filled with a sprig of flowers, and he pulled one of the tea roses from it and presented it to her. 'A rose for my rose.'

She laughed. 'Smooth. What else have you got?'

'That's it. I'm out.' He smiled and sipped his drink. 'Apart from the fact that I arranged a romantic dinner date by the river. What about you? What moves do you have?'

'I guess I've never really thought about it. I suppose I always hoped it would just happen to me. That I would find the right person and somehow, during our relationship, I would be wooed and courted and made to feel special—and that I would do my best, in turn, to make the other person feel the same way.'

She sighed. 'And I want to make you feel special, Caleb, but let's face it—romance is probably going to take a back seat now. We're going to be parents soon—sleep-deprived, exhausted, wearing clothes that ought to have made it into the wash a week ago. I'm going to be wandering about the house in stained pyjamas and unwashed hair, probably smelling of baby vomit. We're not going to have time for romance until they're about eighteen years old, and by then we probably won't even bother. If we're still together.'

'What a bleak future you describe. Maybe you should stay away from writing any romantic stories.'

'I'm being a realist.' Reality worried her. Horrible

things happened in relationships when the newness and excitement had worn off and she and Caleb had not got together the usual way.

'So am I. There's always time for romance. If it's important, you make the time.'

'And is it?' she pressed. 'Is it important to you?'

'With you? Absolutely.'

He wanted to be a man who would remain true to his word. It was a mantra he had always lived by—if he made a promise to someone, then he kept it, as he refused to be like his father, who had always been a man to go back on his word.

He remembered turning seventeen, getting his provisional licence and wanting to learn to drive, and he'd asked his dad if he would take him out driving and help him learn. His dad had vowed that he would find the time. He'd said he knew he'd let Caleb down before, but he would find an hour for that. He managed it twice. They'd clashed in personalities. His dad was an absolute stickler for the rules, yet hadn't made himself clear in his instructions to Caleb—so they'd argued, and his dad had just stopped teaching him. He'd had other stuff he needed to get done and he didn't have an hour every day to take his son out.

After weeks of this, Caleb had simply arranged to have lessons from a proper instructor, and his dad had never even said sorry. He'd clapped him on the back and said, 'Well done,' when Caleb had passed his test first time, but that had been it, and it hadn't been enough. His dad had never been enough and Caleb refused to be like him.

So the next night he presented Rory with a bunch of beautiful red roses when he got home from work. He cooked her favourite meal and took care of the washing up, before running her a nice warm bath, filling the bathroom with candles and piping soft piano music through a speaker. He massaged her feet when she needed. He rubbed her back when she needed. He popped out to get antacids when she got heartburn and always made sure that the house had a nice supply of ice-cream.

At work, whenever he caught her on a break in the staff room, he made sure she ate and had a drink, and he'd raise her feet up onto cushions, because he knew how much she hated her ankles swelling towards the end of the day. In Theatre, he helped her out and kept her amused when the twins began jamming their little feet under her ribcage, making her uncomfortable. He made time for her. He made her feel important. And he began to realise just how much he enjoyed doing so.

Maybe he wasn't like his father after all. Maybe all that fear and worry about turning out like his old man had been baseless. His life could have been completely different. And yes, of course it was easy to be thoughtful now; it was just the two of them. Would he be different when the twins were here and he was juggling sleepless nights and long days at work? That was where his fear lay, so he was probably trying to prove himself too much now, whilst he could. Especially since Rory seemed to have worries that it was all going to go wrong. He wouldn't let it.

'Here you go—strawberry milkshake, extra-thick.' He passed Rory a thick cup that he'd picked up from the milkshake bar down the street. 'You need it before you go into Theatre.'

'Oh. Thanks.' She wrapped her lips around the straw and sucked up the milkshake, moaning in delight as the first sip touched her tastebuds, delighting them.

'You've got a D&C?'

She nodded. 'Yes. Incomplete delivery of the placenta, so I'm going in to remove it.'

'Need help?'

Rory frowned and sighed. 'Don't you have your own patients?'

'I do. But none are emergent. I could help you.'

'I appreciate that, and I appreciate you taking care of me, but I am capable of completing my own surgeries, you know. I'm pregnant, not ill.'

'I like taking care of you.'

'I know, but… I'm okay. You don't need to do everything. I know I've been a lot, and I've been a bit down, but honestly, I'm trying to hold onto my identity before I become Mum—and that means being a surgeon.'

Was she telling him he was being *too much*? Maybe he was over-compensating, but he couldn't help it. He was so afraid of being at the other end of the spectrum.

'Okay.' He wasn't sure exactly how he'd feel about backing off, but maybe this wasn't about him. Maybe this was an issue *she* had. Her jealousies had increased tenfold since she'd got bigger. From what he'd heard about her relationship with Leo, he'd always been distant, and perhaps she wasn't used to so much attention.

'You should finish this off,' she said, standing and passing him the milkshake. 'I've got to go.'

He took it from her and watched her go, rubbing at

the small of her back as she disappeared through the doorway.

Were they going to be okay?

He hoped so.

'Patient's asleep?' Rory asked, before she made a start. Caroline Carr lay on the bed in Theatre, draped in blue, her legs in stirrups. She'd given birth vaginally to a baby boy a few hours ago, and initially the midwives had believed her placenta to be complete. But in the post-natal ward Caroline had begun to bleed more profusely than expected, her womb wasn't fully contracting down the way it ought to and a quick scan had detected a piece of placenta left behind. Without it being removed, Caroline would continue to lose blood and possibly develop an infection.

'Away with the fairies and holding steady with her blood pressure,' Gavin, the anaesthetist, answered.

'Okay, I'm going to make a start.'

Rory loved Theatre. Sometimes, when she concentrated hard and the babies in her belly slept, she could sometimes forget that she was pregnant. But not today. Today, the babies were kicking hard and making her feel uncomfortable, and her lower back was beginning to protest at the extra weight and strain being placed upon it. *Only a few more weeks to go*, she told herself.

She began to dilate the patient's cervix using rods. She felt a little annoyed with herself, having spoken sharply to Caleb in the break room before surgery. He was only being nice, but she really didn't know how to deal with his constant attention. She ought to love it, she knew, but him doing so much… He'd brought her a huge bunch of roses the other day. The only time she'd been bought flowers before was when Leo had done something wrong and he'd felt guilty, so to her bouquets had a bad association. Flowers meant an apology. Flowers meant that the guy felt guilty about something.

Caleb was being *so* attentive! She hated herself for her jealousy getting out of control lately… She wasn't the usually sane Rory she knew, and it was because she was losing control of everything. Her feelings for Caleb were running away with her and she didn't like that. Her jealousy was making her snappy with him, and all because of her hormones. She had wanted to regain some control, to show that she was still independent and in charge. She needed that badly.

'Curette, please.'

Rory knew she would have to ask him to treat her normally. She wasn't fragile. She wasn't precious. She wasn't helpless. She might look like a beached whale, but she wasn't one, and she didn't actually need him to help her back into the water. Maybe if she got him to back off, she would feel better. But if she pushed him too far away…

'Here it is.' The piece of placenta that came out was actually tiny, but it was enough to have caused a problem. She checked the rest of the uterus and, when she was satisfied, she pulled off her gown and gloves and gave orders to the nurses to take Caroline through to recovery and monitor her.

As she scrubbed out, she felt a tightening across her abdomen that caused her to stop moving and just breathe. An early Braxton Hicks. She wasn't even thirty weeks yet, but her womb was the size of a full-term pregnancy already, so it was doing what came naturally. She rubbed her hand over her belly until it softened again and checked her watch. She knew to keep an eye out for any more and she would mention it at her daily scan that afternoon. Maybe she'd tell Caleb she could go by herself. He didn't have to attend every single one.

CHAPTER TEN

'SO, YOU'RE TWENTY-SEVEN weeks and four days?' asked Barb, the ultrasound technician, whom Rory had got to know quite well.

'Yes, though I look and feel full-term. I think I had a Braxton Hicks earlier,' Rory said, lowering herself awkwardly onto the examination couch, lifting up her top and lowering her trousers waistband.

'Not surprising. This can often happen earlier in multiple pregnancies, though I guess I don't need to tell you two that.'

'No,' Caleb agreed.

She'd not managed to persuade him to let her come alone. In fact, he'd looked slightly alarmed when she'd suggested it.

'What do you mean, I don't need to come? Of course I do!'

'It'll just be like yesterday's. And the day before that. And the day before that! It takes five minutes—what's the point in both of us leaving the department?'

'The point is that I get to be with you. The point is that I am there for my daughters.'

'I know you're here for us, Caleb. You don't have to prove it.'

'Yes, I do.'

She'd known she was not going to win this one so she'd backed down. She'd walked down with him to Ultrasound, giving the air that she was simply amusing his weird foible to be there. Secretly, however, she liked having someone to depend on, but she just wasn't used to it. She'd never known anything like the intensity of his devotion before. And, though it should have made her feel more secure, it was having the opposite effect.

As Barb ran the scanner over the twins, Rory lay there, marvelling as she always did at seeing her babies on screen. The daily scans were a comfort and she knew she was lucky to have them. Most women got scanned a couple of times during pregnancy and that was it.

'You're frowning, Barb. What is it?' Caleb asked.

Was she frowning? Rory had been staring at the screen but, now she looked at the technician, she felt her heart rate accelerate. 'Is something wrong?'

'We'd expect to see the babies grow by a few grams every day. I noted yesterday that Baby B had not gained weight like Baby A, and today's measurements confirm that baby B's weight has remained stagnant.'

'You think it's TTTS?' She meant Twin-to-Twin Transfusion Syndrome, in which one baby got more blood flow and more nutrients than the second twin. Most people assumed that that meant the bigger twin would somehow be stronger, but that wasn't always the case. Sometimes too much caused problems, too. 'Why didn't you say something yesterday?'

'Because I wasn't sure, and there was no point in worrying you unnecessarily, but today I can see it and I don't think it's an anomaly.'

Rory felt as if she might cry, but then she felt Caleb's hand grip her own, she turned to look to him for support and felt awful that she'd made him try to stay away. Imagine if she had been successful in making him back off and then this had happened when he'd not been there! He'd have felt terrible, and she would have been responsible for it. 'Caleb?'

'It's okay,' he said. 'They can monitor it, now they've noticed it, and we get daily scans, remember? How are the cords looking?' he asked Barb.

'Good. But do you see here—the blood vessels in Baby A's cord? They're larger than Baby B's—by millimetres, but they're larger.'

Caleb nodded. 'Is Twin B showing any decreased urinary output?'

Barb moved the transducer. 'Bladder looks full. All good for now.'

'So Baby B is the donor twin and Baby A the recipient,' Rory said. 'What can I do? Do I need laser therapy?' Laser therapy would allow a doctor to insert a fetoscope, a small camera, into the placenta under anaesthetic, and the identified blood vessels would be sealed with a laser. Mostly it worked, but sometimes the condition could return.

'I'll get the doctor to check the scans and confirm whether you need that, but for now we'll continue with the daily monitoring. You're booked in for an early delivery, so let's hope that the twins don't develop too diverse a weight differentiation.'

Rory did not feel reassured. She'd known this was a risk from the very beginning when she'd discovered she had morochorionic moroamniotic twins, but everything had been going so well, and she'd begun to believe that everything would be alright. Now the worst was beginning to happen, as she'd suspected it would.

Caleb helped her back up into a sitting position. 'I'll call Mr Atwood-Green. Can you send a copy of the scan to him for me, please?' he asked Barb.

'Sure thing. I'll send it to him straight away and ask him to give you a call once he's reviewed it.'

'Thank you.'

Rory's legs felt shaky when she got up off the examining bed. And she felt sick, too. She should have known that this wouldn't go right! Nothing ever went straightforward in her life and she should have expected this to happen. But she'd allowed herself to be hopeful, to assume that this time, everything would be okay.

It felt as though her world was on a knife-edge.

Caleb stood staring at the CTG tracing of his patient and tried to put the last few hours out of his mind. He'd spoken to Mr Atwood-Green and, after viewing the ultrasound, he had confirmed that nothing needed to be done just yet. He acknowledged that, though it was upsetting for Rory and Caleb to have been notified of the early signs of TTTS, there was no need to panic. It was early. It might not even fully develop into a surgical situation. They would continue to monitor Rory carefully and, as she was having daily scans to check for cord entanglement, then this could easily be done. If it looked as if Baby A, the recipient twin was getting too much of the blood supply, and it looked as if Baby B looked was suffering from that, then they would do something about it before it became a problem.

'But Rory is due for a c-section in just over a month. We might not need to do anything,' the consultant had said.

Caleb knew he was right. Not all TTTS patients developed an issue that needed surgery. Most cases remained mild but, like birth, it was only the horror stories he seemed to hear or remember. So, as he stood monitoring the trace of his new patient, he tried not to think about all of the TTTS patients whom he had seen himself, how many surgical interventions there had been, or how many times the situation had turned into a tragedy. Admittedly, it was a low number, but it did happen, and that scared him. And now he knew for sure exactly how those other parents had felt when they'd pleaded with him to tell them that everything would be alright.

'We're going to keep you on the CTG for a bit longer, Traci. Baby's having one or two decels and I want to keep an eye on them, okay?'

'Is the baby alright?'

He smiled. 'Yes. He's just letting us know that, on occasion, the contractions aren't agreeing with him.'

Traci nodded, but he could see the fear on her face and on that of her husband. This was an IVF baby, a baby who had been wanted for so long, after many years of fruitless treatments and four miscarriages. This was the only pregnancy Traci had managed to carry to term, and he understood her fear of something going wrong at the last hurdle.

Did that fear ever go away? His own mum had told him once that being a parent was the most joyous, yet also the single most terrifying, experience she had ever gone through.

'The amount of times I've had to sit by your bed… fevers, the flu, appendicitis…that time you broke a bone and had to have surgery. You'll never understand what it feels like to get a phone call that your child is in A&E until you're a parent yourself.'

And he thought he'd never have to experience that fear. He had considered himself superior in the knowledge that he wouldn't, because he'd thought he would never have kids. And now he understood. His twin girls weren't even here yet and he was terrified.

But at least he'd been there, holding Rory's hand during the scan. She'd tried to tell him he could stay away, that she could manage on her own, but he'd been persistent and had still gone. Now he was so glad that he had, even though the news had been scary. How would she have felt to have received that news today on her own? She would have remembered it for ever—the day that he had not been there. And, worse than that, one day they would have told their children the story and they would have known too.

He never wanted his kids to think that he had not been there and, even if it killed him to do so, he would make sure he was there for *everything.* He couldn't help but think of his own father in that moment. The man had kept trying to call him and Caleb had ignored his texts, asking him to call him back. Even his mum had said that his dad needed to talk to him. But it was too late for all of that. His dad had had his chance to be a real father; Caleb was not going to let him screw up being a grandfather too. If Callum Stride thought for even one minute that he could suddenly put everything right, then he was wrong, and Caleb would not let his father fill his daughters' lives with disappointment after disappointment.

'I know it's easier said than done, but try not to worry. We have you and the baby on a monitor. Morgan here is a brilliant midwife, and she'll keep an eye on the CTG, and any changes, she's going to let me know. Hopefully, you won't see me again.'

'Don't take this the wrong way, doc, but I hope to never see you again.'

Caleb smiled. He understood. 'Don't take this the wrong way, but I hope to never see you again either. At least, not until after you've safely delivered this one, okay?'

They nodded.

'Got a name picked out?'

'Not yet. We wanted to see what he looked like first.'

'Caleb's a good name,' he said with a smile, then left the room, knowing that Morgan would contact him, or the next doctor on call if he had already gone home for the day.

Rory had already gone home. He'd told her to. She'd been a bit of an emotional mess after the scan and he just wanted her at home, relaxing. It was the best thing after a shock and he knew it would make him feel better to know that she was at home taking care of herself. He'd be there himself in an hour or two and he couldn't wait. He just wanted to hold her close, smell her hair and tell her that everything was going to be okay. Tell her that he would protect her and them, and he wouldn't let anything bad happen to them. It would break his heart if anything did.

He slowed to a stop in the corridor as he realised what he'd just admitted to himself.

It would break his heart. Which meant…

I love her. I love Rory.

He'd never admitted it to himself before. But, now that he realised it, he wanted to tell her! Wanted to tell the world! But…what if she didn't yet feel the same way? He didn't want to pressure her into saying it just because *he* had.

Maybe he would keep it to himself for just a little longer? Maybe now was not the right time to make declarations whilst she was riddled with anxiety and worry for their babies?

So he told himself he would hold the information deep inside for a little while—maybe wait until the babies were here—and then tell her?

Yes. That seems like it's the right thing to do.

CHAPTER ELEVEN

'SO NOW YOU'RE how many weeks?' asked the sonographer.

'Nearly twenty-nine.'

The sonographer nodded as she gazed at the screen, checking the cord as always, and measuring the twins. 'Well, you'll be pleased to know you're holding steady. Baby A is bigger, but Baby B has put on two grams in the last couple of days. Not as much as twin A, but she's growing.'

'So we can carry on as normal still?'

She nodded. 'Yes. You've seen Mr Atwood-Green?'

'Yesterday. He scanned me too; said he was happy and we didn't need surgical intervention yet.'

'That's good, Rory. That's really good.'

'Thanks.' The daily scanning had become a lifeline for Rory. She worried constantly about the twins and it was only the scans that reassured her that everything was alright. Every time the twins moved or kicked, she worried about cord entanglement. With every headache she developed, she worried about pre-eclampsia. Every time someone told her she looked huge, bigger than the day before, she worried that Twin A was suddenly sucking up all the bloodstream and Twin B was being starved. She couldn't help it.

Caleb helped her into a sitting position as she wiped off the gel from her belly. 'Not long to go. A few more weeks. I think we can do this,' he said.

It was easy for him to say! He wasn't the one who felt like a ticking time bomb. Now she could fully understand the fear her patients felt. She'd thought she understood. She could empathise with them, but she had never *truly* known. But she did now. And she knew that Caleb was trying his best to reassure her, but he was still an outsider, looking in. It didn't matter how many times he rubbed her feet, brought her drinks or cooked her food—none of that could make up for the fact that she felt everything could go wrong in a mere moment and they might not know about it until the next scan.

And she'd seen the way the sonographer had looked at Caleb when they'd entered the room. They'd not met her before, as she was new, and she'd blushed. Rory had seen it with her own eyes!

She felt so alone, even though in reality she knew that she wasn't. Caleb was there, and her mum was there phoning her every night, but still she felt alone, cumbersome and unattractive. Despite all her knowledge, despite all her skills, she could do nothing about what was going on inside her own body, and this lack of agency, after being in control of every aspect of her life for so long, was driving her insane!

What if she went through all of this and it still went wrong? What would happen to her then, to the babies, to her relationship with Caleb? *Because, let's face it, we only got together because of them.* If she lost them, how long would it be before he walked out of her life too?

'You're very quiet,' he said as they walked back to the maternity floor.

'I've got a lot on my mind,' she said, more snippily than she would have liked.

'I know what you mean.'

'Do you?' She stopped to turn and look at him, her anger and frustration at the situation coming out, aimed at him because he was closest and she had no-one else she could vent to. 'Do you actually? Because I don't see your body being the one screwing up a pregnancy and putting our children's lives at stake.'

She felt tears prick her eyes and she began to storm off. She'd not wanted to get angry, but it just happened. She was fed up with everyone's fake sympathy, pity and empathy. It wasn't real! They were just glad it wasn't them, and the only way to deal with her was to pretend that they understood.

'Rory!'

He caught up with her easily. Of course he did. He still looked as athletic and as fit as the day she'd met him, but she had grown to the size of a mountain.

'Just leave me alone, Caleb!'

'No! Stop. Rory, will you just stop for a minute?' He stood in front of her, blocking her way past him.

She shook her head, but she couldn't look at him.

'Look, I don't know what's happening right now, but if you're trying to provoke a fight then you're not going to get one. You can't push me away. You can't tell me that I don't understand. I know I'm not carrying those babies, but I would if it would help you. If it would make this easier. But there isn't anything to make this easy! The situation we're in, I get it—it sucks. I know it sucks. You think I want this? You think I want to see you like this, worrying all the time, crying in the shower? Don't think I haven't heard you.'

She flinched at that. She'd not realised that he knew.

'You have every right to be angry at the world for this situation we're in, but you don't have a right to be angry at *me*. I'm *not* going to abandon you.'

'But you could. You could walk away. At any moment, if you wanted.'

'I don't want.'

She stared at him.

'You hear me? I don't want to walk away. I will *never* walk away. I'm not Leo!'

Her tears began to fall freely then, silently, hotly, fiercely. Was this where her anger came from—her fear? She feared losing the babies, she feared losing him. She feared being left alone again. She didn't want to have to go through that again. 'I know you're not.'

'Do you? I'm in this—for ever. Do you hear me? For ever,' he said, so softly. And he reached up and wiped away her salty tears, before pulling her into his arms.

She could feel the babies moving and kicking. They always did when she was in a place of high emotion. She wondered if he could feel them kicking, too.

'They hate it when we fight,' he whispered.

'Yeah.'

'So let's not do that.' And he kissed the top of her head.

Caleb was just coming out of Theatre the next day when he got bleeped to contact Mr Atwood-Green. His first panicked thought was that it was about Rory. He knew she was on shift with him today, but as he'd been in Theatre so long he wasn't sure where she was. On the ward? Still in her clinic?

He went to the nearest desk and asked the staff where she was, only to see her emerge from a ward before he'd got to the end of his question. She was smiling, happy, sliding her pen into her scrubs pocket, before looking up at him. She frowned then at the worry on his face. 'You okay?'

'Mr Atwood-Green wants to see me. I thought it was about you.'

'Nope. Not as far as I know. It's probably for a case he wants to hand over or something.'

'It's the *or something* I'm worried about.'

'Want me to come with? I'm free at the moment, though I am closely monitoring a patient. If I stay on the floor, it should be fine if I get called in to deliver her.'

He nodded and they headed off to their consultant's office at the end of the corridor. Caleb rapped his knuckles against the wood door.

'Come in!'

He pushed the door open and saw James Atwood-Green behind his desk. Opposite him sat a young woman, about six months' pregnant, her face pale and tear-stained, and beside her was a man, also pale, holding the woman's hand.

James spotted Rory behind him. 'It's alright Ms Dotson, I've called in Mr Stride for this patient.'

'Oh, okay. I'll leave you to it.' Rory smiled and slipped away, closing the office door behind her.

'Mr Stride, this is Jennifer Boulter and her husband Hugo. Jennifer, Hugo, Mr Stride.' James indicated he ought to take a seat. 'I've asked you in here because I would like your assistance on this case.'

'Okay.'

'Jennifer is a primagravida mother, currently twenty-five weeks' pregnant with twins after an IUI procedure.'

Caleb nodded, knowing primagravida meant a first-time mother. Intrauterine insemination was when specially prepared sperm was placed directly in the uterus in the hope that the sperm located an egg in the fallopian tube to inseminate.

'She recently has discovered that she has an aggressive form of breast cancer that is oestrogen receptive and has been advised by her oncologist to start treatment straight away. Now, obviously this is a very distressing and confusing time for Jennifer and Hugo, and they are here to discuss an early delivery rather than termination.'

Caleb sympathised. What a terrible situation to find themselves in! 'Have we had a recent scan?'

'I've sent the details of the most recent scan to your email, but basically the twins are non-identical, there's been no complications with the pregnancy, apart from some morning sickness which has now abated and no blood pressure problems. Twin A is measuring at twenty-four weeks and three days and Twin B is slightly larger at twenty-four weeks and five days.'

Ah. 'Okay, well, first let me say I'm extremely sorry to hear of your situation. No-one would want to find themselves facing what you are going through, but we are, so we need to discuss the best things for you, Jennifer, as well as the best things for your family as a whole. Has Mr Atwood-Green discussed the risks of an early delivery with you?'

Jennifer shook her head. 'Not yet. He wanted to bring you in first—he mentioned that you specialise in delivering early babies.'

Caleb glanced at James. 'Believe me, I would prefer not to, but I have had a lot of success in that area. The problem we have is that your twins are measuring at twenty-four weeks, which we class as extremely pre-term. It's four months early and that means that the babies are not as developed as we would like. When I say that, I mean the babies' organs in particular—their brain, their lungs, their heart—are very immature and not yet ready for the outside world. If we were to deliver them at this gestation, they could be, or may become, very sick; they'll most definitely need to stay in the NICU and have oxygen assistance.'

'But it's doable? Babies can survive at twenty-four weeks?' Hugo asked.

'There's an eighty percent survival rate,' Caleb confirmed.

Jennifer smiled. 'That's good, isn't it?'

'Yes, but that also means that one in five babies won't make it. You need to look at the stats that way, as well as positively, and try to prepare yourself for that eventuality if we go down this road.'

'But that's it?' Hugo asked. 'A ventilator?'

'They'll need round-the-clock care. They're at risk of many future complications…' Caleb explained what these were. It was a long list, but important for the parents to know so they could feel prepared.

'How many babies have gone on to have issues, in your experience?' Jennifer asked.

He thought for a moment. 'I'd need to check my figures, but nationally the average is about two in every ten babies delivered early will suffer from a mild disability.'

'Those are national statistics. How many in *your* experience?' Hugo pressed.

'About five in ten.'

'No matter what happens, we'll manage, Jen!' Hugo said, squeezing his partner's hand.

'It can be a difficult road, full of twists and turns, and remember you're also going to be going through treatment, I assume. It's a lot of stress to handle, doing that and also visiting your baby in NICU.'

'I think I can do it,' Jennifer said. 'I can't lose these babies. I've already fought so hard to have them. Do you know how long we tried to get pregnant?'

Caleb shook his head.

'Four years. Four years of hoping every single month. Four years of monthly disappointments. Four years of trying not to be insanely jealous when all my friends seemed to get pregnant and start families at the drop of a hat! Four years of holding *their* babies in my arms and trying not to cry inside because I wasn't holding *my own.* Are you a father?'

Caleb didn't usually like to talk about anything personal with his patients, but in this instance he replied, 'I'm about to be.'

'You probably fell pregnant without trying, huh? It was probably easy for you and now you're about to be a dad without any worries in the world. Life's easy for some. Not for others.'

He was about to put her straight, but he glanced at James quickly, then looked away. James knew, but this wasn't the time to talk about himself. They were here for Jennifer and Hugo. 'When does your oncologist want to start treatment?'

'As soon as possible.'

'I'm sure Mr Atwood-Green would agree with me that the more time we can give your babies in the womb, where they belong, is the best thing for them all round. Even if it's just for a couple of more weeks…maybe get the babies measuring at twenty-six weeks. But we'll need to discuss this with your oncologist; what's their name?'

'Dr Waller.'

'Like Mr Stride says, we'll consult with your other doctors and come up with a plan for your treatment. We have space in our NICU, so that's not an issue, but I'd like to admit you sooner, rather than later, Jennifer, if that's okay with you? That way we have you here and we can keep monitoring you if we're able to keep you pregnant for another week or more. But, if we need to deliver asap, then you're here and there are no delays.'

'But I can go home? Pack, sort out some family arrangements?' Jennifer asked.

'Of course. But once we've spoken to your oncology team we really ought to admit you.'

Caleb excused himself from the meeting, left James to it and went to write up his notes from the surgery he'd performed before meeting Jennifer and Hugo. He really felt for them. What they had to be going through… Jennifer would no doubt want to be there in the future for her babies, but what if she wasn't and it was only Hugo left? Caleb couldn't imagine being in that situation. Losing Rory would be a terrifying prospect. Left alone to raise his twin girls…?

Once he'd written his notes, he grabbed the phone, dialled nine for an outside line and called his grandfather. He'd made a decision. When the babies were here, he wanted to give Rory something special—a gift to show her how much she meant to him. He'd heard the nurses call it a 'push present'. And, if he was going to give Rory a diamond ring, then he wanted it to be the best diamond ring there could ever be.

Rory checked her watch. Where was Caleb? They were meant to be going home together, and she preferred Caleb to drive, as she was really struggling to fit behind the steering wheel. And they had an early ante-natal class to attend. She didn't need to for the information, but more for the fact that she wanted to develop friendships with the other mothers in the group, so that she'd have a group of friends she could call on when Caleb went back to work. She was the only one she knew who was scheduled to deliver early, and she'd been lucky to find a group that had begun accepting mothers from twenty-five weeks' pregnant with multiples.

Her phone buzzed in her pocket and she pulled it free. Caleb.

'Hey.'

'Rory? Sorry, I've been pulled into a consult for a lady with pre-eclampsia.'

'Oh. So how late do you think you'll be?'

'Erm…give me half an hour. Is that okay? When's your class?'

Good, he hadn't forgotten. This was important. She was nervous. 'Starts at seven.'

'Okay. I'll get down there as soon as possible. Can you grab a seat in Reception and wait for me? Or go get a drink.'

'Will do.' She ended the call and sighed. Delays in

their job were inevitable. Just because the rota said a five p.m. finish, it did not necessarily mean leaving at five pm. Often they could still be in a surgery, or needed to stay late because they want to see a delivery through. Or paperwork could delay them, or a quick consult in A&E. She didn't mind waiting on this occasion. They had plenty of time to get to class and she really didn't want to drive, especially not in rush hour.

So Rory grabbed a drink from a vending machine, sat down in Reception and did a bit of people watching. All manner of lives was found here in a hospital, many individual and unique stories. She gazed at a pregnant woman in a dressing gown, wheeling along her IV pole, and wondered about her story. She'd not met her, so had no idea. And what about the guy pacing up and down outside on his mobile phone, smoking furiously and waving his arms about with his voice raised?

She felt the twins kick and she rubbed at her belly and thought about her daughters. They would be here soon, in just a few more short weeks, and one part of her couldn't wait to see them. The other part was terrified. It was again the lack of control that unnerved her. What if she couldn't do it? What if she couldn't be the mother she hoped she'd be? What if, despite all of his promises, Caleb wasn't there for her and she had to do it all alone? She'd never pictured herself as a single mother. She and Caleb were in a romantic relationship, but they'd made no commitment to one another. It wasn't as if they were married. What if it all went wrong? They would have to split custody. And everybody would know, yet again, that she was a failure. That she had been abandoned.

Rory checked her watch, nervously biting her bottom

lip. He should have been here by now! She dialled his number and his phone rang for a moment before being answered by a woman. 'Hello?'

'Who is this?' she asked, worried as to why a woman with a sultry voice had answered Caleb's phone.

'It's Trina, Ms Dotson.'

Trina: one of the midwives who had fawned over Caleb that day, hanging onto his every word as if he were some sort of oracle.

'Where's Caleb?'

'Apologies, he's been called into Theatre on an emergency case.'

'Oh.'

'He said if you were to call that he's sorry, and that he'll try to join you later, but would you mind going to the class on your own?' Trina didn't sound sorry. She sounded fake.

'I'm not meant to be going on my own. He's meant to be there!'

'Sorry.'

Rory ended the call, angry. She knew she shouldn't be. This was part of the job and it wasn't as if he had done so on purpose. It was just having to speak to Trina, rather than Caleb. She knew inwardly that he would be kicking himself for letting her down like this. Or so she hoped. Maybe it was innocent. She had to trust him, or there was no point. But it was so hard!

I guess I'll have go to the ante-natal class on my own, then.

She got up and headed out of the hospital towards the car park. It was quite dark now and, though rush hour traffic would still be filling the roads, she had ample time to get to her class. Squeezing in behind the steering wheel, she adjusted the seat and mirrors and headed off into the traffic. The car was low on petrol, so she stopped off at a garage, filled the tank and treated herself to a pastry to tide her over until after the class, when she could cook herself something proper.

Or maybe Caleb would cook. He liked to and, knowing him, no doubt he would want to for missing out on driving her to class. Maybe they'd snuggle later and she could tell him about her ridiculous reaction to him not being there. Maybe they'd laugh about her hormones playing with her mind.

She arrived at the school hall where the ante-natal class was held and waddled in to join the others. Chairs were arranged in a circle, but to one side there was a table for tea, coffee and biscuits, and she got herself a cup of tea and went over to find herself a chair. But she couldn't help but notice that she was the only single one there. Everyone else had brought their partners.

The class was run by a midwife and, after she introduced herself, she went round the circle and asked them each to introduce themselves too. Rory was pleased that every mother there was expecting twins. Most of them were non-identical, but there was one other mother opposite her, Lyla, who was also expecting identical twins, only hers were boys.

The midwife began talking to them about how to stay active and healthy during their pregnancy. About the importance of good sleep, nutrition and things to avoid, like smoking and alcohol, which Rory was sure they all knew anyway. Even though most of it was information she knew, she sat and listened patiently anyway, because none of these other mothers were doctors or obstetricians, and to them the information was reassuring.

The midwife opened up the floor to questions for a bit and then they were shown simple exercises they could do whilst sitting in a chair and how to treat swollen ankles. Then they were all provided with a beanbag and asked to get down on the floor. They were led through a simple relaxation exercise that Rory actually really enjoyed. So much so, she almost fell asleep, after such a long day on her feet. After that, they were taught simple massages their partners could give to them to help, and how they could look after them to ease any aches and pains as they got into their third trimester.

At the end, they were given time to mingle, and Rory went to talk to Lyla and her husband, Michael. She was a solicitor by trade, her husband was a police officer and their babies were going to be their second and third children.

Rory smiled. ‘You’re having boys, I think you said?’

‘Yes. And you’re having two girls.’

She nodded. ‘We should see if they want to be friends, when they’re old enough to play together.’

Lyla nodded. ‘I’d like that. What does your husband do?’

‘Oh, we’re not married, but we both work at the hospital.’

‘Oh! Doing what?’

‘We’re both obstetric surgeons.’

Lyla laughed. ‘Why are you here? I bet you know all of this already!’

Rory laughed with her. She liked Lyla. 'Yeah, but being pregnant with twins…it's different when it's you, and I don't want to miss out on anything. And I thought it would be good to get to know people who are in my position. None of my other friends have had twins. Clearly slacking on that front,' she joked.

Lyla laughed. 'Same. Michael and I don't actually have many friends that have children; they're all building their careers. Well, there's one, but they send theirs to boarding school, so I'm not sure they count. But hey, you should take our number and we should meet up for coffee one day to whine about our aching backs and swollen ankles.'

Rory smiled. 'Sure!' They swapped numbers, and then Rory mingled with a few of the others, but it was hard alone. She kept telling herself it was fine, but she didn't like it. It would have been so much easier for her to mingle with Caleb at her side. He'd said he'd try to make it, but the rest of the class was already starting to depart and he still wasn't here.

She said her goodbyes and headed out to the car park. She shivered in the cold and pulled her coat closer, before squeezing once more behind the steering wheel and starting the engine. The windscreen took a moment to clear and, once she felt warm enough, she eased into the traffic and began the drive home. Twenty minutes and she'd be back home, if she was lucky, cosy in her jammies, sipping tea and getting herself some decent food. She was starving! And hopefully Caleb would get home soon enough to join her and she'd apologise for thinking badly of him.

Pulling out onto the main road, she saw an HGV parked on her side of the road, delivering something to a shop by the looks of it, and she indicated to overtake as the road looked clear.

She was wrong.

Caleb had been called into an emergency caesarean section for his patient, who had developed a placenta praevia—the placenta detaching prematurely from the uterine wall and beginning to bleed. He'd delivered the baby girl, who had needed to be taken to the Special Care Baby Unit for monitoring, as she'd seemed unable to maintain her oxygen levels. He had thought the emergency part of the surgery was over but then Mum had begun to bleed heavily, haemorrhaging a huge amount. Though they'd tried everything to stop it, they'd had to gain consent from the husband to conduct an emergency hysterectomy, as his patient had been under a general anaesthetic and could not consent herself.

It was a last-ditch attempt to save the mother. Everyone had been on their game, everyone had been focused and Caleb had forgotten everything to make sure that the baby girl he'd delivered had a mother who'd live to take care of her, hold her and love her.

When he made it out of surgery, Caleb glanced at the clock on the wall and realised he'd missed everything meeting Rory, going to class with her and getting home to cook for her.

Damn! I swore I'd never let her down!

Was it impossible never to let her down? The job they did dictated that they wouldn't always get away on time. *Like Dad's did.*

He didn't like comparing himself to his father. It felt extremely uncomfortable. But he comforted himself with the fact that this was just the once, and it was *just* an ante-natal class he'd missed. It wasn't as if he'd missed the birth or anything! It wasn't as if he had missed their first word or their first steps. Rory wouldn't be mad, though she might be slightly upset that for her first time she'd had to go alone. He hoped she'd had a good time.

As he sat there writing his surgical report, he tried to call her on her mobile to apologise, as he wanted to stay at the hospital a bit longer. It was imperative to him that he be there when his patient awoke to explain why she was now infertile and would not be able to carry any more children. He couldn't leave that to someone else. He had made the cuts. He had removed her womb.

Rory didn't answer his call. It rang and rang, but she didn't pick up. Was she mad? Trina had told him that Rory had sounded upset when she'd spoken to her and he knew he'd let her down. He didn't like that he'd made her feel the way his own mother had felt—abandoned, alone. Pushed to one side to make room for her husband's work and patients.

But this was the job! Had he been too quick to judge his father?

And would Rory ever forgive him?

Rory felt as if she was coming out of a deep sleep. She could hear something ringing. A phone…? Bells…? Something sticky was gluing her eyes shut and, as she reached up to clear them, a sharp pain inflamed her shoulder, sickening in its intensity, and its clarifying note brought her back to her reality.

She could hear traffic. Concerned voices. Shouting. Sirens. There was the smell of metal, blood and hot engines. She could feel pain all over her body, and now she was gasping and, despite being unable to open her eyes, realised that *she was upside down* and what felt like a vice was holding her in place.

And then it all came back to her.

She'd been driving, overtaking. Why had she been overtaking? She couldn't think why, but then suddenly there'd been bright-white headlamps glaring at her, a vehicle zooming towards her! The blare of a horn…her horn?…and then a sickening crunch, an impact. She'd spun, felt her head crack against the side window, as her car had flipped and the world had gone black.

I've been in an accident! I'm hurt! I can't get out!

Her seatbelt held her in place and somewhere in the car she could hear her mobile phone ringing. It was Caleb—that was his ringtone. The one she'd assigned to him, to no-one else. *Where is it? Can I reach it?*

But she couldn't see. The sticky stuff holding her eyes closed was blood. Her head hurt. Her shoulder, her hips, felt like white fire…

My babies!

She cried as she tried to stretch out blindly with her uninjured arm to try and reach the phone, aiming in the general direction of the ringing, but she couldn't get hold of it. Her fingertips found its edge, but she couldn't stretch enough actually to find purchase. Rory screamed out in frustration.

And then it stopped ringing. She felt her heart break in despair. Hot tears coursed over her forehead, instead of her cheeks, and then suddenly she heard a voice. A calm, woman's voice.

'Hey there. Hang on in there, we're going to get you out safely, okay?'

'My babies! I'm pregnant!'

'Okay, okay, what's your name?'

'Rory.'

'Okay, Rory, my name's Chantal and I'm a paramedic. You've been in a car accident and you're currently upside down. We can't get your doors open, as they've been crushed by the impact, but we're going to get you cut out, okay? It's going to take some time. Were you alone in your vehicle?'

'Y-yes! I'm alone. Please! Call Caleb!'

'We will, but first we're going to get you out, okay?'

She tried to nod, but her neck hurt. Everything hurt. It felt as if her blood was pounding in her head, but she knew it just felt that way because she was upside down and her blood was pooling through gravity, making it feel worse than it actually was.

As the fire crew arrived to start stabilising her vehicle so they could cut her free, she tried to remain as calm as she could. Tried to test each of her body parts for movement to see what hurt and what didn't. She could wriggle her toes and move her ankles, which was good. Her legs didn't feel too bad, though she couldn't move them much. Hopefully just cuts and bruises. But her pelvis felt on fire and her chest hurt, as did her shoulder, her arm.

Please just let me and the babies get through this!

'Rory?' Chantal was back at the window. 'We're going to try and get you out now. We've given you something for the pain, but this still might hurt a little, okay?'

'Okay.' She tried to calm her breathing through the oxygen mask that was suddenly placed over her face. Tried not to think too hard about how this was going to feel. Tried not to think too hard about what they might discover when she made it to the hospital…

'Caleb!'

He heard a voice shout behind him just as he was pushing through the security door on Maternity to go home.

He turned and saw Trina running towards him, her face flushed and urgent.

'What is it?'

'We've just had a call come in from Accident and Emergency. Jennifer Boulter.'

The mother with twins with aggressive breast cancer. 'Is she alright?'

Trina shook her head. 'She's bleeding. Pretty heavily, by all accounts, and they've just rung up to ask if there's an obstetric surgeon that can take her into Theatre. Rory's not here and, though Mr Michaels is, with his arm in a cast he can't do surgery. Could you do it?'

Caleb nodded. Of course he would, if there was no-one else. And, though he was tired and exhausted from a super-long day and wanted to get home to Rory, he knew that once he got into Theatre all his own unimportant aches, pains and tiredness would go away.

'Would you call Rory for me at home? Let her know I've been called back into Theatre?'

'Of course.'

'And apologise for me. Tell her the situation—let her know, it couldn't be helped. Thanks.'

He turned and headed back into the unit, full of determination, full of guilt that yet again he was being pulled away from the woman he loved to attend a patient. 'And can someone get the admitting doctor to give me a call so I can get Jennifer's admission details?'

'He's on hold right now, waiting for you.'

Caleb smiled. 'You knew I wouldn't let you down, huh?'

Trina laughed. 'You never do!'

No. He did his best to not let anyone down. He just hoped that Rory wouldn't be too mad that he'd missed the ante-natal class and would now miss having an evening meal with her. He would make it up to her. Maybe he'd take her out for a meal tomorrow night instead—one last night out before the babies came in a couple of weeks. Though he felt guilty about letting her down, it was one ante-natal class. He would go to all the others, hold her hand and do breathing exercises with her, even though she was going to have a caesarean. He would be the best partner. He would be the best dad. He wouldn't be like his own.

There was no way he was going to miss anything important.

Rory slipped in and out of consciousness. She experienced snippets. She could remember being strapped onto a back board, the discomfort of the neck collar and the sharp pinch of needles going into her arms. Could feel something tight and compressing going around her pelvis, causing her to black out. Voices.... Chantal's voice... softly encouraging. The glare of blue lights as she was wheeled along. The slam of the ambulance door closing. The rocking as the vehicle drove. The loud blare of sirens. Something tightening around her upper arm. The hiss of oxygen.

She wanted to say something, remind Chantal to call Caleb, but she was beginning to feel fuzzy and it was becoming hard to focus, to form words, to say how she felt.

'She's crashing!'

Who is crashing? she thought. Not her. Not Chantal… though the paramedic sounded concerned. Something… something was being administered into her arm, something cold pressing against her right chest and lower left abdomen. The lights dimmed. Sound faded.

She felt tired. So tired! And the darkness seemed soft and welcoming, reaching out for her, welcoming her in… And she knew that in the darkness there would be no pain and no fear, and it wanted her to go there, to keep her safe…

So Rory let go.

CHAPTER TWELVE

'I CAN'T STOP this bleeding!' Caleb said, frustration washing over him. He'd delivered Jennifer Boulter's twin boys, both small, Baby A weighing just one pound and three ounces and Baby B weighing a little more, at one pound five ounces. He'd removed them from Jennifer's womb with great care and delicacy as they'd seemed so small, like baby birds, fragile and bony. The NICU team had worked their magic, getting the boys hooked up to ventilators and placed in the warmers, and whisked them back to their department for monitoring and further care.

Caleb was still in Theatre, trying his damnedest to stop her bleeding, trying his best not to have to give another woman an emergency hysterectomy tonight. He knew that sometimes it was necessary. Knew that sometimes it was unavoidable. But he'd already sat at one woman's bedside tonight, waiting for her to wake so that he could deliver the news. He had already sat and answered her questions as she'd cried and mourned a future she'd not yet been ready to lose.

The theatre phone rang and a nurse answered it, as he finally located the source of the bleed. 'What is it?'

The nurse turned to look at him. 'They wanted to let us know that there's an emergency coming up.'

'Another one? I'm not done here!' He didn't like to lose his temper, but with being two surgeons down he was really beginning to feel the load. Rory would be at home, thinking he had abandoned her, and he didn't like that feeling. Nor did he want to have to ask her to come in. She needed her rest.

'It's not for this theatre, it's for Theatre Two.'

'Then why are we being called? Who's operating?' He frowned. 'Have they called Rory in? She's meant to be resting.'

It seemed as if the nurse seemed could hardly look him in the eye. 'They've called in Mr Atwood-Green.'

Caleb frowned. He'd thought James had left for an important dinner with his wife. They were celebrating their anniversary and he had left strict instruction not to be disturbed. They *could* have called Rory, so why hadn't they? Why had they called in the consultant? 'What's the emergency?'

'Pregnant woman in an RTA,' said the nurse quietly.

'Does James want me to tag in after I'm done here?' he asked.

The nurse shook her head. 'No. He said to take your time here.'

'Fine.' At least it meant that he didn't have to worry about the other woman whilst he was taking care of Jennifer. He would absolutely get this poor woman through her surgery so that she could see her babies and have enough strength left over to fight her battle with cancer. The other patient was the other surgeon's worry.

When Caleb had finished and the nurses had begun to wheel Jennifer out of Theatre, the nurse who'd answered the phone came up to him and said, ‘There’s a doctor waiting for you outside.’

‘Who?’

‘A Dr Fraser, from A&E.’

‘If he needs a consult, he could have just called up on the phone.’

‘He needs to speak with you—urgently. It’s about… the patient, in Theatre Two.’

James’s patient… He frowned at the nurse. Something was going on that he wasn’t privy to. He dried his hands and left the scrub room, to find a guy in green scrubs stood waiting for him.

‘Mr Stride?’

‘Yes?’

‘I’d like a word, if I may? Is there somewhere we can sit down?’

Caleb recognised the tone in an instant. It was the tone used with a family member, when there was difficult news to impart. ‘Who’s hurt?’

‘Ms Dotson.’

It took a moment for his brain to process the words, as if the world had slowed down exponentially. He noticed the blue flecks in the man’s greyish eyes, noted the tiny scar by his mouth and a thin gold chain around his neck, and then suddenly the world sped up again and his brain made giant leaps. Rory was hurt. She had to be the other woman in Theatre Two with James Atwood-Green! The nurse in Theatre had known and not told him!

The doctor saw the truth dawn in his eyes. ‘We couldn’t tell you, not whilst you were operating. We needed you to concentrate on your patient. It was Mr Atwood-Green’s strict instructions that you not be told who was being brought in.'

He could feel his legs turning to jelly and a wave of nausea washing over him. A hot flush of heat and pounding in his ears made him think that he might pass out.

Rory had been hurt in an RTA. How badly? And the babies? Were the babies alright?

He felt himself be guided over to a seat and felt Dr Fraser's hand on his shoulder.

'What happened?'

'Her car was hit by another car when she went to overtake. I believe her vehicle flipped and rolled and Ms Dotson was trapped inside and had to be cut out.'

'What are her injuries?'

'A fractured pelvis. Dislocated shoulder. She was bleeding heavily and the paramedics got her here as quickly as they…'

Caleb didn't listen to the rest. He had to be with her. He had to know what was going on. He had to be by her side! But before he could get anywhere he felt a hand upon his arm, slowing him down and pulling him back, and suddenly Dr Fraser was blocking him.

'Get out of my way!'

'You can't go in there.'

'That is the love of my life on that table. My daughters!'

'I understand,' said Dr Fraser. 'But Mr Atwood-Green knows what he is doing, and he does not need his focus distracted by having Ms Dotson's partner in Theatre looking over his shoulder and questioning his medical choices. I know you want to be in there, but you can't help her now.'

Caleb wanted to punch him. Wanted to push him to one side and slam him into a wall, just so that he could get into Theatre.

But…he wasn't a violent man and Dr Fraser was right. He would be nothing but a distraction for James and he did not want to have his attention waver from Rory. She needed him more than she needed Caleb right now.

Caleb sank to his knees and felt tears well up in his eyes. He had failed her. He had failed his babies—he should have been with them! And now he could do nothing to save them.

He would never forgive himself for this.

He couldn't sit still. He needed to pace. He went back and forth, back and forth in the small family room, and when pacing didn't make him feel better he sat again. For a second. And then he realised that sitting made him feel worse and so he got up to pace again.

He'd called everyone that mattered: Rory's mum and her sister, Maylee. They were on their way. He'd called his own mum. She'd called his dad who, not surprisingly, said he'd try to make it, but Caleb knew in his heart that he wouldn't see the man, even though these were his grandchildren. He hadn't been able to turn up for his own children, so why would he turn up for anyone else's?

To think that lately he'd been trying to understand the man and give him some grace for the disappointments of his childhood and life. Thinking that maybe his dad had been in situations like Caleb had today—no-one else available to do a surgery. Or with an emergency that had come in at the last moment.

But every single time, every single time Caleb needed

him, there had been an emergency and Callum Stride's patients had taken precedent over his own son. Surely it wasn't possible? Sometimes, maybe, but *every* time? How had the man felt the way Caleb felt now and stayed away? If he'd felt anything at all.

He'd tried to not be like his father, but hadn't he let Rory and his babies down? If he'd been with them, then maybe there might not have been an accident. Maybe they would all be home right now, tucked up in bed, warm, comfortable and fast asleep. Maybe they wouldn't be fighting for their lives if he'd put her first and been with her.

But what could he have done? He'd been needed. There'd been emergencies and no-one else to do them. He'd thought that *this once*, this *one time,* would be okay and that Rory would understand him letting her down. But maybe now she never would. Maybe she would always hate him for not being there. How frightened she must have been in that car—trapped, upside down, hurt, scared for their babies. And *he hadn't been there!*

The door opened and he turned in an instant, hoping it was a nurse with an update, or even better James Atwood-Green come to tell him that everything was alright. That Rory was in recovery and their babies were in the NICU. But it wasn't. It was Rory's mum, eyes red and tearful. She ran into his arms and he hugged her, feeling guilty.

How many people were affected by tonight? Too many.

How would he ever make this good again if one of them was permanently hurt from this? Or, worse, if someone died? How would he ever forgive himself?

How would *they*?

* * *

The door opened again and Caleb looked up, stunned to see his father standing awkwardly in the doorway.

'Dad?'

'Caleb.'

'You…you came?' He was surprised. A little stunned.

Callum Stride nodded, looking uncomfortable. 'Of course I did.'

'You never come.'

At this, Callum looked down and away. 'I've let you down, I know. Many times. But I'm trying to change that now.'

'Not hard enough.' He turned away from his dad. He didn't have the time, or the need, to have this conversation with him right now.

'You're right.'

Surprised, he turned back to look at his father. *'What?'*

'I said you're right. I didn't try hard enough. It was easier to stay at work, to deal with patients, to throw myself into each and every heart surgery, because to me that was easier than facing whatever was going on. I've been cowardly, and most importantly—I've begun to realise through some counselling that I had after my second marriage ended—that I had a responsibility to be there for others and not just for myself.'

'You're having counselling?'

Callum nodded. 'I tried to be there for you all and for your mother. God knows I tried, but the fear that I felt when you were born too soon was too much. I was overwhelmed by my own feelings, my own fears. And yet somehow I had to deal with your mother's too and it was all too much. It made me feel like I was going to explode, and so I left. It was the only way for me to cope. I know that it was wrong, and I continued to be wrong, but I just thought every time you got hurt or injured or sick would make me feel the same way, so I *avoided* it. It seemed easier, even though I knew that it was upsetting to you that I wasn't there. Upsetting to your mother to make her go through things alone.

'The drama of home and relationships was always too much for me, but when you added moments like appendicitis or broken bones… You have to understand, son, that I wanted to be with you, but didn't know how to deal with how I felt. You were this whirlwind of energy for me, and your mum would be crying. and I couldn't cope with that. I hated how it made me feel. And you wanted to be held all the time and I just couldn't… I've always struggled with strong emotions, so it just seemed easier to stay away. I told myself it was easier for *me,* even though I knew it was hurting *you.* I didn't understand it, but now I do. Like I say, it's no excuse, but I wanted you to know that I'm trying to be better.'

Caleb remembered his mother sitting with Caleb on her knee, comforting him after a fall, and saying she would hold him enough for the both of them. That she wasn't used to being held by his father either.

His father was right. It wasn't an excuse.

Dad loved me, he just couldn't show it.

He felt tears threaten at the realisation that he'd been fighting his father his whole life, when they should have just talked! His father had tried to call him, had left messages, and Caleb had simply ignored them. He'd given his father a taste of his own medicine. Had abandoned him. Maybe he was more like his father than he actually realised.

'Can I hug you?' he asked.

His father nodded, tears glazing his eyes, and he ran into his father's arms and began to sob.

A moment after, just after they were both regaining their composure, the door opened softly. 'Caleb?' It was James.

'Are they alright?'

James nodded. 'They're all going to be just fine.'

CHAPTER THIRTEEN

WHEN RORY CAME TO, she was in a hospital room, the steady beep of an ECG monitor beside her, intravenous lines going into both arms, and she felt exhausted; woozy and exhausted. At first, she couldn't remember why she was there, and then the memory of the car crash came cascading into her brain all at once, and the ECG beeps accelerated as she gazed down and realised her bump was gone. Thirty weeks' pregnant and her bump was gone! Where were her babies?

'Hey.'

She turned to her right and realised that Caleb was there, holding her right hand, smiling with tears falling down his face.

'Caleb? Where are the girls? Are they…?' She almost couldn't bring herself to ask the question. 'Alright?'

He smiled. 'They're good. Strong! They're in the NICU and your mum and my parents are with them.'

'They're okay? You promise? You wouldn't lie to me?' She had to make sure.

'I could never lie to you, but I'm so sorry I wasn't with you, Rory. I should have been! But I got called into an emergency and then another and… I'm making excuses, I know.'

'When can I go see them? I have to see them and know that they're alright.' She knew Caleb felt bad about letting her down, but that was the least of her problems right now. All she wanted was to see her babies.

'Not yet. You fractured your pelvis and dislocated your shoulder. You have two fine rib fractures. They want to make sure you're stable.'

'I have to go to them!' She tried to move, to rise and get out of bed, but piercing and intense white-hot pain penetrated the fog of her body and she collapsed back down against the pillows in tears.

'Don't move, Rory.'

'How am I supposed to care for them if I can't move? It's my job to protect them!'

'It's *our* job, and I will make sure they're okay until we're able to get you up there to look at them.'

She looked at him, her eyes filling with hot tears. 'I was so scared and you weren't there!'

He looked down and nodded. 'I know, and I'm so sorry.'

'I felt so alone in that car. In pain, frightened.'

He looked full of guilt, burdened by the weight of all that had happened. 'I'm so sorry.'

'It wasn't your fault,' she whispered.

Caleb looked up at her, surprised. 'You don't blame me?'

'I *did* in the moment, when I was scared and panicked and not thinking straight. I thought if you'd been with me, then the accident would never have happened and I wouldn't have gone alone. But…we're surgeons. And we don't have a normal nine-to-five job.' She frowned then, as a thought came to her. 'Who delivered me?'

'James did.'

'He wasn't at the hospital.'

'We called him in.'

'He can't have been happy about that.'

'I think his wife might have been annoyed. It was their anniversary dinner—twenty-five years. But…I think she understands.'

Rory drifted for a while then. Her eyes grew heavy and she let herself drift into the murky world of dreams. When she came to later, it was dark outside and Caleb still sat beside her, fast asleep, his head resting on her bed.

She smiled at him. At his handsome face. At his dedication to her. Yes, she had cursed him for not being there when she'd had her accident, but it had not been his fault. He had stayed at the hospital to save lives. To make sure another couple had got their family safely. Would she have respected him if he'd walked away from that to be with her at an ante-natal class? No. Because that wasn't who they were.

But for how long would he stay at her bedside? What would happen when he realised that twins were hard work and that they were going to have difficult days? Arguments, perhaps, disagreements over how to raise the girls. He could still so easily walk away from them all and her heart broke at the thought of it.

Whilst she'd been pregnant, and especially in these last few weeks, she'd allowed herself to dream of them having a happy-ever-after. But since this accident, and the fact that life gave no certainties or assurances, perhaps she was being naïve in believing happy-ever-afters existed at all. Maybe it did for James and his wife—twenty-five years and still going strong! But it was never the thing to happen to her. Her life had already been filled with disasters: a non-existent father who'd walked out on her as a baby. A fiancé who had walked out on her and left her standing in the church alone. A car crash that had tried to take her life and that of her children. Was it luck that she was still here? Or just the world seeing how many punishments she could take for believing that she could be happy?

Caleb stirred and rubbed his eyes, before lifting his head and realising that she was awake. 'Hey.'

'Hey.'

'You should go home. Get some decent sleep, if you're exhausted.'

'I'm fine right here.'

'Seriously, Caleb. You don't have to stick around for my disaster of a life. Clearly I'm a bad luck charm and I've already traumatised your life enough. I'm giving you an out before life gets really tough.' She tried to smile and be brave about it. But she would deal with it, if he decided to walk away, because she was used to dealing with life's curveballs all on her own. Better to be in charge of being left behind than just let it happen.

'What are you going on about?'

'It's going to be hard, looking after baby twins, whilst also caring for their mother with a broken pelvis, and working! It's going to be impossible, and it's okay. I'll do it. Mum will rally round, and Maylee, and…we'll deal with it.'

'I don't care that it's going to be hard. And I could never walk away from my children, or you, so stop saying things like this!'

She sighed. 'You never wanted this.'

'Neither did you! But things change. Life changes. People change!' He stared at her. 'Are you telling me that you don't want me?'

She shook her head. 'No. I do. I want you very much, but I know from experience that the people I want to stick around very rarely do, so…'

'I love you, Rory, and I will not let you push me away.'

She stared at him, shocked by his words. He loved her? He'd never said that before!

'Leo might have been a fool, but *I'm* not! You are the single most amazing person in my entire life. Ever since you walked into it, I have not been able to get you out of my mind and my heart, and I couldn't tear you out of them if I tried. *Which I will not!* I love you and I love our girls and I will be here for all of you, for all of our life together. In fact…'

He rummaged in his pocket and then pulled forth a small box. 'I was going to save this until later, but I'm going to do it now.' He flipped the lid and presented her with a solitaire diamond ring. 'Rory Dotson…will you marry me?'

Mouth open, Rory gazed, shocked and stupefied, between the ring and him and then back again. He wanted to marry her? 'Are you sure?'

'Surer than I have ever been in my life! You are my world, and I will dedicate every single day of our lives together to proving to you that you are the very air that I breathe. That I will love you and care for you, no matter what. That I will make you and our girls a priority—subject to work emergencies, of course.'

He smiled, knowing and accepting that of course they were unavoidable. That his father had not deserted him, had not considered his sisters, his mother and him as second best, or somehow less important. That he'd simply been struggling with something that was at the core of who he was. That he hadn't been able to change it.

Rory sobbed a laugh. Shock, surprise, awe and delight all washed over her in a happy wave, and she cried, 'Yes!' as he slipped the ring onto her finger.

Caleb stood and leaned over the bed, kissing her. It felt so good to feel his lips pressed against hers. To feel his love for her embrace her, envelop her, and she felt a fool for not realising the depth of his love before. She'd just been so used to not being good enough that she'd just assumed that Caleb would eventually run from her when things got tough. The way Leo had. She'd seen countless fathers not turn up for the birth of their children, abandoning their partners right at the crucial moment, as realisation hit of what their lives were about to be.

She'd simply accepted the same. She'd forgotten that Caleb was nothing like anyone else. He'd always been different. Always special. And she'd been so afraid to allow herself to love him, in case he ripped her heart out.

Well, not any more.

'I've spoken to the doctors. We're going to wheel you up to NICU in your bed. You can look at the babies through the viewing window.'

'Can I touch them? Hold them?'

He smiled. 'One step at a time, my love.'

In her mind, it took far too long to happen, but hours later, when James was happy that she was stable, he allowed her to be transported up to the NICU. She felt nervous. Excited. Apprehensive. Caleb had told her that the babies were good weights for their gestation, and the fact that there'd been the beginning of TTTS. Twin A, the bigger twin, had weighed three pounds, four ounces, and Twin B just under three pounds. Not huge, but bigger than some babies she'd seen in the NICU.

Then she was there. Her girls' incubators had been moved next to the viewing window and she could see them, wearing little knitted bonnets, one pink, one yellow. They looked so vulnerable and small, covered in wires and monitoring equipment, but they were stable and unhurt by the accident. Her body had taken most of the impact, cushioning them, protecting them—even if, as Caleb had told her, the placenta had been torn and begun bleeding profusely at the scene.

She used to come to this window when life got too much. But now she had been brought here to see her own babies inside and she realised just how strong she actually was. She would heal and her babies would grow.

Rory pressed her hand to the window, straining to see them. She wanted to touch them. 'They should have names. They need their names,' she said, when she saw their cards saying just Twin A Dotson and Twin B Dotson.

'What were you thinking?'

They'd kept lists individually on their phones. They'd occasionally discussed it, but had agreed that they'd need to see them first to see what names suited. 'She looks like a Zoe,' she said, gazing at her bigger daughter. 'It means life, doesn't it?'

Caleb smiled. 'Zoe… I like it. What about our other girl?'

'You should name her. It's only fair we get one each!'

'Okay. What about Brianna? It means strong.'

'Zoe and Brianna.' Rory smiled, tears of happiness falling down her cheeks. 'I want to hold them. Can I hold them?'

Caleb smiled. 'I'll fetch the nurse.'

It took some doing—a lot of arranging of cables and fetching extra blankets to keep the girls warm when they were removed from their incubators—but eventually they were placed into Rory's arms.

With Caleb sitting beside her, supporting the arm on the side she'd dislocated, she'd never felt such happiness! Her world was complete. She didn't need anything more.

She had Caleb, Zoe and Brianna.

Her bones and body would heal. Her girls would grow stronger.

And she knew that, with them all by her side, and her heart filled with love, it could never be broken.

EPILOGUE

RORY WAS NERVOUS as she stood outside the church in her wedding dress, holding her bouquet of freesias, roses and baby's breath. There was no doubt in her mind about Caleb. She already knew he was inside, waiting for her. It was just the thought of standing in front of everyone she knew, having to speak. She'd never had a problem talking to patients, because that was only ever one or two people—sometimes three or four, if family had arrived at the hospital to coo over the new baby in the family. But speaking in front of a full church in front of friends, family and co-workers… She loved them all, but it was still a daunting thing.

And she wanted her voice to ring true, sure and confident as she said her vows, because she wanted Caleb to know that his love for her had made her that way. He'd given her strength that she'd never known she had. The strength to face another wedding day. The strength to be a mother. A wife.

The last year and a half, since the girls had been born, had been difficult only with regard to her recovery from the accident. Her fractured pelvis had caused her an awful lot of pain and she'd not been able to care for Zoe and Briana the way she'd wanted to. But Caleb had been there for them all, lifting the girls and putting them on her lap for story time or cuddles; helping her bathe them and putting them to bed. He'd done a lot of the heavy lifting!

They stood before her now with one of the bridesmaids. Zoe and Brianna were flower girls and they'd practised spreading the rose petals in the weeks prior. Right now they were eager to start throwing the petals about.

'Not yet, girls. You have to wait until you hear the music. You have to wait until you go inside the church and see Daddy.'

Zoe and Brianna adored their father and he adored them. She could hardly believe the fact that Caleb had once told her that he'd never wanted to be a father. He was the best! He'd even healed his relationship with his own father, which had been amazing to see, and Rory had been glad to get to know Callum Stride. He was a talented and dedicated doctor. Yes, he did struggle with social obligations, but he was trying new things. Challenging himself to do things that previously he had avoided or found uncomfortable.

Zoe and Brianna had brought their family neatly together, as if they were the threads that had pulled two halves back into one.

The music began and her nerves became all aflutter.

'Are you ready?' her mum asked.

'I am.'

There was a little last-minute fiddling with the veil, and her bridesmaids arranged the back of her dress and straightened her train so that it would be seen in its full glory as she walked down the aisle.

Then the doors opened and her stomach flipped as

she saw everyone inside turning to look. And then her chief bridesmaid began to lead Zoe and Brianna down the aisle. They looked beautiful, like two flower fairies in their pure white dresses and floral headbands that matched Rory's bouquet, tossing rose petals up into the air and all around, making everyone in the church smile and giggle.

Then Rory began to walk forward, escorted by her mother. Her eyes met Caleb's and suddenly all her nerves and all her worries went away.

This was a day of celebration.

A day of love and unification.

She could do anything she wanted in this world, knowing how much she loved him and how much he loved her.

And they would raise their girls to be strong, confident women, adored by both parents who wanted nothing more than for them to be happy and healthy.

'You look beautiful,' Caleb said as she came to stand by her side.

Rory smiled, her heart filled with her love for him, and passed her bouquet back to her chief bridesmaid. Zoe and Brianna were still throwing out petals, which made her smile.

She turned and faced her husband-to-be and took his hands in hers.

Ready to say their vows.

Ready to commit to the rest of their lives together.

This had to be what bliss felt like.

* * * * *

FAKING IT WITH THE DOCTOR PRINCE

LUANA DaROSA

MILLS & BOON

CHAPTER ONE

Ethan

'JULIAN WILL WIN THIS. I have no doubt about it.' Standing in my father's office brings some old memories back of me growing up and presenting myself for his judgement. Somehow standing in front of his heavy mahogany desk transports me right back into the past, to a time when he lectured me about my family responsibilities, and even though I'm so far removed from the line of succession at this point that they don't list me on my uncle's Wikipedia page any more, I still represent the family.

Not that these lectures have stopped. If anything, that's usually what Archibald Grant-Belmont wants to talk about whenever I need to discuss the cycling team. What we need to do to win our first grand tour. Who we should work with to achieve our goals. How the projections are looking against the other teams that I consider to be our competition even if they don't even perceive us as a blip on their radar.

But that's not what my father wants to talk about. No, all he cares about is—

'Your uncle's birthday is approaching soon. There will be a gala with a dinner at the palace in Lyngholt. Dignitaries and important figures will be present, and he expects us to be there,' my father says, ignoring everything I've just told him about Julian Quintana, our star rider and the man I want to see in one of the winning jerseys this year.

Of course. That's what he wants to discuss. Álben and the duties that await me in our tiny island kingdom in the North Atlantic. He couldn't be less interested in what's happening with the team even if he tried. Yet he also refuses to give me full ownership of the club, hanging onto it despite letting me deal with the day-to-day management.

'Yes, I'm aware. Fairfax already got in touch with me. There are no one-day races on that weekend, so I'm free to come,' I say, remembering the call with Horacio Fairfax, the family secretary. Even after thirty-three years of this life, I'm still put off by the fact that there is a man responsible for scheduling and aligning people's schedules throughout this family for events where my uncle needs us to all be in one place.

And he gets to demand our time because my uncle is the King of Álben. Only in the last few years has he had children of his own, even at his age, which finally pushed his brother—my father—and by extension me further down the line of succession. All the way down to a place that will make it unlikely to require either of us to ever take up the throne.

But apparently he still needs me to show up to events, wave and smile and remember all the royal protocols that I've detested my whole life. Because being a royal ate away so much of my mother's confidence. From an early age, I watched her bend herself out of shape to fit in with our family's expectations and, no matter how hard she tried, the goalpost kept moving.

Only when she focused her time on the cycling team did I see her come alive again, and it's the reason why I'm working so hard on it now. It used to be her lifeline and now it is mine. My way of being more than just the circumstances of my birth.

'And what name did you give Fairfax for your plus-one?' my father asks, and I bite back a sigh because I'm about to tell him the same thing I told Fairfax.

'I didn't give him one because I'll be attending by myself.' I take a calming breath, reminding myself that I'm not responsible for my father's expectations. It's on him to get into his thick skull that I'm choosing to live my life differently, no matter how often he asks me if I'm seeing someone.

'You need to stop struggling against this, Ethan. You're so focused on your career and the team, but you neglect to see that it's not your entire life. Or rather, that it shouldn't be. Your mother wouldn't have wanted that for you,' Archibald says, steepling his hands in front of him.

'You say Mother wouldn't want that for me, but this is her team. She brought me into this sport and ignited my interest. It's thanks to her that *this*—' I put the same amount of condescension in my tone as he did '—is my passion. My life's work. I'll go to any of the family's fancy dress parties you want me to attend, and I'll even look like I'm enjoying myself. But I'm not dropping this team or my work there.'

'And you can have your passion for good if and when I'm satisfied with your life outside work. You and your mother shared a bond through cycling. My bond with her was forged through a life spent together—something we both wanted to see you achieve as well. Cast me in whatever light you want to, but my opinion isn't changing.'

We used to understand each other better; it all changed with my mother's passing. It's like she was the glue between us, a bridge to one another. Now, with her long gone, we stand on opposite sides of the shore, shouting to still hear each other. And with each passing year, the water erodes more of the shore—widening the gap.

'You think holding the ownership of my team hostage will motivate me to find someone? That's how low you're going to stoop to push this ludicrous idea on me? I can tell you right now that's not how it works.' I shouldn't argue, but I do anyway. It's all I can do to push against this idea he has in his mind that I need someone in my life to ground me and show me that I'm committed to my family as much as I am to work.

Too bad for him I'm not. He talks like it's so easy to find someone, when the truth is so far from it. I can count the people I've been in a relationship with on one hand, and none of them were designed to last. Being who I am, people usually approach me because they want to date a royal, not me.

Better to stick to casual encounters while travelling from one location to another during the cycling season. Before they have a chance to recognise me, I'm already gone.

I don't think my father would be too fond of knowing how much of my aversion to dating is his doing. His and my mother's. He defied expectations by marrying a woman he fell in love with regardless of how poor a match his parents thought she'd be. And when she fell ill and died, his grief all but made him disappear for a few years.

Not something I'm keen to ever experience myself.

My father's lips disappear into a thin line, just the way they always do when we have this conversation. He tells me to settle down; I tell him I'm comfortable as I am and a few weeks later we find ourselves reliving the same conversation. It's endless and stupid, but neither of us wants to give in.

'I've had enough of this conversation, Ethan.'

'Good, that makes two of us.' At this point, I don't even care if I sound like I'm eleven again.

'It's clear that this team is distracting you too much. You may not like it, but you do have a minimal responsibility to your family. I've indulged you for long enough, and I blame myself for not putting a stop to it earlier. Your mother…' He pauses and, for a moment, the same flinch goes through us both. We may not get along but we both carry her memory with us and lately she seems like the only thing we have in common. 'Continuing her legacy is the reason I haven't sold the team yet to show you how serious I am about this.'

There's an ominous quality to his voice as the conversation veers off script for the first time. An icy hand clenches around my throat at his last sentence. Sell the team? Throughout all of our contentious conversations, he's never mentioned that. Is he considering—?

'But maybe it's time we let go of it. Your mother wouldn't have wanted it to become something for you to hide behind and you are way past the age of playing around,' he continues, confirming the thoughts that refuse to make sense in my head.

This can't be happening. I have given far too much of myself to see the team sold to the highest bidder just because my father thinks I'm not settled. Just because I'm not bringing a date to my uncle's birthday celebrations.

'How much?' That would be an easy solution. If he doesn't want to lead the team any more—and I know he doesn't because I've been doing it since I became Head of Medical on the team—then I can just buy him out.

But Archibald shakes his head. 'I'm not going to sell the team to you.' Then he sighs, the sternness of his expression softening and suddenly making him look so much older than I remember. He rubs his eyes before he continues. 'It doesn't have to be like this. I don't want us to be antagonistic towards each other, son. Neither do I want to sell the team to hurt you. I've pushed you in the right direction for long enough, and we're getting to a point where I'm out of options.'

Something inside me stirs at his tone. It's not commanding but rather sad. Like he truly means it. I'm still not sure he does because he's right: our relationship has grown more contentious over the years. So much so that I'm not entirely certain I remember what it was like before.

'You want me to find someone to settle down with and I want ownership of the team. The answer to all of this seems obvious,' I say as I try to figure out how to win back the advantage in this conversation.

'I'd thought it was obvious for a while now, Ethan. You just didn't want to hear it,' my father replies, and I know he's not wrong.

'Is that what it'll take for you to hand off the team

to me? I have to show you I'm genuinely trying to find someone?' I ask, wanting to hear the words.

'If you bring someone suitable to the King's birthday and I can see that you are genuinely involved with this person—that this isn't a friend you just asked for a favour—then I'll be happy to give you ownership of the team. I don't expect you to suddenly become all about the family, but I do need to see a shift in your priorities,' he says and I can feel this is as much of a concession for him as it is for me.

'We have an agreement, then. I will let Fairfax know who to put on the guest list,' I say before giving my father a nod and sweeping out of his office.

I will do anything to keep this team going. If that means finding a date, then so be it.

Only, where do I even start? I don't know anyone suitable to be my girlfriend, and even if I did, that's not what I want. No, what I need is a mutually beneficial agreement with someone who can benefit from a connection with me. If I can find someone who needs something I can provide them with, maybe a long-term agreement could be struck.

But who could that be?

A picture flashes in front of my eyes unbidden. Brown eyes peeking out underneath a riot of dark curls. Pillowy lips that never fail to pull into a frown whenever she sees me. Like she's somehow figured out that I can't stop watching her whenever she steps into the room, and she's judging me.

Which is fair enough, since I judge myself for this unwarranted obsession. But instead of pushing the thought of Dr Valerie Torres away, I hold it close as I walk down the familiar corridors of my family home.

Her CV showed up on my desk at just the right time—for both of us. But she's been quiet so far, at least around me. Javier, my head coach, tells me she is quite lively as long as I'm not around.

So I'm not sure why her face pops into my head when I ponder this mutually beneficial arrangement. Even if it's nothing serious, I can't get involved with an employee. And if that weren't a problem, what could I have to offer her in return for this half-baked idea forming in my head?

Grimacing, I slip into the back seat of the car waiting outside to take me to the airport. Valerie Torres is not the answer to my problems. I don't know what—or who—is.

CHAPTER TWO

Valerie

THE SUN IS SHINING. That seems to be about the only redeeming feature of this day. In fact, the sun might even *not* be shining with the rumbling cloud in human form that is Dr Ethan Grant hovering. I'm not sure if something has him in a mood or if he is just being his usual cheerful self, and I've forgotten how grumpy this man is.

I *definitely* haven't forgotten how ridiculously handsome he is. It strikes me as I approach the little van out of which we are working today as a group of our riders do a test ride, involving cycling up the same hill over and over again while we measure their vitals against the time they take to complete one hill. I want to say I only notice him because he isn't supposed to be here. At least he wasn't on the schedule for today.

Not that I was checking the schedule for him. No, I just wanted to know where *I'm* needed today. Yeah, that was it. We distributed the new nutritional plan last night—one Dr Ethan Flipping Grant thought he could just edit without my knowledge. Little does he know I already changed all the values back to their original ones.

If he didn't want me to do my job, why did he hire me?

Not that I'm complaining. Someone like me, whose messy break-up caused her to lose her last job, doesn't really have a leg to stand on when it comes to complaining. And can you really call it a break-up when we were just sleeping with each other, but in a way that *implied* exclusivity?

I glance towards Ethan again. Why is he here? Does he know that I changed the nutritional chart back again before handing it over to the catering team?

Great. I was hoping I could spend some time going through my charity's email inbox while the riders do their loops. I'm only here to analyse some data that the head coach, Javier Salgado, will present at the end. Because cycling is such an endurance sport, nutrition impacts almost all riders' outputs, and even small nutritional adjustments can significantly boost their performance.

'Good morning, Dr Grant,' I say as I approach the van. Inside the vehicle, I can hear Javier talking on the radio to one rider as he points at something on the laptop screen.

A tiny jolt shakes Ethan, as if he was in his own thoughts and my polite greeting shook him out of it. Or, more likely, it was a micro-shudder of revulsion because he didn't realise I would be here too.

His head twists a fraction, the sunshine bouncing off the lenses of his glasses and blinding me for a moment before he faces the street again and gives me a far too enticing view of his chiselled jawbone that makes me clench my teeth in annoyance. I don't trust men who are smart, well-respected and also hot. Alexander, or *Zander* as my kind-of-ex likes to be called, was all three things, and he screwed me over when I was all but ready to commit the rest of my life into supporting his career—his dreams. And in return, he all but crushed mine.

Unlike Ethan, Alexander was very jovial with every person in his team, Team Blue Cow. When I started working for him, I was instantly drawn to his big personality. Turns out, when we started sleeping together and he told me he wanted to keep things quiet so as not to disrupt the team, he actually meant the other women he was sleeping with.

And when I told them about his indiscretions, I got the boot and had to scramble to find a new job. I landed here at Grant Sports Team, working alongside Ethan Grant. The human thundercloud.

At least Ethan doesn't seem to know he's attractive. Otherwise, he wouldn't be such a grumpy goose to everyone around him. Or worse, he would use his appearance to his advantage. Alexander always was a shameless flirt, but I didn't see it as a warning sign until it was too late.

'Good morning, Dr Torres,' Ethan says just as I shake my head like a wet dog to get rid of the Alexander-shaped thoughts creeping back into my mind. A line appears between his far too perfectly arched brows. 'Are you okay?'

'Yes, of course,' I say, my voice squeakier than normal. 'Why wouldn't I be?'

His head tilts towards me some more, a frown now accompanying the deepening lines of his furrowed brow. 'Because you're wobbling your head?'

'Oh, that's—a fly or a bee or something came plummeting at me just as you turned,' I say and bite my lower lip almost immediately as the lie comes out of my mouth. Why did I say that instead of the classic *nothing*?

Now one of his eyebrows lifts high enough to pass the rim of his glasses. 'I didn't see anything.' His tone doesn't hide his scepticism, and I suppress the shiver his stern voice inspires.

'It was small. Maybe too small for you to see, considering…' My voice drifts off as my brain catches up to what I'm about to say. But it's too late. Now the half-finished sentence hangs between us and a burning awkwardness unfurls in the pit of my stomach because I know he's going to follow up and my brain is running empty. Not that I trust a brain that just produced the amazing 'a fly or a bee' line.

'Considering what?' he asks, predictably.

I try—*fail*—not to cringe as I reply, 'Considering you wear glasses. Might be hard to, you know, *see* things.' Oh my God, why am I elaborating my thought process? I cannot be around this man because his brooding nature paired with the stupid hotness seems to send all my brain cells on holiday the moment I spot him.

He blinks—no, he *slow*-blinks, which I feel is an important distinction to make here since a slow-blink is so much worse. The lines on his forehead smooth out as he says, 'I wear these glasses so I *can* see just as clearly as someone who doesn't need corrective lenses.'

I know that. Of course I know that. I'm a doctor. A real one, not like him, who might be a fake one because I cannot find any trace of him in any archives from any medical schools. Despite that, all I can squeak out is a meek, 'Oh, that makes sense,' while praying that he will just let it go before I get even more frazzled.

'Riders are approaching the foot of the hill,' Javier yells out from the van, grabbing our attention.

Ethan's eyes dart down to my mouth where my teeth no doubt left a red mark and they linger there long enough for a flash of heat to flood my body at the sharpness of his lingering gaze. Then he turns just as abruptly, his focus back on the street, leaving me to contemplate whether I could have somehow made this encounter more awkward if I had applied myself a bit more.

Probably not.

'Tell them to crank it up,' Ethan says after our riders pass us for the third time.

He has been ignoring me ever since I managed to stop talking. And I can't tell if that's a good thing or a bad thing. I don't want to be on Ethan Grant's radar, but nor do I want to be on his bad side. Neither of these options is compelling.

'They're slower,' Ethan mutters to no one in particular, snapping me out of my doom spiral.

How does he know that? We're still standing outside as the sun crests over us. We typically do our training rides early in the morning or late at night to avoid the sun's heat. But for today's ride, Ethan wanted to have more realistic circumstances to test them as if they were doing one of the stages.

A tactic I usually agree with, though in this case I'm not sure if we aren't pushing it. Julian Quintana, our star rider and the man most likely to win a place on the podium at the upcoming Tour de France this year, looked tired this morning when I saw him warming up outside, and I'm worried we're running him too thin.

Turning towards Javier and peering inside the van with all its equipment blinking in the semi-dim interior, I see the man's brows dip low and, a moment later, Javier says, 'They're slowing down.'

I start as he repeats Ethan's assertion only a few seconds after he said it. He can tell by feel alone? Is he one of those people who can tell exactly what time it is at any given moment without looking at a clock and also count how many jellybeans are in a jar simply by glancing at it for five seconds?

'What's different today?' Ethan asks as I step into the van to look at Javier's screens, scanning Julian's vital signs.

'He's fine,' I say, pointing at the oxygen levels displayed on the screen. Yet even though he's not pushing at what I know is his maximum, his power output is decreasing. After sprinting up this hill and looping around, he should be faster, not slower.

The scent of fresh laundry and some kind of spice fills my nose, and as I turn my head I almost bump into Ethan. Leaning over my shoulder, he focuses on some charts lower on the monitor—watching the junior rider, Angel Esposito, riding with Julian.

'The bikes are fresh from the service station and nothing has changed on this strip of road. It's a bit more humid today but that shouldn't matter,' Javier says, then looks over at me. 'Did you notice anything last night when you handed out the new nutritional logs?'

I shake my head. 'No, I don't recall noticing anything or I would have flagged it,' I say, retracing yesterday's steps. 'After double-checking the values, I sent them over to the kitchen staff and dropped copies off for the riders. A new nutritional plan shouldn't have this kind of effect.'

Ethan's head turns towards me at the last sentence, his lips set in a frown. He's looking at me as if it's the first time he's realised I exist. Which, again, is not ideal, considering I want to stay employed and the last thing I need is the boss staring at me as if I'm lost.

But no, it gets so much worse than that. 'I changed the distribution of macronutrients on those spreadsheets. Did you send them over after those edits?'

Oh. The spreadsheets. Right. The ones I corrected last night in a fit of rage. Though I'm still convinced that I'm right and he has no business messing around with my spreadsheets. If he really feels so strongly about it, he should have spoken to me.

'Even with the original numbers, Angel shouldn't be flagging like that. Unless the kitchen made a mistake, this isn't it,' I say without answering his question.

Which he apparently notices, because he asks again, 'Did you send them over after I changed the values or before, Dr Torres?' Somehow, him using my last name makes this situation more tense. That's the only way I can explain the bolt of lightning running through me.

I straighten, refusing to be intimidated by anyone, especially this guy. Even having had little to no interaction with him, I can already tell he isn't much better than Alexander. Apparently, there is no shortage of arrogant men believing they're God's gift to the sport. The only thing even remotely divine about Ethan is his jawline.

Wait, what?

Pushing that away, I straighten my spine as I face Ethan. 'Seeing as I am the team's nutritionist, I made sure the spreadsheet reflected what I originally put together. I sent you all the documentation on how I got to my conclusions.'

There. I changed his edits to the stupid spreadsheet and I'm not sorry about it. It might have happened when I was in a less than ideal state of mind, but I stand by it. I know my numbers are right for what we want to achieve with these riders. This prolonged silence that falls over the van as Ethan keeps looking at me with unblinking eyes is not at all making my conviction waver. The numbers are in my brain and I know they're right. *I'm* right.

'You changed the numbers back to the original values, knowing full well I wanted them that way?' he asks, his voice dropping low enough that it sends a shiver skating down my spine.

'I didn't *know*, Dr Grant,' I press out between clenched teeth. 'Not for certain. Because you didn't tell me you wanted them changed. No, you just changed them. If you had communicated your desire to adjust the macronutrients, I wouldn't have changed them back.'

A muscle clenches in his jaw, his frown deepening into a scowl. 'Did you try to get in touch with me to discuss it?' he asks, and I try not to sag my shoulders in relief. I did, and I did that because of this exact situation. Now, to be completely honest, I could have tried harder, but most of the blame in this whole situation lies with him.

'I did. When I noticed the changes, I sent you an email and waited almost an hour before distributing the information,' I say, trying my best to keep the smugness out of my voice. I know I've failed at that when the scowl on his face deepens.

'That was last night?' The question throws me and so I blink at him for several seconds.

'Yes.' What is he getting at? During discussions earlier in the week, he told all of us to ramp our plans to the next phase by this morning, as the training rides would only get more intense. Again, not something I agreed with, but I'm trying to be the least fired person on this team, so unless it's detrimental to the riders, I'm keeping my head low and doing the work.

Except for that spreadsheet. I couldn't help myself.

'I was at an important meeting and I didn't—why didn't you call?'

What? 'I don't think I have your number. And even then, why would I call you? I'm the lead nutritionist. What the riders eat and how much and when and all the other stuff that goes along with that should be up to me.' My temper flares but I'm too far gone to reel myself in. Who on earth does he think he is? 'And if you keep—'

Javier jumps to his feet as a loud alarm sounds through the van. Both our heads whip towards the screen as Javier says, 'Angel's heart rate just dropped below the acceptable threshold.'

'Below?' I ask and gasp when I see his heart rate displayed in the low forties.

'He is bradycardic,' Ethan says next to me, the same shock in his voice. 'We have to help him.'

I nod and follow Ethan out of the van and to his car parked behind it. The moment my seat belt clicks into place, his foot presses down on the pedal and we are speeding down the road.

CHAPTER THREE

Ethan

IT TAKES US less than two minutes to find our two riders. I pull the car over to the side of the road where we see their bikes discarded. Valerie jumps out of the vehicle even before it reaches a full stop, running over to where I can see Julian kneeling beside a motionless Angel, med kit bumping against her thigh with every step.

Pulling up the handbrake, I get out of the car and circle around the back to retrieve the reflective warning triangle and put it down the road from where we approached the riders before returning to them. The roads around here are narrow, winding around hills and down into valleys. It makes this area perfect for training but also dangerous in terms of traffic and visibility.

'What's the status?' I ask, kneeling next to Valerie.

She palpates his neck, resting on the carotid artery there. I can hear her count under her breath as the seconds pass and then she looks up at me. 'Heart rate is still under forty beats per minute.'

'What's happening to him?' Julian asks, his gaze pinging between us as I grab the stethoscope from the med kit Valerie has already thrown open. Looking through its contents, I see we have everything we need to stabilise Angel but—

'Quintana, I need you to call an ambulance and give them our exact location. You know how to describe it?' I look at him for a second even though time is of the essence. He's more freaked out than I like, but that's unsurprising, considering the circumstances. That's why I'm giving him this task rather than doing it myself.

He hesitates for a fraction of a second before he nods, scrambling to his feet as he digs his phone out of his back pocket. When I turn back to Valerie, she's leaning over Angel's face, ear close to his mouth. 'Here,' I say, holding the stethoscope out.

She takes it from my hand, delicate fingers brushing against mine, and I ignore the jolt running through me at that. Instead, I turn back to our med kit and take out the automated external defibrillator. I hope we won't need to use it but, if his pulse keeps dropping, cardiac arrest is an option.

What the hell has happened this morning that one of my riders is in a state like this?

'He's breathing, but it's shallow. Combined with his heart rate dropping like a stone, he might not be getting enough oxygen to his brain,' she says, and I nod.

'Quintana is calling the ambulance already. We're not too far out from the nearest hospital, but we need to stabilise him until they can arrive.' I take a small oxygen tank out of the med kit, looking at the dial at the top, praying it's enough to hold us over until the paramedics arrive.

'Hey, Angel. It's Ethan. Can you hear me?' I ask as I bend over him to put the oxygen mask over his mouth and nose. But the man shows no reaction, his chest rising and falling in shallow, rapid breaths.

'He wasn't responsive to me, either,' Valerie says, and when I hear the oxygen move through the hose and into the mask, I sit back up—and take her measure.

'You said you spoke to him this morning. Did you notice anything then? Any changes in behaviour?' Even though we were going to have an argument about her unilaterally changing adjustments I'd made to my team's nutritional plan, I know it couldn't have been the cause of this. A conversation for later, then.

Valerie shakes her head, her nose scrunching up as she casts her gaze upwards in thought. 'I remember reading his file just yesterday morning and there weren't any mentions of pre-existing conditions.'

I shake my head. 'Because there aren't. I oversee all the health checks and fitness tests of the riders myself. What condition could a—?'

The high-pitched hum of a siren cuts me off mid-sentence and we both sit up straight. I turn my head to Julian, who sits on the ground next to the car in a crumpled mess, head buried in his hands. Another problem to solve once I'm sure Angel is taken care of at the hospital.

'Julian just called. Angel's mother is on the way here. He's asked if he can stay with him until she arrives.'

I lift my eyes off the screen as Valerie's voice filters towards me from my open office door. 'How is Angel doing?'

We stabilised Angel enough that the paramedics only needed to hook him up to their own monitors before driving off with Julian in tow. I'd offered to go myself—and so had Valerie—but ultimately we both stepped aside and let Julian go with him. Having to see a fellow rider crash out is hard on anyone's mental health, and it's worse when it results in an emergency like that.

After we got back from the incident, I went straight to my office to pore over Angel's medical records and latest test results to find any sign that might be helpful to the doctors at the hospital treating him.

'Sitting up on his own and off the oxygen. When Julian saw his energy dip, he made him get off the bike before he could crash. Test results haven't come back yet so they want to keep him overnight for observation,' she says, leaning against the doorframe with her ankles crossed one over the other.

'Good. Thanks for letting me know.' I nod, then focus back on planning around Angel's potential absence. He's one of our best support riders, and if he's out of commission for the rest of the season, I'll need to shuffle things around.

Nothing has gone according to plan this year. During the Giro d'Italia, the grand tour of Italy, we only managed to snag a few stage wins before a handful of riders fell ill with the swine flu and needed to isolate. Then the team nutritionist quit, leaving us scrambling in search of a new one. The one-day races have yielded a few wins for Julian, and the press is buzzing for him, but not as much as I had hoped this close to the Tour de France. And now I'm in this holding pattern, not knowing if Angel will be available for the rest of the season.

Not to mention that I have three missed calls from Fairfax; no doubt to ask about the name of the person I promised my father I would bring to my uncle's event. A name I don't have considering that, one, I don't want to date anyone, and two, I'm so busy with work that I don't even know anyone who could *pretend* to be my girlfriend just to get my father off my case. Never mind that if I really were to go down this route, I would need someone to pretend to be with me convincingly, given my father has already said he'll keep a keen eye on whoever I bring.

A soft throat-clearing rips me out of my thoughts and my eyes whip up again—latching onto Valerie's light brown gaze. Not for the first time since she's joined the team, I lose my train of thought when I look at her. She still has a uniquely *distracting* quality to her, in that, whenever I'm in the same room with her, she draws my attention without saying or doing anything. Which isn't ideal for my productivity. By now I would have thought the novelty of Valerie Torres would have disappeared, but no. My senses still home in on her whenever she enters the room I'm in without me being able to stop any of this.

Inconvenient.

'Is there anything else you want to talk about?' I ask, raising an eyebrow to punctuate my question.

Valerie nods, pushing herself off the doorframe as she says, 'There is, and I've been—'

She interrupts herself, shaking her head hard enough that the tendrils of black hair bounce around her face in a mesmerising dance. 'Actually, I have nothing to say.'

She turns on her heel just as I get to my feet, though why I'm jumping up, I'm not sure. To stop her? That's at least what my outstretched hand is suggesting.

'Dr Torres, if you—'

She turns again at the mention of her name. 'Okay, here's a question: why are you so formal with me?'

Taken aback, I pause before I find my words. 'That's what you wanted to discuss?'

'I've never worked in a cycling team where anyone called each other by their title. Only you do that,' she says, and even though she's facing me again, she still hovers in the doorway as if ready to leave at any second.

'I will take that feedback under advisement,' I say, not sure what words will make her stay—get her to say what I can see she's decided to withhold. Though why I want to know isn't clear to me.

Valerie snorts, her amusement blending into the tension between us. 'Me trying to tell you how you sounded formal only made you sound even more formal.'

'Maybe you could benefit from some more formality. Did you learn at your last position to change riders' plans without involving the medical lead?'

Her eyes flare wide before she drops her gaze to the floor, and I swallow a sigh at her reaction. This is not how I wanted to have this conversation. I'm not oblivious to my reputation as a hard-ass, but there is a reason I expect the best from everyone, even if they don't know it. This team—the work I do here—is the only thing I have left to remember my mother. She gave me the passion and confidence to be something beyond what my birth made me. Anything less than total commitment would dishonour her memory.

'Actually, no—I'm not going to shut up about this.' Valerie surprises me by lifting her head again, a fire blazing in her eyes as her delightful Spanish accent thickens slightly. 'I'm a consummate professional, Dr Grant. Not only have I worked in sports nutrition for the last five years, I also run a food poverty educational charity, Cosecha de Vida. If there is something I know inside out, it's food.'

She pauses, taking a breath, and I'm too stunned by her forcefulness to do anything but sit there as she continues, 'I'll admit I shouldn't have changed your numbers back without communicating that to you, but you altered them in the first place, without discussing it with me. I get that you're the medical lead for the team. However, I'm responsible for overseeing all the nutrition. The kitchen team calls me when they have questions. So do the riders. So does Javier. I need to know what it says on my spreadsheets. You undermining my decisions is a problem.'

Her eyes narrow on me. When my team nutritionist quit, we had to scramble to find someone new within days. We were already in the thick of the Giro d'Italia, and, although the plans were in place, I couldn't risk the uncertainty of not having someone to monitor and adjust everything on the fly. But I couldn't accept just anyone—I needed someone capable, someone who could handle the pressure. When Valerie Torres' CV landed on my desk, I almost didn't trust it. Her credentials were outstanding. Not only had she come in a pinch, she was also the best option, even if it felt like I hadn't had much time to vet her properly.

For example, I didn't know she runs her own charity. Or that she isn't as quiet as she's seemed in the last few weeks.

I clear my throat, fighting down the defensiveness rearing its head within me as I think about the team. She's right to call me out, considering I hired her for a specific reason and that is her expertise in putting together the nutritional plans over long periods of sustained performance. Even though I don't like to admit it, I can see her standpoint. The last thing I need is friction in the team by being difficult.

Something about the fire in her eyes as she spoke right now catches my attention. I want to see more of it. Another inconvenience she brings my way, because I can't remember the last time I was interested in someone outside what skills they could add to my team.

'You're right, and I apologise,' I say as I close my laptop and push to my feet to give her my full attention. Rounding the table, I lean my hip against it while looking at her, immediately sucked into the intensity bouncing off her in chaotic waves.

I look down at Valerie's mouth as her lips press into a line. But she says nothing as the fire winks out—even though I can feel a sudden tension snapping into place between us. Can hear the words rolling around in her head.

'If you have more feedback, I would like to hear it,' I say, keeping my voice even. Is that what she needs? An invitation to speak? Or was this sluice of words a reaction to my behaviour? Not that I can do anything right now to piss her off again and make her speak. And why am I even considering needling her just to hear her voice?

Then something odd happens. Valerie's teeth sink into her lower lip, leaving a red imprint behind. Not that *this* is odd. No, what is weird is my reaction to it. My brain stalls as if some synapses stopped firing, and all my attention homes in on that one spot on her lower lip and how her canine is digging into it. And I need to know what it feels like more than I've needed to know anything else in life.

What is this woman doing to me? How does she have this effect on me when no other woman ever has? Since I shifted my focus to managing the team, that's all I've ever cared about. It's all I still care about, except when I don't have a full grip on my thoughts, sometimes she manages to slip in there. Like after the meeting with my father.

Or right now, when I should be focusing on something else. The thing she wants to talk about rather than my thoughts about her. I know it's not because she's an exceptionally beautiful woman. That's never been enough to hold my attention.

No, it's something else. A quality I can't name.

'I think you're overtraining them,' Valerie says, and that snaps me out of my trance.

It also instantly raises all the defences I've held at bay throughout this conversation. My mouth moves before I can even think about the wisdom of my words. 'If you're going to throw things like that my way, you have no right to complain about overstepping.'

I can hear the edge in my words and I'm about to soften them when I see the wildfire in her eyes come alight again. Oh, is that how we're doing it? Well, I guess another apology is unnecessary, then.

Valerie crosses her arms, her eyes narrowing as she steps toward me, her voice steady but charged. 'Julian's recovery times are getting slower. I've looked at everyone's numbers over the last week—this isn't normal fatigue. You're running them into the ground in your attempt to get to general classification.'

'My training plan might seem aggressive, but Julian's—and everyone else's—rest plans are carefully planned out. You should know that since you made the feeding plan for those days.' The tension thickens and I'm rolling my jaw as I try to relax it. I'm aware the training regimen isn't conventional, but we won't win a spot at the top by doing things like everyone else does.

'Your plan may have put Angel under enough stress that he's in hospital,' she says and, by her flinch, I can tell she immediately regrets it.

Not that it matters. The blow lands and I fight off a visible bristle. This isn't the first time someone has criticised my approach as too intense. I don't usually care because the team sees the results. My father sees it and, except for that one minor snag where he wants me to find someone to settle down with, I know I'm this close to getting control over the team.

Why is it different hearing the same criticism from her? Why does her approval somehow matter to me?

'I'm sorry, I didn't—'

'What's going on with you?' I cut her off before she can apologise.

She takes a half-step back, swaying enough that I push myself off the desk in case I need to reach for her. 'Excuse me?' she asks, blinking at me.

'Outside the interview, this is the most you have spoken to me ever since starting here.' I pause, unable to keep a smirk off my lips. 'Not that I'm complaining. I enjoy you being more outspoken. Just that until now it hasn't happened. So what's going on?'

It's a wild guess and I'm almost certain I'm mistaken. All my skills centre around cycling and medicine and, since my patients are pro-athletes, I've never needed to develop good bedside manners. But some hidden sense—maybe some kind of strange connection?—tells me this was the right thing to ask. That something *is* not going well for Valerie.

'I don't—nothing that should concern you.' Her shoulders slump forward, and she lets out a sigh as she shakes her head. I can't stop the smile from broadening as I watch the emotions play on her face. She wears everything she feels on her sleeve and it doesn't take any effort to figure out something's bothering her.

'If it's about the training plan, I appreciate the feedback, but I'm not changing—'

'It's not about the training. My work is intrinsically linked to the training, so I'm always worried about it, but that's not—' My mind wanders almost instantly, contemplating how the dim light of the office lamp bounces off those glossy locks, giving them a perceived softness that is begging to be verified. By touch and—

I shake my head to get rid of the little voice that's come out of nowhere to possess me, but Valerie takes it as a different sign. She snaps her mouth shut, lips pressed into a thin line again.

'Sorry, I tend to overshare when I'm stressed,' she says and retreats another step.

'No, I wasn't shaking my head because—I want to know what's going on with you.' Wait, no, that sounds far too familiar. 'For work. We're at a critical time, especially with Angel potentially out of the race. Whatever you're thinking, I want to hear it so we can deal with it.'

A myriad expressions flutter over her face again, and I can see her hesitance; can feel it in the tension surrounding us. Is this a personal issue? Does she have some kind of attachment to a rider that makes her more worried about the training plan? Is that why she was there this morning with Angel?

My stomach ties itself into a knot and I force myself to remain still. What do I care if she has any sort of entanglement with anyone on the team? I've got my own complicated dating drama happening. Or rather, the lack of anyone special in my life is causing that drama.

'It's my charity. My goal for this year was to quit my day job at the end of the season and transition into full-time work with my charity,' she finally says, and that's not at all what I expected to hear. But the words aren't lost on me.

'Was?'

She frowns and I can see the battle in her eyes. One she doesn't struggle long with, for she continues, 'When I joined up with Team Blue Cow, they promised me a small patch on their kit to print my charity's logo. Nothing that would detract from their main sponsor, but enough to get people curious. But then I—there were some differences between my vision and the directeur sportif that—' She cuts herself off and all I can do is watch those curls bounce again, the dim light of the office casting them in a warm glow. 'Ugh, I really shouldn't be telling you this. You're my boss.'

'You've kept quiet here because last time you were perceived as outspoken, you lost not just your job but also a sponsorship opportunity?' I take a guess at what she doesn't want to say.

'Pretty much.' Valerie digs her fingers through her hair, causing a tantalising disarray that wipes the words from my brain. I force myself to look away because this reaction isn't just inappropriate, it is completely out of character for me. I *am* her boss and if I didn't know myself any better, I would almost say I'm ogling her.

'Anyway, I'm sorry to dump this all on you. As I said, I overshare when I'm nervous. Sometimes after a long day Alexander would tell me to go talk to his cat and not bother him with—oh my God, what on earth am I saying?' Her hands fly up to her mouth, clasping over it.

I can't help but chuckle though my brain stutters for a second at the name. Alexander? Could she mean Zander Lemoine, Team Blue Cow's directeur sportif? Though the tiny snippet she just shared almost sounds like she knows him outside his leadership position on the team.

'All I needed to do was stress you out to get you talking,' I say, filing that information away. 'Maybe they don't run things like this in other teams, but here I encourage my staff to voice their opinions, especially when criticising my plans.'

'Even if it's to tell you not to touch my spreadsheets without telling me first?' she asked, and I let out a defeated groan.

'You may not be the only one here who's feeling pressure due to external circumstances,' I say, though I don't want to go into any details. Hardly anyone on the team knows my *royal* status, and I prefer it that way. Even though people say they don't care, they always do and then they treat me differently. The whole reason I put so much of myself into managing this team is because I want to escape the stares and expectations from everyone.

Valerie's mouth falls open in surprise, her lips forming an almost perfect O. I can almost see the thoughts moving in her mind though I can't even begin to guess what she's thinking. Nothing about this conversation has gone the way I expected it.

'You need any help with that?' she finally asks, again subverting my expectations.

I give her a trained smile that doesn't feel quite natural to me but hasn't let me down so far. 'No, but thank you. I appreciate the offer.'

She scrutinises me, her light brown eyes sweeping over me as if she has X-ray vision and can see all the mess I keep hidden below the surface. But thankfully she doesn't call me out on my crap and shrugs instead. 'Well, if you want to talk about it, I know someone who just blurts things out without thought and I find people kind of enjoy that when they are ranting.'

With those words, Valerie whirls around and makes for the door, but not without sending me a look over her shoulder. 'Just in case I wasn't clear: I'm that person,' she says before vanishing through the door and leaving me alone with a grin on my face that feels genuine.

Not that it lasts long. The moment I let myself fall back into my chair and my eyes focus on my screen, I see an email from Fairfax land in my inbox, and right beneath it a competitor report on what Team Blue Cow is up to in their training. They'll learn soon enough that Angel might be out of the competition and things will only get more difficult for us from there.

Not to mention that I need to solve this *settling down* problem my father has foisted on me at the most inopportune time. If only there were a way to convince him I'm taking it seriously without actually doing it. I just need him to believe it enough to hand over the reins of the team.

Even though I have a host of my own problems to solve, my mind keeps going back to Valerie and what she just shared. How much she had shared. Not quiet, after all, just lacking an opportunity to talk to me. And, as I stare at Fairfax's email, something slips into place inside me.

I can give Valerie what she wants. The cycling team has always been funded by the trust my mother left behind and we therefore never had the need to find sponsors. In fact, we're the only team that doesn't have anything printed on our kits.

Maybe this is the mutually beneficial arrangement I need and I've stumbled into it without even noticing.

Clicking the email away, I open a browser and input Valerie's name plus the word *charity*, and I start reading about Cosecha de Vida. An hour later I'm certain that she's the solution to my problem and that I have the right incentive to convince her of my idea.

CHAPTER FOUR

Valerie

'I'LL KEEP YOU posted when we hear more about Angel. Were it up to him, he'd be back training with us, but his doctors have advised against it until they—and we by extension—know why it happened. I know this is bad news for the team and a lot of work will go into shuffling things around to fill Angel's big shoes while he recovers,' Ethan says, addressing all the department leads.

I glance around the room, noting the expression of worry on everyone's face, and a pang of something that feels like envy shoots through me. They really believe in the vision Ethan set out for the team and the news about Angel hangs heavy in the air, dragging everyone's spirit down. I, meanwhile, have been more concerned with my own baggage and setbacks for the rest of the season that I haven't settled enough into the team.

Ethan's eyes land on me, as if he can hear my self-admonishments—and my promises to do better. Even though it's hard and I know, because of what happened at Team Blue Cow, I'm now years away from fully launching my charity, I need to focus on what is right in front of me. The chat yesterday helped me realise that Ethan Grant is still a jerk. He's just not *as* bad as I thought he was.

Just because he was reasonable for one night doesn't mean my opinion about him has completely changed. I'm not about to forget that these high-flying team leaders aren't interested in anything but their team's success so they can get more money out of their sponsors.

Except that story falls apart the moment I look at it more closely.

For one, Grant Sports Team doesn't even have a main kit sponsor, so the financing must be coming from Mr Grant himself. Even though I've now been here for several weeks, I still haven't met the elusive owner of this team. Then again, he seems comfortable enough letting his son run things.

And two, the team genuinely cares about their progress. Which again, in isolation, isn't that uncommon. It's not like my colleagues at Blue Cow didn't care about their team's success. But everyone there always had a certain air of superiority. Like their motivation was to be part of the team's history because it would boost their own image.

'Javier, talk to Quintana and see what he thinks about all this. He was on the training ride with Angel, so he's bound to have ideas. Work with him to figure out who we can put in Angel's place. The rest of you—' he looks around the room, making eye contact with everyone, including me '—talk to your teams about this and reassure them that Angel is doing well even if he's not here right now. We'll all have to work extra hard to turn this situation around.'

Everyone around me nods as they meet his gaze with

a surety I don't feel within me. None of my colleagues seem to harbour even a smidge of a doubt about him, which continues to catch me off guard. How come Ethan and I have been butting heads ever since I started here?

As if my thought reached him, he catches my eyes and says, 'Dr Torres, if you could stay back for a minute? The rest of you are dismissed.'

Dismissed. So formal again. Despite working with him for several weeks now, I still can't get used to the way he talks. It's like every time he says something, I'm compelled to listen because his way of expressing himself is so unlike anyone else. It is annoying how much of my attention he monopolises whenever he's near me just because of that.

And what does he want now? As everyone shuffles out of the room, giving me looks over their shoulder that range from curious to pitying, I can't help but feel like the headmaster has called me into his office. Which I know is ridiculous. Ethan Grant shouldn't have this kind of influence over me, and yet I'm here, holding my breath as he levels his stare on me. A familiar current of energy jumps the air between us and zaps into me. It happens whenever I'm too close to him, which is also the reason I've avoided one-to-one situations with him.

He's far too handsome for my own good and my body reacts all on its own without my consent or input.

And that's a problem. The last time I slept with my boss, it cost me my job. Not that I need any reminders of Alexander—or the fact that I will *never* make that mistake again. But maybe I do, because as the door closes behind Lola—the team's physical therapist and the one who took me under her wing when I first joined—she shoots me an entirely inappropriate, conspiratorial wink. My heart rate spikes.

Get it together, Val.

'Thanks for staying behind. I promise I won't keep you long,' Ethan says as he leans back in his chair, crossing his legs.

I know that because he's pushed back his chair a couple of centimetres to accommodate his freakishly long legs. Not to mention that even sitting down he's towering over me—and why is that fact shooting a hot spark down my spine? Is it me? Am I the problem? I see problematic and emotionally unavailable men and my body just does as it wills?

He stares at me and that's when I realise I've been caught up in my own thoughts. Real smooth as always. I clear my throat before I say, 'Not to worry. How can I help?'

He thinks before he speaks. Or maybe that's just what I'm attributing the silence to. When he leans forward, bracing his arms on his thighs, the collar of his shirt slips down and exposes a strip of flesh that I stare at for a few moments. It's so odd that it catches my attention, my eyes darting down to trace the skin there. I force my gaze up when I realise what's wrong with what I'm looking at: his top button is undone.

Unusual for Ethan Grant. I can't remember a single time I've not seen him all put together and ready for business. Because that's all this guy is ever about. Which means that him asking me to stay here is also about business.

Yet that doesn't help with the nervous energy bubbling up within me. Nor does the fact that I can't stop looking at his collarbone sticking out from his shirt, accentuating the pale expanse of his throat that is only interrupted by some dark stubble.

I have to force my eyes back to his face when he finally speaks again. 'I have a suggestion I think could be beneficial for both of us.'

Well, if that doesn't sound ominous. Or…suggestive? No, wait. Definitely *not* suggestive. Right?

Ethan seems to hear his own words as well because he shakes his head, which unfortunately makes the collar of his shirt slip even further down. I can't help tracking the movement with my eyes, unable to untangle myself from the sight. 'This is about the team,' he clarifies, but then pauses. 'But it also has a personal component to it.'

'Okay?' I don't know what else to say, but my mind is already busy spinning the most obscure scenarios that could have led to this conversation. It has something to do with last night. Of course it has. That was the first time we ever really interacted one-on-one.

Ethan lets out a sigh, and my curiosity stirs. What *is* this about? A business proposal with a personal component? Something he doesn't want to address in front of the other staff. What on earth could that be? Seeing him struggle to get out the words only puts me more on edge. Ethan Grant is a lot of things—frustrating, stubborn, stupidly attractive—but he isn't hesitant.

'What? Do you need a date for something?' I ask, grasping at the first absurd scenario that comes into my mind to cut the tension between us.

He lifts his head up, intense brown eyes narrowing in suspicion. 'How did you know?'

My eyes bug out because there is no way I just heard that

right. 'Wait, you're not genuinely here to ask me out?' I say entirely too loud, making my voice echo through the room.

Great impulse control, as usual, Val.

'It's not an industry event. But rather a public function for which I find myself without a companion.' I'm not sure if this is an English as a second language issue or if this guy really does sounds like some aristocratic lord. Maybe that's just how they teach children to speak in fancy private schools and meanwhile I'm here with my peasant English that I learned from watching *Grey's Anatomy* and *ER* with Spanish subtitles.

'You will have to be more specific because I don't think I'm following,' I say, my words coming out haltingly.

Ethan stares at me for several breaths and leans forward a bit more until I have the most unfortunate—and enticing—view down his open collar. I can see a tuft of black hair vanishing into the shadows of his shirt, but it's enough to give me an idea of what lies beneath the fabric. Not that I need to know. In fact, it would probably be better if I didn't know that Ethan Grant's chest is both hairy and spectacularly built.

How is this man so chiselled? I work roughly twelve hours a day before passing out and doing it all over again. But whenever I show up to work, he's already here, and he's still around when I leave.

'You've noticed we don't have a main kit sponsor,' he continues, not really elaborating on the whole looking-for-a-date bit. 'I want to offer you the same thing Zander Lemoine did. Your charity's logo on our kit.'

I mustn't be hearing this right. Ever since I left Team Blue Cow, I've been flip-flopping between impotent rage and bottomless despair at my charity's loss. At what Alexander took from me in a revenge move after I told the other women he was involved with how he'd been playing all of us for fools.

Now, by some strange twist of fate, Ethan Grant is offering me the one thing that I want more than anything in life. And for what?

'You're trading a shoulder spot on the team kit for a date? With me?' I'm pretty sure I'm dreaming right now.

Ethan sits up straight again, which my pounding heart appreciates. I'm already struggling to understand what he's saying while trying to ignore that glimpse of muscled chest he inadvertently keeps flashing at me.

'Not a shoulder spot,' he says, ignoring my follow-up questions. 'I'm offering you the front of the kit.'

My ears ring the moment the words come out of his mouth. I can't even remember what questions I had for him because all I can think of now are those words that have the potential to change my life for ever.

'But wouldn't you rather…?' I stop myself from finishing the sentence as I realise what I'm about to say. Grant Sports Team don't have a front sponsor for their kit. Neither do they have sponsors for the shoulder spots. Or the back spots. Or any other spot that you could think of. Which means that my charity's logo wouldn't just be at the centre of every rider's kit, it would also be the *only* logo.

A subdued smile appears on his lips as he catches up with my thoughts. 'The spot is yours if you want it.' He sounds so casual, amused even. As if he hasn't changed my entire life with this offer. Companies pay millions of euros for these slots and here he is, giving it to me for free.

Well, not *free*.

'In return for a date?' I ask again, because surely I've missed something. Like, I'm all about the 'love yourself' thing, but I can admit that I'm not worth millions of euros. I'm good, yes, but not *that* good.

My eyes dart down to where a muscle is feathering in his jaw. 'This is where it becomes a bit more complex,' he says and my stomach clenches. 'My family is hosting a party and it would be better for me and for…certain others if I don't show up alone.'

His phrasing is so weirdly over the top and ominous that I let out a most unflattering snort. 'Are you part of some kind of mafia, or what?' I ask, relieved when he instantly shakes his head.

'Nothing like that, no. My family is just…important in the circles that we frequent,' he replies, chasing away the short-lived relief with a smile that isn't half as reassuring as he thinks it is.

So not mafia but something else? 'What circles? Cycling?'

Ethan shakes his head again. 'My mother was the only person from my family invested in the sport, and I got it from her. Arch—my father—only got involved with the team after my mother's passing.'

The robotic tone in his voice grabs my attention, and I raise one eyebrow. I really don't know all that much about Ethan Grant, or the Grant Sports Team. Desperate for a job when I had none, all I did was search online to see if this place was legit. Even though everyone in the team works incredibly hard to make it a success, they don't share the penchant of inter-team gossiping I'm used to from other teams. So hearing that Ethan's mother used to be involved catches me by surprise.

And judging by the sudden lack of any kind of emotion on his face, there's a lot of backstory I don't know about.

'I'm sorry to—'

He cuts me off. 'They're having a big event in a few weeks' time, after the Critérium du Dauphiné and before we ramp up for the Tour de France,' he says, making it clear that, even though he's mentioned his mother, I'm not invited to ask any more follow-up questions. Or offer my sympathies.

Fair enough. It's not like I want to talk to him about my parents, either. They're still alive, they're just not relevant to my life and I wouldn't want anyone commenting on that. They're the reason I established Cosecha de Vida, my food poverty charity. Years of making do with whatever leftovers the other kids would let me have in school and being forced to ask teachers for essentials just to keep the hunger pangs at bay long enough for me to pay attention and study left an indelible mark on me. One large enough that I don't want any other child to have to beg for food to survive. Not if I can help it.

Though being too poor to afford food on a regular basis isn't even the reason I'm no longer speaking to my parents. No, that is more…complicated.

'Anyway, I would need you to attend the party with me and pretend to be…*involved* with me.' Ethan clears his throat after he says that, his words still so damn formal that it almost makes me laugh.

'Okay, so one evening of being your arm candy. That sounds simple enough,' I say and just as his nose twitches in the only sign of his true feelings, I realise it is probably not, in fact, that simple.

Ethan tips his head backwards to stare at the ceiling in a strange and unguarded moment. Seeing the long column of his throat isn't that much better than the view down his shirt as far as my stomach is concerned. Because it's twisting itself into an even tighter knot as my eyes dart around the room, seeking any distraction to latch onto but always landing back on Ethan.

Why does this insufferable man have to look like a freaking swimsuit model? I really do have a problem being attracted to inappropriate men.

'The involvement would need to feel credible. It's not enough for me to just show up with someone. A crucial part of this is that my family believes I am serious about my companion,' he says, each word measured and calm. A stark contrast to the fluttering of my heart against my chest.

His words trickle through me, sloshing around inside my head before they form into a request I can actually comprehend. My mouth falls open as the realisation dawns on me.

'Oh, you don't want me to be arm candy just for one event. This isn't a *10 Things I Hate About You* situation. It's a *My Fake Fiancé* situation.' Minus the fiancé part, but those are semantics.

His head drops back down and he looks at me. I don't know why I notice every micro expression rippling over his face, but I do. So I see the slight parting of his lips indicating his confusion. Silence builds between us, and then he says, 'I'm not sure what those are.'

I gasp. 'They're two quintessential romantic comedies. How do you not know these movies?'

He shrugs. 'My household wasn't much into pop cultural phenomena or Hollywood extravagance,' he says with a completely straight face and this time I can't stop the laughter from rippling through me.

'I'm sorry, I'm not laughing at you. This is just such an absurd moment. Like, it's really starting to feel like I've annoyed some cosmic power and they're now just messing with me in the weirdest ways.' My laughter fades into a low chuckle. 'I mean, get this. I lose my job after my situationship—that I'd thought was turning into a relationship—with my boss implodes. Turns out he was sleeping with half the team and when I told those people, he blamed me for the fallout and fired me. So not only did I look dumb for thinking this guy could love me for real, I also lost the sponsorship opportunity for my charity, without which I cannot launch it the way I've always planned. By sheer luck, I find a new job and then you appear, almost out of nowhere, offering me the one thing I've lost and more.' I raise my hands, indicating the space around me. 'I mean, you have to admit that sounds like the plot of a movie.'

An odd thrill races down my spine as his lips twitch, showing off just the glint of white teeth as he smiles. Or rather, he does what is considered the Ethan Grant version of a smile. It's kind of cute.

Whoa. I slam my mental hands down on this word as it bubbles up inside me, pushing it all the way back down again. He is already far more attractive than he deserves. I'm not giving him cute on top of that.

'The way you describe it, it's hard to argue with your assessment,' he says, ever the posh aristocrat. Why on earth do I find that attractive? I must be out of my mind for considering this. 'And I assure you, this arrangement would never leave the bounds of what we agree on. I'm not like Zander Lemoine, looking to manoeuvre you into a vulnerable situation.'

I raise an eyebrow at that, but I don't say anything. Maybe he didn't need all of that context about my life? Well, now he has it anyway.

He knows I don't have another choice and he's trying to assure me I'm not getting myself into another Alexander situation. A front spot on the kit might just give me enough exposure to bring in some wealthy benefactors who are looking for a new pet project. None of them will truly understand the mental and physical effects food poverty has on children, on families, but it doesn't matter. I don't need them to understand, I just need them to fund my work.

Children won't be going hungry on my watch.

'Okay, I'm in. I'll pretend to be your girlfriend in front of your family for the front spot on your kit,' I say and, across from me, Ethan slumps forward as tension leaves his body.

Whoa, he'd been that worried about this? Now I'm really curious why his family wants to see him coupled up. Is it some kind of legacy thing? Is he the only son of an old house and his chronic singlehood is driving his father into an early grave?

The question pushes against my tongue, but I don't say it. It's better if I don't. If I'm forced to spend more time with Ethan, it's better I keep as much emotional distance from him as possible. He already has an outsized impact on my mood, and that's without us being involved. Things can only get worse from here on out.

I have to guard myself from his wicked charm.

'That's…' His words trail off, and he doesn't say anything else for a few breaths. Then he looks at me and his dark eyes create a spark that travels from the centre of my chest right down my spine, lighting my nerve endings up like Christmas lights.

'Thank you, Valerie. I know this is an unorthodox arrangement and I appreciate your willingness to even hear me out. Though, to be fair to you, I want to stress the unorthodox nature of my family. They are a part of the aristocratic circles of Europe, and this particular event will involve the royal families of a few nations.' Each word sounds measured, and I just about stop my mouth from falling open.

Oh, wow. When I'd pegged him as some kind of stuffy aristocrat, I'd been joking but I'm right? So who is—?

Ethan raises his hands, clearly reading my thoughts off my face. 'Take some time to consider. If you're really sure about doing this, I will give you all the information you need about my family. But I'd rather not expose myself more than I have to just yet. Most of the team doesn't know my background and I'd like to keep it that way.' His voice is low, hitting me in places it shouldn't and this decision suddenly feels a lot bigger. I didn't get involved with Alexander just because he promised me a sponsorship, but now I'm no longer sure if he didn't use that to lead me on.

I can't afford to have any doubts. An opportunity like this won't come to me a third time.

My sensory processing overloads with all the information I've just received and I jump out of my chair with far too much speed, sending the office chair rolling into the wall behind me. 'I don't need time to think. I'm in. You found the right incentive to entice me. Just let me know when that family thing is and I'll be there.'

A small smile unfurls on Ethan's lips, and that is the last thing I need. I'd rather he scowled at me because at least I know how to deal with that. 'I'll see you at the race tomorrow,' he says with a nod and from his tone I can tell that I'm now dismissed, too.

But as I walk out, I know this is a turn of fortune for me. I'm going to do it because even though I'd rather not spend my free time fake-dating Ethan Grant, it still beats spending years on the road again while trying to find a way to launch my charity. Even if it means getting trapped in some strange romantic-comedy plot by pretending to be my boss's girlfriend.

And it will only ever be pretending. Falling for Alexander and his lies got me into this mess, and even though I'm glad he showed me his true character sooner rather than later, I'm not risking this opportunity by getting involved with Ethan Grant for real.

CHAPTER FIVE

Valerie

'WAIT, WAIT, WAIT. He did what?' Lola hiss-screams and my eyes dart around as I shush her.

'Would you be quiet?' I whisper back. Thankfully the subject of this conversation isn't here. But Javier is, and I know those two are thick as thieves, so I'm not taking any risks.

Any *more* risks, that is. Last night Ethan said something about discretion, but when Lola walked up to the feeding station we set up at the forty-kilometre mark, the words burst out of me in an uncontrollable deluge of madness. All except the hidden identity part, of course.

'Sorry,' Lola whispers back and takes a step towards me. 'Ethan asked you to be his date for an event? Damn, and here I thought I had a shot with him.'

My eyes bug out. 'Wait, what? I didn't know you were into—you're messing with me, right?'

'Of course I'm messing with you. I mean, look at this—' she waves her hand in front of her face '—do I look straight to you?'

'Hey, I'm not gonna judge anyone's sexuality on their appearance,' I say with raised hands. 'Undercuts are becoming very popular with the wider female population.'

Lola gives me a flat stare. 'My earrings are two pairs of scissors and I always have a carabiner in my pocket.'

'You have a carabiner in your pocket?' I let out a snort as Lola's hand vanishes into her pocket and she comes back holding a carabiner, clicking it open with her thumb. 'Okay, what I meant to say is, why?'

She shrugs. 'Every lesbian gets one when she comes out. It's like a membership card.'

'What, do they just hand them out?'

'Pretty much,' she says, tossing it up and catching it again. 'You show up, say "I like women," and boom—they issue you a carabiner and a flannel shirt.'

'Who are *they*?' I ask.

Lola shrugs again. 'The council of elder lesbians.'

Javier's voice floats through the air as I give up on any pretence of seriousness and laugh with Lola. Then Javier approaches the table where I've already laid out our riders' meal kits to help them get through the rest of the ride. 'Julian and Eddie are on their way here.'

I stare down the narrow road, where fans crowd together, waving flags and signs spelling out their support. I've seen it before in my career, but it never gets old to see how many people come out to cheer their teams on. So much of a rider's success depends on all the people around him and fans are no small part of it.

Glancing at my watch, I raise one eyebrow. 'I wasn't expecting them for another five minutes at least.'

'Julian decided to break away early on. We toyed with the idea last night but didn't commit to anything. With Eddie being his number two now and whatnot,' Javier says with a shrug.

Try as I might, I cannot hide the frown pulling at my

lips. As far as numbers are concerned, Eddie can keep up with Angel, who we're still not sure will be able to join us for the rest of the season. The hospital have pinpointed the incident on the training ride as heart failure, though what the underlying condition is seems to be much trickier to pin down. Ethan hasn't shared any news, and that's not surprising. If this is going to be career ending for Angel, he might not even want the rest of the team to know.

Because of his absence, this race is a high-stress situation and the cyclists should be focusing on learning how to ride with each other in this new dynamic. Not winning prizes. I'm about to ask if this is Ethan's idea when the crowd near us erupts into cheers and the front of the breakaway group comes into view. And they are approaching fast.

'What the—there are fifteen cyclists in this breakaway?' I ask, whirling around to Javier.

He follows my gaze up the hill where the large group of riders approaches, and a line appears between his brows. Our feeding station is set up on a part of the road that narrows before turning left. Not the ideal set-up, but the organisers must have chosen it for a reason.

But still… We are only a few metres into a flat section after a downward hill and the speed at which the fifteen riders are approaching us is not safe.

'Javier…' I say as the warning tingle spreads from my gut through the rest of my body. I grope for Lola, shoving her behind me as I take one step away from our table with the food on it.

Then everything happens in slow motion. At the bottom of the hill, the group of riders slows down a fraction, but one fan running alongside a rider, waving a flag, gets in the way. The fan takes a tumble, falling under the wheel of the rider and taking him down as well. With how narrow the road is, the rest of the breakaway cannot navigate around the two people on the floor and the entire cluster of cyclists crashes.

I gasp in horror and next to me I hear Javier swearing before mumbling something into the team radio. There is no first-aid vehicle in sight, but they can't be far away. At least I pray they aren't as I grab my emergency bag filled with medical supplies and run towards the pile-up.

I stop at the first cyclist, helping him up to his feet. My eyes roam over him, looking for visible signs of distress. He has a nasty road rash on his upper leg, but when he gets on his bike, he doesn't seem to have any other issue.

'Make sure your team car has a look at this,' I say as he pushes off and continues the race.

So do Julian and Eddie, who don't look too much the worse for wear as Javier and Lola help them onto their bikes and push them off. Most cyclists have already dusted themselves off and are continuing the race with only a minor delay.

Everyone except one cyclist, who is still lying on the floor with a gaggle of fans bending over him, shouting with concern. My heart leaps into my throat when I recognise the white jersey, the logos of the sponsors a familiar sight. Not even two months ago, I had been imagining what my charity's logo would look like next to all of them. I glance around again, looking for a support vehicle, but it seems it's just us.

'Excuse me! Please let me through,' I shout as I approach the prone cyclist, shoving my way through the fans.

My heart sinks at the sight of Michael Silver, a junior rider who'd only joined the team a few weeks before I left. He is conscious but in so much pain that his face is contorted.

'Michael, it's Dr Torres. You might remember me from the Blue Cow staff,' I say to set him at ease as I try my best to shut out the crowd of fans that is forming a tight circle around us.

Michael groans, or maybe he is trying to say something but cannot through the pain. I lean forward, putting my ear against his mouth, but all that comes out is another drawn-out groan. Putting the backpack next to me, I unzip it and take out my supply kit. There won't be much I can do other than stabilise him and wait until the ambulance arrives. I'm about to grab my instruments out of my bag when the crowd around me surges and I fall forward, barely able to catch myself to avoid falling into my patient.

I give those around me a sharp look, but it's no use. They are far too wrapped up in the drama of a crash like this, even though all I need right now is space. Time to put on my best mean face and tell everyone to get lost. Turning around, I try to get up, but then the entire peloton zooms past us, creating a new frenzy in the crowd and knocking me off my balance once more. But before I can face-plant into the cobblestone, a firm hand wraps around my biceps and holds me in place. It stays there until I restore my balance and then a familiar voice cuts through the noise.

'I need everyone to leave this area right now. We're dealing with a medical emergency,' Ethan says, his voice thunderous.

I mutter my thanks when he releases his grip on me, ignoring the tingle snaking up my arm and down my spine at his firm touch. Now is not the time to pay attention to any stray signals winding their way through my body.

Taking out my stethoscope, I undo Michael's jersey's zip and listen to his breathing sounds. Ethan pops into my vision as he kneels down. 'What happened?'

'The front right of the breakaway was hit by a fan and came down. The narrow road didn't let anyone else manoeuvre around him, so the entire breakaway came crashing down. Julian and Eddie got back on their bikes fast enough, but Michael is in bad shape,' I explain. 'Breath sounds are okay even if laboured. No pneumothorax.'

'Michael?'

'I worked with Michael at Team Blue Cow. He's one of the more junior riders,' I say, ignoring the prickle of awareness Ethan's proximity sparks in me.

I look down at the cyclist, who is clutching his arm to his chest, each breath a concerted effort. 'I'm going to move your arm, okay, Michael?' I say and look at Ethan. 'When he fell, I think he might've landed on his wrist. Could be a broken collarbone.'

Ethan nods. 'He has abrasions on his palms, too.'

A small amount of blood has soaked into the sleeve of Michael's jersey, indicating an open wound. Pulling a bag of latex gloves out of my backpack, I put on a pair before offering it to Ethan, who takes it with a grateful smile that joins that damn tingling sensation his touch induced in me earlier.

Shaking my head to get rid of it, I carefully wrap my hand around Michael's wrist and pull it away from where he's clutching his arm. He winces and I murmur sympathetically.

'Here.' Ethan holds out a piece of gauze drenched in antiseptic and I take it, mindful not to let my fingers linger on his palm. 'I'll check his collarbone while you patch up his hand. Might be easier to do all the painful things at once.'

I nod and shoot him a look before I swipe the piece of gauze over Michael's palm, cleaning the wound. He lets out a groan and out of the corner of my eye I see Ethan moving to inspect his collarbone. He palpates the space with his fingers; the gentleness catches me by surprise, though I don't know why. With how aloof and straight to the point he always is at work, I assumed that his bedside manner would be similar. But he keeps talking quietly and calmly, explaining what he's doing to reassure Michael.

'Is one of the medical cars on their way?' I ask as I wrap Michael's hand in a thick bandage to ready him for transport.

'I alerted both the ambulance and his team car. The peloton just passed too, so the roads should be clear,' Ethan replies and sets down Michael's arm. 'He definitely needs an X-ray. I'll let the medical team know when they arrive.'

I open my mouth to say something when the sound of a car approaching cuts through the air and a few seconds later a Blue Cow-branded vehicle screeches to a halt at the side of the road.

And the last person I want to see climbs out of the vehicle.

Of course he's here. Why on earth wouldn't he be

here? Looking back at all the crap the universe has put me through this year, I'm surprised it's taken this long for Alexander and me to have a confrontation during the race. How do I know we're about to have a confrontation? Maybe it has something to do with the searing red colour tinting the edges of my vision as he steps out of the team car.

'What the hell happened here?' he barks, his voice loud enough to make me jump.

'A flag-waving fan got under the wheel of one of the breakaway riders, who brought the rest down with him,' I say, clenching my teeth hard enough that I hear a grinding noise reverberating through my skull.

Great. Can't wait for this to turn into a tension headache.

'And you of all people just happened to be here to render first aid?' Alexander sneers at me in a highly predictable jab, and I tell myself not to rise to the bait. He might be here to check on his rider, but I know this man won't pass up an opportunity to antagonise me. Something about toxic males.

'I was here when it happened,' I shoot back with venom in my voice. 'Would you rather next time I don't intervene and we'll just see how one of your riders deals with a broken collarbone by himself?'

The nerve of him, accusing me of somehow deliberately staging this? That's the only way I can interpret his words and the rage it fires through my system burns so hot, I can hardly speak.

'Oh, you really want me to believe that this is all just—'

'Our team got this place assigned as our feeding station, Zander. As a directeur sportif, you should know how that works.' Ethan's voice is deep and stone cold as he cuts in, interrupting Alexander mid-sentence. My ex-*something* shifts his attention to where Ethan is wrapping Michael's arm in a sling and securing it to his chest for transportation.

His eyes flare wide, only noticing Ethan's presence now. The sneer returns to his face and somehow it's even more vicious than the one he gave me. Enough for me to recoil, but Ethan remains unbothered.

'I see the prince of cycling himself has deigned to help one of my riders. Do you expect me to curtsey? What are you going to do if I don't?' Alexander mocks, and those words are enough for me to know that he has completely lost the plot. Prince of cycling? What kind of weird pissing contest is he trying to start here? Wait, is Ethan really a—?

'I'll make sure the paramedics know how concerned you are for Michael once they arrive,' Ethan replies, not rising to Alexander's taunts. 'As Dr Torres has said, he most likely has a broken collarbone and abrasions on his palms and legs.'

I can see the signs of Alexander's temper getting the better of him. His nostrils flare and his hands ball into fists at his sides. Then he turns to me again, because why not? In his story, I'm the villain. Never mind that the people he was cheating on deserved to know the truth as much as I did. If he thought I would keep quiet about something like that, he didn't know me as well as I thought he did. Didn't *see* me at all. 'Valerie, if I catch even a whiff of interference from you, I promise you—'

The wailing of a siren interrupts him this time as the

ambulance comes into view and I raise my hand to flag them down. I get to my feet as the paramedics come over with a stretcher and we move Michael onto it. Ethan updates the paramedics as we do that and when the doors to the vehicle close, I turn to face Alexander again. But before I can challenge him to a verbal sparring match that I know won't end well for either of us, Ethan takes one step forward and levels an icy glare at him.

'You might want to follow the ambulance to the hospital,' he says, and I'm just marvelling at how even-keeled he is when his eyes narrow before he continues. 'And if I ever hear you talking to Dr Torres like that again, Lemoine, you'll learn *exactly* what I can do.'

That sentence follows me around for the rest of the day as we clean up the station and head for the finish line just in time to see Julian cross it first. Which is why everyone on the staff side is crowding the hotel bar and celebrating at such obnoxiously loud sound levels only the winning team could get away with.

In the centre of it all stands Ethan.

I try to muster a smile whenever someone glances my way and thankfully no one tries to drag me into the noisy crowd. News of me handling a medical emergency must've spread, and maybe they think I'm tired. It's a good excuse for me to sneak upstairs and call it a day. Because I'm not feeling celebratory.

Not after that encounter with Alexander. Thinking back, it makes sense that he'd be in the team car, but that thought didn't occur to me at that moment. Not that it matters. It's not like I would have walked away from Michael just because this guy appeared.

'Are you calculating Julian's protein intake to the seventh decimal in your head?' Ethan's voice pierces through the celebrating crowd, and I jump out of my skin when he appears right next to me.

'What?' The smells of alcohol and food hang heavy in the air, yet they aren't enough to distract me from the fresh scent of pine enveloping me as Ethan takes a step closer to me. Close enough that I can feel his presence in my space at the base of my skull. Awareness rushes through me, settling in a warm puddle in the pit of my stomach.

'In a sea of very happy faces, your severe expression really stands out,' he says and chuckles, the corner of his mouth kicking up in a small smile. 'Or maybe your face just stands out to me.'

What? The same question forms in my head again, but this time I don't think I voice it. Instead, the warm pool of awareness that came to life in my stomach just a few seconds ago explodes through me.

Ethan looks at me, head tilted to the side as if he hasn't just said that he finds my face pretty. No, wait. That's *not* what he said. Is it?

'I can't tell if you just called me pretty or ugly,' I blurt out.

Oh God, does that sound like I'm fishing for a compliment? I'm about to correct myself when Ethan lets out another low laugh, amusement sparkling in his eyes.

'I don't think there's anyone out there who could call you ugly and mean it,' he says, ever the straight shooter.

'Oh.' That's all my brain has to offer. Because it's scrambling to figure out what to do with this unexpected compliment—from my boss. The boss who I have been ogling since I started working here, but who I have also been butting heads with recently. So I'm not entirely sure I'm hearing him right.

Just as I can't forget what he said to Alexander. Did Ethan really mean it as a threat? Or is this somehow my delusional brain grabbing onto something that doesn't exist?

Despite the celebratory mood around us, I can feel the awkward silence sinking into the space between us. What am I supposed to reply to the compliment when Ethan and I have only recently started talking like actual adults that don't hate each other and the only reason we're doing so is because we've somehow got the exact thing that the other one needs?

My eyes roam over his calm expression, looking for the irritable man who's been bugging me since I started working here. He didn't just vanish because I agreed to be his date.

'Are you okay?' he asks and oh, boy, my heart slams against my sternum at the simple question.

I should play it cool. No need to wear my heart on my sleeve. This guy is still my boss and if today's bin fire taught me anything, it's that getting involved with your boss is a very bad idea. Not that we're getting involved right now—or ever. The reason I'm even in this emotional trap is because I word-vomited all over Ethan after the whole Angel situation.

Taking a deep breath, I prepare the words that will let him know everything is okay and he should get back to celebrating with the rest of the team. 'No, I'm not okay. Like, I knew I would meet Alexander eventually. But I can't believe that he accused me of somehow staging

Michael's fall. Because that's what he did, right? And it would be one thing if he did that to me in private, because at least I could deal with it on my own. But he did it in front of you. My new boss,' comes out instead.

I think we're both hearing my verbal word salad in real time together. Because our eyes grow larger in the ensuing silence.

'You know what? I should leave,' I say, scrambling at an excuse when Ethan continues to stare at me. 'I forgot I have to…mow my cat.'

His eyebrow shoots up at that, and then he looks at the glass of lemonade in my hand. 'How many of those did you have?'

'Believe it or not, but I'm sober. My poor impulse control is all natural,' I say and even though I just told him I'm leaving, I don't. Something in his eyes ensnares me. He seems to know it too because one corner of his lips tics up.

'If that is how poor impulse control manifests in you, I quite like it.' He nods towards two armchairs next to a large window and I follow him with a glance cast behind me as he sits down.

Nobody should care that I'm sitting down with Ethan for a drink but some important part of me needs to check anyway that nobody is looking. Or that, if they are, nobody is really talking. I don't need any weird rumours to spread through the team.

Not that I can focus on whatever is going on behind me when my brain is playing Ethan's last words on a loop. He likes that I don't know when to shut my mouth? That inevitably everyone else usually knows how I feel about five seconds after I know how I feel?

'Are you mocking me?' I ask, taking a tone I normally wouldn't dare to pick with a superior. But he already knows everything from my weird ramble, so there isn't really much to hide at this point.

'Please, sit.' He waves his hand towards the empty chair, his long fingers almost curled in a way that compels me to move towards him rather than the chair.

A sigh escapes me when I plonk myself down and sink into the plushy cushions. Another tic of his lips as he looks over at me and it must be because of how ridiculous I look in this oversized chair.

'I'm not mocking you, and I'm sorry that's how it came across. I find your propensity to say whatever is on your mind disarming.' He takes a sip from his glass, the large ice cubes clinking. My eyes follow the liquid as it pours into his mouth, and his throat bobs and it's only then that I realise I am staring at his throat. With heat staining my cheeks, I wrench my eyes back up to meet his.

'And here I was thinking you find me unbelievably annoying because of how much I disagree with you in front of the team,' I say, as if I need to prove to him I indeed just say whatever pops up in my head.

He chuckles and I'm not prepared for what that sound does to me. With how uptight he is at work, I didn't even know he was capable of amusement. You can imagine my surprise at this genuine laugh and how it vibrates through the space between us and right into my bones.

Oh no. That's not good. I'm not supposed to *like* him. Combined with his ridiculous attractiveness, that is a deadly cocktail that I should avoid. But how can I do that when I've agreed to be his fake girlfriend? Ever since that conversation in the conference room, we haven't really discussed the details.

Is that why he's asked me to sit with him?

'I don't think those two sentiments are mutually exclusive,' he says as he takes another sip.

'So I'm annoying, but in a cute way?' Oh my God, can somebody shut me up? Did I just call myself cute in front of my boss?

'That's one way of putting it.'

My heart reacts to his words before my brain has the chance to even comprehend what they mean. It drums against my chest as if looking for a way out and sends waves of heat through my body. I can feel the next slew of ill-advised words crawling up my throat and, to stem their flow, I take a few sips of my drink and then desperately wish it weren't carbonated.

If Ethan notices my struggle, he's too polite to say. He saves me from myself by continuing, 'My family is… reserved about sharing their thoughts, let alone their feelings. So it's not the most natural thing for me to do so myself or hear other people do it so freely.'

His family isn't big on sharing feelings—if he's not used to expressing his thoughts, let alone his emotions, it makes sense that he wouldn't share his opinions on my work. If that's how he was raised, Ethan probably thought it easier to make changes himself than risk a discussion that could turn into a disagreement.

The heat coursing through my body flutters. It doesn't quite wink out but settles down into a gentle simmer. This conversation isn't at all what I expected. In front of the team, Ethan is always so stalwart, almost unapproachable. His confidence unrivalled to the point where at least some of my wariness of him stems from the simple fact of how easy he makes everything seem.

'Thank you for defending me in front of Alexander,' I blurt out when quiet settles in between us. I've never been good at handling silence, be it in school or at the dinner table when growing up, when all we could afford to eat was two-day-old bread and a can of luncheon meat. Along with only one or, on some nights, neither of my parents. Mum always worked the nightshift, but sometimes Dad would pick up random jobs for the night if the opportunity arose. Leaving pre-teen me to figure out my own hunger.

Ethan clearly didn't expect my words, his brows shooting up. Then they draw down until a line forms between them. 'Mr Lemoine should be more careful what he says, especially when it's his rider's health on the line,' he snaps, and I can sense the same rumble from him I heard earlier when the confrontation happened.

So I didn't make it up under the stress of the situation: Ethan and I have a common enemy in Alexander. Only why he doesn't like my ex isn't clear to me. Time to go on a fishing expedition.

'You don't like him,' I say, getting straight to the point. When choosing between slowly baiting a line and waiting for a fish to bite or using dynamite, I choose dynamite. Subtlety has never been my strong suit.

Ethan shrugs. 'I think little about Zander Lemoine.'

'I don't think much about him, either. But when I do, it's usually to imagine how I'll crush him under my heel like the pathetic bug he is and how he will regret taking things away from me to hide his own misdeeds.' My hands ball into fists all on their own and when another silence settles between us, I take a deep breath. Why am I saying any of this? I'm not about to bore Ethan with any more details of my affair with Alexander. 'Sorry, this guy—he really gets under my skin.'

'I can see that.' The side of his mouth kicks up in amusement, and I'm almost certain I've overshared again. Has it always been this easy to talk to him? I've never thought so, but somehow he's turned things around with that one conversation in his office. One conversation and a deal to be his fake girlfriend for a night in front of his family.

Something we haven't really talked about since. But before I bring that up, Ethan continues, 'I think Mr Lemoine takes the rivalry between teams far too seriously. With how common it is for riders and staff to shuffle around teams between seasons, I don't exactly see the point in it. But he seems to enjoy that dynamic.'

I can't stop a very non-sexy snort from escaping me. 'You can say that again. It's not enough for the team to be competing. He has to be right there with them.'

I pause, thinking back to the moment earlier. The only reason Alexander accused me the way he did was because he wants me to pay for exposing him and causing a huge fallout within the team.

We need to stop talking about Alexander. Every breath I waste on this man is too much. I'd much rather discuss why Ethan wants to talk to me alone. There can be only one reason.

'So, are you ready to tell me who you are?' I ask.

Ethan's hand pauses halfway to his mouth, the glass hovering suspended in the air. Then, instead of taking that sip, he sets it down on the chair's arm. 'You're right.

We should talk about our arrangement. Since you're bringing it up, I gather you haven't changed your mind?'

'Were you expecting me to change it?'

He shrugs. 'No, you seemed certain, but I wanted to give you a chance to at least think it over for a bit. Then let's talk about the rules.'

Rules? I hadn't even thought about rules. The only thing I want to know is who this man really is. Especially for him to get such a reaction from Alexander. *Prince of cycling.* He'd mentioned that his family mixed with royal circles, but could he really be a prince himself?

'You're the one who needs to convince his family. What will convince them?' I ask, because I honestly have no idea what he's envisioning.

'We can leave the team out of this. The only people that need to believe we're together are my family and the people associating with them. I keep these two lives separate as it is, so I don't foresee them mixing. As to what will convince them…' He pauses, his eyes sweeping over me in a gesture that feels almost assessing. 'Some nearness can't be avoided, I'm afraid, or they won't believe it's genuine.'

My stomach flips at the vague concept of *nearness*. 'What will that entail?' Although nothing he says will change my mind because I need that sponsorship money.

'Nothing too intimate, I assure you. At the event I'll have my hand on your waist and I might kiss you on the cheek. More flagrant displays of affection wouldn't be appropriate in that setting. Everything should be restricted to that one evening, but since part of my story will be that we've been seeing each other for a while, we'll have to act like it whenever we're interacting with each other outside the team.' His voice takes on a low, detached quality, yet it doesn't help the anxiety bubbling up in my chest.

'Will they watch what we do at work?' I ask, and he shakes his head.

'They might, but it's work. We can get away with the excuse of keeping things professional.' Ethan has thought about this, and I wonder for how long. But what's more, I need him to finally answer the question I asked him.

'So, you're a prince? Is that why Alexander called you that?'

I'm still half joking, but Ethan drums his fingers against the glass and when he finally looks up at me, those dark brown eyes are different. Sharper. A clear warning to accompany his next words. Though I'm not sure what he's warning me about. Him?

'My full name is Ethan William Grant-Belmont of the Grant-Belmont family. Few people know that because I try to keep it out of my professional life as the head physician and soon-to-be owner of this team.'

I blink slowly at him, unravelling the information. Some dusty memory sparks inside my brain and I recall an event a few years ago when Spain got a new king and I was in Madrid when the entire procession kicked off with lots of foreign dignitaries flooding into the city. Including the royal families of other countries. I stood there, listening as the announcer read out the names and far-too-ridiculous titles of people as they entered the venue. Including his.

'Holy sh—'

Ethan surges forward and clamps his hand over my mouth to stifle my shout. A few of our teammates look our way, which can't be good, and I don't even want to think about the reasons they might come up with to explain it. Not that my brain is able to think of anything other than Ethan's hand on my mouth, my lips pressing against his surprisingly calloused skin.

His scent drifts up my nose, sandalwood and something smoky mixing with the alcohol on his breath. My eyes are drawn down to his throat when he swallows. We stay like this for a long moment and when I finally look back up at him, I can read the words in his eyes as clearly as if he'd said them aloud: *do not breathe a word of this.*

And apparently I need the reminder, because even though he told me to be chill, I've almost shouted my surprise to the whole bar.

Ethan's eyes keep darting between my face and our colleagues still standing to the side at the bar. 'I'd better go before they start talking about this,' he mumbles, almost as if he's talking to himself rather than me.

As he gets up, I wrap my fingers around his wrist, holding him in place. 'Wait, you can't just drop this on me and then walk away. You really are *a prince*?' I hiss the last two words under my breath. Even though I'd thought he might just possibly be one, the confirmation still rattles me. 'Like, a real flipping *royal*? Do you have a crown?'

Somehow *that* seems the most important question right this moment. The picture of him wearing a diamond tiara pops into my mind and a shrill giggle escapes my throat before I can reel it back in.

From the glower he levels at me, he doesn't seem half as amused as I am. 'Yes, I'm a real *flipping prince*. But you can infer from your complete lack of knowledge that I don't go around advertising this fact. Quite the opposite. It's bad enough that Zander Lemoine seems to have somehow found out. Though he's unlikely to talk; he definitely won't want to give the press any reason to focus on my team rather than his.'

He shakes his hand, and I relax my grip on him. When his gaze strays towards the group at the bar, he flashes them a quick smile. No wonder he always sounds like he's just walked straight off the *Downton Abbey* set. I thought maybe his father was rich enough to hire some high-class British nanny to raise his son in his stead and that's why he's so formal with everyone.

'But you didn't even tell me if you have a crown.' My brain is still so busy processing this new information that this is all it can latch onto.

I gasp when Ethan steps away with an audacious eye roll directed straight at me as if *I'm* the unreasonable one for asking this when he'd literally revealed that he is a prince.

'We'll talk later,' he says as he walks away. But then he stops and looks over his shoulder at me. The smile tugging at his lips is small, near invisible, yet it slams into me and pushes all the air out of my lungs. Then he adds, 'It's called a coronet and I usually avoid wearing it. But I might just put it on for you.'

CHAPTER SIX

Ethan

'YOU DON'T JUST casually wear it when you're out and about? How will people know to treat you differently?'

I huff out a laugh through my nose, giving Valerie a sideways glance. She's become obsessed with the idea of me wearing a damned coronet, and somehow it's more endearing every time she mentions it—which she has at least three times today.

I'm not about to tell her I don't even own a coronet. As far down the line of succession as I am, my father would no doubt see it as some kind of protest that he wasn't pedestrian enough to understand. Considering I rarely show up to these big events and when I do, it's in the one suit I own with no sashes, badges, or other gaudy regalia.

'The entire point is for people to *not* treat me differently,' I say, and then I usher her through the door of a shop where three sales associates are already waiting with an eager smile on each of their faces.

'Your Royal Highness, welcome,' the woman slightly to the front says, and I try not to sigh when they all attempt a curtsey. But before I have time to correct them and nip this nonsense in the bud, the woman turns to

Valerie and gives her an equally bedazzling smile. 'And welcome to you too, Miss Torres. We have already pre-selected some gowns for you to try on. Mr Fairfax was so kind as to brief us on the overall requirement of the event and what outfit would be best suited for you as His Royal Highness's…er…consort.'

Consort? Fairfax didn't say that, did he? Of course, my father's secretary would have done his best to make as much of a spectacle of this as possible. But something else grates on me, specifically how they addressed Valerie. Because when I'd finally given Fairfax the name of my date for the event, I had made *one* thing absolutely clear.

'It's *Dr* Torres,' I cut in, before Valerie can say anything. When I shoot her a sidelong glance, I can see her stunned expression. 'Consort' wasn't the word I would have picked for her.

My hand slips onto the small of her back and I give her a gentle squeeze to reassure her. Before we arrived I told her we had to treat the people at the boutique as if they might report anything back to Fairfax or my father. This was officially our first outing as a fake couple.

Four pairs of eyes home in on me, all varying degrees of surprised. But then the woman who greeted us—Elisabeth, according to her name tag—nods, dragging the other associates out of their stupor. 'Of course, Dr Torres. If you would both follow me, I will get you situated.'

I only get to steal a brief glance at Valerie before Elisabeth ushers us along through the shop and into a section that they've made more private by putting up some screens. Two comfy-looking armchairs stand to the side, along with a small table with refreshments laid out.

Valerie's eyes go wide as she looks around, first looking at the chairs and then at the racks around this partition that are laden with dresses of different shapes and colours. Finally, she inspects the platform in the middle as if it's a pit of snakes.

As far as 'extra' is concerned, Fairfax really couldn't have done more. The irony of me claiming not to want special treatment only for us to walk into all *this* is not lost on me. Valerie picks it up, too, because she turns and stares at me.

'Your Royal Highness?' she asks in a whisper when the two other sales associates—Magdalena and Paula—start shuffling around under Elisabeth's close watch.

'It was Fairfax. This reeks of him. He probably gave them my entire family tree to make sure they knew exactly who they're talking to,' I reply.

'So this is your idea of low-key? Because when you told me we needed to get me an appropriate dress for this party thing, I clearly remember you using the words "low-key" and now I'm in a private section of a shop I'm pretty sure have shut down their usual operations just for us.' She keeps her voice low as she speaks, and I glance over her shoulder, looking at Elisabeth, who is moving dresses around from the racks, eager to get the presentation started.

'This *is* low-key. It's only us here. How much more low-key can it get?' I don't really believe this myself, but I sense what she needs from me now is reassurance that none of this is over the top and weird. Which it definitely is if you're not used to this life.

'I'm pretty sure I can't even afford the lacy thongs they have in their displays over there and those are tiny strips of cloth. How do you imagine me affording a dress?'

She sees my eyes dart over her shoulder and follows my gaze, sending Elisabeth a sweet smile before returning her eyes to me.

My stomach does a loop when my brain misfires and I imagine her in one of those aforementioned lacy thongs and how the material would caress her with a gentle touch; soothing her right before my not-so-gentle-touch would make her—

'Ethan?' Valerie's voice interrupts and I blink the haze away, my mind snapping back into the present.

'Pardon? What did you say?' Heat creeps up my neck but I push it away, not wanting her to know just how far my thoughts have strayed away from decent. What the hell am I doing even letting myself think about her in such a way?

'The dresses don't even have price tags on them,' she says, raising her arms in an exacerbated gesture.

'Oh, of course. Everything today is paid for already. The gala I'm asking you to attend has very specific attire and so it's only right I foot the bill for it.' If I'm being completely honest, this is a small price to pay for finally getting my father to hand the team over.

Something crosses her face. A brief flinch that she quickly contains behind thick walls before I even get the chance to figure out what it means. Does she find it distasteful that I'm buying her clothes? Or is it the sheer necessity for a new wardrobe that is turning her off? Damn it, it's always something once people find out. People either start treating me differently because they hope to be in good with the King of Álben or they flee for the hills because they can't handle all the *extra* that is the royal family.

With Valerie, I hoped she'd fall into a third category that I haven't discovered yet. Since she knows me in a different context, I wanted to believe that she would continue to see me in the same light once she'd learned the truth about me.

Judging by that tiny flinch, she now belongs in category two. Though I'm not sure why I care. The struggle to understand people's motivations when they get close to me is the reason my father is always on at me about finding a special person to share my life with. A part of me gets why. His marriage was a love match. But we live in a different time now, one where I can never be sure if whoever is approaching me isn't after something other than me.

I've long made peace that it's not worth the risk and casual flings will be all I get in my life.

'Considering you've never had a kit sponsor, I assume you have more than enough money to pay for some dresses,' Valerie eventually says, and I swallow my sigh of relief. I'd already steeled myself for an argument about who is going to pay. Not that it would have been a real argument. The store is already under instruction to send the invoice to me.

'Seeing how you're doing me a favour here, this is the least I can do for you.'

Behind us, I can hear Elisabeth and her associates shift on their feet, keen to begin. I look at Valerie, raising one eyebrow expectantly and lowering it almost immediately when her face turns from blank to thoughtful. 'Do you—' I'm not quite sure what I'm trying to say. Is this a situation where it isn't just a bit extra, it's a completely foreign concept to Valerie and she needs guidance? '—need anything before we start?'

Valerie sighs and shakes her head. 'No, sorry. I know I'm being weird. Just—ignore me.' She pauses, raising her hands to her face and slapping both of her cheeks. Then she spins around and nods at Elisabeth. 'All right, since you already know more about the event than I do, how about you suggest something for me to try on?'

I grab my phone when Valerie slips behind the curtain again with Elisabeth in tow to peel her out of the awful salmon-pink number they put her in. This is the third unbelievably unflattering dress they have forced on her and if I didn't know any better, I would have said it's on purpose.

'Lola sent a message. Angel is going to be released from hospital,' I say loud enough for my voice to carry over to the fitting room.

The rustling of fabric stops. 'Oh, really? That's such good news. Did he feel comfortable sharing a diagnosis?'

I nod, then stop abruptly when I realise she cannot see me. 'Intermittent high-degree AV block. His cardiologists are currently determining if he needs a pacemaker. He'll miss the Tour de France, but over the summer we should be able to figure out if he can get back on the bike.'

'Poor Angel.' The genuine sadness in her voice taps at my breastbone and tries its best to find a way inside. 'I hope we'll see him back in his seat for the Vuelta. One of the stages goes past my home town, and I promised I would show him where to get the best churros.'

My ears perk up at this small detail of her life. Outside the circumstances that brought Valerie into my team and that she is working on launching her own charitable organisation, I know exactly nothing about this woman.

If we want to fool my father, we need to exchange a few more notes about one another and this is the perfect moment—if these sales associates could just leave us alone for a bit.

Maybe I can send them to grab refreshments before they subject Valerie to the next hideous dress. I don't like playing the prince card but it is fairly effective in dealing with situations like this one.

'Valerie, maybe we can take a short break and—'

The words die in my throat when they move the curtain and Valerie walks out and onto the podium, somehow in an even uglier dress than before. The skirt of this dress is layer upon layer of cerulean tulle, creating the impression of a dark cloud.

'What do you—?' Elisabeth begins, but stops when she looks at me and then back at Valerie. At least the saleswoman's astute enough to understand our opinion without making us say it.

The discomfort on Valerie's face prods further at the soft spot right between my ribs and I turn my gaze to Elisabeth, indicating the racks of dresses around us. 'How about you give us half an hour to sit down and have some refreshments? Meanwhile, I would appreciate it if you could take all this away and come back with a plan for dresses that enhance Dr Torres' natural beauty rather than shoehorning her into whatever guidelines Fairfax gave you.'

'Of course, we'll get right on that. Any particular style you're looking for?' Elisabeth asks and when I glance over at Valerie, she shrugs.

So I take the reins and say, 'Let's try something form-fitting, no tulle or petticoats. Sequins or crystals to elevate it. Floor length but if it has a side slit that might make it even better.'

All the sales associates nod in unison, then one of them hurries around the corner and re-emerges with a tray laden with all sorts of refreshments before disappearing again. Valerie, still wearing the hideous dress, quirks an eyebrow as she looks at the selection. 'I guess she was too scared of you to ask what we might want and brought everything.'

I blink at her. 'I'm not scary.'

'Meanwhile, why don't you come back with a plan for dresses that enhance Dr Torres' amazing body?' she says, lowering her voice to imitate mine, and I push against the imagery her words create.

'That's not what I said.'

She waves a hand in front of her. 'You said something to that extent. Which I appreciate because I'm such a people pleaser, I would have said yes to the first dress and called it a day.'

'Fairfax probably told her to provide dresses in that style. His fashion sense is stuck in the last century.'

'Who is Fairfax? You've mentioned him a few times now.'

'Oh…' I pause because even though I'm quite used to the existence and idea of Fairfax, it's one of those things that tends to weird other people out. *Normal* people, who haven't grown up thinking they are special just because they were born into a certain family.

But she's going to meet him, and the whole point of this break is so we can achieve the other objective of the day: learn more about each other. So I explain while I point at the chair next to me asking her to sit. 'Fairfax is my family's private secretary. He mostly works with my father since it's just me and him on this side of the Grant-Belmont line. But occasionally he inserts himself into my life as well—like organising this entire thing.'

Valerie steps down from the platform, the tulle of the skirt rustling with every move she makes. When she comes to a stop in front of the armchair, she frowns. 'I'm not sure I'll be able to get up again if I sit down.'

'I will make sure you do. Please sit. We'll be here for a while. They don't have anything prepared in the style I gave them.' My smile turns into a huffed laugh when she all but collapses into the chair and the skirt of the dress puffs up around her.

'So you don't have any siblings?' she asks, picking up the piece of information I put down.

'No, only child. What about you?'

'Same. My parents had me young and I think when they realised how much one child cost, they quickly got a lot better at birth control.' She sounds flippant as she says that, and I pause. That we grew up with different perceptions of wealth has been clear from the start, but her words make me think money might have been more than just tight for her.

'I see. And you grew up in Spain?' I still remember the information on her CV. Which was weird, considering I read it weeks ago, but, then again, not a lot of things make sense to me when it comes to Valerie Torres.

Even before we made our deal, I could hardly stop myself from looking at her whenever she entered a room. Now that we are sharing something beyond work, it's like this small tug towards her has grown into something much more insistent. It's not just my gaze but my hands too, wanting to find out what she feels like underneath my fingertips.

'Yup. Spent all my life there. First time I really left was when I started working in cycling.' Valerie leans back and when I laugh, she shoots me a narrowed glare. 'I look like a bucket of candy floss.'

'We're going to fix it. There will be some press at the gala. They rarely bother to stop me since I've been flying under the radar so long, but with someone on my arm, they're bound to pay attention.' I shudder at the thought, but it's unavoidable. 'Feel free to talk about your charity work when they ask you questions. That's probably the best value you can get out of this.'

'Other than helping you,' she says, and my eyebrows draw together.

'If you consider helping me to trick my family into believing I'm in a happy relationship a worthwhile endeavour, then yes. There's certainly that.' The moment I say the words, I regret them because it invites questions to answers I'm not willing to provide.

'Why is it so important that your family believes that we're together?' she asks. Of course she does, because I all but invited that question. Because outside the overarching plan and the need to dress her up, we haven't really spoken about *my* motivation for needing my father to believe this relationship. She doesn't know that my ownership of the team hinges on it and I don't want her to know.

Reaching for the tray, I busy my hands by pouring some water into two glasses and taking the time to place a lemon wedge and some ice cubes into them. I don't know what to say. On the one hand, I don't want to lie to her.

Something about the very suggestion pushes at a spot in my chest, making it harder to breathe.

But I can't tell her the truth, either. Agreement or not, she is part of the team and I don't want to burden any of the team members with the knowledge of a potential power struggle between my father and me.

'The way my family is run is quite archaic and, even though I wish they didn't, they place far too much value on things like marriage and raising one's family.' I go with a version of the truth I feel comfortable sharing. 'When I decided to go to med school and become a doctor, none of my family thought it would last. But since I'm far enough down the line of succession, my father was happy to let me go and "get it out of my system" after my mother insisted I should follow my mind. Except for her, they all thought it was just a phase, and sometimes I think even now they're resentful of how I picked my own path rather than sticking to the one someone from "my station" should follow.'

I hate talking about my family because it sounds so removed from reality. People would kill to have these problems and somehow I'm complaining. It's the reason I've lived my life playing things close to my chest.

But when I look over at Valerie, I don't see any of the usual disbelief or judgement on her face. She tilts her head to the side, examining me with an intensity that sends a shiver down my spine.

'My parents also didn't want me to go to med school,' she says after a beat of silence. 'They both worked multiple jobs just to make ends meet, so I spent much of my childhood looking after myself. School became my entire focus because the teachers gave me the attention

I couldn't get from either parent, and it was one of my teachers who told me if I kept my grades up, I might be able to get into med school on a scholarship.'

Footsteps sound through the store and hushed whispers arguing with each other. Elisabeth no doubt struggling to find something that fits my requirements while also adhering to the limitations Fairfax thought he needed to impose. Did he really think I would show up with a date dressed like Princess Leia while imprisoned by Jabba the Hutt? Why they think so little of me is beyond me. Like somehow following my own path painted me in a light they don't appreciate.

'And your parents didn't like that?' I ask, leaning on the image I have in my mind of what supportive parents would be like. They'd want their child to become a successful doctor, wouldn't they?

'They wanted me to drop out of high school and start working. One of my mother's employers had a position open. I think it was a warehouse or something. Their hope had been that once I got old enough to work, my mother could quit her daytime job and work full-time at night to earn more money. But I didn't want to work. I wanted to go to med school—become a doctor. They told me it was foolish to go into debt for something that might not even work out.' The fabric rustles when she shrugs, and I can see how much she doesn't want any of this to affect her even as her frayed edges show up around her words. 'Anyway, I defied my parents by staying in school and, in doing so, made their lives much harder for the years it took me to get through med school. Though ironically, now they seem quite the fans of that plan, given how much I help them out financially.'

Her tone is carefully blank and I recognise it instantly. I've used it too, talking about my father and family obligations when I needed some emotional distance from everything simply to feel like myself. If I didn't let all of this be a part of myself then it couldn't hurt me.

My arm moves before I can consider whether this is a smart choice to make. Stretching across the small space between our chairs, I reach out and wrap my hand around hers to give it a squeeze. Electricity lances down my arm, setting tiny fires underneath my skin as our palms rub against each other. Our fingers flex and bend—a tentative dance as we both try to decide if we want to do this. A charged sense of significance that wasn't there a few moments ago settles on us as the tips of our fingers brush against each other in a quiet acknowledgement: we might have been raised under different circumstances, but family obligations have bound us both in some way.

'What inspired you to put so much of yourself into Cosecha de Vida?' It's a thought that's been stuck in my mind since our first conversation about this arrangement. This charity is clearly her passion, yet I don't know why.

Valerie stares down at our linked hands and for a moment I worry she will pull away. But she doesn't and shakes her head instead. 'I told you my parents realised how expensive one child was so they didn't go for a second one, right? Well, they didn't even have the money to feed one child properly. They…tried their best, but when you are so far below the poverty line the way we were, even everyone working two jobs often isn't enough to make ends meet.'

She lets out a breath that has the heavy meaning of her words wrapped in it. Still, I can't help but marvel at her. At the ease with which she shares tender parts of herself. It's such a foreign concept to me to be this open, yet I crave it from her.

'I got by on school meals, though they weren't the best nutritionally. Sometimes teachers would give me food packages to take back home, but when the other kids noticed, I got bullied a lot. So I learned how to live with hunger throughout my childhood, along with my absent parents. When I moved to Madrid, got into medical school and became responsible for cooking my own meals, I was so overwhelmed, I had to get help. And if I hadn't found that help at the food bank, I don't know if I'd have made it. That's when I realised that once I reached a moment in my life where I could give back, I would. And that is how Cosecha de Vida was born.'

Another parallel in our lives coalesces between us. The way she thinks about her charity is how I feel about the cycling team. Both things being the focus that helped us find something worthwhile beyond the circumstances of our birth.

'Thank you for sharing this with me,' I say before I can think better of it. This is supposed to be a simple exchange of information, yet somehow we've slipped into a place that is much more intimate than that.

Valerie shakes her head. When she looks back at me, her smile doesn't quite reach her eyes. 'I might have disappointed my parents with my choices some years back, but if I can stop children from going hungry like I did, then I believe it's money and time well spent.'

A disappointment? 'It's probably obvious to you now, but it would be remiss of me to not say that disappointment is—'

Elisabeth circles around the partition shielding us from the rest of the store and drags with her a garment rack, its squeaky wheel ripping us both out of this moment. Valerie pulls her hand back and leaves mine dangling in the air with nothing to hold onto.

'Sorry for the delay. I've put together a few sample dresses that should be more to your liking, Your Royal Highness.' The title is like a bucket of ice water dumped over me, dousing what flickering embers I may have felt coming alive between us.

Good. What am I even thinking, reaching out to her like that? This is a business arrangement and the stakes are too high to let anything get in the way.

Including myself.

'Let's see it, then.' I get off my chair and step in front of Valerie, who is trying her best not to look like she's struggling to stand up on her own. As predicted earlier, the dress is making it much harder on her.

Suppressing a shiver as the memory from mere moments ago ghosts over my skin, I hold out my hand. She hesitates, looking at it and then up to me before sighing and clasping it the way she hadn't wanted to just now. Expecting the touch does nothing to lessen its impact and this time the heat surges through me with such ferocity that I stagger back, pulling Valerie with me. She stumbles forward into my chest and I wrap my hand around her upper arm, steadying her.

The scent of lilacs drifts up my nose, and I yank my head back before I do something stupid like follow the trail of that scent down her neck. Valerie shifts, looking up, and we're stuck in this semi-intimate, semi-awkward position where neither wants to move even though we both know we should. We must.

But more than that, a new thought bubbles up within me: Valerie feels it, too.

The tension between us that has built up over the last few weeks of working together. The clashes and challenges that have somehow brought us closer together and now this deal we've struck has distilled it all into something tangible.

'Are we ready to start?' Elisabeth asks, snapping us both out of our stupor.

Valerie blinks twice and a hint of blush rises to her cheeks, giving them an even darker tone. Heat I feel reflected in my own body; in the reluctance of my hands as they let go of her once she's steady on her feet.

'Yes, we are done with this,' Valerie says and I'm not sure if she means the dress—or whatever moment passed between us a few seconds ago.

It takes them so much longer to get her into this dress and a part of me worries we're going to be here all day. Not that I have any other plans, but, with what I saw in Valerie's eyes when we touched, I need to walk this bubbling heat off before I do something stupid. Or maybe I need to be as far away from her as our deal allows, since her proximity is clearly messing with my brain chemistry in a way I cannot understand.

Attraction isn't an unfamiliar concept for me. I've been attracted to plenty of people throughout my life. No, this is something else. In my experience, attraction is fleeting and not this consistent current pinging between Valerie and me whenever we get too close to each other. It's distracting and making me doubt if we can get through the gala in one piece.

The rustling behind the curtain finally stops and I sit up straight when they pull it back, revealing Valerie in the dress. It's dark red, and, unlike the other gowns, it clings to her body without any unnecessary thrills or embellishments. It's like the fabric is fused with her skin, becoming part of her as it dips into every single valley and stretches over her curves, casting them in a light that is irresistible.

And dangerous.

'What do you think?' Valerie asks. There's a large mirror next to her where she could make her own impression of the dress, but instead she looks straight at me—eyes dark with a spark of *something*.

I take a step towards the podium—when did I stand up? Somehow I don't remember. The back of my neck prickles as I take a few more steps until I stand right next to the podium. It's high enough to put us at eye level and her eyes are so round, I can almost see my reflection in them.

'You look…' My voice trails off because I don't know how to end that sentence. No, that's not entirely true. I know exactly what I want to say, but some sense of self-preservation stops me from uttering the word.

Ravishing.

'Is it that bad again?' She turns her head—or at least she tries to, but I stop her by putting my hand on her cheek.

'This is the one.' No doubt it's nowhere near what Fairfax would consider appropriate, but, then again, he doesn't seem to live in the current century.

Her cheek is warm underneath my fingers and a shudder I've suppressed all this time emerges, reacting to the proximity of this woman. This woman, to whom I am irresistibly drawn, is now permanently in my life, as agreed. Not just for the night of the gala, but also in my team.

I should walk away right now. It's the smart thing to do for both of us. I can't give her myself and she…has been in this situation before where her superior changed their relationship without acknowledging or addressing the power imbalance between them.

Except my body refuses to listen to my brain and my thumb gains a will of its own as it brushes over her cheekbone in a wide arc. Valerie doesn't pull away, either. A few seconds go by where we remain locked like this and then—she shifts her head ever so slightly, pushing against my palm.

The fire coming alive within me is instant, surging through me and making each breath harder to inhale, each thought more nebulous until I can't remember why I should keep my distance.

The fabric of the dress is a soft silk with tiny beads of crystal stitched all over. I know that because my hand finds its way onto her hip, gliding up until it rests in the dip of her waist.

'You are beautiful,' I say, my voice loud in the silence despite only whispering.

My eyes dart down to her throat when she swallows. 'You mean the dress is beautiful?' she asks.

'That's not what I said.' Her lips part, forming a small O, and I lean forward as if drawn in by a magnet. Even under the harsh lights of the store, her mouth looks soft and pliable, just waiting for me to verify these impressions.

I move my face closer to hers when her hand lands on my shoulder, gripping at the fabric of my shirt. The space we are operating in for our deal becomes more narrow and plausible deniability more of a problem with each touch. But her hands playing with my shirt and her panting breaths skittering over my skin disable all my defences; all I can think about is what her mouth will feel like against mine.

My eyes bore into hers, looking for *something* to still me. Or worse, make me act on this idea that's unravelling in my mind. Her gaze flicks to the side where two of the women, Magdalena and Paula, are pretending not to glance at us. I follow it, though I don't understand the gesture. With my fingers on her cheek and her scent in my nose, I don't have the space to process anything else.

And then Valerie gives me a shallow nod that rocks through me like a bolt of lightning. It could mean a hundred different things, but when her eyes slip down to my mouth, I know it means what I need it to mean. Dread it, too.

Her eyes flutter shut as my grip tightens around her waist, pulling her closer. When I slide my mouth over hers, her softness presses against me and it has to be the most delicate thing I've ever felt. Even so, the hunger that sets in at that small touch is all-consuming and I have to stop myself from sliding my hand to where I know I'll find smooth skin.

This isn't supposed to happen. Not when this isn't more than a business arrangement rooted in mutually beneficial outcomes. Yet I can't stop my other hand from coming up, framing her face and then—

A metallic clatter rips through the air, and we jump

apart, turning towards the noise. Elisabeth is sprawled on the floor, tangled in a clothing rack that must have gone down with her. Magdalena and Paula rush to her side, their faces pale and frantic, but their hands hover uselessly above her.

I step away from the platform instantly, Valerlie right behind me, the fabric of the dress swishing softly as she moves. 'Elisabeth?' she asks as she kneels down, then looks over her shoulder at the associates standing a few paces away, their eyes wide in horror.

Paula wrings her hands, her words stumbling. 'I—I think she said she felt dizzy and said she'd go sit in the back for a moment and then she just went down. She has…diabetes, I think.'

Valerie doesn't waste a second. She waves at me to kneel on the other side of Elisabeth and I tilt her head back slightly. 'She's breathing. Pulse is weak but steady. Hypoglycaemic? Since she might be diabetic.'

Her eyes flick to me and then to the two women beside us. 'Can you get me her handbag? If she has diabetes, she will have a glucometer and maybe even some glucose tablets or gel,' she says.

Both women scurry away, Magdalena coming back an instant later and holding out a black leather bag. Without any time to care for her possessions, I turn the bag and spill its contents on the floor, scanning through everything that falls out. Lipstick, receipts, a half-empty packet of mints—and then my fingers close around a small tube of glucose gel. I toss it to Valerie.

She catches it in one hand and unscrews the cap. 'Elisabeth,' she says softly, leaning in close. 'You're going to be fine, but I need you to swallow this.' She squeezes a small amount of gel into the corner of Elisabeth's mouth and gently massages her jaw to encourage her to swallow.

Paula speaks up, her voice trembling. 'Should we call an ambulance?'

'Not yet,' Valerie says without looking up. 'Let's stabilise her blood sugar first. Do you have juice or fizzy drinks here? She might want to eat once the gel kicks in.'

The woman nods and bolts away again.

For a few seconds, we both hold our breath. Elisabeth stirs slightly, a faint groan escaping her lips as Valerie administers another small dose of gel.

'That's it,' Valerie murmurs, her voice low and steady. 'You're coming around.'

I crouch down on Elisabeth's other side, scanning her face. Her colour is still off, but her breathing is evening out. 'She's responding,' I say, glancing at Valerie.

'Good,' she replies and I can see the tension draining out of her. She doesn't glance up, her full focus on Elisabeth, but I catch the faint tension in her jaw, the way her fingers tremble just slightly as the associate rushes back with a bottle of orange juice.

Valerie takes it, twisting off the cap. 'Take small sips.' She holds the bottle to Elisabeth's lips, coaxing her to drink.

Elisabeth's eyelids flutter open, her gaze unfocused but alive. 'What—what happened?'

'You had a hypoglycaemic episode. When was the last time you ate?'

Elisabeth winces, clearly embarrassed. 'Skipped lunch,' she mutters. 'Busy day.'

Valerie presses her lips into a firm line, but her voice remains even. 'Finding breaks to eat can seem impossible, but I don't have to tell you that you can't skip food with your condition. Low blood sugar can be dangerous. You're lucky this wasn't worse.'

I find her glucometer in the bag and hand it over. Valerie works quickly, pricking Elisabeth's finger with practised efficiency. She reads the result on the small screen. 'It's 42 mg/dL. Low, but you're stabilising.' She glances at the associates. 'She'll need to sit and rest for a while. Can you get her a snack?'

Paula nods, her earlier panic subsiding. 'Right away.'

Elisabeth manages a weak smile as she takes another sip of juice. 'Thank you,' she whispers. 'Both of you.'

Valerie steps back, brushing her hands against her thighs as if to clear the moment from her skin. Her face is calm, professional, but there's something in her eyes—something soft, almost shaken. The comment about food sticks with me. Her charity is all about food poverty, both in education and in more tangible work like helping food banks. Something as simple as a missed lunch seems to have had an outsized impact on her. Now I understand why.

'I owe you both…an apology,' Elisabeth says, her voice hoarse but steady. 'You look so pretty in that dress and clearly His Royal Highness liked it, too. And then I had to go and ruin your moment.'

Valerie freezes, her back to me, but I catch the way her shoulders stiffen. When she turns, her expression is as smooth and unreadable as polished glass. 'I think we'll take this dress. I'm His Royal Highness's girlfriend, after all. So I'd better look the part,' she says, straightening the dress and stepping back onto the platform.

But her eyes flick to mine for the briefest of seconds,

and the look towards the two women before our kiss clicks into place for me. I told her that we needed to pretend to be a real couple around anyone that's in touch with my family—that included the boutique employees since Fairfax organised all of this.

This wasn't a real kiss for her. She gave me permission to hold up her end of the agreement. Rightly so.

The kiss couldn't be real for me, either.

CHAPTER SEVEN

Valerie

'We should talk about this, right?' I really wish I sounded more convinced than I do and as far as first words to Ethan are concerned, I know I could have done better. But sitting in the passenger seat of the team car while Ethan is driving isn't exactly the most relaxed of circumstances. At least not after that day in the boutique. After the kiss.

Ethan raises his eyebrow in a way that is far too familiar to me already. He does this when he disagrees with a piece of information he just heard. Or when he thinks we're not seeing the right approach in a team situation. Either way, I've come to know this particular bend of his eyebrow as the 'not going to happen' shape.

'What specifically is *this*?' he asks. Of course he would. Why did I think this man would be merciful enough to, one, not make me bring up what happened between us at the boutique, and two, not feign ignorance when I eventually do bring it up?

'You really going to make me spell it out?' I ask, and the stubborn part in me wants to take his lead on this and be quiet. But it's the compulsive part in me that needs to talk about her feelings all the time that is winning that fight. She always does and I end up starring in another episode of 'things Val shouldn't have said but couldn't help herself because tension makes her uncomfortable'.

I watch as his eyes dart over the road, following the signs the organisers of the Critérium du Dauphiné set out for team cars to follow. It's the final stage of the race and Julian is wearing the green jersey today and has been for the last three days after gaining points for some tricky sprints he won along with finishing high every race day. The entire team has been working tirelessly this week to make sure Julian can stay in the green jersey and get us the win we're craving. The win *I* need. Because when Julian crosses that finish line wearing the green jersey and thus becoming the breakout star of the season, my charity's logo will be front and centre on his chest.

Seeing the logo appear on everyone's jersey has been an unreal experience and, every now and then, I still have to pinch myself to make sure I'm not making this all up. After spending years working nights and weekends while putting whatever of my own money I could into this, I've finally got the sponsorship I wanted. Donations have been trickling in over the last few days, and every time I see the number jump up by a few digits, a burst of butterflies comes alive in my stomach. It's not much, but it is a start.

When we join a queue of other team cars waiting to park to go to the finish line, Ethan turns his head towards me. His expression is inscrutable, the way it has been ever since the race started. I know I have no business feeling this way, but, after spending so much time with him in an effort to get to know each other, the distance stings.

It shouldn't. I know it shouldn't. But it does.

'I don't see how there's anything to talk about, Valerie. I appreciate that you saw an opportunity to make our romance believable and you made me aware of it. What else is there to talk about?' We pull into our designated parking spot and, before I can reply, Ethan shuts off the engine and gets out of the car with me scrambling to keep up with him as he strides towards the waiting area.

'Where is Julian?' I ask, eyes flicking to the digital clock behind the finish line. They can't be far. Maybe another half an hour?

'Race radio is down,' Ethan replies, checking his phone. 'Javier is on one of the support bikes trying to catch up to the breakaway.'

So all that's left for us to do is wait. Wait and, well, talk.

I'm not sure where this particular outburst is leading me, but I'm committed to it now. 'Why are you so hung up about the kiss? It's the kind of stuff we agreed on doing for the sake of this arrangement.' He doesn't need to know that the memory still makes my heart flutter. Because that reaction was *not* part of the deal.

Ethan looks straight ahead as he says, 'I'm not hung up about anything.'

'Shut up, you liar. Since our trip to the boutique, things haven't been the same between us. You barely spoke to me after buying me an overpriced dress I'll never wear again after this gala because, let's be honest, I don't go to events fancy enough.' I remember a moment too late that I'm talking to my boss here. And that people from other cycling teams waiting for their own riders surround us. Some heads turn in our direction and I wince. Stupid me and my loud mouth.

If Ethan is bothered by it—or even notices the stares—he doesn't let on. He turns towards me, leaning his hip against the balustrade with his arms crossed in front of his chest. Like some kind of Pavlovian response, my eyes dart down to where his muscles bunch underneath the button-up shirt. So ridiculous that even on the road he dresses up like that when we're all wearing T-shirts and jeans. It's something I noticed about him from the very beginning, giving him such an unapproachable air. Though now that I know him better, I can see how wrong I was.

He's been a lot of things to me in the last few weeks, but unapproachable hasn't been one of them. Not until now, after that kiss.

'You realise I'm still your superior, no matter what we might have agreed on doing outside work?' he asks, clearly reading my mind. A hint of a smirk tugs at his lips and my heart falls out of step when I see that fleeting expression, realising that I've kind of missed it.

'Well, you're also my fake boyfriend and, in this case, that is the aspect of Ethan I want to speak to,' I reply, conscious to keep my voice low this time. Does he realise I enjoyed the kiss more than I should? Which, obviously, is not at all since it's supposed to be fake?

He frowns and, even though it's the opposite of a smirk, I'm here for it. Anything that is resembling an expression from him is an improvement over the days of stony silence, and he says, 'Go ahead, then. I'm all yours.'

He drops his voice low to match mine, but instead of sounding quiet and conspiratorial he's giving me a husky, just-rolled-out-of-bed-after-a-fantastic-night kind of vibe and it's messing with my focus. Argh, how does he keep doing that to me? Didn't I dislike this guy just a few weeks ago?

'Well…' My voice trails off when the truth lodges itself in my throat. If I say this now, I'm admitting to something I haven't even dared to think through at all. But the need to have him understand—to see me for who I am—is too strong for me to keep things inside. 'Because maybe for a fraction of a second, I forgot it was just for show, okay? You told me I'm beautiful, which got my head all turned around, and then the two women started whispering and I couldn't hear them other than the word "cute" and then your hand tightened around my waist. And I realised that they might feed this information back to that Fairfax guy. That you were only looking at me like you meant it because of our deal and not—'

Mercifully, I can swallow the rest of the words popping up in my head about how I had really *wanted* it to not be for show, but it would be so damning to our charade that he'd probably call it off. That's something I can't risk. This week alone has already given me so much more traction than I've gained in years. So whenever I start thinking I might be genuinely attracted to Ethan, that's what I need to bring to mind: I'm resisting for a reason.

That and he's just said it himself. He's my boss. And I'm not about to make the same mistake twice.

Surprise flickers over his features, as if he mentally prepared for a few scenarios and this one wasn't any of them. I'm not shocked by that. Everything I've ever seen him do has been deliberate and planned. Meanwhile, I'm so used to living my life day by day, I can easily get lost in my own thoughts. Or in a particular moment in a high-end boutique where I definitely shouldn't have been losing sight of the plan.

'You thought I—'

I interrupt him before he can finish his sentence because I don't need to hear his incredulity. I'm already beating myself up over this enough. 'I know that's super dumb because clearly you wouldn't ever be interested in someone like me. It was a heat-of-the-moment thing. With all the dresses and the fussing of Elisabeth and her team, I just lost my head. I'm not used to getting *any* attention, so when I get *all* of it, I struggle. Okay? Just… say we're good.'

I let my gaze drop to my feet when the last words come out, a tone more akin to a desperate squeal.

'Valerie. You shouldn't—' He stops abruptly when his phone goes off, and I catch a glimpse of Javier's name flashing across his screen. At the same time, staff of the competing teams move closer to the balustrade. Damn, I got so caught up in whatever this is between us again that I forgot where I am—again. My eyes dart to the clock just as Ethan raises the phone to his ear.

I crane my head towards the finish line, my heart leaping into my throat when the first cyclist comes around the bend and sprints towards the finish line. The royal-blue jersey is a familiar sight, yet my stomach is already falling through my body while my brain is still busy processing what I'm seeing.

'Wait, Julian is wearing green. Ethan…' Now the crowd around me surges, as if they've just reached the same conclusion. I look ahead at the rider, then back at Ethan, who slowly lowers his phone.

'Ethan. What's happening?' I've never seen his face

so expressionless. Even when he's being severe, I can at least tell that. But his face is blank, not letting me guess at a single one of his thoughts.

I think I know what's happening. I'm seeing it right now as the rider approaches the finish line a few metres ahead of the rest. His head whips up as he comes closer, checking how much further it is to the goal before looking behind him at the competition.

Then Eddie Burgess sits up on the saddle, showing off the logo of my charity in its full glory as the domestique that replaced Angel just a few weeks ago snags the final stage win at the Critérium du Dauphiné.

'Fantastic win for Eddie Burgess, but it comes at the cost of your star rider, Julian Quintana. Are there any worries about Julian this close to the Tour de France?' the reporter asks Ethan, and I wonder how he's staying this cool after everything that's happened in the last half an hour.

With the race radio down, neither of us had any idea that Julian had been in a crash bad enough that he couldn't go on. He's currently being treated at the hospital, and I know that Ethan is itching to finish up all the press interviews so we can head over there and get a status report. Thankfully, Julian was conscious when they shipped him off, but he couldn't stand on his own.

'It's a testament to Javier and the team dynamics within Grant Sports Team. Our domestiques rival the general classification riders of other teams and Eddie is the proof of that. Now we have the green jersey and a stage win for one of our up-and-coming riders,' Ethan replies, giving another variation of the same answer he's given to three other outlets.

Standing a few metres behind him and out of the chaos that is the press area, I can see him flagging and I'm about to step up and suggest we leave when another reporter pushes her way to the front, shoving her microphone in his face. 'What is your relationship with Cosecha de Vida, Ethan?' she asks, and my heart stutters when I hear the name of my charity uttered like that.

Ethan blinks several times, brows dipping low. His pause makes me nervous. 'I don't—How is that relevant?'

My stomach drops by several centimetres. Has he *not* prepared for this question?

'Grant Sports Team has never had a kit sponsor before, which brings up the question of what it is about Cosecha de Vida that made you commit to a sponsorship.' Oh my God, she's asking about my charity. Live on air. This interview is on TV right now, and Ethan has no idea what my charity is even about. I know we discussed it when I got way too real way too fast with him, as I tend to do when it comes to Ethan Flipping Grant, but there's no way he remembers any of that incoherent ramble about my parents and how I never knew where my next meal would come from.

'Cosecha de Vida does important work to educate people about and prevent food poverty in poorer communities. In the European Union alone, we have almost a quarter of the population at risk of food insecurities. Did you know that?'

The reporter stares at Ethan as if he's just grown another head and, to be fair, that is how I feel as well hearing his forceful reply. Is he defending me and my charity? The thought rushes through me, filling me with a heady sense of closeness. All my life, I've struggled to make people see me and somehow Ethan is showing me time and again that he just does. As if it's instinctual for him to see me. Like he can't help it.

'What made you choose Cosecha de Vida as your first official sponsor?' another person with a microphone asks and both of us look towards the new person.

It's not someone I usually see among the body of reporters waiting to interview both cyclists and staff at the finish line. Instead of a big handheld microphone with her station's logo on it, she holds a small microphone between her thumb and index finger while holding her phone in the other hand. Unlike the previous reporter, she sounds excited, as if, in her opinion, it's about time that Ethan picked my charity as a sponsor.

'This team is in the very fortunate position of not needing a kit sponsor. And since we do have visibility, we should be using that space to promote good causes.' I nod along with Ethan's reply, feeling a rush of pride. This is exactly what I've always wanted to achieve. If even just a few people who are watching this live now go and check it out and donate, I'll get closer to my goal. My fingertips twitch with the need to check my phone for where I'm currently sitting with donations.

But then the gaze of the reporter slides to me. 'You're the owner of the charity, right? Dr Valerie Torres?'

I stare at her for a few seconds before I remember how to nod. When she holds the microphone in my direction, I instinctively take a step back. Except someone's hand on the small of my back keeps me in place and then pushes me forward so I'm in front of all the cameras and microphones. Twisting my head, I see Ethan is now standing behind me with an encouraging smile.

'Yes, this is Dr Torres, and she is far better equipped than I to tell you more about the charity,' he says to the reporter. He stays close to me and his hand doesn't leave my back. Feeling the closeness rush back to me, I lean into the touch as I make eye contact with the woman.

He has prepared for this question, after all, and I don't have time to wonder why my first thought was that he might not have. Probably because even though Alexander agreed to give me a shoulder spot in lieu of a part of my salary, he never really listened when I spoke about why I've put so much of myself into this charity.

Ethan knows after one conversation about it. Knows *me*.

'I started this charity because food poverty is an issue not often talked about. Not only are there people who can't afford a daily meal, but when they can afford it, it's ultra-processed and not fresh. I don't think many people understand that eating healthy and nutritionally rich food is a luxury and how much it actually costs to be poor.' The words come easier as I speak, and I'm encouraged by the eager nod I see from the reporter. Is she interested in the topic of food poverty? Is that why she's here and not because of the cycling?

She answers my question with her next words. 'Have you seen that you've gone viral on TikTok this morning?'

'What?' Ethan and I say the word at the same time, and I feel him step even closer, his chest so close to my back now that his heat jumps over the tiny space remaining between us.

She turns her phone towards us and shows us a clip. It's me, kneeling on the ground next to Michael, the Team Blue Cow rider who crashed. I can't hear the narration, but my eyes widen as I read along with the subtitles. They're describing me, my work in cycling, but, more importantly, the work I do in nutritional education. As the video goes on, a snapshot of my doctoral thesis appears on the screen, which talks about the socioeconomic division in nutrition.

Then my charity's homepage appears on the screen and in front of it the face of the female narrator, talking about all the work Cosecha de Vida plans on doing—that *I* want to do—and calling her followers to help. I look at the woman closer and then back at the reporter, recognising her face. 'You…but why?'

I look down at the video again and then I see the name at the bottom. *Chelsea-NutritionDecoded.* A name anyone on social media with an interest in nutrition immediately identifies and the second I read it, recognition dawns on me.

'I got many other people in the network to share the video and we're almost at ten million views. And look.' The woman's cheeks—Chelsea's—flush, the excitement clear in her voice as she takes the phone back and swipes up. When she turns it around again, it shows my website on the donation counter.

The number pushes all the remaining air out of my lungs, and everything goes quiet. All the people around me stop moving, and my focus narrows until I perceive only my own heartbeat—the rushing of blood through my ears, the gentle pressure of a hand tightening on the small of my back.

Ethan.

I spin around to face him and the part inside me I keep guarded because of the countless people in my life who have let me down is afraid of what I'll find reflected in his eyes. Will he want to claim this success like my parents now do even when they weren't at all supportive of my career choices?

His eyes are as wide as mine when he looks at the screen. Then a big grin appears on his face when the information sinks in and my breath hitches at the sight. Ethan, who keeps his thoughts and feelings close to his chest, is sporting the widest smile I've ever seen on him, and it breaks a cold and ancient wall inside me.

My throat burns as the reality of this situation hits me. I throw my arms around Ethan's neck, burying my face there and breathing in his scent that's already so much more familiar to me than it should be.

'Thank you.' I breathe out the words. Or maybe I shout them. I'm not entirely sure because my ears are ringing. But that alone doesn't seem adequate to express my gratitude for the opportunity he's given me by putting the logo on the kit.

Ethan's arms come around me, squeezing me close to him. One of his hands is still on my back, but the other one follows the path of my spine up to my neck, cupping my nape. A rush of heat trickles through me and, mixing with the incredulity and excitement already brewing inside me, everything explodes in a cocktail of heightened emotions.

An electric current jumps from my body to his when I lift my head up and pull his face close enough to slide my mouth over his. Ethan stiffens underneath my hands for one heartbeat, then he pulls me closer, and I melt against him, getting lost in the intoxicating quality of this kiss.

It's not because I'm grateful to him. I *am*, but this is

something else. An accumulation of both small and big moments we've shared since I joined up with the team that now seems to so clearly point into this direction—one where we take the next step.

My hands dive into his hair, seeking purchase. There's no space left between us and still it feels like it's too much. I lose myself in this moment, licking over his closed lips and in response I can feel his groan vibrating through me. But his mouth stays closed, denying me what I want. Then his arms around me slacken, his hands coming down on my shoulders and pushing me away. It's less than a centimetre that's between our mouths, but the sudden chasm feels insurmountable.

The distance is also enough for reason to rush back at me and when it does, I stumble back with a gasp. If it weren't for Ethan's hand still on my shoulder, I would have fallen—right into the pack of reporters still standing in front of us. With their cameras pointing right at us.

Oh God. What have I done?

CHAPTER EIGHT

Ethan

'TRULY IMPRESSIVE, WHAT Eddie managed to do,' my father says, and I nod absent-mindedly.

Though he's always remained interested in the affairs of the team, Archibald Grant-Belmont isn't the type to summon me to his office just because my team has done something impressive. Otherwise, I would have spent far more time in this office. Or should I say hotel room, since it seems he's come all the way to Lyon to talk to me. Only what it might be about eludes me. I've done everything he's asked of me, including getting Valerie involved in this ridiculous ruse to convince him I'm—

The reason my father is here rushes at me and I bite the inside of my cheek to stop myself cursing out loud. He's here because he, like everyone else, has seen the press coverage of Eddie's win. Except some publications have decided that the more interesting thing to report is Valerie kissing me. Not even an hour after we packed up and drove back to Lyon, Javier sent me a link to one of the pictures showing us locked in a passionate embrace, with far too many question marks attached to the message.

'I'm very proud of him. He stepped up when Angel

needed to drop out and he's grabbed at the chance when confronted with it. We're hoping we can get Angel back on the team for the Vuelta, but if Eddie keeps it up, we're facing some tough conversations on who gets the top spot next to Julian,' I say, keeping my tone as detached as possible. What objections could my father possibly have at this point? He's been the one to push me towards dating, so, if anything, he should be satisfied that there is physical proof out there that he can show the rest of the clan that I am *taking this seriously.*

He won't ever find out how serious this really is. How the deal Valerie and I agreed on didn't include kisses at the finish line of races. No, that was a spontaneous moment—and a mistake.

'Eddie reminds me a lot of you, my boy,' Archibald continues, leaning back in his armchair and studying me over the rim of his glasses. 'You've never been satisfied with what was allotted to you in life. Always wanting more. It's the same tenacity that drew me to your mother.'

I let out a sharp exhale at the mention of my mother. Even so many years on, speaking about her isn't easy for me. My father makes it look so easy to reminisce about the good times they had without falling down the deep hole of grief that lives right next to the pleasant memories. I haven't learned how to do that yet, so I just nod.

'I appreciate you coming all the way here to watch the team. Though not everything went according to plan, we managed to snag an important victory for both Eddie and Julian.' I hope my words are signalling clearly enough that I'm done with any pleasantries and we can get straight to whatever he has to say about Valerie and me. There's no doubt in my mind that he's found some tiny thing to criticise, just how he always does, and, in doing so, pushing the ownership discussion away for another few years.

'Of course. I know we've had our disagreements around how much time you put into managing this team, but I couldn't be prouder of the results, and I know your mother would have been, too.' The hint of a smile plays on his lips and the wrinkles around his eyes soften. 'Fairfax told me the woman you were photographed with is also the one coming to the gala as your date.'

Taking a surreptitious breath to steel myself for whatever commentary might come next, I nod. 'Her name is Dr Valerie Torres. She joined the team a few weeks into the season as part of the nutritional team.'

'I know. Even with Eddie's extraordinary win, some of the publications have focused almost an equal amount of time on the work Dr Torres does. I understand it's her charity that you put on the front of the jersey?'

His tone is even, not letting me guess what he thinks about that decision. Not that I care what he thinks. Even as Valerie and I agreed to this ruse, I knew that helping her with her charity was the right thing to do. But the more I read about not just her work but food poverty in general, I've become convinced that there is so much we could all collectively do. Giving her space to advertise her charity was a no-brainer, and when I agreed to it, I could never have anticipated the results that we saw earlier today.

'That's right. It's something we agreed on when she came on board as our head of nutrition for the team. Part of her compensation package was getting the front kit sponsorship,' I say, the lie coming out smoothly. He doesn't need to know the details.

'And you two were involved from the very beginning as well?' he asks, and I tense at that question. They've all been mild, but if I know anything about this man it's that he'll be aiming towards something. The whole reason I'm in this mess with Valerie is because of his relentless prodding into my affairs, going as far as withholding the one thing I want more than anything in life.

Except now—

'No, that's a more…recent development,' I reply, shoving the intrusive thought away before it can find purchase anywhere within me.

The kiss at the finish line was impulsive and ill-advised and even though I can still feel the brush of her lips against mine when I close my eyes, I can't let myself hold onto the memory of how much I enjoyed it. How it didn't feel like a mistake, but rather the natural progression of this thing between us.

And that is the mistake in my thinking. This can't be the next step in a series of steps because none of this is real. It's all choreographed to convince this man sitting in front of me to finally hand over the team. That needs to happen sooner rather than later, because after this season Valerie will be gone, busy managing her charity, and our split will become apparent the first time I'm forced to attend another big event as Prince Ethan.

'Well, I can tell she means a lot to you,' my father says with a chuckle.

More than you realise.

The thought pops into my head unbidden, and I push it away just like all the other thoughts that have plagued me since that kiss a few hours ago. I wish I could hide behind the fact that it was just for show—another layer to the lie we need to tell my family. But while it worked to some extent in the boutique, the excuse falls apart now. We didn't plan this. Seeing her dream come true right there—being part of the reason it happened—unearthed something inside me.

A magnet that's been quietly humming away ever since I met Valerie, growing stronger as I got closer to her, as if it had found its polar opposite within her. And the more time we spent together, the closer it came to the surface. Now, it has broken free, and I can't stop it from reaching out to her.

She kissed me, but I know that, if she hadn't, I would have closed the distance between us a second later.

'Thank you, Father.' Is this the moment he'll tell me all the reasons he doesn't approve of her? Luckily, most of the immediate family have moved away from the notion of only marrying within the nobility, but I can still see the stigma surrounding those my extended family doesn't consider one of them.

My mother was such a case. Because she hadn't gone to the right schools and known the right people in life, she'd spent most of her time being *other.* Watching her struggle for the wider family's approval while I was embraced with open arms because I'm still my father's son was an eye-opening experience once I was old enough to understand. Hell, the entire reason I've refused to date anyone publicly is because of what my mother went through.

And now I'm about to subject Valerie to it. It will be only for one night and in an environment where we hopefully won't have to spend excessive amounts of time near anyone. A quick round of the room so people can see us together, so if my father asks about us, he gets the answer he wants, and then off we go in our separate ways. For anyone asking, we'll still maintain our relationship ruse for a few months. But one event is all she agreed to and it's all I can ask her to attend.

Going by what Archibald is saying, the moment at the finish line might turn out okay. As impulsive as the kiss was, maybe it will play in our favour if my father is here now to scope out our supposed relationship.

'And I'm glad to see you taking my request seriously. Work is important, and I'd never want to take that away from you but rather steer you in the right direction while I still can,' Archibald continues, and my gut twists at the genuine warmth I hear in his voice. 'I look forward to getting to know Dr Torres better and hearing about the work she plans on doing with her charity. Watching the interview she did, I think she seems like a good person.'

'She is.' I say it without hesitation, the truth such an easy thing to release, yet guilt chases right after it. He sounds excited, and that's not something I expected. But maybe I should have. Has his incessant bugging really just been about me finding a person while I've always thought it was about finding the *right* person to add to the family? But did he really *just* want me to find the right person for me?

'I also look forward to seeing both of you at the gala. I know the Tour is coming up and you don't have much time, but if you can stay a bit longer, I would enjoy that.' My father gets up and so do I, glad to be dismissed. This conversation has brought up far too many confusing things, and I need time to sort through them all. After opposing him so many times throughout the years and his stubborn refusal to yield, it finally feels like we've broken some new ground. I don't know how I feel about that yet.

He follows me to the door and when I turn around to say my goodbye, he hands me a blank envelope. Not even the family crest or the address of his office are on it. 'What is this?' I ask as I flip it around, flipping the flap open to peek inside.

'Ownership of the team. Today showed me you know how to juggle both aspects of your life, so it belongs to you now.'

CHAPTER NINE

Valerie

I SHOULD GO back to my room. Even under normal circumstances, it would be weird to find me pacing up and down in front of the door of Ethan's hotel room. After basically throwing myself at him in front of live cameras, it's downright stalkerish to do that. Especially since he's clearly ignoring me.

He's not answered my text that I spent two hours composing and it's led me on an epic doom-spiral.

That kiss…hell, why did I do that? Of all the stupid decisions I've made this year, this one has to take the top prize. Because after everything Alexander put me through, I've gone ahead and kissed my boss—again. As if the first time around didn't already go horrifically wrong, I'm apparently chasing a follow-up lesson with Ethan Grant.

Like, I don't even know what to say to him if he shows up. *Sorry I kissed you. I was too overwhelmed with reaching my funding goal and apparently the one way I wanted to celebrate was like this?*

No, what am I even thinking? It was an impulsive decision that I will not repeat. I'm just here to apologise and make sure that he knows this isn't some kind of attempt to get on his good side because I've learned that he is a bona fide prince.

Sure, chances are high that I'm going to overshare far too much, but hasn't he said he likes that about me? So this should be right up his alley as far as—

'Why are you prowling up and down the corridor?' Ethan's crisp voice pulls me out of my thoughts and I freeze mid-step, my eyes snapping to his.

He's standing in front of his door, the black keycard dangling between his fingers. Awareness rushes at me the moment our eyes meet and I shiver as the memory of his fingers on my skin ghosts over my flesh again. The very vague apologies I prepared evaporate from my brain and I'm left only staring at him. Then my gaze narrows on his mouth, on those lips that I can still feel on mine.

'Valerie?' The edge that was in his voice is gone now, and I'm not entirely sure that's a good thing. Because now it sounds too similar to the voice he used at the boutique, where he was neither Ethan Grant, head physician of the Grant Sports Team, nor Prince Ethan William Grant-Belmont. Just Ethan.

And that's the man that is the most dangerous to my resolve. The one that smiled so broadly when he absorbed the news of my charity's success. Not that I should be thinking about *that* moment again, because that will get me to melt against him all over again.

'Sorry, what did you ask?' I say, my voice husky in a way I hope he doesn't pick up on.

The hand still hovering over the door lock drops down to his side and when he turns around, I see a spark in his eyes that wasn't there a second ago. Damn it, he did hear it and now he knows I've been indulging in inappropriate, lusty thoughts about him. Oh God, why have I come here?

'I asked why you are prowling up and down the corridor.' His voice does that thing again where it drops low enough that I can feel it resonating inside my bones.

'Oh, I was looking for—' I stop myself because I'm no longer sure it's a good idea to tell him I was looking for him. He *knows* I have been, but admitting to it feels dangerous. Like if I say those words, the tangles around us will tighten and I won't find my way out of them; out of *him*.

He looks at his door and then slowly turns to me. The spark in his eyes catches flame, burning higher and higher when he locks eyes with me and whatever the reason was for me coming here, it no longer matters. I'm rendered speechless, nothing more than a moth drawn to this enticing flame that is now so close to me I can feel heat licking through my entire body.

Ethan closes the distance between us with two long strides and then his mouth is on mine again. And this time, there is no hesitation in his actions. His hands dive into my hair, pulling at the messy bun I had put it into until the tie loosens and my dark curls tumble over my shoulders. He fists a handful of them, pulling my head backwards to deepen the kiss, and this time his tongue slips into my mouth.

The taste is overwhelming and I slump against the wall for support as I grab at him, pulling him close again in a mirror of what happened a few hours ago. It was wrong then, and it's wrong now. Nothing has changed in our circumstances, yet I still can't stop. My hands wander down his spine all the way to the base, where I hook my fingers underneath his waistband.

His skin sizzles beneath my fingers and when I lock our hips together, his head rears back to let out a low hiss.

'You are so…' Ethan leans his forehead against mine, pupils blown wide as he looks at me. 'This is all I've been thinking about for days now, even though I know I shouldn't. When I'm near you, it's hard to remember that this is supposed to be for show. That you're not actually mine to keep. That I shouldn't think about kissing you or undressing you or want to make you come.' His voice reaches an even lower register, the sensuality lacing it running through me like a river of lava and igniting everything it finds in its path.

'What if you could do all those things?' I say, though I don't even know where this is coming from. All the warnings and rationalising of what's been brewing between us since we entered into this agreement float away as if they never existed; inconvenient fragments of the truth that won't stop me from getting what I want right this second.

Ethan doesn't reply—at least not with words. No, he lets out a throaty growl that sends a spear of need straight through my core and my internal muscles clench.

'Val.' He straightens just enough to look at me and what I see in that darkened gaze is enough to break down the tiny amount of resistance I managed to claw together since our last kiss at the finish line.

'Let's pretend that this is real. For one night, how about I don't just ask you to kiss me and touch me…' Emboldened by the unveiled desire I see in his eyes, I push against him again. 'But I beg you to do it all to me.'

Ethan presses his mouth against mine again, his tongue

fuelled by the frantic knowledge that this moment—this one night—is all we'll have. Tomorrow we'll go back to our old selves, and Ethan will be free to do with these memories whatever he wants. I know I'll keep them close to my heart, because even though none of this was supposed to happen, I can feel him there already.

His hands slip out of my hair, down my exposed arms and onto my hips. Each of his index fingers slips under the hem of my T-shirt and grazes over the sensitive skin there, making me gasp as he wrenches his mouth away from mine again.

For a few seconds, he remains still, only his fingers drawing small circles on me. Then his grip tightens around my hips and he lifts me up. My gasp turns into a yelp, but he steadies me when I wrap my legs around his middle and my arms around my neck.

'One night—but there will be no begging,' he says hoarsely. 'Whatever you desire, it's yours. Tonight.'

I bend down until our foreheads touch again, my fingers twining into his hair and messing up the still perfectly styled locks. His scent washes over me, spices and clean laundry, and it's enough to send my heart into a gallop—making me clench around nothing.

'Your room or mine?' I say and capture his lips with mine before he can reply. Gooseflesh crawls down my arms when Ethan groans, his grip slipping down to my bottom and pressing me against him.

Instead of answering my question, he hefts me higher and then walks the few steps to his door. The electronic lock beeps as he swipes the card across it and before the door clicks back shut, he's turned us around—pressing me against it while he kisses me again, deep and hungry.

Ethan kisses me like a man starving, and I'm not just the first meal he's seen in days. I'm the one thing he's yearned for his entire life. I don't think I've ever been kissed like that before. His grip on my thighs loosens as he sets me back down, his body still caging me against the door.

Whatever you desire, it's yours. How can I tell him he is all I want? His lips on mine, his fingers twining with mine, his taut length inside me.

The heat pooling between my legs burns so hot it cascades through my body in a wave so intense, I'm sure he must feel it rippling underneath my skin. My head falls back when Ethan's lips leave my mouth to trace my jaw, pressing hasty kisses all the way down my neck. When his teeth graze over my pulse point, I let out a moan and grip his jacket, desperate to tear it and every other piece of clothing off him.

'Off,' I say as I fumble with the lapels of the jacket. 'Who even wears a dinner jacket on race day?'

His breath rasps over my too hot skin when he laughs, and I moan again when his tongue darts over my collarbone. 'This is not a dinner jacket. It's a sports coat. Perfectly appropriate to wear to a sporting event,' he replies without taking his mouth off my skin. Every word he says turns into a kiss and I need to do something to ease the tension building up in me.

He chuckles when I continue to fumble at his jacket, then takes a step back and lets me push it all the way down his arms before he catches it. A flash of white drifts through the air and then an envelope lands on the floor, visible even in the dark of the room. Ethan follows my gaze and before I can reach for it, he bends down and tugs the envelope back into his jacket, which he throws onto a chair behind us.

'What's that?' I ask, even though everything inside me tells me to ignore it and throw myself back at him.

Ethan's eyes dart to the jacket, then back at me. His hands reach up to his collar, undoing his shirt one button at a time. 'A note from my father,' he says, or at least I think that's what he said. I'm not sure because all my attention is focused on his fingers as they glide down the front of his shirt, exposing more and more delicious skin.

'What does it say?' I'm not sure why I ask.

Ethan huffs out a laugh, pulling the now open shirt over his shoulders and slipping his arms out of it. It lands on the floor with a soft whisper. The moon's light is the only thing illuminating the room, bathing him in a soft blue glow that throws dark shadows in all of his valleys while highlighting the ridges of his muscles.

I swallow and the sound can be heard in the silence between us. He reaches his hand out and, when I take it, his fingers wrap around mine and he pulls me closer. Then I'm pressed against him, my chest flush against his and my head bent back so I can look up at him. Fire rages in his eyes, his arm coming around me and settling on my hip again.

'Is that really what you want to talk about right now?' he asks and, before I can answer, his hand slips under my T-shirt and caresses my stomach for a second before coming up to my breast. He cups me over my bra, squeezing me with just enough force for it to vibrate down my spine and between my legs.

I arch my back towards him, leaning into the touch and letting out another needy sound when he gathers me close enough that I can feel the ridge in his trousers pressing against the part of me where I really need him.

'No.' I breathe the word out, along with the tiniest kernel of curiosity that the white envelope raised in me. I know their relationship is contentious and if he came here with a note from his father in his pocket, does that mean they just had a meeting?

When Ethan lets his other hand slip under my T-shirt as well and pulls it over my head altogether, that curious part shifts, focusing exclusively on how his eyes rake over my body, drinking me in. His gaze fills with desire.

And then, as if standing has become too much for him, Ethan takes a few steps back while pulling me along with him, until his knees bump against the bed and he sits down on the edge. Our height difference is enough that he only has to tilt his head slightly to look up at me, but the sight is so different—so profoundly *erotic*—I can't help but clench my thighs together when a new wave of need crashes through me.

When I make to straddle him, Ethan stops me with a hand on my stomach. The other hand caresses up my back, leaving a renewed path of gooseflesh along the way and even in the warmth of his room, I shiver. His fingers slip under the band of my bra, moving around for a few seconds and then the pressure around my ribcage loosens, and the bra falls forward, sliding down my arms.

'Now we're on more equal footing,' he says as he peels it from my arms and throws it on the floor next to his shirt.

I chuckle. 'There is no way we are anywhere near equal footing. Have you looked at yourself in the mirror lately? Half the time, even the press slips in something about your devilishly good looks.'

'You know, I think you're the most beautiful woman I've ever laid eyes on,' he says in a low rumble that shoots right through me, riding that wave of need he pushed through me just a few seconds ago.

'I am?' This must have been some kind of message hidden in the subtext of work because if Ethan Grant told me he thinks I am the most beautiful woman he's ever met, I'm certain I would remember. Might even get a tattoo somewhere commemorating the date.

He doesn't reply. His hands, stroking my back until now, settle on my hips and pull me closer so I stand between his open thighs. A growl escapes his throat when he looks me up and down, studying me up close as if he can find the evidence of his claim written right on my skin. I brace myself for the tension to set in, the discomfort of having someone inspect me so closely, even in the dim light of the moon outside. It's been like that before, with me feeling more comfortable under the sheets, when things were too busy to think about hiding.

But with Ethan, I'm already there, burning so hotly for him I don't know if I'm even going to survive past the first touch.

His mouth traces a line of kisses up my stomach, pausing here and there to graze his teeth over my skin before moving up to the valley of my breasts. He pauses, leaning his forehead against my sternum as he takes a deep breath. 'I wasn't complimenting the dress when we were out shopping,' he says, his voice so near to my skin that I shiver.

'I know you say that and mean it. But desiring someone in a dress that's designed to make them look good and wanting them when they're wearing day-old sweatpants is a very different thing.' A trickle of ice slices through the heat he's conjured up in me. 'Not that these are day-old sweatpants. I put them on after getting back to my room. Which I think you know since I wasn't wearing them earlier and—'

My words turn into a moan when his mouth closes around my breast, lavishing me with indulgent kisses that are all tongue and teeth and delirious suction. The sensation is so unexpected, my knees buckle and I put my hands on either side of his shoulders to steady myself. He glances up at me through lashes that are ridiculously long for a man and would have anyone eating their heart out with jealousy as his tongue circles around my nipple for one last round. I think he's about to say something, but then he simply does the same thing again on the other side.

Whatever was left of my mental faculties flees under the onslaught of sensation, and I'm left with nothing but the tightness building between my legs to guide me.

'Seems I have one night to convince you I mean it in every conceivable way. No time to waste.' Ethan nudges my chin with his nose and I bend down to slide my mouth over his. With our positions the way they are, I should be the one leading this kiss, but I'm not. With all these sensations washing over me, I'm at his mercy and Ethan—he is so gentle with his kiss even as desire barrels through us both.

He could have me right this moment. I know I'm ready, can feel the wetness pooling between my legs. But he wants to do more than make me feel good, though what that more is, I can't tell.

Still, a part of me wants to challenge him, though I'm not sure why.

'I'm sure you can convince me for one night. But I won't believe there's any compatibility here beyond that. The whole outing in the boutique showed how we're from different worlds that don't fit together. Forcing it will just cause more issues.' I don't know how he could deny this. He knows now how I grew up, knows why I've worked so hard to launch my charity. Meanwhile he's lived a life of luxury the likes I've never dared to dream of. Surely he needs someone equally refined next to him. That's why we agreed this would only be temporary.

Ethan seems to pick up on what I'm saying. His hands stall for a second and then I gasp when they dip underneath the waistband of my sweatpants and he pulls them all the way down to my ankles. My grip around his shoulders tightens when he gently lifts up each of my legs and places them back on the carpet as he pulls my clothing away.

'The boutique is an outlier and doesn't reflect the real world. We don't know each other in the context of big events requiring white tie. We know each other from hotel buffet breakfast and treatment plans for injured riders and sharing snack pouches while out on training rides.' I gasp when his mouth connects with my skin just below my navel. His tongue darts out, caressing the spot, and my head falls back. My fingers dig into his shoulders as I force myself to keep them there and not grab his head to guide it downwards—where the need is building with such ferocity, I'm not sure I can wait much longer.

'But other than just now, you've only ever told me you thought I was beautiful when I wore that dress,' I counter, though I don't know why. Which is becoming a concerning theme between me and him. Somehow, being near him overrides all the carefully constructed safety mechanisms in my life and I become a creature of instinct, of emotion. I react to him without thinking.

Ethan kisses that spot again and then lays his cheek against my abdomen. The stubble of his beard grazes over my skin, evoking a brand-new sensation that trickles through me and rips a moan from my lips.

A moan that turns into a cry when his thumb presses down on the front of my underwear and swipes upwards. My knees buckle and I lean harder on his shoulders. Ethan does it again, slow and agonising and, even though there is still fabric between me and his fingers, the edges of my vision begin to blur.

'That's fair enough. I evoked that impression by only telling you then what I've thought about you for a long time.' His voice vibrates through my skin and he swipes his thumb over me again, sending a spear of lightning through me. 'But I also thought the exact same thing when I saw you pacing up and down in front of my room. And when you gave me an earful for changing the macronutrients for Julian on your spreadsheet.'

I want to call him out for the lie I know that last one is, because I was there when it happened. Does he think I don't remember how cold he was towards me? But my entire brain shuts down when with the next swipe of his thumb, Ethan slips underneath the fabric and strokes me. This time, even my arms can't save me from falling over. My knees come down on the bed on each side of his thighs and even though I shift to straddle him now, Ethan doesn't stop stroking.

'I've imagined so often what you would sound like when I finally got to touch you, Val. But this—' He captures my mouth, pulling me into an indulgent kiss that's amplified by what his fingers are doing to me. His fingers nudge at my entrance and when they sink into me, my hips buck. I don't recognise this person as myself, but the friction is so good—so long overdue—that I'm not even able to care what I look or sound like. My hips move on their own as he pleasures me, and his lips keep pulling me back into kisses that are all tongue and teeth and desire unearthed from the depths of our souls.

It takes me by surprise when tension suddenly gathers at the base of my spine and then I clench around his fingers. My climax barrels through me, gripping me with an intensity that pushes all the air out of my lungs. Below me Ethan whispers sweet nothings near my ear as he strokes me through it and, when I can breathe again, I fall onto him with my entire weight, pushing him down onto the bed.

I try to sit up, still wrapped in the heat of my orgasm, with only one thing in my mind: more. More of this; of *him*. In whatever form I can get it, I'll take it.

Climbing off the bed on unsteady feet, I hook my fingers into the elastic of my underwear and push it down. When it pools around my feet, I step out and look down on him as he props himself up on his elbows. The way his eyes rake over me sends a wave of desire through me, and the truth that shows me is almost undeniable. What he said about me, what he thinks about me—how he sees me. It has to be true. Passion glazes his eyes, but it's not *just* that. And it's that something else I see, something that eludes any description, that rips through the final barriers inside me that were stopping him from seeing all of me.

'Take that belt off,' I say with a voice that doesn't sound like my own.

Ethan's lips twitch into a smile and then his hands go down, unbuckling the belt and pulling it out of the loops. Stretching out his hand, he lets it fall down the side of the bed before he settles back down.

'Now undo the button,' I say as I step closer. He does as I ask and before his hands can settle back down on the bed, I add, 'And the zip.'

His smile broadens into a smirk that I feel reflected on my own face. 'Now push down your trousers.' I take another step when he lifts his hips off the bed and I pull on both trouser legs until the garment lands on the floor with all of our other items. 'Your boxers, too,' I say before I can change my mind.

Not that I *want* to change my mind. I won't. But I'm running so hot, I'm not entirely sure I'll be able to savour this moment if I bend down to take off his underwear myself. Instead, I watch him push it down to his thighs until he can kick it over the edge of the bed and onto the floor. Then he settles back onto his elbows, his eyes filled with promises of more pleasure.

More Ethan.

But first: 'I'm on birth control and I've been tested several times since my last relationship.' I don't say that the reason for that is because Alexander might have been having unprotected sex with other people while being with me, but by the way Ethan's brows draw together in anger, I can tell he understands the subtext.

And his anger is somehow only fuelling the needy fire in me. Seeing this man disgusted and indignant by what was done to me unlocks a new dimension in me.

'I don't do casual sex without protection.' There are so many layers to that one sentence that I pause. What we are about to do is the very definition of casual. One night to get it all out and then we are going back to how things were between us. But something inside me balks at the idea that anything between Ethan and me could be classed as casual. It's not casual, and somehow it's never been, but if it's not casual—what is it, then?

Ethan is not telling me I should go. No, he's stating what this is to him and that I still have a choice. He doesn't do casual sex, so this one night we have given ourselves will be meaningful. We will wake up different people after crossing this line, and he's making sure I know that.

Crawling onto the bed, I slide up his body and when I get to his erection, I wrap my fingers around him. My mouth dries out as I give him a pump and underneath my hand Ethan strains, a strangled groan coming from his throat. When I look up at him, I can see the leash he's kept on himself so far—and how one touch from me is already enough to break it.

The thought is such a turn-on, I feel my own dampness growing and one thought obliterates all others: he has seen me come undone and I want the same.

Letting go of him, I sit up and straddle him with my knees on either side of his hips. His length presses against me, nudging me in a way that if I let myself sink down, I would take him all in. But his hands dig into my flesh and hold me in place, even though I want to let go. To cross that line we've been flirting with since we started this thing.

'Val.' He says my name as a plea. Does he want me

to stop? Or is this the same warning I hear echoing inside myself? That we cannot uncross this line and if we do this now, we will for ever change things between us.

His gaze draws me down until my chest touches his, and my face is in front of his. When I kiss him, I put all the words I can't say into it. That we don't know what will happen tomorrow, but tonight is in the palm of our hands and we can make of it what we will.

Not casual. But not for ever.

One by one, his fingers loosen their grip and skate up my bare flesh until he reaches my face. Cupping it on either side, he deepens the kiss. When I feel him pushing against me again, I shift my hips and gasp into the kiss as he sinks into me in one deliberately slow stroke.

My vision fractures when I bear down, my breath coming out in pants. So does his and our kiss turns more into mouths pressing against each other as we struggle to process the new sensation. The sheer *rightness* that floods through me as Ethan moves inside me is something I'm sure I will never forget. Sex isn't supposed to feel like this, like the melding of body and mind until I lose track of where I end and he begins.

Then again, nothing with Ethan has been how I thought it would be. He's defied my expectation at every turn, forcing me to revise my opinion of him more times than I can count. Layer by layer, he's let me uncover the man beneath the masks. Not Ethan Grant, my boss. Not Prince Ethan William Grant-Belmont, a man of royalty.

'Ethan.'

'Val.' He says my name again, and this time I know exactly what it means because I've said his name the same way. Not plea or prayer, but promise.

Pressure builds at the base of my spine as he picks up the pace, our breaths mingling in between frantic kisses that try in vain to match the rhythm of our bodies. I feel him twitch underneath me, his eyes burning into mine and letting me see all the squishy and soft parts he keeps hidden from everyone in his life. Everyone except me now. I'm the only one who knows *this* Ethan.

Not casual. Never.

A new level of heat bursts through me when his hand shifts down between us, finding that sensitive spot and rubbing it in steady circles. Lightning zaps at the touch and Ethan groans when I clench my muscles, gripping him even tighter. And as the wave inside me crests and crashes down into another orgasm and I feel Ethan surging and then shuddering underneath me, one thought follows it all.

How is one night supposed to be enough?

CHAPTER TEN

Ethan

IT WAS NEVER going to be one night. I don't even know why I agreed to it because the moment I did, I knew I was going to go back on it. That I would rather cut off my own arm than let Valerie walk out of this hotel room and back into a life where this thing between us didn't mean anything.

I haven't slept a wink all night but I feel more alive than ever. Because Valerie is lying curled up next to me, her even breathing syncing up to the beat of my heart. She looks like she hasn't slept this soundly in an age, and I'm not entirely surprised by that. She didn't do much sleeping either. Occasionally she dozed off just to wake up to my hands on her body and…well, we might have said one night, but that didn't mean one *time*.

With the team now fully under my control, I feel like for the first time my life is exactly as I want it. The only thing that's left to do is go to my uncle's gala and then all my family obligations are done.

Valerie stirs when I reach out and touch her shoulder, relishing the special warmth only sleep brings to a body. I could stay in this bed for ever and watch her drift away into slumber. But our departure is approaching and before we get back to Girona, there's something we need to talk about.

'Hey,' she says, voice a little raspy from tiredness.

Instead of replying, I gather her closer to me and press a soft kiss to her mouth. She drapes her leg over my hip, our legs interlocking the way they have all night. Her heat radiates against me and I stir in response, feeling her ready—*needy*—just where I want her and it's a challenge not to forget about everything and simply sink into her again until we are both spent.

Judging by her wiggling against me, I can tell she's of a similar mind.

'We need to head out soon. Our plane leaves just after lunch,' I mumble into the kiss when she surges against me with clear intentions.

'I'm all packed up so I only have to grab my luggage and I'm good to go,' she replies, her hand diving below the covers.

My chuckle turns into a kiss when she wraps her hand around me. My eyes flutter closed and everything inside me tells me to just give in. There's still time to talk later when we're back in Girona. Only later is no good. I have to tell her now before either of us has time to panic; to question what we've both witnessed happening between us last night.

'Val, please…' I chase after her hand and wrap my fingers around her wrist.

She stills, brow furrowing for a moment. Abruptly, she sits up, covers falling from her naked body and, of course, my lizard brain yells at me to forget everything I wanted to discuss and just have her again. 'Oh, right, because the sun is out, I have to leave. We agreed to that and here I am, trying to score some extra sex.' Her voice pitches higher as she speaks and I lose balance when she attempts to get out of bed with me still holding onto her wrist.

'No, that's not what is happening here.'

Valerie turns back towards me, eyes narrow. 'I get it. You said one night, and that's what you want to insist on. I agreed to it, after all, so let's not draw this out unnecessarily.' I can see her swallow, her words coming out in a rapid fire that betrays her real feelings. Despite the serious discussion, I can't stop the smile from spreading across my face. Inside, I'm sagging in relief because this discussion could have gone either way. Having stayed away from relationships because of my difficult family dynamics, I wasn't sure I was reading her right.

But I have. She wants this, too.

'Why are you smiling?' Her tone shifts from embarrassed to indignant, which I much prefer to deal with. After today, I never want her to feel anything close to embarrassment in front of me ever again.

'Because we're not stopping after this,' I say, giving her wrist a little tug until she settles back down again.

Her eyes are still wary when she says, 'Oh, yeah?'

I nod. 'This may have started as a mutually beneficial agreement for us to each get what we want while helping the other. But that's not what's happening between us any more.' I reach for her hips, dragging her closer until we are flush against each other.

'But we said—'

I silence her with a kiss and Valerie melts against me, her mouth opening for me so I can tease those throaty mewls I'm already addicted to out of her. 'First of all, *you* were the one to insist this was only for one night. I accepted it yesterday, but, now that I know what one night with you has done to me, I can't walk away. Not without trying for more.'

Her gulp is audible as she swallows, and her gaze flitters away to the window. 'There's a reason you only wanted a fake girlfriend in your life. I don't see how that could have changed in such a short time.'

'The reason I didn't take dating as seriously as my father wanted is because of how recognisable I am. Women in royal circles don't interest me and finding someone the conventional way has always led to me meeting people who already knew who I was.' I pause, remembering the few dates I went on before realising that modern dating didn't work when your family ruled over an entire country. 'They never wanted to be with me for me but for the prince side of things. But you…'

When I kiss her this time, she leans into it and gives me another moan that shoots straight through me and into my groin. It's with great reluctance that I pull away from the deepening kiss because even though I know she wants this, the possibility she might not admit that is still there. 'You've only ever known the man I want to be—unburdened by any royal matters and simply managing this cycling team. So if you want me the way I want you, then let's try.'

Her fingers dance over my collarbone, tracing the dip there to the middle of my chest before stopping. My stomach clenches when she lets out a deep sigh. 'I've got involved with my boss before and it didn't turn out well. I—what if this isn't a good idea? The power balance between us will always be off.'

I thought that, too, but after what happened yesterday, that won't be a problem any more. 'Your charity exceeded its funding goal. After this season, you don't have to renew your contract with my team. I will keep you as the main kit sponsor for as long as the charity remains in operation. But us working together directly won't be an issue after the Vuelta.'

A smile appears on her face, her eyes briefly catching on mine before she looks away again. 'I can't believe that influencer, Chelsea, spoke about my charity in front of the press. Or that it was less than twenty-four hours ago. How is me reaching my funding goal not the craziest thing to happen to me yesterday?'

Valerie shakes her head but then softens against me, her hand tracing the hair running down my stomach. I shiver against her as each gentle caress of her finger stokes the flame of hope higher in me. She's not a cruel person; surely she wouldn't stay in bed with me like this if she meant to reject me.

'I'm not asking you to marry me or move in with me or stop everything to be the perfect princess by my side. I just—why don't we try? We have the gala two weeks from now, then the Tour de France and the Vuelta after that, and then we're free to explore this.' I lean my head down, nudging her forehead with my nose and, when she looks up, I draw her into a kiss that says all the things I don't dare to say just yet. How crazy I am about her. How much I want her in my life. How I won't stop at anything to prove to her that this can work.

Valerie threads her fingers through my hair, pulling at me until I roll on top of her. My hips rest in the cradle of her thighs and my best intentions slip through my fingers when my erection presses against her. Straining my hips, I get onto my elbows to put a fraction of space between us.

'Val, please. I can't be this close without us—'

'Yes,' she says, interrupting me.

I blink at her. 'Yes?'

'Let's try. I—want to try. With you.' She wraps her arms around my neck at the last words, pulling me down towards her mouth. This time, I don't resist, and our mouths crash together as I slide into her.

Her mouth, her soft skin, the sounds she makes as I bring her close to orgasm—everything is *right*. Valerie is perfection.

I've never fallen in love before in my life, but I'm sure this is it. What else could it be?

CHAPTER ELEVEN

Valerie

YOU READY TO *go in?*

Ethan asked me that a few seconds ago. Or maybe it's been a few hours? I don't know for sure right now because I'm completely focused on what's happening outside this car.

Lights from cameras flash brightly enough to reach through even the dimmed windows as we slowly approach the front of the line of vehicles bringing guests to the King's palace in Lyngholt, the capital city of Álben. Ethan had warned me ahead of time that there would be press, that we would be photographed. Somehow, I'd convinced myself it wouldn't be any different from the post-race press I've participated in since becoming the main kit sponsor.

But *this* is on a different level and it's only dawning on me now as I stare outside. How can these people be so interested in me? They don't even know me.

'I think that's part of their interest, as much as it pains me to say,' Ethan says next to me, making me realise I was rambling out loud. Smooth move, Torres. Why don't you just tell him all your innermost thoughts while you're at it? That won't negatively affect your new relationship energy. Just as debuting as a real couple in front of his judgemental family will be easy. A cakewalk. I'm not worried at all.

The last few nights, Ethan has given me a crash course on the gala, royal etiquette and also experiences he's had in the past. Mainly about his mother and her struggles to fit in. I know he did it to calm me down and let me know he's on my side, but I'd be lying if I said it didn't freak me out a little.

Wasn't that foretelling *our* story? How will I manage to fit in with everyone?

'Why is that?' The nervous energy simmering within me all day bubbles over when my eyes dart across to Ethan, long enough to see how gorgeous he looks in his suit. It's as if the designer searched the entire planet to find the most flattering fabric and colour to put on this man's body to enhance his already natural beauty and strength.

Real. On returning to Girona after the Critérium du Dauphiné, we hardly left each other's side. In the hotel he asked us to try, telling me he is not looking to have me move in with him, but it's basically what I've done. There hasn't been a single night we've spent apart since *that* night and a part of me knows I should pump the brakes. I guess the thing inside me is the *absence* of worry. I know that Ethan means the things he says and does. Unlike Alexander, he's never played games with me. It's something I didn't realise worried me until last night, when he opened up about his concerns around *my* comfort at this gala.

Ethan even gave me the option to back out of it if I

wanted to. I told him no, that I wouldn't leave him by himself when this was clearly causing an unusual amount of anxiety in him. But as I look out of the window at the assembled crowd of people walking down a literal *red carpet* towards the palace entrance while cameras flash at them, I wonder if I should have accepted his offer to stay away. Because I don't really belong in this world he calls home.

Like, I didn't even have a dress to wear to such an occasion and the way I mean to live my life—devoting my time to charitable work—I will never have a wardrobe that is adequate enough for regular events like this. Nor do I have the correct manners. Or the conversational acumen.

I'm *completely* out of my depth here and it hits me square in the face as we approach the drop-off point. It didn't matter to me when this all started, because I didn't care about him. Now the stakes are so much higher. What if I make a total idiot of myself and Ethan too realises how I don't belong in this world? Or by his side.

'You're the first person I've brought to one of these events,' he replies, and my head whips around to stare at him before I can remember that I shouldn't be doing that.

The look of intensity on his face—and the realisation I'm way too attached to this face already—hit me all at once, and it takes me a few seconds to understand the meaning behind his words. I blink several times in an attempt to shake the memories from the last two weeks before I get distracted. Alone time with Ethan is easy, and so is working with him. It's the family time that I'm dreading. Whenever he talks about his extended family, and his royal duties, he frames it in a way as if they simply don't understand him. That his appearance here with me is just to satisfy a tick box and then we'll be on our way.

But that can't be true, can it? Family is never that easy. I know that because, well…my family is a mess. But at least they wouldn't judge Ethan for using the wrong fork or wearing a budget dress. Will his family come around to accept me, or will this cause more of a rift? He's already not on the best terms with them and the last thing I want is to cause more issues with my *otherness*.

'The first person since when?' My voice comes out all husky and I clear my throat in an attempt to get a grip on what's happening. On me. I can't be all up in my head if I mean to impress people today.

The smallest of smiles tugs at his lips and his eyes flick towards the window, as if he's contemplating his words. When they settle back on me, a cascade of sparks trickles down my spine and dissolves into a fiery pool settling around my stomach.

'Ever,' he says, and the concept is so absurd, my eyes bug out because surely I'm misunderstanding what he's saying.

'Ever? As in, you've never brought a girlfriend with you to a family thing?' Great, that's exactly what my panicking brain needs: more pressure. Turns out Ethan has never brought anyone back home to meet the family and the first person he does show up with is some Spanish nutritionist who works for him.

'I told you, in my position, there isn't really such a thing as dating. I'm lucky that most of the time the tabloids aren't all that interested in my activities, especially since I started working for the Grant Sports Team. But that always changes when someone else is involved. When a new member joins the royal family. Suddenly everyone is far too interested in the business of the person who is fifth in line to the throne.'

He looks out again, his face illuminated by the flashes of the cameras. 'I managed to attend medical school incognito by going to the United Kingdom and, of course, I met people there, but it never seemed fair to start anything serious when I knew what life I'd be luring them into. And now…' He pauses, and my insides lurch at the thought of the women he's dated in the past in an irrational bout of jealousy. 'Now I have you. To think all of this happened because my father warned me not to attend this event alone. I almost feel like I owe him something.'

Ethan's laugh rings out and I try to wrap myself in it, but I fail to find the usual comfort. I realise we've never spoken about why he needed someone to accompany him here. Only that it was important for his family to believe the relationship was real. Only now that it *is* real, so much more seems to be riding on it.

A lump appears in my throat and before I can help myself, some of my insecurities spill out of me. 'And they won't think me too…common?' The word feels weird on my tongue and I hate what it does to me. It brings out a flavour of anxiety I'm far too familiar with from other aspects of my life. With my work as a nutritionist and finally getting enough money to fund my charity, I thought I'd left that part of me behind. But now I'm not even among his family and yet I feel doubt and worry unfurling in my stomach.

'My father was happy to hear about our relationship, and he's the only one whose opinion matters to me. When we first made this arrangement, I warned you it needed to be convincing because there are so many people here who feel I've not been living up to what it means to be part of the royal family.' He pauses, reaching out his hand to squeeze my thigh. 'But now that it is real, we have nothing to worry about. Their opinion didn't matter to my father when he chose my mother, and, because I saw her struggle at times, I'm going to make sure it doesn't happen to you. They don't matter to me. You *do*.'

The flutter in my stomach is kept at bay with a simple question that I almost voice: how are you going to make sure of that? But the mention of our previous arrangement prickles at something in me. 'Why was it so—?'

The car lurches to a halt and before I have a moment to steady myself, the door swings open and Ethan steps out, then turns and helps me out. Lights flash and my brain goes completely blank at the overstimulation, so I trust in Ethan as he rests my hand on his arm and walks me along the line of photographers.

After we are seated in the grand dining room of the Far Too Fancy Palace and eat our Far Too Many Course Meal, I genuinely think the hard part is behind us. All that's left to do is to smile politely, have inane conversations that will be forgotten five seconds after they've occurred and eventually Ethan and I can be on our way.

Turns out, I don't know anything at all about these events. Eyes follow us as we make another round of the ballroom and I know I'm not being paranoid when I hiss, 'They're still talking about me. Like, *a lot*.'

If that concerns Ethan on any level at all, he doesn't show it. His arm underneath my hand is relaxed and his face doesn't show anything other than regal indifference. The contrast between my boyfriend Ethan Grant and Prince Ethan William Grant-Belmont is so strong, I can actually look at him right now and feel…less. And the longer we go on having bland conversations, the less I like this version of him. The less I like the version of *myself* I'm projecting outward to meet these people's expectations of the person Ethan finally decided to bring to the gala. Like I'm some kind of Mediterranean Cinderella just waiting for the clocks to strike midnight and having my utterly common self exposed for everyone here to point and laugh at.

'It's really me they're talking about. You're the unfortunate focal point of my presence,' Ethan says, the smile he gives me subdued but reassuring. 'I'm sorry. Try not to listen, and we'll take the first opportunity to get out of here.'

'But why are they being so unkind? And that's coming from me, who is the poster child of a dysfunctional family,' I say. He warned me about this, but it still shocks me to see it in action.

Ethan only shrugs at that. 'You're not the only one with a dysfunctional family. They're angry with me for neglecting what they think is an essential part of myself.'

I snort what I'm sure is a very unladylike laugh at the sheer thought anyone would make *this* a part of their personality. It makes me glad that I met Ethan in his element rather than in the context of his princely duties. 'Sounds to me like they're just jealous. You went out and forged your own path, while putting on nice dresses and smiling for the cameras is the best they can do.'

This time, his chuckle reaches through my skin, calming some of my nerves. So does his touch when he drops the royal facade for a moment to pull me closer to him. He places a delicate kiss on top of my head and I shiver at this smallest of touches.

'That's sweet of you to say, even if I don't think it's entirely accurate. I went against the norm and so my family doesn't really know what to do with me. I'm almost certain most would prefer it if I stayed away from these occasions.' There's no tone in his voice, no indicator to tell me how he feels about that. Does he wish he were closer to his family? Or is he happy staying on the outside and inconvenienced by his need to appear here?

'Why come, then? Seems like everyone is losing in this arrangement.' Ethan takes a step away but keeps his arm around my waist and guides me towards a row of standing tables tucked away to the side of the ballroom. The light is dimmer here, the music quieter, and one of the many strings tying themselves around my chest unfurls and I revel in the breath that comes just a touch easier.

'It's important to my father and uncle,' Ethan simply replies, and something in the back of my mind comes back to me. A fragment of a conversation we've never had.

'And why was it so important for your father to believe we're involved?' When we were still pretending to feel nothing for each other, this question didn't bother me because it was none of my business. I was getting my spot on the kit and he was getting whatever he needed. But now that we're real—that we are trying—it feels like information that I should know. Maybe even information he should have already volunteered.

Ethan leans against the standing table, elbow on top

of it as he turns to the crowd and scans it. 'My parents married for love and their story always struck me as extraordinarily sad. They met as two strangers on a train across Europe. She didn't know who he was, and he was intrigued by that. But the moment they became more serious, she was sucked into this world. Her one link back to her "old" life was the cycling team my father had purchased for her.'

He pauses, eyes drifting down to the floor. 'Even though they often led separate lives, I could tell they were happy. And then my mother died, and my father was never the same again. For the longest time, it seemed so terrifying to me how much of himself left with her. And yet my father kept insisting all my life that I needed to balance my passion—ground myself in a marriage like he had. But after watching him have his entire life ripped apart after my mother's death, it wasn't something I was interested in.'

My heart stutters in my chest and I'm glad we are standing off to the side because I'm not sure I would be able to give him all of my attention while having people file around us, each of them giving me a dirty look. Things are so fresh between us, and it feels like I'm learning something important about him. But his words also send a pang of panic down my body, my stomach swooping. This sounds so different from what he told me after the race in the quiet of his hotel room—about how he wanted us to be together.

What's changed? These are the words I want to say, but instead what comes out is, 'But why did you want to trick him with a fake relationship?'

He looks at me and something passes over his face.

The kindness I've got to know over the last two weeks—and even longer—is still there, but it's mixed with a sharp pain. My breath comes out in a stutter and, for a few seconds, I think he's not going to tell me. That this relationship is too new for him to confide in me in such a way. No, worse than that. That these are royal problems for royal people and, as such, I simply wouldn't get it. Because I don't belong here and one event has been enough to expose the truth of that.

'He and I have a difficult relationship, one made worse by my mother's passing. But he's not a bad man, he's just always had a particular vision for my life. I think he's always wanted to see me find the same love he had. Believes that my life would somehow be less without it,' he says, and I don't know why, but breathing becomes harder. I can sense something is coming, like writing on a wall far away, and with every moment that passes, I get closer to seeing it fully. And something in my gut tells me I'm not going to like it.

He looks at me with a subdued smile and continues, 'A few weeks ago, he and I made a deal: I would—'

'Your Highness.' The words interrupting us are soft yet float above the surrounding noise due to the urgency with which they are spoken. Both our heads turn towards the newcomer—one of the palace waitstaff. Even after I've heard it over and over today, it's still weird to hear people referring to Ethan by his title. I'm not sure I'll ever get used to that.

Ethan's eyes dart up and down, taking in the man standing in front of us. Then a muscle in his jaw clenches 'Is something the matter?' he asks, and I can't pin down what I'm hearing in his voice. All I know is that it increases the roiling of my own stomach. What was Ethan about to say?

'If you could come with me, Your Highness.' There is a slight hesitation in the waiter's words, as if even though he is using that ridiculous title, he still might be being far too familiar. But why would that matter when someone has clearly sent him to fetch Ethan?

The reason hits me right as the waiter's eyes focus on me, expression apologetic. Apparently, I'm not invited.

'There's a—' Ethan starts, then interrupts himself and shakes his head. 'Sorry, Valerie, it seems I'm needed. I promise I won't be long and then we'll continue this conversation,' he says, and then he leans in, placing a gentle kiss on my cheek before withdrawing and walking after the waiter.

Leaving me to puzzle over this entire conversation. He made a deal with his father, but what could that have been about for him to take such a drastic measure as making his whole family believe he's seeing someone? And now that I'm real and tangible, how does that change things for Ethan?

As Ethan disappears into the crowd, I'm left standing at the edge of the ballroom, surrounded by glittering strangers who don't even try to hide their whispers. Their eyes flick to me and then away, their judgement pressing down on me like the weight of the grand chandelier overhead.

The knot in my chest tightens and, for a moment, I think about leaving. Just walking out of the door and never looking back. I could send Ethan a message later—something polite but detached—and remove myself from a situation I should have known better than to step into.

But the thought of walking away leaves a sour taste in my mouth. This isn't just a ruse any more. We said we would try being together and I want to because, despite all the warnings to myself, I'm falling in love with him. I *want* to live in this future I'm imagining, but even one night in this company throws me into a place of uncertainty.

Taking a deep breath, I push myself off the table and square my shoulders. I'll wait. For now, I'll wait. For Ethan to come back. For the rest of the story he started telling me. For the moment this night will finally be over, and I can figure out how to piece everything together.

Turns out waiting is not my strong suit and after half an hour that feels like three, I need to do something to get rid of the nervous energy bubbling up inside me. So I start walking around the ballroom, trying to look like I belong. Only that turns out to be an even worse mistake than coming here in the first place, because now I can hear them. And without Ethan by my side, the tongues seem to have found a new sharpness.

'Did you see the slit of her dress?' The voice drifts towards me as I circle the room for the third time, looking for something to do while Ethan is God knows where instead of finishing that story that keeps gnawing on my mind. But when I toss a look over my shoulder, I can't see who said it. Which must be some sort of upper-crust sorcery because I can hear them continue.

'He must have brought her on purpose to annoy Archie. You know that boy will do anything to rile up his father—including this, apparently.' The ambient noise around me swallows the tittering that follows these words.

But I know there's tittering, because something like that can only be accompanied by a derisive laugh. And I don't know if it's because I'm by myself or that my mind is coming up with increasingly bizarre ideas why Ethan might have wanted to trick his father with a fake relationship, but the words find a soft spot and burrow in.

It's not like I haven't asked myself that same question. Did he bring me here only to defy his family's expectations? He looked around and picked me because I'm so unrefined that I don't even know which fork to pick up? Why are there six different forks, anyway? What possible advantage can this slightly smaller fork have that makes it easier to spear chicken?

No, that's my insecurities talking again. Ethan likes me. To deny that would be to deny every moment that's happened between us in the last few weeks. Every night spent together, every stolen glance and small smile as we prep for the Tour.

When I begin my fourth round of the room without a single glimpse of Ethan but with a lot more comments about *that woman*, I decide I've put myself through enough. I can only participate in my own humiliation for so long before it becomes beyond pathetic. Time to find a quiet corner and jump down a random TikTok rabbit hole to take my mind off all this while I stoke that simmering anger at Ethan having left me alone for so long, right after warning me how unpleasant his family could be.

Stopping the first waiter that passes by me, I ask, 'Can you point me towards the service exit? I need somewhere quiet.' I hope the desperation in my voice is enough to convey that I *really* need to be somewhere else for a few minutes.

The man hesitates long enough for my stomach to give a flutter before he nods, and then ushers me away from the crowd and through a door. The silence that envelops us when the door swings shut behind us washes over me. My muscles almost instantly relax and each step feels a bit easier as he leads me down the empty corridor and points at another door.

'This leads to a side entrance, but there might be some other staff there,' he says, and I wave off his explanation.

'Trust me, this is where I belong.' Without parents to put me through med school, I had to spend most of my free time working odd jobs and the cater-waiter life is a familiar one. Funny how all the people inside there could see that, but somehow a fancy dress and some professional make-up could convince this waiter otherwise.

I nod at him in thanks, pushing through the door and blinking several times when I step into the gentle light of the lamp illuminating the small, secure outside area.

'Val?' One of the human shapes says my name in a tone that's far too familiar for my liking and the tension snaps straight back into place. Wait, has he ditched me at the party so he himself could find some quiet time?

Anger runs through me in an electric burst. 'You've been hanging out here while I had to fend for myself in there?' I blink a few more times until Ethan's shape takes form enough for me to round on him. 'You know, I get you saying it's all posturing, but that doesn't really help someone like me, who is so out of place in this world that I might as well be from another planet. What was the point—?'

My mouth snaps shut with an audible click when I look at him. He and the person sitting on a chair next to him with her arm wrapped in a bandage. My blinking this time is due to surprise and not poor vision. 'Oh…' The sound escapes me as a breath more than an exclamation. 'What happened?'

The woman sitting on the chair looks at Ethan with wide eyes and then shakes her head. Why does she not want me to know what happened? Ethan, seeing my questioning expression, turns to the woman and says, 'She's a doctor, too. And someone you can trust if you see her around.'

The woman still doesn't look convinced but nods. I stay rooted in my spot, because I don't want to startle her, as she's clearly already spooked. But I'm also not sure what I'm looking at. Why is Ethan seemingly treating a wounded staff member outside the service entrance? Surely they have a first-aid room that is more suitable for such a procedure?

He helps her off the chair and as she walks towards the door I'm standing next to, she rolls down her sleeve, fixes the button and then throws on her uniform's jacket. She spares me a glance as she pushes through the door and when it falls shut behind her, silence settles between us. We're somewhere on the ground floor, but this staff entrance must be far enough away that any external sound can't reach us.

Ethan is the first to break the silence. 'I— Apologies for disappearing on you. The staff here know they can pull me aside if they need anything.' He's still standing next to the chair, both hands stuffed in his pockets and shoulders slightly pushed forward in an uncharacteristically shy move. That, in combination with the knowledge of why he left me like chum in shark-infested waters, is enough to evaporate most of my anger.

Most, but not all.

'Why are you fixing someone up here? Don't they have a staffroom or first-aid area where you could treat them?' I know Ethan well enough to understand there is a reason for this. I just can't conceptualise it.

Ethan looks down at his feet, and I can feel the tension rippling off him. 'My family always uses the same company to hire extra staff for these large events and because they usually involve royal families from several countries across Europe, the staff needs to be on the ball one hundred per cent of the time. More than once, the company has fired people for minor mistakes—like cutting yourself on a piece of broken glass.'

My chest tightens when he looks up at me. It's clear that it isn't the first time he's helped someone at one of these events. But that it's even necessary… 'I don't understand. People would complain about an injured waiter and that would be enough for them to get fired?'

'It's messed up, and it's one reason I try to help whenever I can. I'd rather set tongues wagging than be complicit in this.' The edge in his words slices. Not because they're aimed at me but because I'm like the staff and I always will be, no matter how expensive a dress I put on. Just like Ethan will always be one of *them*—and why is this even bothering me? He told me he doesn't care what they have to say.

Yet the words these people so brazenly spoke within my earshot still echo in my head and I can hear them again as I look at him.

Ethan frowns, his eyes scanning my face, and he takes a step towards me. 'How did you get here? Did someone tell you where to find me?'

I'm not sure if the concern underpinning his words is because I'm here or because he thinks someone might have given him away. It doesn't matter either way and yet my heart squeezes inside my chest at the thought that he might not have wanted me to know this about him.

Another secret, and, paired with me still not knowing the reason why he needed to fake a relationship for his father, I'm unable to shake the sinking feeling in my stomach that something is *wrong.*

'I didn't know you were here. A staff member led me here when I asked them where I could get some fresh air by myself.' I swallow the ever-growing lump in my throat as Ethan's stare remains on me, seemingly picking up on every tiny detail he can read off my face.

'Why did you need some fresh air? Did something happen?' His eyes narrow on me, kicking a shiver down my spine. 'Did someone upset you with what they said?' he asks, his voice impossibly low.

Not the question I was expecting, but my throat tightens anyway. 'They certainly didn't get nicer to me once you left,' I reply, sounding far more accusing than I mean to.

'What did they say?' He steps forward again, but it's different from the other times he's closed the distance between us. He doesn't vibrate with barely contained desire, but something else.

'That my dress isn't appropriate and that you're probably only with me because I'm someone your father would disapprove of you dating.' I say everything in one breath, not giving myself a break because stopping would give me an opportunity to overshare as I'm prone to do.

As he looms over me, I can feel his breath ghosting

over my skin when he exhales, and my stomach tightens at the low sound coming from his throat. It's a dangerous growl, unlike what I'm used to hearing from him.

'I'll set them straight.' He makes to push past me, but I'm not letting him get away with another unfinished conversation. Not when the unsaid things hanging between us are turning my stomach sour.

'No, you won't.' I shift at the same time he does, and his hand comes down on my arm, which is now blocking the door handle. He releases his grip on me for a second, then he flexes his fingers again, letting them encircle my lower arm.

'If they want to run their mouths about me, I'm fine with that. But making you think that I—'

'What were you going to say? Earlier, before we got interrupted?' I need to know and the longer things between us are left unsaid, the more I drift away into a space I don't want to be in. These people have already made me feel like an alien, and Ethan being cagey about stuff isn't helping. What if he really only picked me because his father would hate me?

Ethan's grip on my arm loosens, his gaze dropping to the floor. For the first time tonight, he doesn't look like the composed prince who always has the right words, the perfect smile. He looks unsure—like he's trying to untangle something too complicated to say out loud.

'I was going to say…' his jaw tightens, and the pause stretches until I want to scream '…that my father and I had a deal. About the team.'

The words hit me like a gut punch, and for a moment, I can't breathe. A deal about the team? This has something to do with our team? The thought has never occurred to me before, but it makes sense. Archibald isn't involved in any of the decisions, but we all know he's somewhere in the background. Ethan even told me he bought the team for his late wife because she enjoyed the sport so much.

'What kind of deal?'

He steps back, releasing me, and the space between us suddenly feels like a chasm. 'He wanted proof. Proof that I could handle more responsibility. That I could…' He rubs a hand down his face, the movement jerky, uncharacteristic. 'That I could represent the family, not just myself. The team was always my mother's, and he was reluctant to give me ownership of it unless he saw I was—' He breaks off, shaking his head, his voice dipping lower. 'Settled. That was his condition. And for a while, I thought it mattered.'

He exhales slowly, like he's trying to steady himself, and his next words come softer. 'I didn't tell you because it stopped being about him,' he says. 'But that's what started all this. He wanted me to prove I could balance everything in my life. That I was ready to take on the team. And…' He hesitates, his jaw clenching as he looks away. 'He gave it to me two weeks ago.'

'Two weeks ago?' I echo, my voice brittle. 'So you already have it. You've had it the whole time we've been sleeping together, and you just…didn't tell me?'

Ethan's shoulders sag, and he runs a hand through his hair, his expression torn between frustration and regret. 'I didn't know how to,' he admits, his voice strained. 'I thought… I thought if I told you, it would look like everything between us was still tied to that deal. Like you'd think none of it was real.'

The cold washes over me, creeping in through every

crack in my carefully constructed composure. 'So that's why I'm here,' I say, my voice flat. 'I was just part of your pitch to your father. A means to an end to get what you want. Only a prop.'

His head jerks up, his expression twisting. 'You're not—' He stops himself, exhaling sharply, like he's reining something in. 'That's not what this is.'

'Isn't it?' My voice rises, and I hate how unsteady it sounds. 'You told me you wanted this to be real. That it *is* real. And now you're telling me you brought me here because of some deal you made with your father? How am I supposed to believe anything you say?'

Ethan's jaw tightens, his shoulders squaring as he takes a step forward. 'Because I meant it. Every word I said. I wouldn't have asked you to try if I didn't—' He cuts himself off, his voice dropping to something quieter, rougher. 'I didn't tell you about the deal because it didn't matter any more. It stopped being about him the second I—' He shakes his head, like he can't find the right words. 'It's not what you think.'

I let out a humourless laugh. 'I— This is ridiculous. From the second I put on this dress, I've not felt like myself, and spending a few hours in the company of these people was enough to get into my head. When I agreed to give this a try, I didn't know what I was buying into.' This has been rubbing me the wrong way the entire evening. In theory, I knew who he was—what he was—but seeing it in person… 'Maybe this is a compatibility problem. This world is so foreign to me. I mean, I don't even know which fork to use.'

He pauses, turning away from me and taking a few steps. Then he turns abruptly back to me, and the betrayed expression on his face almost breaks me. 'So you're just like everyone else in the end,' he says and his words slice through me. 'I can't change who I am, Val. This—' he throws his arms out, gesturing at our palatial surroundings '—is what you get with me. If you don't like it, try being born into it.'

'Born into what? Exorbitant wealth where your biggest fear was how to convince your father that you're not working too hard, so he literally hands you a cycling team?' Ethan means so much to me, but somehow I've lost the connection to the man standing in front of me, and I don't understand how that even happened.

Ethan's face hardens at my words, the vulnerable man I've come to know retreating behind a mask of practised composure. 'You think this life is easy?' His voice is low, taut with barely contained anger. 'Do you think any of this is what I wanted? Do you think I'd choose this—choose to constantly have my life dissected, my decisions questioned, my relationships treated like transactions?'

'Then why bring me into it?' I throw back, my voice trembling. 'Why drag me into a world you hate so much, knowing I don't fit into it? Knowing—' My breath catches, and the next words come out quieter, but no less raw. 'Knowing it would make me feel like this?'

'Because I thought you'd stay,' he says, the words landing heavy between us. 'Because, for the first time, I thought someone might actually want to stay.'

I freeze, the ache in my chest tightening into something sharp. 'Stay? Ethan, you didn't even trust me enough to tell me the truth. How was I supposed to stay when you couldn't give me that? Would you ever have told me about this deal or just let that detail fall into obscurity?'

'I gave you the option to not come today, didn't I?' he says, his tone softer now, like he's forcing himself to stay calm. 'And it sucks to say it, but this right here is my life almost as much as the team is. I *need* you here. Because I'm crazy about you, Val.'

His words chip away at my anger, but they don't erase it. 'Please don't say anything more,' I say quietly, sensing he's about to go into depth about his feelings for me. Because I know I can't hear it. If I do, I'm going to lose my resolve. 'You don't get to keep important things from me and expect me to be okay with it. I've been standing in a room full of people who don't think I'm good enough, and now I'm standing here wondering if, deep down, you feel the same.'

His expression falters, as if I've struck a nerve. 'You really think that?' he asks, his voice low. 'That I don't feel you're good enough?'

I don't answer right away, because I don't know how to. The words stick in my throat, a tangled mess of fear and doubt. 'I don't know what to think,' I admit finally. 'I don't know if this is something I can do, Ethan. Not like this.'

Ethan takes a step towards me, his hand lifting like he's going to touch my face. I see the hesitation in his movements, the flicker of uncertainty in his eyes, and it breaks something in me. I know if I let him close the distance, I won't be able to step away. Not from him. Not from the man who, despite everything, makes me feel like I'm the centre of his world.

But I can't let him do it. I can't let him touch me, not when my heart feels like it's being split apart.

'Val…' His voice is barely above a whisper, and it's

filled with so much pain, so much longing, that my resolve wavers. I clench my fists at my sides to ground myself, to stop the part of me that's screaming to let him in. Just one touch, one reassurance that this is still real, still ours.

'No,' I whisper, shaking my head, even as my voice cracks under the weight of it. 'Please don't.'

The hurt that flashes across his face is immediate and visceral, as though I've reached into his chest and taken something vital from him. His hand drops, his shoulders sagging. Throughout all of our time together, I've never seen him like this, and the need to console him is almost overwhelming me.

'Okay,' he says, so softly I almost don't hear it. He swallows, his gaze flicking over me like he's trying to memorise every detail, and then he takes a step back. 'I'm sorry, Val. For all of it.'

I nod, but I can't bring myself to say anything. My throat feels tight, and my chest aches so badly I feel suffocated. I watch him turn away, his movements slow and deliberate, like he's holding himself together through sheer force of will.

'I'll get the car,' he says, his voice hoarse. 'You shouldn't have to go back in there.'

The offer stuns me into silence. He's giving me an out, knowing full well it'll leave him to face the whispers and stares alone. It's too kind, too selfless, and it makes the ache in my chest unbearable.

I shake my head, my voice barely audible as I reply, 'You don't have to do that.'

'I know,' he says, his gaze dropping to the ground between us. 'But I want to. Just…wait here. I'll be quick.'

He steps around me, his movements careful, like he's afraid to spook me. When his hand brushes the door handle behind me, I can feel his hesitation—just for a moment—before he pushes it open and steps inside. The sound of the door clicking shut echoes in the quiet space, leaving me alone with nothing but my thoughts and the weight of everything that's happened tonight.

I press my back against the cool brick wall, letting out a shaky breath as my arms wrap around me. The ache in my chest spreads, sharper now, like something inside me has splintered. I close my eyes, willing the tears to stay at bay, but it's no use. They come anyway, silent and hot, sliding down my cheeks as I replay his words in my head.

The door behind me clicks open again, and I flinch, expecting him to have come back. But it's not him. Just a waiter, stepping out for a breath of air. I blink at the intrusion, wiping at my face hastily before turning away from the light spilling out of the doorway.

Because I can't handle the possibility that Ethan might come back through that door. Or worse, that he might not.

CHAPTER TWELVE

Ethan

JAVIER STICKS HIS head through my door with an inquisitive eyebrow raised. 'You all right in here?'

I twitch at the sudden noise and look up from my monitor to see my head coach walking into my office. Well, not *my* office precisely, but the small broom cupboard I designated as my office during our Tour de France campaign. There had been hardly any rest before we had to hit the road again, packing up our entire operational base in Girona and moving it to a compound just outside Paris. Not that I'm complaining. Quite the opposite. A busy schedule leaves less time for stray thoughts to gather.

'Sorry, I was just thinking through some stuff.' With varying results. Thinking about the team and running around all day doing everything that needs to be done to make this Tour de France count occupies most of my waking hours. It's the sleepy ones I don't have any control over, and my dreams seem to delight in tormenting me with visions of things I can't have.

Someone I can't have, no matter how much everything inside me aches for her.

'I can tell. I stood out there for a few minutes knocking

up a storm.' Javier sits down on the chair opposite me. Then he extends his arm and drops a folder on my desk. 'I ran into Torres, and she asked me to deliver this to you. She said it's all the plans for the rest days and who needs to adjust their weight before the competition starts soon.'

My stomach roils at the mention of her name and seeing her work sitting on my desk, delivered by an unsuspecting messenger. Again. It's been like that since the night of the gala when everything came unravelled without me really knowing how. Sure, I'm the first to admit that all the minor royals can have sharp tongues, but in the grand scheme of things they don't matter. Though clearly they did. Enough to make Valerie doubt we could make a life together.

'Tell her thanks if you see her. I'm going to be stuck in this office until the first day,' I tell him, vaguely pointing at the paperwork piling up on the makeshift desk I put together out of two foldable picnic tables.

I go back to reading through the competitor report and Javier clears his throat. He's not moved and I straighten up. 'Did you come here to discuss something?' I ask, because I'm not sure why else he would be lingering.

'We've been doing this for a long time, Ethan. I was one of the first riders your mother brought on as a youngster, and even though cycling didn't work out for me, I stuck with the team. And I'm glad we built this together.' He raises a hand, and I know he means to point at all the achievements of our team, but it looks like he is specifically pointing out the cramped broom-cupboard-turned-office. The snorted laugh escaping my throat surprises me for a second and when Javier grins, I know he's done this on purpose.

'Quintana is looking good. A coloured jersey might be possible, even if it isn't the yellow one,' I say.

'I think we can even do yellow with how motivated the squad is after Eddie's win. Julian says he's all better, but I can see he's still holding back on the sprints at times,' Javier replies, and I nod. His crash at the Critérium du Dauphiné wasn't the worst we've seen, but even a small bump can turn into something larger with a cyclist.

I pause. 'But we have a variation of this conversation every morning when we talk to the team. That can't be why you're here.'

Javier barks out a laugh. 'I'm here because apparently I've become Torres' messenger pigeon, and what I wanted to ask is if that comes with an increase in salary.'

Despite his jovial tone, I'm immediately on edge, not just at the mention of Valerie, but at how hard it's been to even be around her. Not that I would ever let the team sense it. We're both professionals and I'll be damned if I treat this break-up the same way Zander Lemoine behaved after their split. But Javier wouldn't be sitting across from me if the tension between Valerie and me hasn't interfered with the team in some way.

'Javier…'

He lifts his hands in a defensive gesture. 'Listen, Ethan. You're like a brother to me and I'm not here to admonish or criticise or anything, okay? This isn't the first time people within this team had to learn to work with each other again after something's happened. We'll all be fine.'

His words do little to placate me. 'I'm sorry things have been awkward enough that anyone outside me and Dr Torres has even noticed something going on. I will…

talk to her about it.' Have I been kidding myself that we've been nothing but professional?

'Before you do that, can you tell *me* what happened? Because from where I'm standing, I'm still pretty confused about what even went on. For the longest time, I wasn't even sure you liked her until one day you make out in front of the entire press pool and seemingly come out to the team as a couple.'

I let out a sigh, burrowing my face in my hands. 'She surprised me with that kiss. The excitement of the situation got the better of both of us. At that time, there wasn't even anything going on.'

'You're telling me that when you made out at the finish line, you two were not a thing?' Javier doesn't try to hide his scepticism, and I can't really blame him. I've seen the photos taken that day and this was not some quick peck on the lips to celebrate a success.

Is there any point in discussing this? 'Have people been talking about us?' I ask instead of answering his question. The last thing I need is this becoming *the* thing people talk about. Javier isn't really a gossip so if he is concerned…

He shrugs. 'Maybe a little bit? People know to mind their own business and since the vibe between you two is pretty clear, no one wants to get in the middle of it.' Javier pauses, giving me a meaningful look. 'I'm not bringing this up as the head coach, Ethan. I'm talking to you as your friend. You know, in case you want to talk about this instead of quietly brooding in whatever corner of the training grounds you're in.'

As my friend. I know that's what Javier is to me but the words still strike at me. I've poured so much of myself into the team, I haven't stopped to consider how much more there is to it. That these people are more than employees and their reaction to all of this isn't actually the one I feared. That they're actually worried for me.

'I'm sorry, Javi. Things have been chaotic. My father—' I interrupt myself when I sense the familiar resistance in me, the need to keep things inside. To pretend to be okay because if I don't, I might lose the team and my mother's legacy to boot. But I have it now. It's mine to keep and yet it feels hollow. 'After seeing the pictures of Valerie and me, he gave me full control of the team.'

Javier tenses in his chair, eyes wide from the shock of the news he didn't expect to come out of this discussion. He's the only one who knew that my father was holding onto the ownership of the team as an ill-guided means of controlling me. Though now that he's relinquished it with such ease, I'm wondering how harshly I may have judged his actions. If I was just too wrapped up in wanting things my way that I didn't stop to consider his point of view.

'That's amazing news. When did that happen?'

'A month ago. Right after the Critérium de Dauphiné. It's officially mine now.' The last words hang between us, a moment I've been working on for so long. But the satisfaction at having all the pieces falling into place and finally arriving at the end of a long road doesn't come. The road just goes on, the forks I missed behind me for ever.

A line appears between Javier's brows, as if he too is tracing the work of the last few weeks and wondering why I haven't made a bigger deal out of this. How can I tell him I'm waiting for the broken edges inside me to stop stinging before I can feel anything else?

'There's no way he did that just because of the photos of you two,' he finally says, catching me by surprise.

'Of course that's why. I may have asked her to pretend to be my girlfriend before that moment, but Archibald couldn't possibly know that. Nobody…' My voice trails off when Javier's eyes once again become saucers, and I realise what I have admitted.

'You asked her to *pretend* to be your girlfriend? Like proper *10 Things I Hate About You*?'

Now it's my turn to scowl at him. 'I still haven't watched that movie, but I highly doubt it's about a man needing to convince his father that he's settled down enough to deserve ownership of the team he's been developing for the last six years.'

'It's more or less that, to be honest. Just cut out all the cycling and royal stuff and make it teenagers and there you have it,' he says in a tone as if any of this makes *any* sense.

'The "cycling and royal stuff" are pretty big parts of my life,' I reply through gritted teeth. How have we gone so off-topic suddenly?

Javier waves a hand in front of his face. 'Cycling okay, I'll give you that. But the royal bit isn't really something I see with you. Sure, your father wants you to show up to a few things, but that's not really too much to ask, is it?'

'He withheld the ownership of my mother's team—*my* team—from me because he wanted me to become more involved in that "royal stuff". It's why he wanted me out there dating. Are we even having the same conversation?' My shoulders tense and I wish I knew how to stop talking about this. Somehow Javier has me jumping from one topic to the next, speaking way too freely for my own taste.

'Did he though? Or does he not actually care about your involvement outside those few events? Your mother wasn't involved much beyond that. What if he just wants you to have what he had and that's why he's been pushy?'

I don't reply because…what do I say? The endless conversations my father and I had about this topic are fuzzy in my memory and I don't recall what either of us might have actually said. All I remember is what meaning I took away from his words. But was it the right meaning?

Javier leans back in the chair, his gaze steady on me as if he's waiting for something to click. 'You really think your dad handed over the team because of some kiss that made the tabloids? Come on, Ethan. That man's not exactly swayed by a couple of headlines.'

I cross my arms, leaning back in my own chair. 'Then what was it? He's been holding onto this team for years, dangling it like a carrot. The timing lines up. What else could it have been?'

Javier raises an eyebrow. 'Maybe it had something to do with the front of the kit.'

I glance towards the pile of jerseys folded in the corner of the room. 'What about it? It was part of the deal I made with Valerie. She helped me and in return she got to put her logo on the kit.'

'The *front* of the kit. You could have given her any spot and yet you gave her the front? After leaving it blank? Maybe it was because of your deal, but it's also a choice you made and people have noticed. Archie saw you make a decision—one that wasn't about sponsorship money or politics, but about something you believed in. You put her charity there, front and centre. Don't you think that's what guided his decision?'

The front of the kit. Is that what my father noticed? Not just that I put her logo there but how I spoke about the charity and its owner? Was this really all about pushing me towards a life with someone worthy rather than seeing me settle down with just anyone for the sake of the family?

I stare at the jerseys in the corner, the weight of Javier's words settling over me. I thought my father needed proof I could handle the responsibilities of my station, that I was 'settled', so I could contribute more to any events, show my face more often. But ever since he's handed the team to me, he hasn't mentioned anything in that regard. No, all he asked about was Valerie and I still remember my throat feeling tight as I lied to him.

'All he wanted is for me to find someone the way he had. But I thought it was about the family, about his legacy. That it would be good enough for me to fake it and then—I wasn't supposed to fall in love with her.' The words tumble out unfiltered and at some point they've stopped being for Javier and morphed into my own consternation about this situation. 'I took Valerie to the gala to spend the evening in a room full of people who didn't deserve to breathe the same air as her, because I thought I owed my father some kind of performance. That it was the exchange we made.'

I press my palms into my eyes, groaning. 'Hell. I put her through all of that for nothing. And now it's disrupting the team or you wouldn't be here moonlighting as my therapist.'

Javier doesn't say anything for a moment, just lets the

silence hang between us. When he finally speaks, his tone is gentler than I expect. ‘You made a mistake. It happens. The question is, what are you gonna do about it?’

I drop my hands, looking at him. The answer feels both painfully obvious and impossibly daunting. ‘I need to fix this. I need to tell her I'm an idiot—for not telling her the truth when she deserved it and for putting her in an uncomfortable situation where she didn't feel like herself. That's not who I am, either.’

Javier nods, a small smile tugging at the corner of his mouth. ‘Good. Now get out of this broom cupboard and do it.’

I stand, grabbing my jacket. My heart's pounding, but there's no hesitation in my movements. ‘Thanks, Javi. I appreciate…whatever this was.’

‘Don't thank me yet,’ he says with a grin. ‘But before you go, I have an idea how you can fix this.’

CHAPTER THIRTEEN

Valerie

THE SUN HANGS annoyingly bright in the sky. I used to enjoy the run-up to the Tour de France when all the teams flood into the city and you can tell by the excited current floating through the air. I'm not excited this year, and it's becoming a problem because other people around me are noticing. That's the only explanation I have for Lola all but hauling my butt through the doors of a tiny gelato shop tucked away in a side alley of Paris.

Once we have our order—white chocolate for me and pistachio for Lola—we sit down and my friend pins me with a stare that's a mixture of comforting and inquisitive. I fail not to squirm under those dark brown eyes that are wordlessly peeling away the protective layers I've built up ever since my relationship with Ethan imploded.

When she remains quiet, I let out a deep sigh. 'Can we just enjoy our ice cream and not go all deep and real and all that?'

She frowns, the shake of her head almost regretful as she says, 'I wish I could do that. But I let you mope around for a while, hoping you'd figure it out on your own, but clearly you haven't. Which unfortunately means that we do have to talk about it.'

'I knew this was a trap,' I say as I spear my spoon into my scoop of white chocolate gelato as if it's somehow betrayed me.

'And yet you came anyway. So on a deep, subconscious level, you must want to talk about it as well.' Lola looks smug as she says that, and something inside me bristles.

'You intercepted me and quite literally forced me to follow you for some "work stuff you needed help with".' I raise my hands to mime quotations as I recall her words. 'And then five minutes into our walk, I realised you were abducting me.'

Lola pops a spoonful of gelato into her mouth, her eyes fluttering shut for a moment, and she lets out a moan that's almost too graphic. Except everyone around us seems to have a similar reaction, so I'm actually the one standing out with my glower.

'Listen, I was immediately on board when you told me about the Ethan thing. I probably was on board even before you told me. This whole rivals-to-lovers thing you had going on with him the moment you joined resulted in such—' Lola raises her pinched fingers to her lips, kissing them before splaying them out in a chef's kiss '—delicious tension.'

I let out a snort. 'We were never rivals. I'll admit I had less charitable thoughts about him when I started out and made him work a bit to change my mind. But in my defence, he does lean into the entire "brooding and unapproachable" trope, so I'm not willing to take the entire fault on this one.' It's the first time I've let my thoughts dwell on Ethan since our break-up, but only because it's a memory I enjoy. The connection we shared has turned the initial rough landing into an anecdote I hope I can some day tell while laughing.

I had this boyfriend once that was stupidly attractive but had the emotional capacity of an ice block. Through working together, I learned more about him and what hidden depths there were behind the ice. And I've been in love with him ever since.

Oops. That's not how the story is supposed to end.

Jamming another spoonful of gelato into my mouth, I let the coolness spread through me to banish any thoughts of Ethan. How could I have forgotten that the nice memories are now interlaced with thorns, waiting to sting and drag me down into the place where I'm no longer sure I made the right decision?

'It's not about—' I start, but Lola's withering glare silences me.

'Don't give me none of that "It's not about Ethan" crap because that's insulting. You've been walking around like a storm cloud given human form and Ethan hasn't been seen outside his broom cupboard since we arrived here.' Now it's Lola's turn to snort. 'I don't get it. You've been chasing each other since you joined the team and when you finally had it, it fizzled out before any of us could get invested.'

Her phrasing catches me off guard. 'I'm sorry I ruined this for you.'

'Ugh, you're right. I'm making this about me when I wanted to make it about you. About your ridiculous choice of dumping Ethan like a hot potato.' Lola shakes her head, the disappointment in my choice clear as day. A choice I don't ever remember communicating to her.

Neither have I ever really confirmed the real relationship with Ethan, so her well-informed opinion on what exactly went wrong between us is surprising. Have we been this transparent?

The question must have been written all over my face for Lola laughs again. 'Please get over your shock. We all knew what was going on. Probably even before you two did. Which is really odd from Ethan's side because he's never shown interest in anyone since I've started working for him.'

I shake my head—both to dissuade Lola from her ideas and to get rid of the ones popping into my head the moment I hear the words 'Ethan' and 'showing interest in anyone' in the same sentence. 'No, that's not—what you saw wasn't real.'

Lola's spoon halts halfway to her mouth and she tilts her head. Okay, so most of the things she's said here were lucky guesses, and she didn't actually know the whole thing. When I'm done telling her about how our fake-dating arrangement spilled over into genuine feelings, her jaw drags on the floor and the precious gelato sits melted in her cone.

'You two really went about this in the most complicated way possible,' she concludes and, even though she makes it sound like we put *any* thought into this scheme beyond the rewards we both craved, I have to admit that Lola isn't wrong.

But I don't need her to tell me that. Waving a hand in front of my face, I let out another sigh. 'It doesn't matter. We both got caught up in thinking things might work out for real. Only took me two weeks to realise I was fooling myself, at least.' Letting out a groan, I press the heels of my hands into my eyes. 'I can't believe I fell for a guy so quickly. I'm such an idiot.'

Lola remains suspiciously quiet and when I look at her, I'm not seeing the usual sharpness in her features. 'It sounds to me like you did the "getting to know each other" part of dating during the pretend phase. You knew him for a lot longer than that and then you spent a few weeks "dating".'

I'm not sure I agree, but I wave her away. 'It doesn't matter. It's over now.'

Again, her features soften in a way I'm not used to from Lola. And then she poses a question I'm not prepared for: 'Why, though?'

I blink at her several times. A laugh bubbles up in my throat—a defensive mechanism slamming shut before any of the answers to her question can escape the deep recesses of my brain. 'I don't have to explain breaking up with someone to you, do I? It's when one or both people in the relationship decide that they no longer want to be in that relationship.'

Her lips disappear into a thin line, and my stomach flips over when she doesn't relent. 'You know, we can sit here all day with me staring at you while you avoid talking about your feelings. Or you can tell me and then we get to move on.'

Her words hit me in a soft spot, a tiny hole in the shoddy defences I've put together ever since that evening when it all fell apart. 'I *don't know* how to move on,' I say far too loudly, judging from the heads swirling in our direction. But the truth explodes through me because it's the reason I've been working on autopilot during the run-up to the biggest cycling event of the year. 'But I know

I have to. And you should know, too. You were my first friend here at the team and got to witness first-hand the kind of mess Alexander made of me. Dating the boss is never a good idea.'

I can tell Lola isn't buying it even before she rolls her eyes. 'That's not good enough. You won't be working here next season, so it hardly counts as a workplace romance.'

'It's not just that. There's also his family, who are a bit on the intense side, and they don't really like outsiders,' I say, struggling to keep my tone even. Even as I say it, I can feel how flimsy that excuse sounds. But how do I explain the other parts? The parts that have less to do with his family and more to do with me?

Lola narrows her eyes, studying me. 'You've been on the team long enough to know the cycling world isn't exactly sunshine and rainbows. You've dealt with intense people before, Val. What makes this situation different?'

I hesitate, my spoon swirling through the melting gelato as I try to find the words. 'Because they don't see me as someone who belongs there. At least not someone who belongs with Ethan. The way they talked about me… like I was this—this nobody pretending to be something I'm not. They'll never stop seeing me that way. How can I put myself in such a place? I'm still struggling to accept that my plans for the future might finally succeed. I don't need extra critics. No, I'm doing that on my own just fine.'

'Who cares what they think?' Lola says bluntly. 'I know Ethan and, even though you think you two were being super slick, I've seen how he looks at you. There's no way *he* cares about any of that.'

'But I do!' This time I shout properly, my hands ball-ing into fists tight enough that my nails dig into the flesh of my palm. People start shooting me looks varying from pity to disturbed. 'I care, Lola. For all my life, I've been adrift. First with my parents having to work so many jobs that I was left to raise myself with barely any food. Then I lost what flimsy support I had from them when I decided to strike out on my own in med school. And just when I'd started to feel like Team Blue Cow was where I belonged, Alexander not only destroyed our relationship but also somehow turned everyone against me. I can't get attached to Ethan and go through the same thing again. There's only so much rejection I can take before I've had enough of it.'

The frown on Lola's face deepens and my gut twists as she asks, 'So this doesn't mean anything to you? The people you met here outside Ethan?'

I let out a groan, slumping back in my chair. 'Ugh, no. Of course not. I care about the team. About you. About… all of it. But…' My voice falters. 'I don't know how I'll ever be enough. I've spent my whole life chasing after some idea of what "enough" looks like, and every time I think I've found it, the goalpost moves.'

Lola's gaze sharpens, cutting through my self-pity like a scalpel. 'Has Ethan ever said you're not enough?'

I freeze, the question burrowing under my skin. 'No, but—'

'But what?' Lola presses, leaning forward with a no-nonsense look that makes it impossible to squirm away.

'But it's only a matter of time, isn't it? He's… Ethan. He has everything. And I'm just me,' I say, my voice softening at the end, barely above a whisper.

There it is. The truth I'll have to learn to live with

for the rest of my life. That I found the man I could see myself growing old with, but I aimed so far above me I can't reach him. Lola opens her mouth, but I shake my head. 'I would spend the rest of my life trying to reach him and always falling short. I can't do that to myself.'

Lola's eyes narrow. 'That's such bullcrap, Val.'

I blink, startled by the sharpness of her tone. 'Excuse me?'

'Bullcrap,' she repeats, leaning forward and jabbing her spoon in my direction for emphasis. 'You're acting like Ethan's up on some pedestal while you're stuck on the ground. That's not how love works, and it's definitely not how he sees you.'

I shake my head, looking away. 'You don't understand—'

'No, *you* don't understand,' she cuts in, her voice unwavering. 'Ethan doesn't want someone who's perfect or someone who's already got it all figured out. He wants you. I have never seen him this gutted the entire time I've worked with him. He is head over heels in love with you, and I can't understand how that's not enough for you. What else is he supposed to do to show you that you're worth it?'

I open my mouth, but no words come out. Something twists in my chest—half denial, half hope. Because I can't answer the question. I don't know what to say. What else *is* he supposed to do? Is there a world in which Ethan has said all the right things? One where my past is different, and I don't struggle with these self-doubts?

But if I can acknowledge that, what's stopping me from fully embracing my feelings? Self-doubts are a normal part of life, and a large part of the education I want to do around nutrition involves mental health issues as well—these two things go hand in hand. How come I'm so stuck when Ethan and I could be—?

'He said he didn't tell me about the conversation he had with his father about the team because he didn't want us to become all about that. That it might be how it started, but it's become so much more to him,' I say, thinking back to the conversation at the palace. Was it only two weeks ago? Somehow, it feels both so far away and fresh.

I'm not sure Lola knows any of the background with Archibald and Ethan, but I'm too far in my own head to consider what's a secret and what isn't. Maybe that's part of the problem as well: too many secrets. 'But I don't know how to be this person in front of his family. This highly refined version of myself that knows how to talk about Premium Bonds and never uses the wrong fork.'

'Aren't these really small things to worry about in the grand scheme of a happy relationship?' Lola asks, and I don't know what to say to that. Apparently, that's becoming a trend in this conversation since it's at least the third time I've been rendered speechless. If that's not indicative of my entire mindset right now.

Before I can answer, Lola asks another question: 'Has Ethan ever told you he needs you to fit in with his family?'

The answer falls like a boulder into my stomach. 'No,' I say, shaking my head. 'He said they don't matter.'

But for some reason, I decided they do. I let my personal experience—the years of hurt I'm still carrying around—make the decision for me by running away from Ethan. *I* decided for him that what these people think is relevant despite him explicitly telling me it isn't.

I took that decision in my own head rather than listening to him. And that's kind of also what I threw at his head that night.

'Oh God, I'm such an idiot.' Hiding my face in my hands, I let out a long sigh. I've been miserable since the day he closed that car door behind me with nothing but longing and regret on his face. 'All this time I've been rationalising that I made the right decision, so it doesn't matter how I feel—because it's the right thing. But actually it was the *easy* thing. Disengaging and pretending it's all for the best rather than facing why I feel this way.'

How do I even begin to fix this? Is it possible? If I were in Ethan's shoes, would I even hear myself out? Ugh, what am I thinking? Of course he would. He'd be kind and gentle and generous about it because that's who he is.

'Do you love him?' Lola asks, getting me to lower my hands and look at her. Have I ever seen her look so serious?

I hold her gaze as I nod, barely able to get the words out. 'Yes.'

She lets out a dramatic, relieved sigh that turns into a grin. 'Good. I thought the whole plan was about to blow up.'

'What do you mean?' I ask, my heart leaping into my throat.

Her eyes slip past me, focusing on a point behind me. I whirl around and my heart now stops dead in my chest. Ethan is standing right outside the window, looking far more windswept than I've ever seen him. I'm pushing off my chair before I notice. 'How long have you been there?' I ask, even though he can't hear me through the glass.

Our eyes meet and there's a flash of hesitation in his, as

if he is unsure I even want to see him. How could that be possible when he's been nothing but gracious through this entire episode while I've behaved like a stubborn donkey? I turn back to Lola, asking, 'Did he ask you to get me here?'

Lola shakes her head. 'No, this idea is all on me and Javier. He had a similar talk with Ethan, and I think he's here now because he reached a similar conclusion.' I keep staring at her, unable to understand what's happening until she waves her hand in a shooing motion and says, 'Will you go talk to him already? You two are driving the entire team nuts.'

My feet move on their own and then I'm standing outside, in front of the gelato shop, and Ethan is just…there. The muscles in my body go taut when he leans in ever so slightly, tension snapping into place between us. There are dark circles underneath his eyes and his shoulders slump forward. The urge to reach out to him and press him against me thunders through me.

Instead I say, 'Hi.'

'Hey,' comes his reply.

And then we're staring at each other again. My cheeks heat under his gaze and I can't believe how good it feels to just stand here and drink him in. It's only been a fortnight, but it feels like an eternity. How did I ever walk away from this man?

We're both quiet, the noise of Paris swelling around us. Then we both say at the same time, 'I'm sorry.'

Both our mouths snap closed and then, miraculously, we're both laughing. Genuine laughter, not the automatic response I've been faking since our break-up. It's so startling and freeing at the same time that neither of us seem to be able to stop.

'How long ago did you speak to Javier?' I ask when we both calm down and already the tension feels like it's changing. Not disappearing but…relaxing.

He raises an eyebrow in surprise. 'How did you know I spoke to him?'

'Lola told me. Apparently, they both decided they'd had enough of this and stepped in.'

Ethan chuckles and it's the most amazing sound I've heard. It slips down my spine in a trail of warmth, settling down in the pit of my stomach. 'A few hours ago,' he says.

'Okay, then please let me go first. I word-vomited all over Lola not even fifteen minutes ago, so it's fresh in my mind.' Some of the amusement in his eyes fades. So does the levity our laughter brought him. A part of me wants to move on, not lay myself bare but rather skip to the good part where we've both worked through some stuff. But I know we won't get there if I keep hiding from him.

'I walked away from you without giving you an explanation—at least not a real one. Turns out I'm pretty messed up because of all the parents stuff I told you about. And the Alexander thing still has me hung up, too. But I let my insecurities make decisions for me that night. That place, those people, all the glamour… I thought: how can I even compete? You'll realise what an insecure mess I am eventually, so why drag out the hurt?' I pause to take a deep breath when my voice wobbles and that sound snaps something in half between us.

One moment I'm staring up at Ethan with a pleading look, the next I'm in his arms, my face pressed against his neck and fighting to stop the tears from slipping down my cheeks. I can't cry just yet, not when I still have so much to say.

Except Ethan doesn't let me. His hands snake up my back and head. His fingers fist into my hair and draw me away from him until our eyes meet. 'I won't let you walk around one second longer thinking this was on you. It wasn't. I was the one who changed things between us without fully understanding you and how it would make you feel. Instead of listening to you, I pushed ahead with what I thought *I* needed to do for *my* success.' The same shake infusing my voice trembles through his and I feel his muscles strain underneath my hands. 'I'm so sorry, Val. I did this and you were right to call me out.'

I try to reach out to his face and brush over his cheek, but his arms are now wrapped so tightly around me that I can only wiggle my fingers across his broad chest. His hand is still cupping the base of my neck when I shake my head, warmth trickling through me from that touch. 'All my life I've tried to live up to expectations—so much so that I sometimes still struggle to understand who matters and who doesn't. I should have listened to you when you tried to calm me down before the gala.'

'How can you be sorry when this was all on me?' He sounds so sincere as he says that, his eyes boring into mine. It's only been a minute, but we're already stuck in a loop, and I can't help but laugh.

So does Ethan. With a shake of his head, he continues, 'You're the first person to ever see all of me. Everyone knows one aspect or the other, but not you. You see the whole and now that I know what it feels like to love you, I can't let go. Not without knowing that I put it all out there first.'

My eyes go wide, the words setting off a cascade of fireworks inside me. 'You…'

I can't finish the sentence and so Ethan does it for me. 'I love you, Val. So much it's ridiculous, and I promise you if you take me back, I will spend the rest of my days making sure I live up to those words.'

'Take you back? No, wait.' His breath comes out in a shudder and I realise he's only heard the words, not my tone of voice. So instead of replying, I stand up on my toes and slide my mouth over his in a kiss that has been building inside me since the day of the gala. Ethan relaxes against me enough that I can free my arms and slide them around his neck to bring him closer to me.

'I love you, too. And I should be the one asking you to take me back. I can't promise you I will be whole, but I'm trying to be better and I want to try with you.' I kiss him again, my lips lingering against his as if we're the only people here and not standing in the middle of a busy street.

When we come apart, he smiles at me and it's so Ethan that a shiver runs through my body. 'So we try again. For real?'

My heart flutters inside my chest, and I nod. 'We try again. And we'll keep trying. Until we get it right.'

EPILOGUE

One year later...

Valerie

THE ROAR OF the Champs-Élysées crowd crashes over me in waves, but my entire focus narrows on the man standing at the centre of the podium.

Julian Quintana in the yellow jersey. Winner of the Tour de France.

Next to him, Angel, back after his near career-ending health scare, takes the third-place podium, lifting his arms in victory, and my chest squeezes with pride.

Even though I'm no longer part of the team, I still feel the thrill of victory run through me, and it's intoxicating. Next to me, Ethan's lips kick up in a smile—and I laugh because that is just so *him*. He's achieved the greatest milestone he could with his team, and a subdued smile is all that anyone will catch on his face.

But I know better. I know exactly what it means to him to be here at this moment, watching all the team's hard work fall into place.

'You did it,' I say, leaning into him. His arm comes

around my back, pulling me closer to him. I shiver when he brushes a kiss on top of my head.

'*We* did it,' he says, and I know he's not just talking about the team.

Earlier today, an article in *El País* went live. They'd interviewed me about Cosecha de Vida, highlighting some of the recent milestones the charity has reached. I'm still buzzing from the notification.

Cosecha de Vida: The Charity That's Changing Nutrition for an Entire Generation.

The visibility from the team sponsorship was life-changing, but it was the sheer momentum of that first viral video, of people seeing the issue of food poverty framed in a way they'd never considered before, that pushed it into something bigger than I ever dreamed.

I let out a breath. 'The new Madrid centre opens next week.'

'I know,' Ethan says, glancing at me. 'You're speaking at the launch.'

I hum non-committally. There is something he doesn't know. Things I have kept to myself so as not to distract him from this thrilling moment of victory that has been in the works for so long. 'They've asked me to do a segment on national television. A full hour, not just a sound-bite,' I say, and Ethan turns to me, one eyebrow raised.

'You didn't tell me that.' There's no sharpness in his words, just a genuine curiosity, and even though I didn't think it was possible, this moment makes me love him even more.

'I didn't want to steal your limelight,' I reply, and, predictably, he shakes his head.

But before he can say anything else, Julian and Angel

descend the podium, moving towards us. Julian's grin is wide and full of triumph. When he reaches Ethan, he throws an arm around his shoulder, still breathless, sweat dampening his curls. 'We did it.'

Ethan grips his back. 'You did it.'

Julian laughs, then turns to me. 'Are you proud of your man?'

I shake my head, feigning exasperation. 'Proud doesn't even cover it.'

Angel smirks, eyes flicking between me and Ethan. 'And to think I missed your *10 Things I Hate About You* era. Best origin story ever.'

Ethan groans, and I bark out a laugh. Because, really—he's not wrong.

* * * * *

If you enjoyed this story, check out these other great reads from Luana DaRosa

Falling for Her Miami Rival
Hot Nights with the Arctic Doc
Pregnancy Surprise with the Greek Surgeon
Surgeon's Brooding Brazilian Rival

All available now!

MILLS & BOON®

Coming next month

SINGLE DAD'S CHRISTMAS WISH
Alison Roberts

'I want to buy new decorations for the house this year. I'm thinking of doing it online and having them delivered but I might need a bit of help choosing them.'

That glow that had been missing from Eva's face today had already returned – probably during that ride on the carousel. But it had just gone up a notch or two and she looked genuinely joyous, her eyes shining and her lips curving into the happiest smile ever.

'I can help.' Her words were an excited whisper. 'I *love* Christmas.'

Noa was smiling back at her, watching as she caught her bottom lip between her teeth. As if he didn't know that already.

And then it happened.

He was caught.

He couldn't look away from Eva's mouth. He didn't dare raise his gaze to her eyes because he might see what he'd thought he'd seen in the on-call room the other day – that she might be seeing him as something other than a colleague or the parent of one of her patients.

That she might have been aware of what he'd been thinking. Or rather, feeling. That *attraction*.

The desire to touch her. To hold Eva in his arms. To *kiss* her…

Continue reading

SINGLE DAD'S CHRISTMAS WISH
Alison Roberts

Available next month
millsandboon.co.uk